PROLOGUE

*T*HIRD PERIOD.

One minute left on the clock.

Every muscle in my body convulsed from exhaustion, but I have to push through. All the hits I took throughout the game were a constant reminder of my age. My limbs were burning, and the excruciating pain from my fractured kneecap had returned after months of recovery.

My vision blurred as I slashed across the skating rink in search of the golden puck. Seconds later, I located it, but Inzo Padovano charged at me, relentless in his pursuit. He was twenty-four years old and ruthless, with youthful legs, sharp as a damn blade. He smirked at me, brazen. We're both aware of what's at stake.

"Gonna need a walker after this shift, Callahan?" He sneered, circling me like a shark as I struggled to get back on my feet.

I ignored his taunts, but inside, I felt it – time slipping away, my shot at the championship cup, the one thing I'd chased for nearly two decades. The last game of the playoff season had devolved into utter chaos. Referees ejected players left and right. Visor shields flew off in frustration. Bodies collided with bone-jarring force, and hockey sticks clashed like swords, slicing across the ice. The incessant echo rever-

1

berated in my ears. For a moment, I stood still to catch my breath, coasting on the frozen surface as the thundering crowd grew muffled and distant. *Why does it seem as if I'm swimming underwater?*

That's when I spotted it. The puck was loose with Padovano already on its trail, his eyes ablaze. He was determined to complete his mission. His goal was to send me packing without a championship. He wanted to humiliate me in front of my city, but there's no chance in hell I'll let him do it.

My ribs screamed with every breath, bruised from an earlier hit, and my knees were about to buckle, but I refused to give him the advantage. I bent my upper body and dug deep, forcing myself to rip through the battlefield beneath me. My skates carved trenches in the sheet of ice as I rushed to cut him off in the shooting lane.

Thirty seconds to go and a one-point lead on the scoreboard. I sensed Padovano approaching as the puck sped toward our zone like a high-velocity bullet. He took a swing, his stick slicing through the air, but I intercepted it. Pain shot up my forearm as the hockey disk slammed into my stick, and for a split second, everything froze. I could hear his shallow respiration, his frustrated growl, see the shock on his face as I deflected it out of bounds.

"Better luck next time, rookie," I muttered with gritted teeth, writhing in pain.

The horn blared.

We won.

I fell onto the ice, my chest heaved from my racing heart. I let the weight of it settle in. We'd done it. The Glory Cup was ours, and I was going out on top. My teammates lifted me up to celebrate our victory. I removed my helmet and waved it at the crowd. Drenched in sweat, I welcomed the champagne shower on my face. Surrounded by a sea of friends turned family, and longtime Vipers fans, I couldn't have asked for a better ending to my career than this.

If only I had something to show for it.

We entered the tunnel where we were bum rushed by the media. News reporters eager to secure the first interviews off the ice with the

A PINCH OF PUCK AND SPICE

SUNFLOWER FALLS
BOOK 1

LEIGH RYANN

A Pinch of Puck And Spice

Copyright © 2025 by Leigh Ryann

All rights reserved.

CONTENTS

2024 NHL champs cornered players with their mics and cameras along the wall, blocking our locker room.

Cheryl Brooks, my on and off again press conference fling, made a beeline in my direction before my swollen feet could hit the ground. A nurse on staff handed me a crutch to lean on while my manager pulled a championship T-shirt over my head.

"Congrats, Kota! That was one hell of a game." The lanyard dangled between the cleavage of Cheryl's low-cut blouse tucked in a form fitting A-line skirt that hugged her curves in all the right places.

She hopped up on her tippy toes in a pair of six-inch strappy heels to throw her arms around my neck, but I offered a casual side hug instead. Anything more would have led her on. I'm retired and in my thirties now. No more mixed signals. Brody the Bear, my right-hand man, shoved his way through the bustling crowd right on time for the save.

"You did it, Ace!" he interrupted, embracing me in a bear hug as I winced from the pressure against my rib cage. He was several inches taller than me, and at least fifty pounds heavier. Bone crusher is an understatement. His thick beard and neck length shaggy haircut dropped into his face at all angles, covering his deep-set brown eyes.

"No, *we* did it. Those Ravens never stood a chance, brother."

"Yaaahhh-hoo! Number one, baby!" Bear revealed a gummy smile. Overwhelmed with joy, he forgot to replace his front dental bridge. He passed me a cigar before we were both pulled away for post-game interviews. I placed a 2024 New England Vipers Championship cap backwards atop my head, grinning from ear to ear as a cameraman hovered his microphone above me for crispier audio.

A middle-aged woman, with a sharp, blunt cut with a mixture of blonde and silver strands, put a thumbs up for the green light after adjusting her earpiece and swiping confetti off her navy-blue pants.

"What an explosive match tonight here at the Skylight Arena. I'm now joined by none other than Dakota Callahan, who has played multiple positions for the New England Vipers over the past five years. Coach Flannigan asked you to step in as a defenseman for the closing minutes of the game. How do you feel about pulling off the winning move?"

"My plan was to go out with a bang, and that's just what we did." I swallowed hard, still trying to steady my breath from the adrenaline surge throughout my body. "We played as a unit tonight, as we do every game. We went in with the disadvantage of having several starters benched in the opening half, but we still pulled through."

The reporter jumped from the loud cork popped beside her. With her palm cupping her ear, she continued, "At the start of this season, you predicted the New England Vipers would bring the Glory Cup home just in time for your retirement. Any plans on your next move?"

I smirked as she held the microphone closer. I lowered my head to help her out. "There aren't any talks about contract renewals. Vipers are by far the best team I've played for in the league. My team will always be family, but I'm ready to settle down and have a few littles of my own."

"Sounds like a plan. Big, big win tonight, although just a few months ago you experienced a significant loss in your family. Did that weigh heavily on your final decision to retire?"

"Fran..." I smiled, wagging my finger. "You get me every time, Fran. Losing my meemaw was an unexpected dagger in my heart. Definitely a blindside, but I know she's always with me, carrying me, and smiling down on me from up above right now. I promised her I would exit the league after I won a championship, and I plan to honor that. So, Grandma Massey, this one's for you." I kissed two fingers, a signature gesture I used to make on television to let my grandmother know I was thinking about her.

"Will you be sticking around town for the foreseeable future or?"

"Nah, my home's back in Sunflower Falls. I'm searching for my soulmate." I rubbed my hands together with a light-hearted chuckle.

"Well, ladies, you heard it here first on Premium Hockey News. Dakota Callahan won't be with us for long. He's returning home. Congrats on the win, over to you, Charles!"

1 / THYRI

Hues of pale blue, orange, and crimson painted strokes throughout the sky as a warm, subtle breeze kissed my cheek. Streetlamps hovered, resembling oversized fireflies above the sunroof. Sticking my head out of the passenger window, I inhaled the smell of wet dew from the culmination of summer's end.

Calico Hills felt unreal.

A decade ago, I stepped foot onto this movie set with no intention of leaving. Modern homes crafted from steel and glass lounged on rolling hills. Some nestled away on hanging cliffs with floor-to-ceiling windows that only twinkled at dusk. Coffee shops and cafes occupied each corner. Outdoor patios jammed with wiry metal tables and umbrellas filled pockets of sidewalks, accessorizing city lights, and a score of palm trees that shimmied at the slightest touch.

We turned right on the corner of Suncrest Boulevard and Monroe, two street names I've grown way too fond of. It's been ages since I took a stroll on the sleepy side of the city I once called home. Memories of long Sunday walks wearing matching Alo sets and gossip sessions with my coworkers at The Red Taco floated above me like bubbles before dissipating into thin air.

A part of me still wanted to knock on our Mahogany-stained

doors, jump into my husband's arms, and end this one-sided lover's quarrel. But I carried our marriage on my back for six arduous years until our vows were ridden with dust and broken beyond repair. Now I'm spending my final night in Calico Hills playing get back with my ex, Noah Edwards.

"Okay, can someone please tell me why we're back in your old neighborhood?" Sebastion lifted his foot off the brake and exchanged glances with our best friend, Kels, in the backseat.

"And explain why we're dressed in all black?" Kels' eyes darted to mine as I dangled three ski masks in my hand with a mischievous grin.

"There's one last thing I must do before I hit the road back to hell tomorrow," I said.

"Now see, this is not the type of divorce party I had in mind. We need to be downtown at the Ritz, or poppin' bubbly over in Santorini somewhere, bitch." Sebastion gripped the steering wheel and pursed his glossy lips.

"Boy bye. None of us have money for a trip to Greece. Let's start there."

"Let's not," Kels said with a slight tremble in her voice. "Thyri, you weren't serious about playing that sick kidnapping trick on Noah, were you? I mean, he was a pretty shitty husband, but he doesn't deserve to be locked in a dark room and burnt with cigarettes—."

"Hold up, that sounds kind of fun." Sebastion bit his bottom lip in contemplation.

He and Noah never got along. They were frenemies at best, and only tolerated each other because of me.

My eyes narrowed at Kels. "Of course not. I've got something better in mind."

"Ya' know, back in the day when we were younger with shit for brains, I'd be down for something like this. But now that I'm a mother of three, I'd rather go home without silver bracelets slapped on my wrists."

"Three kids?! Girl, since when?" Sebastion curled his upper lip, adjusting his royal blue, two inch thick-framed glasses to look over them. "You knocked up again?"

"Hell no! I had my tubes tied when the twins were born. If I squeeze another child between these thighs, I'll blow up like a sumo wrestler."

"She's talking about Antonio," I clarified with a blank stare.

"I almost forgot your husband's an infant, too," Sebastion added with a light chuckle.

"He is. I'm just hoping Anjel can prevent the boys from burning down the house until I get back. I'd be living my best life if I never had kids."

"You always say that." I flicked my eyes up, knowing Kels was all talk and no action. When Sebastion parked across from 638 Vino Ave, I couldn't help but notice the multiple rays of neon colors flashing on the living room ceiling.

It's the only light emitting from the classic Tudor-style home, with Italian inspired details on the exterior. Textured stucco walls in sun-washed tones. Six pairs of arched wooden shutters. My olive-green Mazda CX-5 sat at the far edge of a cobblestoned, circular access road that led to a three-car garage.

Noah's home.

Doing nothing other than what he does best—gaming. I bet he hasn't showered in days.

"I keep tellin' y'all I lucked out with Rujnik in London," Sebastion teased, wagging his tongue. He pushed imaginary strands of hair behind his ears while sporting a low taper fade.

He's cuter than Kels and I combined. Only Sebastion can sculpt the perfect brows, create a minimal makeup beat, and still make a plain black turtleneck, black slacks, and lace up brown leather boots look like Versace.

He's blessed with the perfect butterscotch complexion, baby soft skin, and not an ounce of dirt under his manicured fingernails.

Sebastion smelled like a fresh bar of Irish Spring soap topped with notes of smoky woods, Cardamom, and cedarwood. A replica of Le Labo's Santal 33 perfume, he learned how to make from scratch.

"Alright, guys, this is my divorce party tonight, remember?" I folded my arms across my chest. "No boy talk."

"Then tell us why we're here? My knees are going numb. Shoot! They already sound like a bowl of Rice Krispy treats every time I bend them."

"My neck is starting to hurt, too. Got me all hunched over in this clown car." Sebastion massaged his shoulder.

Neither of my friends were the ideal size for my 2011 FIAT 500, but it fit my five-foot five frame just right. Sebastion was slim, and I weighed less than a buck fifty, give or take a few pounds. While Kels was the shortest yet fluffiest out of all of us.

She resembled a squashed blowfish in my backseat with waist length, shiny jet-black hair and hints of gray highlights around her crown. Her petite pre-postpartum body never returned after she gave birth. She complained non-stop about how all of her Filipino genes skipped out of her life by her mid-twenties.

I met Curly and Larry in a developmental math class during our second semester at Hartman Liberal Arts College. We flunked the course, formed a weekend study group, and we have been inseparable ever since.

Noah and I crossed paths at a skateboarding park my sophomore year. We connected over our love for body art, rock band concerts, cooking, and our dreams of dropping out of school to travel. Umber skin, a long ponytail, charming smile, and sexy tattoo sleeve went as far as the River Nile with me. We were best friends first, lovers second.

Everything seemed perfect until it wasn't.

He proposed in a hot-air balloon, which threw me for a loop. We ended up stuck in the clouds, and I felt pressured into saying 'yes,' dreading the long way down.

We graduated college months before, and I had no clue what path I was on. Most people don't at the tender age of twenty-three.

But with everyone pairing off around us, marriage appeared to be the logical next step. Noah got down on bended knee and popped the infamous question. Trapped with nowhere to run, I twisted my mouth and shrugged. "Okay...I guess." The romantic moment turned into four cruel hours of terrifying dread that foreshadowed what was ahead.

"We're going on a scavenger hunt."

"Nun-uh, Thyri. Not this shit again. I'm not figuring out no hard ass Harry Potter-head riddles, getting lost in the middle of a damn forest at midnight again. It's Friday. We've been at work all day... And I don't want to think." Sebastion frowned.

Kels' big round milk dud eyes blinked back at me in solidarity.

"Not that type of scavenger hunt. We're going to break into the garage and steal Noah's most prized possession."

"Steal what? I know you're not talking about that damn dog?" Sebastion yawned.

"Sure... Yeah, Beanbug, too." My voice trailed off. I had every intention of taking Beanbug with me. So as a favor, I asked my favorite couple next door, Mrs. and Mrs. Seymoor, to put him up in Noah's garage with fresh water and dog treats. This morning they jumped on the task without hesitation. The Seymoors weren't fans of Noah nor his disturbing streaming parties.

"You said you never liked that dog."

"That's not true." My eyes shifted. Kels' sharp memory is a gift I wish she never possessed.

"No, you told me Beanbug was a permanent eyesore in the house. You said he reminded you of a Boston pug with a terrible stroke. You made fun of his botched haircut, and questioned if Noah had him on steroids."

"Kels, seriously? I said nothing like that... Beanbug's just fat and old. He's got missing teeth on the bottom and nerve damage that makes his tongue sag from time to time." I winced at the visual.

"Chile, please. Beanbug needs to audition for a permanent role at Halloween Horror Nights. You know Noah's dog is not cute. Got every excuse in the damn book," Sebastion quipped, and I shoved him in the arm.

Did I wish to drag Beanbug along with me back to Sunflower Falls? Not really.

I'd rather leave every remnant of my failed marriage behind, but Beanbug's been my support system since the pandemic. After getting laid off, Noah picked up a PlayStation 5 controller and never put it back down. He traded in his Software Engineering career for a set of VR glasses, a headset, and numerous gaming consoles. His video game addiction surpassed a new level of pathetic when he transformed our master bedroom into GameStop overnight. He stopped applying to jobs and stayed up gaming all night.

But Noah's ironclad prenuptial agreement, I had no recollection of signing, put the final nail in the coffin. He kept me in the dark about his assets throughout our entire marriage. I slaved away at a toxic non-profit, overworked and underpaid, while Noah sat on a hidden goldmine.

Thanks to his smothering mother, I signed our divorce papers and walked away with nothing, because I filed first with no evidence of infidelity or foul play. Noah reluctantly agreed to pay my attorney's fees after months of sparring. Tonight will be my sweet revenge. I'll take Beanbug and the one thing he can't live without—a stash of vintage video games. I kept a spare key to the garage underneath the mat outside of the door. I just need another pair of eyes to find what I'm looking for.

"Okay, well, Beanbug's in the garage. Which one of you is coming with me?" I pulled the ski mask over my face.

"Don't look at me. I'll stick out like a sore thumb." Sebastion opted out, just as I expected. Despite his lanky, five-foot eleven frame, he's always been the scariest.

"Great, then you'll be the lookout and getaway driver."

Sebastion squeezed his hands around the wheel like he was prepping for a million-dollar heist. "Fine. But I'll only honk twice. If anything looks sketchy, I'm out." He checked the rearview mirror, then turned the headlights off. "I'm getting too old for this shit."

Kels needed more convincing. "You guys know this is breaking and entering, right?"

"Kels, can you please remove your Law & Order hat for a second? We'll be in and out. Besides, it's our last night together. We can at least make it memorable."

"Girl, just because you work desk duty at *District Thirteen* doesn't make you an expert at fighting crime." Sebastion flicked his eyes upward.

"Hey, I'm due for a promotion."

"And once you get it, we'll throw you a party." I took one last glance at the house before opening my door.

"...I'm still not sure about this, Tee." Kels unbuckled her seat belt.

"Oh well, tagged, you're in, bitch!" Sebastion snickered in the front seat, and Kels popped him on the back of his head. "Ouchh!"

Windmilling over the seats ensued, and I pressed my lips together. "Not now, you two."

I helped Kels squeeze out of the back of the car as she lowered her balaclava. "How can we breathe wearing these?"

"Just come on." I started a light stride up the driveway, ducking behind Noah's brand-new Ferrari F80, careful not to set off any silent alarms.

Kels followed suit, watching over her shoulder like there was someone after us. "Wait, I brought these just in case." Kels reached into her back pocket to retrieve a pair of black gloves before I touched the doorknob. Her addiction to detective dramas reached a new low. The floodlights switched on as soon as we set foot inside.

"I think we're busted, Tee, we gotta go!"

"They're on a timer, relax. I'm sure Noah's either chugging down beers or arguing with twelve-year-olds on StreamGeek. That man ain't staring out no windows."

"I'm shocked you all have come to this. I remember when you all were the perfect couple everyone envied."

Were we, though? I didn't know Noah and his toxic mom were a package deal until after we tied the knot. I fell in love with Noah's representative, but his mask slipped the moment life got rocky.

When we were dating, Noah would deliver lunch and fresh flowers with cute handwritten notes inside. He cooked dinner on a whim, and we swapped schedules for cleaning. And although his performance fell short in the bedroom, he found other ways to satisfy me.

On the day of our wedding, Noah wore a tuxedo jacket, black bow tie, long sleeve white shirt, and frayed denim shorts. My ivory skater dress cut several inches above my knee and a long lace train cascaded from the top of my head and gathered at my feet.

Our sneakers matched, and we flashed the biggest smiles on our faces. He swept me off of my feet as we walked down the rice-covered aisle. On the night of our honeymoon, his mom urged us to return home early because of her emergency. When Noah's mother finalized her second divorce, Noah started running every single decision we made together by his mommy dearest first. I thought I could deal with it, maybe even sway him out of their enmeshment, but I always came second to Elodie. Perhaps third, his excessive gaming took first place.

I bent down on the opposite side of Noah's weight bench, moving cardboard boxes and bins stacked underneath his custom heavy-duty shelves. "I know it's over here, somewhere."

"Uh oh, Tee. Come here. You need to see this."

"I can't right now. Just tell me what it is."

"I think... Beanbug is dead."

"What?" My head whipped around as I rose to my feet, bracing myself for the worst. "That can't be. It's only been a few hours." I was so busy looking around for Noah's box of keepsakes I didn't notice that Beanbug didn't run up to greet me. No barking, sniffing, sneezing, or scratching, just silence penetrating the drafty air.

"He looks... frozen." Kels' expression was a mix between petrified and disgusted.

Beanbug's four legs were stiff as a board, pointing upwards with his off-kilter tongue locked in place. I walked over and clapped my hands three times near his right ear. "I forgot to mention he's partially deaf."

On cue, he rolled onto his distended belly in defense.

"Oh shit!" Kels jumped back while I rubbed his head.

"He's not dead. That's just how he sleeps."

Beanbug snarled at Kels.

"Does it have a cage?"

"No, you want to hold him?"

"Fuck, no. Keep him far away from me." Her body shivered from the idea alone.

A frown creased my face, and I glanced upwards. "He just needs a little grooming. That's all."

Hiding behind Kel's short stumpy legs was a cardboard box tucked away in the corner with 'confidential' scribbled in a black Sharpie marker across it.

"The jackpot." Beanbug released a weak yap and grunt when I dropped him back onto the concrete. He snuggled back into his comfy bed.

"You hear that? I think that's Sebastion." Kels scurried to the side door. "All the lights are on upstairs. There's a shadow behind the drapes. Shit, it's Noah. He knows someone's in here!" The rain drenched half of Kels' sweatshirt as she ran in place.

"Okay, let me just grab this box." I struggled to pull it out on my own. "Lend me a hand, will ya'?"

"We've gotta get out of here now, Tee. Breaking in and trespassing is illegal. I'm not going down for this." Kels threw her hands up and paced back and forth.

"Really? I should have made you the getaway driver, you're just as scary as Sebastion."

Kels shrugged in agreement.

"Girl, if you don't get over here and help me."

"Oh, alright. Fine!" Her sneakers shuffled in place before she even moved. We pulled the box out together, almost falling to the floor, when a flicker of light shone through the window.

"What's in here? A load of bricks?" Kels kept her voice low.

I opened the box to double check.

Kels took one look inside and placed both hands on her hips. "Video games?! I know you're shitting me?"

"Shhh. Get Beanbug, I think Noah knows we're in here." Sebastion's horn grew louder and more incessant. After closing the box back, I located Noah's foldable dolly cart against the back wall.

"There's no way in hell I'm touching that dog."

"Help me lift these boxes on the cart, then."

"I know you didn't bring us all the way here to steal a Nintendo 64?"

"No, we got Beanbug."

Kels balled up her fists with a scowl.

"Okay, I'll tell you later. We've gotta go." Kels and I lifted the foldable cart over the threshold just in time. Rain obscured Noah's vision.

"Hey! Who's out there?!" Noah's voice boomed through the open window screen.

"Kels, if you'd rather not spend a night at your job, you better push with all your might." With Beanbug tucked underneath my arm, I placed my feet shoulder width apart. Just as on a skateboard, I remained steady.

"On three, Kels."

"Say less!" she screamed.

Without my countdown, we flew in the rain, my tresses wafting in the wind. "Woo-hoooo!!"

"Thyri!! Thyri!!" Noah poked his head out the bedroom window as the flood lights served as our spotlight.

"So long, momma's boy!"

The moment we reached the sidewalk, Sebastion grabbed both boxes and threw them in the trunk. Breathless, Kels crawled into the back seat. Noah ran out of the house, and Sebastion hit the gas while Beanbug grunted in my lap. "Say goodbye to Daddy!"

"What the hell?!" Noah clasped his head with one house shoe on while he kicked up a patch of grass on the front lawn. "Thyriiiii!!"

Sebastion honked the horn as we made a wide left turn, burning rubber from the slippery fresh sheet of rain on the asphalt. He rolled down the window and stuck out his middle finger while Aerosmith's *Crazy* bellowed over the speakers. I closed the chapter to the most cringeworthy era of my life, with a ninety's coded ending.

———

The murmur of crackling timber and hissing film played subtly in the background as Sebastion, Kels, and I took turns refilling our glasses with twelve-dollar Chardonnay. I rubbed my feet together on the cherrywood floor while leaning against the coffee table I plan on leaving behind.

Gold flames reflected in the lenses of Sebastion's frames as he stuffed his face with another slice of sausage and pepperoni pizza. A subtle glow lit up the living room of my temporary apartment rental. Cardboard boxes towered in corners with several pieces of my luggage scattered throughout.

Kels lounged on two oversized bean bags while Sebastion sat on an uncomfortable futon I slept on the past few nights. I sold all of my possessions on Trade Hive except for my car. It's the only physical reminder I'll have left from the decade I lived on the West Coast. In a few hours, movers will arrive to follow me back to my sleepy home-town of Sunflower Falls. A place I never thought I would return to— at least not at thirty-two, divorced and unemployed.

"My nephews are going to love Noah's old gaming systems. They never saw an original Gameboy or Super Nintendo in real life," Kels said.

"I can't believe you put us through all of that just to burn his entire video game collection." Sebastion sent another text on his iPhone with his legs sprawled across the floor.

"Knowing Noah, he probably has a few backups somewhere. But if he doesn't, I don't care. I lost count of how many nights I had to sit in bed alone listening to *Call of Duty*, *Grand Theft Auto*, and *NBA2K*." I shuffled through several cases of games, removing CDs and cartridges, tossing them into the fire.

"Isn't that the game he tried to use for a bootleg date night?" Kels squinted at the old *Fortnite* case in my hand.

"Plenty of times. He memorized every single dance move, then thought I was interested in learning them."

"Bunnie Barbie, or whatever the hell her name is, better have her dancing shoes ready, then." Sebastion snapped his finger, and Kels pierced him with a glare.

"Noah can have his way with as many barely legal gaming chicks as he wants now. *I. Am. Done.*"

"I know that's right!" Sebastion's head tilted as he raised his glass. "To new beginnings, bitch!"

We clinked our glasses together and exchanged horrific dating stories for the remainder of the night.

Noah replaced me within a blink of an eye. The ink on our divorce papers hasn't even dried. Weeks after I moved out last year, he had another woman take my spot as his personal vacuum. Except I didn't enjoy cleaning up after his mess. Dirty laundry. Past due bills. Unpaid therapy sessions. Career coaching. Beyond my role as a housekeeper, sex kitten, and private chef, I devoted my twenties to fulfilling all of Noah's needs. And still, I ended up as the third wheel in our marriage.

I should have taken a bow when my husband face-timed his mother at the top of every hour during our honeymoon in the Maldives. All the warning signs were glaring right in front of me, but I wanted to make us work.

Noah portrayed himself as the perfect gentleman at the onset of our relationship; opening doors, frequent check-ins, planning date nights, and never missed a 'good-morning' text. He was the unicorn I stumbled upon before he turned into a complete stranger in my bed. That's the downside of marrying too young—you quickly grow apart.

"You know, your last day in Calico didn't turn out too bad. I was picturing something a little more luxurious than greasy takeout and watered down wine, but I'm going to miss our little sleepovers."

"I agree. Our triangle won't be complete without you." Kels rested her hand on my knee, snapping me back into the present.

"What's up, Tee? You alright over there?" Sebastion talked in between mouthfuls, placing his phone down on the table.

"Yeah... Just thinking." I closed the wool shawl over my chest.

"Why are you feeling so down about this move? It's a brand-new start." Kels attempted to cheer me up.

I sighed, dreading my inevitable encounters with everyone that made my life a living hell growing up.

"Okay, I wish my family had a nice big house to come home to where I could live rent free and work in a cute lil' bakery. Sign my broke, bourgeois ass up, puh-lease!" Sebastion added.

"You know I'll be down in a few months to celebrate the holiday with you and Aunt Jacquee. I can't wait. Sunflower Falls reminds me of a romantic, small town right out of a Hallmark movie scene."

"It looks like one, too." Sebastion found my yearbooks while rummaging through my open cardboard boxes. He licked his fingers before opening my senior yearbook. "I thought you said there were less than a thousand people that lived there. Why does your high school look like a university?"

"Magnolia is the only school there." I shook my head.

"Oh, it's Pleasantville, huh?" Kels pursed her lips to the side, skeptical.

"Yeah, but ten times worse..." I stood up to gather the empty pizza box and Poppoli cans. In the kitchen, I guzzled down the corner of wine and tied up the trash bag, relieved to put some distance between me and those old yearbooks that linked to my embarrassing past. Four long years of terrible memories, torture, and regret.

Why didn't I burn them when I had the chance?

"Ooh, now who is he? I wish I graduated from Magnolia High. Y'all had all the Brads and every single one of them is hot." Sebastion swiped his pointer finger across his tongue and made a sizzling sound while holding it up midair.

"Give me that." Kels snatched the yearbook out of his lap. "Why do I recognize some of these names?... Jett Avers. Xander Nichols. Logan McDermott."

Here we go.

"You went to school with professional hockey players?"

"Hockey?!" Sebastion scrunched up his nose.

"Yeah, unfortunately," I said.

"Ain't nothing unfortunate about these boys, honey. Look at this one, showing off his abs." Sebastion traced his fingers down the page.

I knew which picture they were looking at.

"*The Dakota Callahan?!*" Kels' head whipped back in my direction.

My eyes narrowed at the mention of his name. I walked over to the futon they were sitting on. Exactly as I expected, Dakota was center stage, smiling at the camera with a twinkle in his left eye.

He flaunted a slab of abs underneath the orange Magnolia Falcons' hockey jersey he lifted just enough to tease. A pack of teenage girls surrounded his legs on ice with their jaws dropped. It's the most cringe-worthy high school yearbook photo I've ever seen. Dakota staged it on purpose. I know, because I'm the one who took the picture.

"Tony is going to flip out when he hears this. Dakota is his all-time favorite NHL player. He's never skipped a Vipers game, and you should see his new man cave. There are pictures of Dakota plastered all over it. Actually, he almost had me worried for a minute." Kels paused.

"Don't look over here. Even if Tony swung my way, I wouldn't pitch him a ball," Sebastion retorted.

"Alright, you two, that's enough digging for now." I struggled at prying the yearbooks from Kels' hands.

"Hold on, is this you?" Kels spotted the only yearbook picture of me that was published by accident. My small face was tense and devoid of a smile. Sporting a head full of kinky ringlets pulled into a pair of buns, blemishes from a cystic acne outbreak on my forehead glistened from the sun beating down my brow.

Daria in the flesh. My drawstring camouflage shorts hit right above my knobby knees, and the black *Rolling Stones* rock band shirt I wore had holes all over it as a trendy fashion statement. My high-top red Converse sneakers matched the lettering, and the skateboard standing upright was my permanent accessory. After a minute of playing tug-of-war, I gave up and took a seat beside them.

"Thyri...you were so cute."

"Okay, space buns, come through." Sebastion glided his finger across the caption, then stopped. "Most likely to portray Casper in a Broadway musical—what the hell is this?"

"I don't get it." Kels rolled her eyes.

"They're trying to say she's invisible." Sebastion put up a thumb down. "Corny."

"Yeah." I pressed my lips together as my cheeks burned hot from the memory. "It was a running joke that I could never live down. As the newspaper photographer, I was everywhere and nowhere at the same time. Aside from the taunting, they didn't pay me any mind."

Well, except for one person who I can't stand to this very day.

Sebastion sucked his teeth. "To hell with them, boo. I hated the kids from my high school too."

"Now I see why you never share much about your past. What a bunch of jerks?" Kels frowned.

"What sucks is that a lot of them are still there..." Forever stuck in Sunflower Falls. That's something I'd never wish on my worst enemy. "It's one of the reasons I'm dreading my return."

19

"With all that eye candy there, you can sign me up for the next flight. Kels, what day are you taking a trip out there?" Sebastion pursed his lips as he drooled over another photograph of the Magnolia Falcons team altogether at the ice-skating rink my sophomore year.

"Be careful. The girls were cutthroat about their favorite athletes back then. I can only imagine how they are now," I warned.

"Where are the other sports teams?" Sebastion thumbed through the yearbooks.

I shrugged. "That's it."

"What do you mean, that's it?"

"Your school has an unhealthy obsession with hockey." Kels wrinkled her nose at the pages filled with Magnolia pride.

Our undefeated Falcons were the focus of every photo, with indoor and outdoor ice rinks in the background. And how could I forget our infamous mascot, *Flash the Falcon*? Sunflower Falls' very own celebrity. You could find the unruly bird on the front of T-shirts, caps, flags, car bumpers, and other miscellaneous Sunflower Falls memorabilia. The residents painted my hometown in hues of orange, beige, and chestnut brown. Magnolia's school colors were a terrible combination, but they fit the aesthetic.

In Sunflower Falls, we only experienced two seasons. It either felt like summer or the dead of winter. There was no in between. It wouldn't surprise me if all the neighborhoods still look the same. The townsfolk loved absolutely everything but change.

My eyes shifted before I answered Sebastion's question. "Because hockey is the only sport there is."

"That's different." Kels leaned back, covering her legs with the fuzzy knitted throw I left on the futon.

"Yeah...Weird. I've heard of small towns going all out for football and Friday night lights, but hockey?" Sebastion closed my yearbook and handed it to me.

"Now you all see why I refuse to watch it? It's the only sport I watched until I left home for college. I found refuge in skateboarding and never turned back. That's the one and only photo credit I received underneath."

Thyri Richards, Sophomore.

I hate Sunflower Falls.

I hate hockey.

But I hate Dakota Callahan even more.

2 / THYRI

Sebastion waved goodbye in my rearview mirror while Kels buried her face in his chest. We'll see each other soon for Friendsgiving and the annual *Whisk It To Win It* competition in Tennessee, but there's a finality in our farewells. Only God knows when I'll return to Calico Hills, so I waited until they were out of sight before I shed my tears.

Sunflower Falls is a quaint small town on the opposite side of the country and a three-day drive from here. I'm not in a hurry, so I'm sure the U-Haul truck will beat me there. It's the furthest I will be away from what feels like my second family in years.

You would think I'd be rejoicing about my divorce, but my life has been spiraling out of control ever since I served Noah his papers. It's as if I'm on a rollercoaster ride traveling at the speed of light in reverse. Every job opportunity, every professional connection, every relationship I cultivated from scratch—gone.

I spent the past ten years building a house of cards. I could check the box next to everything a woman my age should have, and I did so with pride.

Wedding ring? *Check.*

Loyal husband? *Check.*

Homeowner and financial security? *Check, check.*

Then I pulled the trigger and my life changed for the worst overnight. Codependency was a foreign concept in my world growing up. My elders taught me that relying on men for survival was for the weak. Being soft, feminine, and carried just wasn't a reality for women that looked like me. All of that went out the window when I met Noah. My doting unicorn of a husband that would be a safe landing every time I fall.

Boy, was I wrong?

A few years after our honeymoon phase ended, our marriage went from sugar to shit. He wasn't the knight in shining armor that he portrayed himself to be. Noah turned into the roommate from hell that I bumped bellies with from time to time. Never in a million years would I have imagined living paycheck to paycheck after dropping my last name to an able-bodied man.

Footing half the bills with a Senior Software Engineer that worked at a top Fortune 500 company was insane to me. I gave Noah permission to walk me down the aisle as his bride and ended up with a toddler in return.

I may be low maintenance, quiet, and non-confrontational, but I'm no pushover. Like any other wife, I expected to be led by my husband, not the other way around. And Noah skipping the fact that we never had a mortgage was the final straw. He half-listened to me complain about the bullshit I experienced at work every night, encouraging me not to quit because we needed to keep the lights on.

Bastard.

The entire time, I was funding his gaming habit. That's what I get for being impulsive. I usually make good decisions—most of the time. But accepting Noah's hand in marriage came back to bite me. When I realized I made a mistake, I cried on the phone with Aunt Jacquee for two weeks straight. One minute you're sitting on top of the world, then the rug gets pulled from underneath you.

All of my friends and family say none of this is my fault. People grow apart, yadda, yadda. But I have to take accountability. I always knew Noah wasn't the *Neo* to my *Trinity*. We have too much in common. Those pairings never work out. Before Noah coasted his way into my heart, kick-pushin' on that damn skateboard, I fell head-over-heels for men that were total opposites. I'd be the perfect Siberian to somebody's Golden Retriever. Noah was more of a Border Collie. Obnoxiously smart, flighty, and neglectful as hell.

Well into my forty-eight-hour journey back home, my dreadful life status hit me like a ton of bricks. I'm divorced, unemployed, and childless. Going back to Sunflower Falls without any of those notches on your belt was tantamount to social suicide. I can see the rumorville spinning its wheels right now.

They were notorious for churning out watered down gossip. From the Sunday Service pulpit to the gritty bars lining Palomar Street, stale tea traveled like wildfire in a circular ten-mile radius. The uppity sorority mothers in pearls and NHL *WAGs* took pleasure in playing a real-life game of telephone wherever they went.

I would like to believe that the townspeople have changed, but deep down, I feel they never will. The elderly pass the torch to their adult children, who end up messier than them. People don't grow up where I'm from, they just master the art of hiding their flaws.

Every small town has its diamonds in the rough, but they're a rare find. Here and there, you'll stumble across a shiny new object, someone who appears to be as harmless as a sunflower until you uncover all the rust underneath.

After a few rest stops and hotel stays, I veered down a narrow road lined with bog birch trees. The fall foliage was stunning during that time of year. It looked as if I were on a scenic route, heading back home to find my lover in a cheesy romance dramedy. Beanbug awakened from his nap just in time to scoff at the faded blue 'Welcome To Sunflower Falls' billboard along with me.

"Wow. A whopping one thousand population increase since I skipped town in 2010." I inhaled the gentle breeze that made my hair dance in the wind. Wildlife lurking in the shadows of Red Maple trees caused the leaves to rustle. Two red-tail hawks cleared the skies, as their resounding kee-eeeee-arr made the forest preserve grow still.

I eased my foot off the gas to take in the beautiful scenery. There's an old saying that goes 'if you leave Sunflower, you won't be gone for long.' Maybe that curse is true. The additional residents were likely former townspeople returning to lay roots.

A trickle of them grandchildren, or obsessed sports fans enamored with the idea of living in a small hockey town. Our NHL players put such a spotlight on Sunflower Falls that it's now a tourist trap year-round.

I'm not surprised there aren't many people on the road during a lazy Sunday afternoon. This is how I remember it. No traffic, just nature, and a shit ton of crazy hidden behind closed doors. I cruised down the winding roads, rolling my windows down as a wave of nostalgia overcame me.

I peered over at the cedar log bridge that sagged with time. Covered in green moss and weeds, it loomed over the edge of the murky riverbank that would turn into a thick layer of black ice by winter.

Further down, I spotted a chapel and gazebo in the center of Fox Park. Both had a fresh coat of white paint, and they were an instant reminder of what every Sunflowerian valued. *Religion. Marriage. Family.* People frowned upon anything outside those three pillars. The level of hypocrisy never ceased to amaze me here. While shaking my head, I jumped the cracked asphalt to ruin Mrs. Dozoryst's flower beds that she grew on the front lawn of her mid-century yellow brick ranch.

My aunt Jacquee always complained about the unpleasant encounters she'd had with that old cow. I'm certain she's the one leaving multiple one-star reviews about my family's bakery on that *Flour Power* app, too.

"Sorry!" I yelled outside my window, although no one on the empty street could hear me. The way these people watched their doorbell camera footage for entertainment, it was only a matter of time before they found out it was me.

I suppressed the urge to drive through a few more picket fences and sideswipe the luxury cars of culprits who had been giving my aunt a hard time as of late. The colorful quaint cottages that rested on tiny hills and acres of land didn't require HOAs. Manicured lawns, freshly cut Privet and Indian Hawthorn hedges, and the occasional garden party are still staples around here.

I have one more stretch of road to go before I reach my final destination. Beanbug yawned and stretched in the passenger seat, unphased by the rough drive. I rolled the window up to silence his yapping at the cattle, munching on grass and fescue hay at Old Eden's Farm.

I steered the wheel to the left to avoid the pothole the township never filled. That ditch caused all the bumps, scrapes, and bruises I got skateboarding as a kid. I turned into a cul-de-sac with an island of Hickory trees swaying in the middle. A large hanging pole sign reading "The Raspberry" in script sat in my childhood home's front yard. Our block still hasn't lost its charm, just the few good people in it. Aunt Jacquee relocated to the cookie-cutter new homes of Sommerville, a gated community across town, two years ago. I never saw the appeal of paying an arm and leg in fees to live in a village that has an endless list of rules and regulations.

Aunt Jacquee and my uncle couldn't afford to live in Sommerville when I was growing up. They always dreamed of building a retirement home from the ground up and waking up to the murmur of the river spring in their backyard. Aunt Jacquee promised never to sell our home and put it in my name when she moved away. She turned the first floor into a Parisian inspired cafe that sold baked goods seasonally.

We may not be located downtown, but the tasty, authentic home cooked items on our menu are world renown. The Raspberry's name speaks for itself. Aunt Jacquee grew the bakery into a Cloverly neighborhood staple, with local honorary awards and non-stop recognition across various media outlets for three decades and counting. People used to travel far and wide from all corners of the South as soon as she opened the doors for the holiday season.

After accepting a cookbook deal from a major publisher, she bargained with me to take over the family business. Arthritis and a rare form of retrograde amnesia affected her baking skills, causing the food quality to decline overtime.

A wave of uncertainty washed over me as I considered her proposal. I told Aunt Jacquee that simply leaving my job would be irresponsible. For months, she had dangled the promise of free housing and business ownership as a potential career pivot, but going back home always felt more like a setback than a stepping stone.

She pressured me into changing my perspective until I had no choice but to give in. Three months ago, Bright Futures served me my walking papers because of my spotty attendance. Management insisted that I was a liability and lacked punctuality. Human Resources requested an exit interview, but I declined with no explanation. I just gathered my belongings and left.

When they hired me, I was an advocate for the company's mission. I loved helping underserved communities, but the mistreatment of youth and mishandling of donations rubbed me the wrong way. I showed up for the students as much as I could before my marriage catapulted downhill, but my passion had weaned after five years in.

My brakes screeched as I pulled into the only empty parking space on Bananaquit Street outside Miss Massey's classic white farmhouse with the wide grey porch and black wooden shutters. Except now it's rundown, with curled shingles on the roof that need to be replaced. Chipped robin egg blue paint revealed the weathered vinyl siding. While wilted flowers drooped over the brim of cracked resin window boxes.

Beanbug rapped his tiny paws against the passenger window and growled at the passerby. To my surprise, the bakery is already open. The 'We're Open' sign swung from side to side behind the fiberglass on the oak wood door with every entry and exit. I recognized a few old faces, but most of them are new. I stepped outside of the car, cradling Beanbug taut in my arms while inhaling the aroma of streusel pumpkin bread. The corners of my lips tugged at a smile from the familiar sound of Mr. Fisher's wind chimes two houses down. And that's when it hit me.

I don't hate my hometown, I just despise everyone in it.

"I love Miss Jade, but I'm unsure how much longer I'll be patronizing her business."

"Yeah, you're right. I've been coming here for years and never seen the quality go down this bad."

"I hope she's not cutting corners on the ingredients."

"For those prices, she shouldn't be."

"Last week, I purchased several jelly and butter croissants for thirty-dollars. I didn't notice the charred bottoms of all the croissants until I arrived home."

My eyes bucked at the criticism I heard from all the patrons leaving out of our front door. She was Aunt Jacquee to me, but everyone else knew her as Miss Jade, because of her love for the color. The movers left my boxes on the porch as I instructed, so I pretended to rummage through them.

"You know what? I think this will be our last visit for a while." Mr. Rucker and his frail wife rushed down the steps.

"My black coffee tasted like dirty mop water. Bless Miss Jade's heart, but she should close up shop until she can get more help."

"Well, she needs to close her doors soon." Mr. Rucker ripped into his raspberry scone with his dentures and frowned before throwing it on the ground. He stomped it underneath his leather boat shoes and my jaw dropped.

"What's wrong, hon?"

"The scone tastes stale, too." He frowned and a roadmap of deep lines and ridges etched into the cracked skin on his sun-spotted cheeks and forehead.

The elderly couple marched off dressed in their Sunday's best, arm in arm, grumbling along the sidewalk. I don't know how Mrs. Rucker still puts up with that old goat. Mr. Rucker always took pride in being a grouch, but this was a new low.

I dropped Beanbug on all fours and hurried down the porch steps to tidy up after him before anyone else could see it. The trash bin is within arm's reach. I narrowed my eyes while watching them waddle like penguins down the street and yelled, "Rude!"

"Now look who we have here."

My aunt's soothing voice instantly calmed me. Every time she spoke, it sounded like the strum of harp strings crafted from silk creating a melody. She stood with the door open wide, grinning from ear to ear, wearing loose fitting jeans, leather clogs, and a 3-pocket apron with a light gray cashmere sweater underneath. Strawberry paste and flour created an abstract masterpiece down her arms and manicured hands.

Aunt Jacquee was naturally petite, with smooth mahogany skin that had creased and stretched with time. The extra folds, freckles, and Crow's feet lines around her eyes may have multiplied in number, but her cherubic face remained.

She used bobby pins to secure the silver strands of her bowl-cut bob from falling into her face. Aunt Jacquee's eclectic style and costume jewelry matched well with her profession. When she wasn't kneading dough in the kitchen, she was hosting art galleries in French or touring exhibits across Europe. But I preferred the toned-down version of my aunt the most.

"Hey Auntie!"

"I was just about to pull out my phone to call you, but I forgot to put the stupid thing on the charger. The movers tried to leave everything outside, but I paid them a little extra to carry your larger boxes up to your room."

"You didn't have to do that." I walked back up the steps as Beanbug chased his curly tail.

"Who else was gonna move 'em?" She shot me a glare over her square-framed royal blue glasses. "What did I tell you about all that heavy lifting? You're just as stubborn as I once was. You never want to ask for help."

"I know, Auntie, I know," I said, smiling from the inside out.

"Look at my beautiful niece." She squeezed me as tight as she could, rocking me in her arms; a comforting, homegrown hug I hadn't experienced in a while. With her hands around mine, she raised my arms. It's the very first thing she does when she hasn't laid eyes on me for months—counts my tattoos.

"You haven't made any more trips to that tattoo artist, have you?"

"No, Aunt Jacquee, those days are behind me."

"Mmm. Hmm. The last time you told me that I discovered a vine of roses crawling up your thigh and Japanese symbols on your side. Did you ever find out what they even mean?"

"Auntie, that was for my thirtieth birthday. I was going through something."

"Well, we all know that's nothing new." The slits of her eyes resembled pools of dark chocolate as she squinted down at Beanbug with disdain. "So, you decided to move forward with bringing Satan's spawn along with you, huh?"

"I did." I rocked back and forth on the balls of my feet, readjusting the fitted baseball cap on my head.

Beanbug lifted his leg to mark the porch as his territory, but decided against it when Aunt Jacquee clapped her hands, gritted her teeth, and growled, "You better not!"

He wept and found the neighbor's patch of grass to relieve himself instead.

"I have a special place just for that one."

"Ooh. I hope it's not the basement." I picked up a box of my belongings while she held the door open for me to follow her inside.

"His only other choice is the attic. That scraggly thing makes my skin crawl just looking at it."

"Oh, you'll learn to love him. He just takes some getting used to." I whistled and Beanbug trotted up the cobblestoned walkway. "Come on, this is our new home."

"I've got a few loads of laundry I need to check on downstairs. Our old bedroom is all yours. We made it up just for you. I'll come upstairs to help you get settled in." Aunt Jacquee's dimples twinkled with excitement as she hummed her way through the kitchen. Aretha Franklin's 'Until You Come Back To Me' played over the vintage gramophone in the living room.

One step into the foyer and I no longer recognized the place. Aunt Jacquee's contractors did one hell of a job. Wooden tables and chairs, small enough to fit several pairs of two, filled the living room. Our repainted brick fireplace now matches the color of the plush ivory sofas.

After sitting the cardboard box down on the bottom of the staircase, I noticed an old man dressed in a three-piece suit with short white hair staring off into space in the corner by the window. A sprinkle of streusel crumbs decorated the saucer in front of him, but the mug of hot chocolate remained untouched.

"Helloooo," I sang to announce my presence, but he didn't bother to look in my direction.

"Yeaaah, and he scores!"

The sound of a puck crashing into the wall startled me and Beanbug, too.

"What the hell..." I returned to the hallway to discover a young hefty boy, maybe four feet six inches in height, wearing an oversized hockey jersey with shin guards to match. The sight of his hockey stick alone brought back unpleasant memories as he skid across the floor in a pair of dirty crew socks.

"Excuse me, are you with someone?"

He flipped open the gasket of the helmet much too large for his head, compelling me to step back. I'd seen those striking mossy green eyes before, I just can't remember where. He flashed a gappy smile. Some teeth were smaller than the others. His olive skin was clear, but his wide-bridged nose, ginger brows and curly hair gave him a distinct appearance.

"I'm waiting for my mom to pick me up." His hoarse voice, heavy breathing, and the chocolate brownie residue staining his chubby cheeks told me all that I needed to know.

"Right." I turned on my heels to leave him to it.

My aunt is running this bakery like a local community center. The floors are dusty and unpolished, and all the tables sit empty. Thankfully, Beanbug is keeping himself occupied by sniffing dusty corners and licking up old food. Aunt Jacquee agreed to hand over the reins, so I'm taking the first step to enforce change.

I twisted the 'Welcome' sign to 'Closed' and locked the front door. Three lonely cupcakes and a banana nut muffin are all that's left on the countertop's carousel. The labels in the empty glass container don't match any of the menu items listed on the chalkboard overhead. I bent over for a closer look and shook my head.

Apprehensive, I made my way around the counter to discover that the rumors and reviews about 'The Raspberry' are true. My aunt's pastries were no longer up to par. Uneven pie crust. Dense bread that's charred on the outside but doughy in the middle. The croissants were flat and deflated with patches of pale undercooked dough clinging to its layers. Her mouthwatering macaroons are now misshapen, cracked, and rubbery. And the batch of blueberry muffins in the wicker basket looked even worse.

They have sunken tops and overdone edges, as though they gave up midway through baking. I cut a slice of my aunt's show stopping raspberry pie. There's no way in hell she can mess this up, but the filling is sloshing beneath the browned crust. From the strudel's limp shape and the bread's charcoal edges, it was clear Aunt Jacquee's osteoarthritis and memory loss have gotten the best of her.

She must have spent the entire morning trying to bake every one of these recipes just right. No wonder there's nothing in the display case and no customers. Now I owe Mrs. Dozoryst an apology for messing up her flower beds earlier. Witnessing my aunt's health decline in real-time put me in a somber mood. I began the clean-up process, wondering, "What the hell have I gotten myself into?"

3 / DAKOTA

I STOOD in front of the floor-to-ceiling windows watching the cityscape of Marigold's Rowe flicker like a distant constellation below. Cradling a glass of Bourbon whiskey in my hand, engulfed by silence, I surveyed the penthouse suite and its immaculate design. Polished hardwood floors. Modern art. Chrome fixtures. The modern decor is a far cry from the charming aesthetic I'm used to seeing in my hometown a few miles away.

The downtown district, alive with its busy streets and sleek high-rises, shrank against the backdrop of towering tulip trees that bordered the city's edge. Beyond them, the landscape transformed into a vast and wild stretch of land that felt like another world entirely.

The outskirts, with their winding roads and rolling hills, seemed like they belonged to a different time, a different life. One sip of liquor sent a burning sensation down my throat, making me aware of how far I've come from Sunflower Falls and how much of me remained.

I traced my finger along the rim of the glass, gazing down at the city that sprawled beneath me. My hometown is a short drive from here, but why does it feel like another lifetime away? The thought of moving back to my old neighborhood sent a chill down my spine. I spent so many years running away from my past that an invisible line has formed, separating the man I am now from the boy I used to be.

I threw back what's left of the Bourbon whiskey in my glass, allowing its warmth to spread through me as the faint memories slipped away.

"Mr. Callahan, your guest has arrived," a soothing voice of a woman belted over the smart embedded speakers above me. There's a gentle precision in her tone. Every word is crisp and perfectly timed. It's neither too human nor robotic, with just enough familiarity to comfort.

"Let him in."

Bear bounced off the elevator next to the state-of-the-art kitchen, disrupting the silence in the room. His voice was a powerful, booming baritone that echoed with a hearty, unmistakable energy. It's deep and gravelly, with a bit of gruffness to it, but it's inviting.

The corners of my lips crawled upward at the mere sound of it every time. Bear could motivate a team or share a good-natured joke, all with the same magnetic charm. He massaged his shaggy beard while shaking his head in awe as he surveyed the splendor of my temporary humble abode.

The penthouse suite is a masterpiece of modern design, with sleek lines and a minimalist aesthetic that felt both luxurious and futuristic. It's dominated by tall stone pillars that add a sense of strength and grandeur to the room. Ambient lighting reflected off of the pristine wooden floors and ran discreetly along the walls and fifteen-foot ceilings.

Futuristic decor accented the space. Floating shelves, suspended lighting fixtures, and smart glass walls shifted between transparency and opacity at a touch. The furniture is low-profile and angular, with sharp edges, softened by high-end fabrics in muted tones of grey, charcoal and metallic silver.

An Ai-powered home automation system controlled everything

from lighting to temperature, responding to voice commands with little to no effort. Every detail, from the holographic art displays to the sleek, stainless-steel kitchen, reflected innovative technology and refined taste.

"So, this is what it feels like when you've made it?" Bear stood in the middle of the living room like Superman, slowly turning in a circle as he took it all in.

"I wouldn't know, because none of this is mine."

Topanga Luxury Lofts and Hotels offered me a three-month stay at no charge as long as I promoted their discounted packages on my social media pages and website. I can hardly afford a one-night stay in this hotel, let alone the custom, hand stitched Egyptian cotton sheets they change for me to sleep on every night.

"It's yours for now." He rubbed his hands together in contemplation.

"Whatever you're thinking, Bear, I don't want to know."

"This would be the perfect after-hours spot."

"How many times do I have to remind you? Those days are behind me."

Bear is the buck wild, fearless younger brother I never had. Sometimes, I have to rein him back in, but I give him grace during the off-season. He's still on the Glory Cup high while mine has raced down after being raked over the coals by the media.

"Did you get hitched and not tell us about it?" Bear's chaffed lips parted halfway, but at least this time his partial is in.

It's hard to distinguish the real teeth from the fake ones. At first glance, you wouldn't guess Bear was one of the top, highest-paid NHL players in the league. He carried his humble beginnings like a badge of honor on his shoulders and preached about modest living. Given my current state of financial ruin, I regret not listening. The only time Bear splurged was on women.

Something we both have in common. Except he hails from a large family and is the only son out of eight older siblings. My mother perished from a rare form of brain cancer by the time I turned eight years old. Growing up, I dreamed of living a life in the fast lane, far away from my childhood home, where I shined under bright lights, and people chanted my name.

I experienced all of that and then some just to end up feeling like a hollow well. Now you can hear my name at the end of every punch line on ESPN news. Sowing my wild oats yielded a fruitless career and my reckless lifestyle is to blame.

Meemaw's untimely death was the icing on the cake. She left me with a hole in my chest that's impossible to fill. I built up hefty savings during my last stretch in the league, but it wasn't substantial enough to live off of long term.

With ill guidance, I made some lofty investments—fifty percent of them were mistakes. So, when concerned fans inquire where all my money has gone? I promise I didn't flush it down the drain. Okay, maybe the first couple of contracts. They were a bust. But I was young and naive then, and investing was a foreign concept. Don't worry, I eventually hired the wrong people to do it for me. That's after I purchased two Bugattis and more real estate than I could afford.

My biggest regret is working with Gangsley's Sports Management Agency. Turns out, they are literally a gang. From breaching contracts, fraud, mishandling contract negotiations to unethical business practices and misappropriating funds, you name it; they did it, with some of the most powerful owners in the NHL involved. I won't even touch on the number of fake paternity suits and settlements that fell right into their hands. My grandmother warned me that a fool and his money will always part—and it did.

Instead of responding to Bear, I smirked and shook my head. "I thought you were dropping by to treat me to dinner. Why are you dressed like you're on your way to the beach?"

Bear walked towards me with his oversized hand extended for a shake in camouflage cargo shorts and a Coca-Cola T-shirt. "It's warm out, brother, if they won't accept me for who I am, then I'm not patronizing them."

Who was I kidding? Bromine "The Bear" Pulkovich was a household name. You could spot his six-foot burly frame from a mile away. Upscale establishments treated Bear like a god, even if he showed up in only swim trunks and pink bunny slippers. Out of all the new eight-figure contracts he could have signed, he moved forward with the Sunnyvale Kings.

They purchased him for a fraction of that price. He recently moved into a lush condo half a block away from here. When I move back into my old house, there's no way I'm getting rid of him. Deep down, I know he accepted the contract solely to keep his eyes on me.

"I'll never leave you, brother." That's what Bear said after sharing the good news and learning that my grandmother passed. His sisters made him a softy, but he's the complete opposite on ice. A raging grizzly described his playing style to a tee. His teammates in high school coined him with the nickname after he slammed his opponent's body so hard into the ice the rink parted.

Bear. It's stuck like glue ever since.

"Who's sending you flowers and cigars?" Bear nodded over at the dining room table.

"Take one guess."

"With your roster, is that a trick question?"

"I've cut them all off. My slate is clean." I rolled up the sleeves of my black sweater, took a seat on the couch, and leaned backwards on the suede, cloud-like cushions. "They're from my old assistant, Lala. Who else?"

"Weird shit, man. I still don't know why you hired Logan's little sister to be your assistant. Everyone knows she's not working with a full deck."

"You're telling me. I felt a little sympathy for her. I knew Logan's family growing up in Sunflower Falls before they split."

"Those are some of the ugliest flowers I've ever seen. Are they dead?"

"Yeah, she sent them that way..."

"Okay. Cryptic." Bear sat on the opposite side of the couch.

"I mean, I appreciate the gesture and all, but she just won't take a hint."

"They usually don't after they get hooked."

"Don't you think I know that? But it's not like I'm stringing her along. We spent one drunk night together, which is still a blur. She claims we had a romantic evening but all I can remember is falling asleep on the couch. I never touched her." I released a sigh. "It doesn't matter either way. I just want her to leave me the hell alone."

"She sent a card, too?"

"Yeah, but I'm not opening it. I sent Lala flowers with a note in it when the season ended as a farewell gift."

"What did you say?"

"Take care." I shrugged with a frown, flustered by Lala being the stubborn thorn in my side that I couldn't rid myself of for good. "There's enough on my plate right now. I figured ignoring her may do the trick, yet here we are months later."

"Tell her you've got some other chicks on the board and she ain't one of 'em."

"Why would I do that? I've got enough bad press as it is. She's got connections."

"True." Bear nodded in agreement. "Anyway, this isn't what I had in mind when we discussed celebrating your retirement. We should be at the nude beaches in Brazil, surrounded by enormous boobs and booze, a man can only imagine."

"I got dressed up for a New York rib-eye and the only thing we discussed is you coming with me next week to help clean out my granny's house."

"That depends. How hot are the women in your old neighborhood?"

"How would I know? I mean, they were cute when we were growing up, but that was ages ago."

"You haven't looked at any pics?" Bear's upper lip curled as he leaned forward.

"Well, yeah, but they're older with mom bods now."

"Hey, hey now. I don't discriminate." He held both of his ashy hands up as if to surrender.

"You date women with kids?" My eyebrows stitched with concern, but I'm not surprised. No one was off limits with Bear, midgets included.

"Yeah, why not? I come from a blended family myself. The more the merrier. And quiet as it's kept, some of the best sex I ever had was with this sexy ass milf."

"The one that was married?!"

"I did not know until after the deed, alright? Why do I have to keep explaining myself to you, assholes?"

"I can tell you one thing. They definitely aren't the type of dingbat chicks that you're used to."

Bear twisted up his lips until they resembled a pink bow. "Enough on me. How's everything else going?"

"Not bad. All the press is dying down since training has started but..." My eyes cut in his direction. "I'm sure you've heard?"

"That you're moving forward with the civil suit against Gangley's firm?" He squinted as I nodded in confirmation.

"Yeah, about that." Bear grunted while pinching his bandaged nose. "Are you sure it's worth the fight?"

"It's the only shot I've got."

"You mean to tell me companies aren't blowing up your phone for sponsorships and brand deals? We just won the Glory Cup, for Christ's sake."

"I'm on my way out of the league...that's a risky investment." My tone remained flat. Bear and I had crossed this bridge one too many times before.

"Not if you stay visible. There's always coaching, commentating..."

"I only love hockey on the field." I cut Bear's brainstorming session short. "Too much red tape and politics will kill the game for me."

"Understood..." He backed down. "You know if you ever need

anything." Bear rested his elbows on his gigantic knees while peering back at me. "I got you."

I rose from the couch and walked over, holding out my fist for a pound. "I know, brother, but this is something that I have to do for me."

4 / THYRI

Aunt Jacquee and Uncle Kai turned my old bedroom into a stockroom. The twin-sized canopy bed, white desk, and matching computer chair were all gone. A textured accent wall and a calm wheat color replaced my lavender wallpaper.

Roll away metal racks filled with empty jars, blank labels, boxes of straws and napkins, bags of flour, and condiments my aunt ordered in bulk were against the wall. I walked over to the small window and cracked it open to let in some fresh air.

A crack marred the murky window on the side of Miss Massey's home. Except there's no longer any light or movement in her kitchen. And the broken window Dakota once hit his puck through is now boarded up. Memories of us bickering across the fence resurfaced, and a faint smile tip toed across my lips as tears filled the rim of my eyes.

As kids, we were at each other's throats nonstop, but Miss Massey always took my side. When puberty hit, the tension between Dakota and me only thickened. Girls were crawling in and out of his bedroom window, and I ratted on him countless times for sneaking out. The more attention people gave him, the cockier he got. It didn't help that he was one of the top hockey players on every NHL scout's radar since the sixth grade.

But as Miss Massey aged, her health naturally declined. Diabetes. Arthritis. Mild strokes. Dakota spent more time at our house until she got well. My aunt treated him like a king even after I begged her to make him stay elsewhere. One time, we fought over who could have the last corner of Yummie-O's.

Our argument got so heated, it turned into a brawl on the front porch for all the neighbors to witness. When Dakota got the upper hand, I used everything as a weapon: eggs, a paint gun, broken dishes, and his hockey sticks. When Aunt Jacquee and Miss Massey returned to see the disaster we created, they grounded us for weeks.

By the time I entered high school, Dakota was starting his junior year. He and I exchanged little to no words unless we were shoving each other in the hallways or arguing on the way to school. He hung out with the popular jocks and cheerleaders while I stuck with the same group of rejected emo friends I'd known since middle school.

I'm what many would consider a late bloomer. All of my firsts occurred during my later years: my first kiss, my first love, my first you-know-what. I didn't become boy crazy until my sixteenth birthday. Junior year is when I blossomed. I got my braces removed, my breasts sprouted out of nowhere, and I developed a few premature curves the hot guys in school couldn't keep their eyes off of. Now and then, I would catch them checking me out in the hallways and during gym.

As soon as Dakota moved away to college, all the boys in our neighborhood started noticing my presence. I never understood why until I caught wind of Dakota cracking jokes and spreading lies about me. He was the annoying older brother I never asked for. Twenty years later, my cheeks still burned red from the mere sight of him.

I never followed Dakota's whereabouts, but seeing his Colgate smile plastered across countless billboards and sports ads online makes it hard to miss. I scoffed and shook my head while inspecting

Dakota's old bedroom window on the first floor, across the red berry bushes planted along the fence in our backyard.

But this time I can only see streaks of sunlight reflecting off wooden floorboards, and the casement windows covered by tattered screens in Miss Massey's sunroom. That's where the EMT found her unresponsive with a faint pulse. I still remember the morning my aunt blew up my phone to deliver the devastating news.

Dakota requested a wellness check after not hearing from her for two days straight, so my uncle and aunt traveled through the storm to check on her themselves. But when they arrived, it was too late. The ambulance rolled Miss Massey out on a stretcher with a white sheet covering her entire body and face.

For minutes, my aunt's words were indistinct, but I could hear her heart breaking like a glacier inside of her chest. They were close friends, more like sisters. Tears rolled down my face just imagining Miss Massey suffer from a heart aneurysm alone with no one to help. My heart softened towards Dakota as soon as I learned about it.

She was a second mother to me, and the only family member Dakota had left. Her spunkiness, wisdom, southern hospitality, and witty sense of humor is what I'll always remember her for. I pulled my head back inside, overwhelmed with regret.

How could I allow my divorce to prevent me from attending her funeral?

In the corner of my room were a metal headboard, a mattress, and a black futon with dust ridden photo albums and cracked old frames stacked on top of each other inside of a cardboard box.

I opened up one of the album covers to find a picture of a young couple laughing with vibrant smiles, and wedding cake smashed all over their faces. My uncle Kai's dashing features haven't changed since his prime. Aside from a thinning silver goatee, and much less hair, he's kept his muscles strong with only a few inches shaved off his six-foot height. Aunt Jacquee swears he and Barack Obama were twin brothers in another life.

The sky-blue tuxedo and ruffled shirt fit him just right. The thick sideburns, curly hair on his chest, platforms, and skinny gold chains around his neck were a stark contrast to the knitted sweaters, Ferragamo moccasins, and boring slacks he wears now.

Aunt Jacquee's infatuation with this man was clear from the sparkle in her eyes. And despite the many challenges they've faced throughout their twenty-nine years of marriage, she still looks at him the same. Sometimes I wonder if I'll ever look at a man like that again.

"Riri!!" Aunt Jacquee yelled from the bottom of the stairs, locking the front door of the bakery behind her. She agreed to close up shop and reopen when we have enough inventory and a revamped menu.

"I'm upstairs! I'll be down in a few minutes!"

To my surprise, she gave little to no pushback when I suggested it. Maybe she's finally ready to let go. After hopping in the shower of the remodeled master bathroom, I sniffed the fresh eucalyptus dangling from my filtered shower head. I'm late to our one o'clock meeting, but the clanking of pans downstairs lets me know my aunt isn't in a rush.

I insisted we postpone my pastry training to review QuickBooks instead. I'm certain our profits aren't exceeding our debts. The heated stone floors compelled me to wiggle my toes. My aunt and uncle had outdone themselves with the upgrades.

Farmhouse style wall paneling, marble floating sinks, a vintage chifferobe, and natural lighting made me feel as if I stepped right into a Homes and Gardens magazine. But the twelve-foot skylight ceiling, custom walk-in closet, and loft reading nook adorned with crane-patterned wallpaper were the true icing on the cake.

"Riri!! Any day now, your uncle Kai and I have doctor appoint-ments scheduled at five."

"I'm coming!"

Life never allows enough time to prepare you for its shifts. All the obstacles make you feel as though you're stuck in a kayak on a raging river that never ends. One minute you're cruising, or teetering on the edge of a drop that's beyond your control. You resolve one problem just to discover there's another hidden right behind it.

Uncle Kai's health has done a complete three-sixty. Years of smoking non-stop almost did him in. Aunt Jacquee worked around the clock to pay my college tuition and his hospital bills. He required three surgical operations to remove non-cancerous nodules off of his lungs. My aunt hasn't seen him spark a cigarette since.

The revving of a fake engine and action figurines in battle greeted me as I descended the stairs. The chubby boy with the hockey jersey has returned.

"Where is this child's momma?" I thought to myself with a brow of volition raised. I stepped over Beanbug, who was wagging his curly tail, barking, and jumping up and down from the sound effects.

At least one of us has made a new friend.

"You look...refreshed." My aunt glowered at me over the rim of her new eyeglasses, the Cajun-red cat-eye frames adding bold flair to her black wide-legged pants and ivory silk long-sleeve shirt. "The O-O-T-D could use a little work, though."

Aunt Jacquee peered at my Spandex biker shorts, boxy graphic t-shirt, crew socks, and suede Birkenstock clogs with a curl in her upper lip. Little does she know, this is as good as it gets.

"What do you know about an outfit of the day?" I continued down the steps.

In the past, she would have told me to go back upstairs and change. Aunt Jacquee believed in looking presentable everywhere she went. A quick run to the grocery store required a face full of makeup, two David Yurman stacks, and a stylish ensemble. She pieced her clothing together like a work of art. But I'd always been a tomboy at heart.

"Haven't you heard? I'm all the rage on social media for the fifty-somethings these days. Everyone loves my fashion sense, and they always compliment me on how youthful I look for my age."

"I bet they do, but for a day of baking I don't feel I look too shabby myself."

Aunt Jacquee shifted her gaze up at the tray ceiling with crown molding.

I won.

"Did you stumble across any of my recipe books upstairs, by any chance?"

I shook my head. "I didn't see them. Are you sure you all didn't take them with you to your new house?"

Aunt Jacquee pursed her lips together as the folds in between her brows rippled. "I could have sworn I told Kai to put those boxes in the basement. We practically tore the house apart looking for them."

"Worst-case scenario, Auntie. We'll have to write them from scratch."

Bewildered, my aunt staggered off into the kitchen. "Let me go check on these cookies. I'm sending a batch home with Jace."

Jace?

I chewed on my bottom lip to keep my mouth shut as I observed him from afar. I'm not sure what irked me more. My aunt being taken advantage of for free daycare services, the fact he was here on a Saturday, or the Avers hockey jersey he wore over his clothes every day. *Number 8.* I had a history with the man behind that number. Horrific memories I've tried my best to forget. I watched Jace make several failed attempts at throwing a tennis ball for Beanbug to catch.

"He doesn't play fetch."

Jace looked up at me with a contorted expression, and I continued walking past him into the living room. I flipped back pages of two yellow notepads and placed calculators and pens on two of the tables I pushed together the night before. I opened my laptop and signed into QuickBooks, then noticed the same old man from yesterday sitting on the loveseat near the fireplace. He was holding a cup of hot chocolate in his hands.

What don't these people understand? We're closed. If Aunt Jacquee keeps this up, she's going to drive me insane. I took a seat and blew out my breath to calm my nerves. An hour later, Aunt Jacquee finally joined me in the dining room after getting a lemon meringue pie recipe just right to include in her cookbook.

"Taste this." She placed a slice of the pie in front of me, and I did as I was told.

As much as I wanted to find something negative to say about it, I couldn't. The crust was delicate with just enough crunch and the creamy lemon mousse kept you craving another slice. I used my fingertips to clear every single crumb off of my plate and returned to the kitchen for seconds and thirds.

"Good, ain't it?" Aunt Jacquee smirked as she put a load of soiled dishes into the sink.

I nodded between mouthfuls. "It's... delectable." I completed an entire budget plan for the bakery before Aunt Jacquee finished tidying up.

"Okay, I'm ready when you are?" My aunt pulled out the wooden chair in front of me like I was a reporter waiting to get first dibs on an exclusive interview. She placed a plate of pie on the table and dug in.

"I was ready two hours ago," I grumbled, keeping my volume low. "Auntie, how are we supposed to discuss finances with all these people here? You—"

Several loud honks from a car outside interrupted me mid-sentence.

"What people, dear?" My aunt moved aside the sheer drapery for a better view outside of the bay windows. There was an overcast outside from the looming storm on the way.

"Hold on, Jace's mother is here. Jacey, grab your things!"

"Those people..." I uttered, patiently waiting for Jace's mother to come inside so I could give her a taste of my mind.

If I don't make it known that we're officially closed until October, my aunt sure as hell won't. Jace trudged down the hallway with a hockey helmet on his head, and a tattered bookbag over his shoulder, waving goodbye. I signaled a weak salute instead.

"Well, what's wrong with you?" Aunt Jacquee sat back down, gathering a ruffled shawl around her shoulders as she unwrapped a mint.

"That lady allows her son to stay here all day long, but doesn't have the decency to come in?"

"Be nice, Thyri. It's just a part of our little routine."

47

"But it's not my routine, and it won't be. There's no way I'll be able to get this place up and running alone in less than six weeks with someone's child running around."

"He's not a problem. You can barely even tell when he's here." Aunt Jacquee dismissed me with a light flick of her wrist.

"Auntie, I don't like kids, especially ones that don't belong to me."

"Your mind will change once you have a few of your own." She flipped through the pages of her notepad, stopped on a blank page, and scribbled the date in the corner.

"I don't know about a few, if any at all."

Aunt Jacquee's fiery glare left me with no choice but to look away. After all these years, the topic of children was still tender. She learned she wouldn't be able to bear children in her late twenties after several miscarriages. It's the reason she welcomes them with open arms.

I stirred in my seat and selected my next words carefully. "My concern is his safety. I'm also not a part-time nanny."

"Then, his mother can drop him off here and I'll come pick him up then."

"Auntie Jacquee, you live over an hour away. You also have your upcoming art tour in Europe. How are you going to babysit while traveling overseas?" I scratched my head to hide my frustration. "Who is his mother, anyway?"

"Just someone in need of a helping hand."

Her endearing tone and judgmental gaze compelled me to switch gears.

"And what about..." I pointed towards the dining area so the creepy old man couldn't overhear.

Aunt Jacquee looked over her shoulder with a frown like no one was in there.

"The man...that old guy." I reduced my tone to a faint whisper.

"Oh, Mr. Henry?! He doesn't bother a soul."

"Can he hear?"

"Thyri, the man isn't deaf, just sad, that's all," Aunt Jacquee whispered back.

"Oh-kay..." My eyes shifted from left to right. "Soooo, what happened to him?"

"Life." Aunt Jacquee's head canted to the side while scooping up the last bite of pie on her fork. She licked her thumb before continuing on. "After his wife died, his sons moved to the Upper East for college, which left him with his baby girl. The bad seed."

"Is she in jail or something?" As creepy as the old man was, I feared the behavior might run through their family line.

"No. She's not." Aunt Jacquee rolled her eyes, and I leaned back. "The last time he saw her was in here. I can't exactly remember, but it was over a year ago. They had a heated argument about her dropping out of college and running off with some professional hockey player. Left him distraught, but she was always into some mess. And it's such a shame because he's all alone but a really nice man. He stares out that window, hoping she'll make her way back home someday."

"I'm moved and understand his plight, but what does any of that have to do with us closing down the bakery?" I squinted while covering the side of my mouth with my hand. "You can't ask him to come back when we reopen?"

"Thyri, how is he in the way?" She scowled like I was the one getting on her nerves. Frustrated, I threw my head back and ran my fingers through my hair.

I almost forgot how bullheaded and stubborn my aunt used to be when she wasn't in charge. If my marriage didn't teach me anything else, it was setting boundaries.

"Now, Auntie Jacquee, this isn't what we discussed before I came." I kept my tone firm.

"Yeah...I know." Her lips clenched while looking off into space.

"I need to get this place in order." I turned the laptop around to show her the income statement. "These are the profits from the past year. We're still in the red."

"I trust you will turn The Raspberry around, but I have some loyal customers. This is more than just a local bakery to many of them. It's a nostalgic memory, a place to build community, and for some...a second home."

"I get that, but we need to rebrand to get ahead of the competition—"

Aunt Jacquee patted me on the arm to knock me off my high horse. "That's fine and all, baby, but I show compassion for everyone that walks through the door."

Maybe that's the problem.

Her stern look was a warning shot. Don't get ahead of yourself, Thyri. She still has part ownership of the bakery. I leaned back to retreat.

"Very well then." I dropped the subject and pulled up a list of scheduled dates that painters and cleaners would be out. "They will finish everything by the fifth. I just need to find someone for the roof."

"Look at you." She grinned in approval. "I'm leaving this place in good hands."

My smile faded after remembering Miss Massey's beautiful home. "You think we can have the contractors fix up Miss Massey's roof, too?"

"That would be sweet, but I believe Kota's got everything covered."

"Really?" My brows bent. "What does he plan on doing with it?"

"The last time we talked, he said he wasn't sure. I don't think losing Miss Massey has hit him yet."

"Is he holding up okay?"

She nodded slowly. "He's in better spirits these days. Which reminds me, I want to make him a special batch of pumpkin spice donuts when he gets here."

"Wait, what do you mean by here?"

"He's retired now, honey, where have you been?"

My eyes bulged out of my sockets. Dakota was the last person on Earth that I wanted to see.

"I don't keep up with that man." My palms moistened at the thought. "Why would he be returning to Sunflower Falls out of all the places he could choose from as a multi-millionaire?"

"I don't know how long he'll be in town. When he reaches out, I do my best not to meddle. He's ordered everyone in the neighborhood not to touch Miss Massey's property, and that's what I plan to do. Now, write this recipe down."

Aarrggh! Suddenly, the room was spinning and I felt winded, like someone just caught me off guard with a punch straight to the gut. If she told me this six months ago, there's no way in hell I would have agreed to stay here. I begrudgingly grabbed the pen like a defiant toddler.

"One-fourth teaspoon of salt. Two sticks of softened unsalted butter...or did I use salted butter?" Aunt Jacquee tapped a finger on her chin. "Anyway, one cup of golden-brown sugar, two cups of flour, one-half cup of pumpkin puree...I think."

I massaged my temple and made another scratch out on the paper.

"Shoot, I completely forgot about the time." Aunt Jacquee hopped up from her seat after looking at the dainty watch bracelet on her wrist. "Your uncle and I are going to be late."

"What about Mr. Henry?" I pointed to the living room in a panic.

"Thyri, get a grip. I'll have a talk with Mr. Henry on Monday."

Before I could say anything else, the front door slammed.

Great.

My worst nightmare has come true, and I'm stuck in the house alone with Michael Myers.

5 / DAKOTA

I woke up gasping for air. Frostbite lingered on my lips as if I'd just stepped off the ice. I'm drenched in sweat. And my heart is an unyielding drum inside of my chest, beating fast enough to break through my ribs. The eerie dream gripped me again, tighter this time, as if it would never let go.

In it, I'm back where I used to belong—on the ice. A wave of sound crashed over me as the roaring crowd chanted my name.

"Kota! Kota! Kota!"

They shouted with enthusiasm, their faces glistened under the harsh stadium lights. I beamed with a smile so wide it hurt my cheeks. My teeth sparkled like the blade of my stick reflected on the light just right. I remember taking off my helmet, running a hand through sweat-soaked hair, and basking in their adoration. For a moment, everything was perfect.

Then it all changed.

The lights went out, plunging the rink into a darkness so thick it felt alive. The noise from the crowd died down, leaving a vacuum of silence that pressed down on my shoulders. I turned in slow circles, the empty stands staring back at me like hollow eyes. My teammates were gone. My coach, gone. The puck, my lifeline, had vanished. All that remained was the sound of skates slicing through ice, sharp and eerie, circling me in the void.

I spun around, desperate to find the source, and there they were. At the far end of the rink, standing together like a beacon in the gloom, were the two people I loved the most. My grandmother with her favorite knitted shawl draped over her shoulders, and my mother, her heavenly face soft with the warmth I barely remembered. They were smiling and waving. Their presence filled me with a bittersweet ache.

"Dakota, we miss you! Come with us," they called out, summoning me closer.

But the ice stretched between us like an impossible chasm. No matter how fast I skated, I couldn't reach them.

"Wait! Wait!" I yelled. My voice cracked as my legs pumped harder. My muscles screamed in protest. "I'm comin', just wait for me! Please!" By the time I got within arm's reach, the ice beneath them cracked and splintered. Before I could save them, they fell. The emptiness swallowed them whole.

The loud knock at the door jolted me awake. I shot up from the couch with ragged breath and sweat sticking to my skin. The familiar scent of stale beer and cold pizza mixed with the faintest whiff of my meemaw's sandalwood and vanilla perfume still clinging to the fleece blanket draped over me. I blinked as my vision adjusted to the streaks of light filtering through the curtains.

This house felt like a ghost itself. Stacks of unopened mail covered the coffee table, and a sea of crushed chips and beer cans littered the floor. I had reduced my life to this wreckage, a pathetic monument to everything I'd lost. I rubbed my face. The scratchy stubble on my chin grounded me in the present. The knock came again, pulling me to my feet. My legs felt like rubber as I stumbled toward the door, stubbing my toe on a moving box I left in the middle of the floor.

"I told Bear to drop by tomorrow. I'm not in the mood for visitors."

I swung the door open, expecting a delivery guy, or another neighbor dropping off more sympathy flowers.

Instead, I found *her*.

For a moment, my lungs collapsed. Thyri stood on the opposite side of the screen door with her wavy hair strands tousled by the wind. Her almond-shaped, brown eyes carried a quiet determination that made me feel like maybe I wasn't completely alone just yet.

She opened her mouth to speak, but I didn't hear a word. All I could think was that for the first time in weeks, I felt something other than despair.

Hope.

A fragile, flickering hope that our past isn't beyond repair.

"Heyyyy. Is this a bad time or?" Thyri peeked through the screen to see if anyone else was in here with me. "... You look like you've just seen a ghost."

"Can't say it doesn't feel like it. I was just getting ready to tidy up a bit." I lied, unlocking the screeching screen door to welcome her in.

"Oh, there's no need. I just stopped by to drop these off." Thyri lifted a baby pink cake box with *The Raspberry* logo printed on the top, sporting a painful smile. "Aunt Jacquee's been begging me to get them to you every day since she learned you were back in town."

She did all that knocking just to deliver some treats... Nothing else? I sighed. "What's in it?"

"They're pumpkin spice donuts. Something new on the menu we're trying."

An uncomfortable silence evaded the space between us as I stepped out onto the porch to accept the gift.

My lips twisted to the side as I opened the box to a dozen donuts doused in crystallized brown sugar. "They smell delicious." I nodded in approval. "Send Aunt Jacquee my love."

"Yeah. Of course. I'll do that."

In true Thyri fashion, she's looking everywhere else but in my direction.

The clear sky. Leaves waffling from the gutters. A handful of

Common Grackles fluttering their wings and chirping across the street.

It's official. She still hates me.

My lips twisted into a lopsided grin as she fidgeted and shielded her eyes from the relentless sun. Thyri's the only woman I know that's reserved, hypersensitive, and socially awkward until she's crossed. Maybe she's tamed the dragon raging inside of her over the years. I felt her scorpion sting once. I never wanted to feel it again.

"Soooo." Thyri released a deep sigh before finally looking me in the eye. "How have you been?"

"I'm okay, but if you asked me some months ago, it would probably be a different story."

"Yeah. I...ummm...can understand that." Thyri rocked back and forth on the balls of her feet. "I wanted to share my condolences with you in person at the...you know..."

Funeral. I'm glad she doesn't say it. The reminder that my grandmother is buried six feet under is still jarring to hear. I haven't accepted it yet. My attention drifted to the mail carrier sprinting off the porch next door, a small dog yapping at his feet as he hurried down the sidewalk. Then I turned my gaze back to Thyri.

"Yeah. She would have wanted you there."

Thyri's flushed cheeks are still a signature sign of her discomfort. She tugged at the stretchy heather gray biker shorts, riding up her toned butterscotch thighs. Her heart-shaped face had matured like fine wine, and a natural glow shimmered on her dewy skin.

Thyri's pillow soft lips and high cheekbones truly set her apart, but there was something about her mocha brown eyes that were hypnotizing. Eventually, my eyes roamed down to her perky breasts, slim waist, and rotund cheeks that she tried to hide underneath an old N-Sync T-shirt. The colorful artwork adorning her right arm was new to me, but fitting for her personality.

Thyri always possessed striking features, except they're a far cry from the teenage version of her I remember. Now she's poking out in all the right places. I brushed my fingertips across my lips to stop myself from drooling. To mask my physical attraction and the boner growing in my jeans, I redirected the conversation.

"What brings you back here now?" I asked.

"I guess you can say some unfinished business."

"It's not the divorce?"

"Who told you about that?"

The tip of Thyri's upturned nose wrinkled. I hit the wrong button. Right question, wrong timing.

"Aunt Jacquee and my grandmother were like this." I crossed my middle finger over my pointer. "If you came around more often, you would know that. Plus, there's no wedding ring on your left hand."

Thyri rubbed the finger where her wedding band used to be. Divorce is still a sore topic to breach, I see.

"I don't need you in my business."

That quick, she turned to walk away, but I called after her. "Why didn't you make it?"

"Seems like you already know the answer to that question."

"My grandmother was worried sick about you."

Thyri placed a hand on her stomach like her heart had sunk down from her chest. Guilt etched into her expression.

"Listen... I wanted to come back. I had a lot going on, and losing Miss Massey was just another nail in the coffin."

I smirked and folded my arms across my chest, unable to hold in my chuckle.

"What's funny?" Thyri shook her head while resting a hand on her hip.

"She said you visited her like three times. It's been a decade, Thyri."

"Okayyyy..." Thyri threw daggers my way. "I've always hated this town. Your grandmother knew I had no intentions of coming back."

"It wasn't all that bad." I walked over to the post with peeling paint and leaned against it.

"I hate to burst your bubble, *Big Time*. But a lot of us didn't grow up with fans. Unlike you, we don't have the fondest memories of this place."

"Here we go. There she is. That's the Thyri I know."

"You're such a toddler." She grimaced. "You know I haven't forgotten the terrible things you did to me growing up."

How could I forget? Thyri's infamous grudges lasted a lifetime. Cross her once and there's no coming back from it. I flicked my eyes at the deteriorated roof above the porch. "And what might those be?"

"Depends on how much time you have?"

"Not that much." Indifferent, I folded my arms over my chest. I would rather watch paint dry than listen to Thyri complain about our past.

"I can produce an entire scroll if you'd like."

"Hit me with your top three."

She rolled her eyes as I leaned forward. "For what? It's not like you care."

I stepped a few inches closer, leaning down low enough for her to hear me. "So you can hear how silly you sound."

"Oh, whatever! You're not the one who had to hide a bald spot in the back of your head for months, because a certain someone stuck a piece of chewing gum in your hair."

I slipped my hands inside of my pockets. "If I'm not mistaken, I told you to move out of the way. I spit my gum out over the gate and the wind blew it in your direction."

Thyri's eyes shifted back and forth. She didn't even remember herself. "That's not how it happened!"

"Uh, yeah, Sherlock, it did." I could see the steam rolling off her shoulders and felt instant gratification.

"Okay... Okay." She paced back and forth, clapping her hands. Seeing her riled up like this reminded me of how cute she looked when she was upset.

"Well, what about the time we were at Gazelle Park and you hid my bikini top at the public pool?"

"It was a five hundred dollar bet." I shrugged.

"So that made it right?"

"Uh, yeah. I was sixteen. What did you expect me to do? Turn it down?"

"You humiliated me. I ran home in a beach towel."

"It's not like there was much to see."

"You know you're much cuter when you're not talking," she quipped.

Was that a back-handed compliment?

"Everything isn't about you, Thyri." I opened the box of donuts and ate them while she whined.

"What's that supposed to mean?"

"All you think about is yourself."

Judging by the solemn look on her face, I struck the wrong cord.

"You don't know me." She scoffed.

"You're still a brat." I ripped my teeth into the tender donuts, savoring the melt-in-your-mouth texture, unbothered by Thyri's senseless meltdown.

"And you're still an obnoxious, arrogant prick that only thinks about himself!" She stomped down the steps.

"I did nothing but look out for you."

"Yeah?" Her head whipped around like Linda Blair. "And who asked you to do that?"

"Take one guess." I used my foot to push off the post.

Thyri's eyes blinked rapidly, like she had an epiphany.

"You've always had people to clean up your mess." I continued antagonizing her from the top of the porch.

"Please. You made it your mission to ruin everything I touched."

"If this is about you know who, you were better off."

"That should have been for me to decide. No one told you to chase my prom date away with a hockey stick."

"You're over thirty complaining about a prom date and I'm the one who needs to grow up?" The ripples in my forehead multiplied.

Thyri's nostrils flared as she charged at me, but I didn't budge. She tried to snatch the box of donuts out of my hand, but I grabbed her wrist instead. She snatched it back after I prevented her from falling backwards down the porch steps.

"I baked those donuts. Give 'em back. I don't want you to have them."

"You did?! No wonder they taste bland." I held the box up high enough so she couldn't reach it, shaking my head.

"You're such a dick!" she snarled while bending over to grab her keys that fell into the grass. It's the best view I've seen all morning.

"See you later, sunshine." I reopened the screen door with a mischievous grin and winked.

"Stay out of my way, Kota!" She sprinted over to her front porch, flipping me the bird as she picked up the neighborhood's new terrorist. I'm not surprised that the rowdy mutt belongs to her.

"As long as you stay out of mine!" I yelled back before I shut the door.

Man, I've missed her.

6 / THYRI

"Helloooo." The bakery was too quiet for comfort on a Tuesday afternoon. No pucks were flying across the floor, and the living room was empty except for Beanbug napping near the fireplace. I closed my eyes to appreciate the silence, but the clinking of pots and running water alerted me to Aunt Jacquee's presence in the kitchen.

"Hey, Auntie. Where is everyone?"

"We're closed, remember?"

"Oh, yeah." I ignored my aunt's snarky tone. I had gotten used to seeing the back of Mr. Henry's balding head and his three-piece suits. He stared off into space while I ran around like a chicken with its head cut off. "You told him he could return on opening day, right?"

"I did." She continued swirling the bristle brush around the inside of an empty mason jar.

"How did he take it?"

"No hard feelings. He'll be traveling to spend some time with his sons soon, so he won't be in town during renovations."

"Well, that's good to hear. What about Jace?"

Aunt Jacquee removed the yellow rubber gloves from her hands. She frowned at me without blinking. "His mom knows I'll be going on tour soon. Now that the twenty-one questions game is over. Where have you been?"

"I had to run a few errands." I took off my jacket and hung it on the brass coat hook on the wall near the door.

Aunt Jacquee removed a fresh batch of Arlettes from the oven. The comforting smell of cinnamon wrapped me in a warm hug as soon as I reentered the kitchen.

"You said to meet you here at noon. It's a quarter past three."

Why is she the only one that's allowed to be late?

I spun around one time so she could see my entire outfit. "So, how do I look?"

Aunt Jacquee's pensive glare wasn't a good sign. "I love your hair. Those small box braids have always suited you."

"I'm talking about my dress." I lifted the frilly hem as I curtsied. "It's called cottage core."

"You sure it's not called a 'cottage mess?'" Aunt Jacquee's surly expression put an instant damper in my mood. "And those platform wooden sandals? Just why?"

"I called myself, taking a page out of your book."

She snorted. "Then you must have picked up the wrong book, baby girl, because I would never."

"I meant by creatively expressing myself through fashion." I made a fluid motion with my hands, then posed like I was at Paris Fashion Week.

"I mean... it's...interesting. But prints and florals have never been your thing. You don't even like flowers."

"That's not the point. I went thrifting to try out a new style. You're always ragging about the athleisure I wear, so I took myself shopping."

"Well, it's a definite miss, but you should have told me you were into thrifting. I've got tons of boxes in storage with just about every article of clothing from my heyday."

I took a seat on the stool by the front counter and propped my chin up with my hand. "Diahann Carroll in bell bottoms and striped chromatic dresses isn't quite the look I'm going for."

"*Pardon?*" Aunt Jacquee ripped off a piece of saran wrap, staring at me like she just took a bite off of a sour apple. "Point to the picture outside of Halloween where you've seen me dressed like I was auditioning for Soul Train? Don't worry, I'll wait... Tuh. I was a fox back in my day."

I giggled while clicking my wooden sandals together. "What don't you like about the shoes? I think they're cute."

"They're fine if you're a hippie time traveling back to 1968."

"That bad, huh?"

"Horrendous." Aunt Jacquee pressed her lips together with a spatula in hand. "What brought on your sudden interest in style?" Her eyebrows raised with suspicion.

"Nothing, really. When we reopen, I'll be the face of this place. I figured I should at least dress the part."

The high-pitched hiss of the griddle and aroma of smoked turkey, eggs, and mini silver dollar pancakes made my stomach roar. Breakfast in the middle of the day used to be our thing. I'd been up since eight o'clock this morning without a bite to eat and no sleep.

Reuniting with Dakota for the first time in years knocked me off my square. I couldn't stop thinking about him for some strange reason. I spent every waking moment trying to retrace every curve and line of his striking face and over analyzing every word that rolled off his lips. But what made our reunion even worse was that he knew something that I didn't.

"Unless you've booked a one-way ticket to Denmark or live in a castle I don't know about, then I suggest you go back to the drawing board. The only thing you're missing is two straight-back braids with baby blue ribbons tied on the ends and Dorothy's red glittery shoes."

"Ha-ha." I rolled my eyes while pouting as she peered at me above her frames.

"You sure this new look has nothing to do with Dakota moving back in next door?"

I could feel the heat rising on my cheeks. "The day Dakota has any influence on my appearance is when the Earth stops spinning on its axis." I hopped up from my seat and grabbed a glass plate from the cabinet. "What made you ask me that anyway?"

"He told me you all ran into each other yesterday."

"O-kayyy...and?"

"He said he loved the donuts and ate them up in one sitting. He thinks we should permanently add them to the menu."

"How strange... He told me they were dry and bitter."

Aunt Jacquee chuckled to herself, shaking her head. "Don't tell me you two are still at each other's throats after all these years?"

"Not me...I don't hold grudges." I stuffed my face with a strip of bacon and eggs.

"Now, we both know that's a lie." Aunt Jacquee removed her apron and brought her plate over to the counter. "Speaking of grudges..." She stabbed her fork into her eggs out of habit before taking a bite. "I spoke with your mother the other day."

My eyes widened before they turned into tiny slits. "What does she want now?"

"Surprisingly, nothing."

"... How did she sound?"

"She sounds like she's in a better place."

My aunt had a habit of buttering me up before dropping a load.

"So, she just called to check in before the holidays? Or does she need a place to crash again?"

Aunt Jacquee shook her head. "No. She didn't ask for a place to stay, either."

Her lingering glare gave me the answer I was fishing for.

"She would like to visit you."

"Why can't she just take a hint?"

"You only get one mother, Thyri." Aunt Jacquee's tone remained flat as she returned her focus to her plate.

"Yeah, that's easy for you to say. Grandma never chose a bottle of gin over you. I had to compete with Jack Daniels, Remy Martin, and Hennessy every night."

"How your mother treated you was wrong, but she was also very young when you were born."

"And somehow her irresponsibility is my fault?" My lips twisted into a pretzel.

"No, but you can extend a little more grace... Forgiveness can be healing."

"Forgive my mother?" I sneered.

My sudden loss of appetite compelled me to push away from the counter. "She showed up to my college graduation with the smell of cognac seeping from her pores. Uncle Kai had to carry her out of the auditorium. Do you remember how embarrassing that was for me? How much of an embarrassment she's been my entire life?"

"Your mother grew up in a tumultuous environment."

"You all lived in the same house," I retorted as I emptied my plate into the garbage disposal.

"Going away to college saved me, but I wish I could have taken her with me."

"You never want to hold her accountable." I blew out a ball of hot air.

"Oh, I do and I have. Plenty of times, but I was seven years older than your mother when I left home at eighteen and much less vulnerable to our toxic environment. There's a part of me that still blames myself for leaving her behind. If I stayed, the trajectory of your mother's life may have been much different." My aunt's glassy eyes glazed over with guilt.

"I don't know." I shrugged. "I'm just glad you rescued me in time. I had lost track of how many times I had to empty liquor bottles and flasks she hid in stashes around the house. Inside the cookie jar. Flowerpots. Cereal boxes. Laundry hampers. By second grade, I was cooking all the meals, because she either wasn't home or passed out somewhere. And I'm the only one who made sure she was up in time for her graveyard shifts when grandma got sick... But that car accident..." I turned around and leaned against the sink as a Rolodex of horrific memories flashed before me. "I remember it like yesterday."

"Unfortunately, I don't think that's a day we'll ever forget."

I allowed the sunrays seeping through the lace cafe curtains on the window to beat down on my face.

"Sometimes, the smell of burnt rubber or gasoline triggers my memory. Everything happened so fast. Flames engulfed the tree branch stuck on the hood of Dauntrice's Oldsmobile. She tried to get out, but the door wouldn't open. And when the latch finally released, all I remember is her stammering outside like a drunk toddler with blood trickling down her forehead away from the car. I thought she would come back for me. That she would turn around when she heard me screaming her name and outstretching my hands from the back seat. I tried to escape on my own, but the safety lock was on and my seatbelt had jammed. My tiny hands slid down the window, as I cried out for help, but she was in a trance."

"She was in shock."

"Is that still her excuse for leaving her only child trapped in the backseat of a burning car?"

"Listen... My sister's trauma has affected us all in more ways than one. And you, my dear, have every right to feel how you do."

"Then tell her that the next time you talk to her." I was over the conversation before it even began.

Aunt Jacquee shook her head like the weight of my mother and I's estranged relationship was pressing down on her shoulders. "I can't..."

I looked over at her. "You can't, or...you won't?"

"Both. I've played referee between you two for far too long. If she shows up on this doorstep, just remember, all family is welcome in my home. You're an adult now, Thyri. I no longer need to protect you. You're on your own with this one, kiddo. Besides, I'll be somewhere relaxing on the Gulf of Saint Tropez come Thanksgiving Day."

"Lucky you," I put my plate in the dishwasher and walked over to the gigantic mixing machine frothing dough back and forth. "But I'm confident that my mother won't show up, just like she hasn't shown up for me the past thirty-three years of my life."

"All I ask is that you remain respectful if she does. Like I said before, she's still your mother."

She's still your mother. I mouthed behind my aunt's back. "Auntie, my mother and I switched roles a long time ago. Now, how in the heck do you work this machinery?"

"If you're looking for an off switch, there isn't one."

I stood upright. "I don't get it. You remodeled this entire house, but didn't think to install a dough mixer or stove?"

"I'll have you know my appliances are top of the line and built to last."

"Are you sure about that?" I walked over to the white, red, and silver antique gas stove for an impromptu demonstration. "This front burner on the left always gives me the flux."

Aunt Jacquee raised up from her seat and walked over. "Maybe if you stop fidgeting with it—" She tapped my hand away and turned on the other three burners while keeping the one in the left corner on low. "Just give it a few seconds and it'll throw properly. Might as well give you a quick training while we're at it."

"I've been cooking and baking in this kitchen for two weeks now. I have a handle on it." I wasn't in the mood for any of my aunt's long-winded tutorials.

"It's for safety precautions. This old thing has a mind of its own."

"What's wrong with it?"

"Besides these old pilot lights, nothing really. I mean, it's a little clogged, compared to the other three, so it gets hotter than it should when you leave it on for too long."

"And what happens then?"

"Flare-ups...sooty flames. And we don't want either of those. Just remember to keep it clean to avoid grease build up, but if you don't have to, don't use it. Do you need me to revisit the routine?"

"Mmm. I think I've attended this lecture before." I tapped my finger on my chin. "Prep in the evening and bake in the morning before sunrise. Have all the dishes cleaned by noon."

She glanced over at the double oven. "And never exceed two hundred and fifty degrees for the top oven. Stick with the bottom one and you'll be just fine."

I opened up the drawer with Aunt Jacquee's artsy kitchen instructional guides inside. "I've studied this from cover to cover."

"Good." Her eyes lingered on me for a few seconds. "We don't need you burning down the house while we're out of town."

I frowned, narrowing my eyes behind her back as she walked away. "What do you mean by that?"

"Do I really need to spell it out?" Aunt Jacquee never backed down from a potential spat. "You and fire are like oil and water, girl. Y'all won't ever mix."

"I was seventeen, Aunt Jacquee. The fire starter jokes are getting a little old, don't you think?"

"If my jab bothered you, I suggest you thicken that layer of skin back up once we reopen. Because Sunflower townspeople don't forget a thing."

Tell me about it. I released a deep breath. "I know I'm not a fan favorite around here."

"Are you sure living on the West coast hasn't softened you up a bit?"

"Out there, I didn't really have to keep my guard up."

"For someone who claims to be chronically unbothered, you sure are concerned with what people think of you lately... What's going on?" Aunt Jacquee walked through the kitchen to do a final wipe down, gathering her scarf, car keys, and wristlet wallet to go.

"I'm not exactly the same person I was over a decade ago. I developed a hard exterior because I needed to protect myself. But that's not who I am at my core." My eyes shifted.

"We all have feelings, Tee. But your strength is one thing I always admired about you. Miss Massey used to talk about how resilient you were all the time." An endearing smile spread across her thick lips. "Not caring what anyone thinks about you is a gift."

And a curse. "I do care...sometimes."

"If you say so."

"Miss Massey..."

Aunt Jacquee pulled on her rubber Prada boots while sitting in the chair. "I'm listening."

"When did you all become close?"

"That's a good question."

"You always called her a nosey know-it-all, but Dakota told me you two were inseparable. That's not what I remember."

"You were just a moody teenager back then. I never disliked her."

"You weren't very fond of her, either. When she kept chastising you about landscaping the backyard, you were ready to rip her a new one."

Aunt Jacquee chuckled. "Alright, you got me there. I never understood why she was so obsessed with our yard. Years later, she finally admitted she called the village officials on me for not keeping my lawn and bushes trimmed."

"That doesn't sound like something she would do." I grinned, stifling my laughter. Dakota and I had our own rivalry, but Aunt Jacquee and Miss Massey had a few squabbles of their own.

"Oh, it definitely does. I'm not the only one she called on. I was never a big fan of her or her passive aggressiveness until we got to know each other."

My eyebrow arched to the high heavens. "When did this happen?"

"After your incident, your senior year of high school." She cocked her head to the side and my eyes lowered to the floor. "But I'd have to say we got much closer after you left for college. Dakota was already gone, and I noticed she was alone a lot. We started inviting her over for dinner, and brunches, so we naturally bonded over time."

"What did Miss Massey tell you about that night?"

"What night?"

I sucked my teeth. "Prom, Auntie."

"Nothing really. She just apologized for Dakota's behavior."

"That's it?" I prodded to see how much she knew, or at least remembered.

"I can't think of anything else. She came with us to meet with the principal when they threatened to not let you walk across the stage for graduation. To this day, I still don't know what she said in that office that changed their minds, but your uncle and I were grateful. Miss Massey was also the only one who supported us when many of these rigid old townspeople just wanted us out of the way."

"Because of me?"

"I hate to burst your bubble, sweetie, but they disliked us way before you came along. When we first moved here in the seventies, the community did not welcome us either. And once 'The Raspberry' opened up, we had all odds stacked against us."

"As far as finances?"

"No, baby, they didn't want us here. We were too different, if you catch my drift." Aunt Jacquee pointed to the back of her hand. "They refused to support our business for years until we got the church's support and started winning all those baking competitions."

"What?! ...You never told me any of this."

"They robbed you of your childhood for enough years. Worrying you about the mess we had going on was unnecessary. We handled it as best as we could and they came around eventually, but a tiger never changes its stripes."

"I get that." I shook my head. "So, it took Dakota and I leaving for you and Miss Massey to hit it off, huh?"

"To be honest, we actually bonded over disliking some of the same people."

"I should have known. Miss Massey complained about everyone behind closed doors, but was always pleasant with them in public."

"Yeah. She played nice-nasty well, but push the wrong buttons and there would be hell to pay." Aunt Jacquee clapped her hands as she reminisced.

"I think I've seen that side of her before."

"Now I let a lot of things slide, because I prefer to keep it cute. My bark is definitely louder than my bite, but Miss Massey turned out to be a sweetheart. I remember one day I came home from a two-month work trip to find our front lawn manicured. I went to the backyard and there were fresh vegetables and flower beds springing up everywhere. Miss Massey didn't want to take credit for it, and she refused to accept any payment, so I eventually let it go."

"I miss her."

"We all do. She was a real gem around here. You don't find many like her in this lifetime."

"Don't I know it?"

Aunt Jacquee's subtle smile transitioned to compressed lips as soon as I kicked off my clogs. As if she caught a waft of an unsettling stench. She walked over to pick them up.

"What are you doing?"

"I was waiting for you to hop out of these." She shook her head and threw them in the trash bin. "Follow me downstairs. I've got some things I'm sure you can fit. That Little Bo Peep dress is next." The basement door flew open, and Aunt Jacquee pulled on the string to turn on the light. She shouted from the bottom of the stairs, "Come on, girl, I don't have all day."

"I'm comin', I'm comin'." I glanced at the small kitchen window to see if Dakota was back. Judging by the dark windows, nobody's home. I tugged at the frilly dress and shook my head. *What was I thinking wearing this out in public?*

Last night I fell down the rabbit hole of Dakota's hockey harem after stumbling across an article posted online for Valentine's Day earlier this year. It was a brief interview with Dakota shedding more light on his dating life.

He definitely had a type. Brunettes over blondes. Dark brown, sultry eyes. His exes' physical appearance ranged from somewhat plump to athletic. Nerds with glasses, visible tan lines, and sun dresses paired with casual sneakers seemed to be more his speed.

If Dakota ever saw me in this ridiculous outfit, he would never let me live this down. And the fact that I was comparing myself with women he likely still had on his roster made my stomach churn. I held onto the wooden rail as I made my way down to the basement, scrunching my nose at the putrid smell that slapped me in the face. Black mold and rotten wood were hard to inhale.

"Look in these boxes over here." Aunt Jacquee had labeled every box by categories and years. She had stacked at least twenty cardboard moving boxes against the concrete wall, with some wedged between the water heater and double sink. A vast improvement from the mountains of toys and broken furniture we used to hoard from wall to wall.

"Are you planning on donating these soon?"

"Now, why would I do that?"

I pulled a moth-eaten maroon negligee from the box. "Oh, I don't know. What's the point in keeping stuff like this?"

"Give me that." She snatched it out of my hands and folded it neatly. "It's from our honeymoon."

"I'm sure a few Polaroids would suffice."

"I have those, too."

"Auntie, are you still a hoarder?" I pulled out a pair of fishnet stockings and bell bottoms and threw my aunt a disapproving look. "Maybe I'm looking through the wrong boxes."

Aunt Jacquee frowned and removed the box from my reach. "I'm not a hoarder. I just...hold on to things that feel sentimental to me."

"You didn't hold on tight enough to that recipe book."

"Why do you think it's so organized down here?" Aunt Jacquee rolled her eyes. "We searched high and low. Hell, we almost tore this place apart looking for my family's recipes."

"Maybe it's still hidden down here. It wouldn't just get up and walk away."

"I'm hoping it'll show up eventually unless your uncle accidentally sold it at the estate sale."

"Not the estate sale? Those sound like rich people's problems." I

71

spun around to find more boxes and bins with lids filled with old items. A broken record player, vintage radio with antennas, a cassette player, chipped oriental China sets, and old phones.

"When do you plan on using this teapot? The stout is missing?"

"Your grandmother gifted me that in '72."

"Alright, I don't think I'm going to find much down here. Plus, basements make me lightheaded."

"Don't worry. When you get older, you'll wish you hung on to old things that reminded you of good times."

"...I prefer to live in the present."

"Am I not breathing right now?"

"You know that's not what I meant."

"Ain't nothing wrong with reminiscing. As a matter of fact..." She held up a finger with an elegant, square shaped yellow gemstone sparkling from it. "I've kept quite a few things from your childhood around here."

"Donate them. I have more than enough photographs to use as memories." My aunt pulled a green dress from another box and flicked off the dust.

"Do you remember this dress?"

"How could I forget it?'"

"Oh, my god. You were so cute that night. It was your first school recital. You had one simple line we practiced for weeks."

"And I still stumbled through it."

"None of that matters, Tee. It was a special moment for you on stage, and your uncle still has the VHS tape."

"I was terrified."

"Now look at these hippie jeans and off the shoulder sweater?"

"Low-rise flare jeans. They're making a comeback. But...I don't know about the sweatshirt. The gold glitter is a little too much."

"That's because you don't know how to style an outfit properly. You never have, if I'm being honest."

"Thanks for the compliment." I pulled out a tie-dyed shirt with slits down the back and arms and threw it back in.

"First rule of thumb. You wear the clothes, don't let them wear you. We can cut this sweatshirt up and make it more modern. Paired with the right heels and subtle jewelry pieces. This would be the perfect look for the grand opening. You can put your hair up in a bun. Cinch these pans in to show off your cute shape."

"Heels at a bakery? That's a stretch."

"Those wedges you love so much are out of the question, honey. You'll be comfortable, I promise. Maybe three inches, two straps for your pedicured toes to show, not too much."

I nodded in return. I could see the vision, but I wasn't confident in how I presented myself these days. Sure, I have a cute face, toned body, but what else is there to love about me? I stayed in a loveless relationship for so long I questioned what was wrong with me.

"Why the long face?"

"Nothing, just thinking."

"About something or someone?"

"Someone like who?" I walked around her before meeting her gaze again.

"Dakota seems interested in catching up with you." She folded the clothes back while I dug deeper into the boxes with my name scribbled on it.

"What makes you think that? He hates my guts and vice versa."

"Well, you could have fooled me. You haven't been yourself ever since your encounter with him yesterday."

"I have not."

"No, I can tell. Look, you're blushing right now." She giggled.

"You're grasping at straws." I flipped an old Tamagotchi keychain over in the palm of my hand. Dakota is still cute, I can admit that, but outside of physical attraction, there's nothing there. "Did he mention how long he'd be sticking around? The sooner he gets out of dodge, the better."

Aunt Jacquee cut her eyes at me with her lips upturned into a smirk. "I'm not sure. He'll be helping out around here while I'm gone. You can ask him yourself." Aunt Jacquee busied herself by pulling out different cashmere and wool sweaters, blouses, overalls, terry cloth tracksuits, high-waisted denim, skinny jeans, and cargo pants from her boxes underneath the stairs. For a few seconds, I stood frozen, unable to comprehend what she said.

"I'm sorry. I don't think I heard you correctly. What does Dakota need to help me with?"

"Not you, silly." She took the pile of clothes and plopped them into my arms. "The contractors will be out to work on the roof soon. Our landscaping company will have to keep the front lawn and back-yard in tiptop shape. So, he's offered to manage them both."

"Oh, so he and I won't have to interact?"

Aunt Jacquee shook her head. "No. I've let him know about the stubborn bathroom door upstairs and putting up more cameras inside and out."

I stifled my laughter. "Dakota is far from a handyman. He's never picked up a hammer a day in his life."

"You don't know that. He's not a little boy anymore. Dakota is a grown man now, a very handsome one at that. Instead of pushing him away, why not give him a chance?"

"Trust me, Auntie, I'm the last person he'd ever be interested in."

"Please, he's always had a school yard crush on you, but you were so mean you couldn't see it."

"Did I grow up in an alternate universe of something? Dakota picked on me for sport."

"Most boys do that. Men, too, Tee." Her eyebrows lifted. "You'd be surprised."

"Who put this idea in your head that Dakota was ever into me?"

"Miss Massey knew Dakota better than he knew himself."

"She told you this?" I frowned.

"Plenty of times. Besides, his presence in 'The Raspberry' will be good for business."

"I know you're not trying to use his name for publicity?" I folded my arms.

"There's no harm in letting people know he's using our space to sign autographs. They'll get a signature and a treat."

"Auntie, you know that ain't right."

"Seems like a fair exchange to me."

"I told you I was working on a marketing plan."

"Yeah? With what? Pebbles in a bucket for a budget." Aunt Jacquee pushed up her glasses. "Having Dakota around will give us a much greater return. You know this town eats, craps, and breathes hockey. I squirm every time I watch those games with Kai. They get on the ice just to pummel each other like cavemen."

"I'm pretty sure he just wants to torture me."

"You two are adults now." Aunt Jacquee's tone inflected. "I will not be meddling in your business, but I expect you both to act your age. Understand?"

As much as I wanted to open my mouth to refute her decision more, I decided against it.

Why did Dakota have to get finer with age? From his sexy smile, salt and pepper hair, convex wrinkles in his forehead to his shallow beard, strong jawline, and undeniable strength, my temperature rises every time I think about how he pulled me into his chest. When my head hits the pillow and I close my eyes at night, all I see is him.

I should have accepted his invite inside. I'd been touch deprived for quite some time, and I'm not opposed to a few back shots from behind. My only request is that he keeps his mouth shut the entire time.

"Tee, Tee! Girl, you hear me talking to you?!"

"Uh. Huh. Yes, ma'am." She snapped me out of my trance.

"It's getting late. What did you want to eat for dinner?"

"You can head home. I'll just get a pizza delivered."

"Are you sure? I can whip something up real quick."

There was nothing quick about my aunt in the kitchen. Baking and cooking were her art. An hour's dinner would turn into a five-course meal.

"No, I'm sure. Get back to Uncle Kai. I don't want him to stay up late worrying and waiting."

"Okay. Don't change your mind at the last minute. You may know how to bake, but your cooking needs practice."

"Alright. I got it." I planned on following her upstairs, but the bubble pink tulle fabric sticking out one of my boxes caught my eye. The patter of claws I heard on the wooden stairs was none other than Beanbug arriving to join me.

"I can't believe she found my prom dress." I removed it from the box. Surprisingly, it appeared to be in fairly new condition. At the bottom of the box was Dakota's Magnolia Falcons hockey jersey. Miss Massey pulled it over me that night to combat the inclement weather. Right after the fire. The orange, brown, and beige colors were as ugly as I remembered them. I picked the worn jersey up to examine it.

I could still hear Miss Massey's raspy voice whispering in my ear. *Your secret's still safe with me.*

7 / DAKOTA

I FLIPPED the light switch on in the garage, but the light bulbs had burned out. Inside, I stubbed my foot on an ugly plaid couch, with no cushions. The same couch I hit several home runs on in the basement as a young chap. I pressed the button to open the garage door, but of course, it's still jammed.

The sunlight will have to suffice. For years I promised meemaw I'd get it fixed, but never got around to it. Maybe that's why she settled on using it as a storage space. She stopped driving shortly after I graduated from college because of a decline in her vision. Instead of keeping her favorite car, she donated it to someone who could use it.

Everything of sentimental value is still inside the house. I took the next few hours digging through dust-ridden boxes scattered on top of a wooden workstation and broken weight bench I haven't used since high school. Dirt and cobwebs coated my old hockey sticks, helmets, and protective gear.

Closest to the garage door in the corner was a pre-lit snowman, two large boxes with Christmas trees, decorations, and tangled string lights dangling outside of a smaller box. To my surprise, our beach cruisers hanging on the wall are in fairly good condition. They were our only means of transportation on the vacation trips we took down to Bombay Beach every summer.

A family of defrosted dead mice curled up like croissants in the corner let me know what the rest of my day would entail. After slipping on my dust mask and gloves, I pulled up my favorite John Mayer playlist on my phone.

Four hours later, the large dumpster I rented was half full and I could see the pavement again. While cradling a box of my grandmother's old electronics that I intended to repair, the sound of someone shouting compelled me to turn my music down.

Sandoval's team was doing a fine job of repairing my grandmother's roof in such a short amount of time. They even had a ladder against Aunt Jacquee's home next door. I made my way through the chain-link gate, as an irate, barefoot woman in a white robe stomped across the front lawn, yelling my name.

"Dakota! Dakota! I know you're in there! Dakotttaaa!"

By the time I made it to the front, I saw Thyri screaming at the top of her lungs, loud enough to wake the dead. She's been avoiding me for some days, so this display isn't what I expected to see. I put the cardboard box down and leaned against the brick siding of 'The Raspberry' while she ripped me a new one.

"Dang, I've got you screamin' my name this loud already? We haven't even made it to the bedroom." I stepped out to reveal myself with a smirk on my face.

Startled, she stumbled back off of my porch. Thyri never got her clumsiness under control, but I found it rather cute. I lifted my head towards the roof.

"How long have you been standing there?" Flustered, she folded her arms across her chest.

"Long enough." I shoved my dirty hands inside the pockets of my cargo pants. Thyri's silk pajamas left little to my imagination and the brisk air didn't do the untamed melons on her chest any favors. If we were on better terms, I'd pick her up right now and give her something to scream about.

At a loss for words, I could only smile as she fidgeted with the terry-cloth hooded robe. She adjusted the purple satin bonnet slipping off her head and curled her toes in the grass. If only she knew she could walk outside wrapped in a plastic shower curtain and I'd still find her attractive.

"If you're not doing all the banging up there, then who is?"

I pointed to Sandoval's vans parked across the street.

"Next time, give them a later start time and me a heads up, will you?"

"You say that like you're easy to find."

"Maybe I don't want to be found." Her upper lip curled like it got snagged on a hook. "And why are you looking for me, Kota? I thought we had an understanding." She threw out her hip and cocked her head to the side for emphasis.

Sassy. I hope she never changes. "We do, but Aunt Jacquee said she left me a spare key."

"For what reason? Why would you even need that?"

"Sandoval's team and I are doing some work in the basement and around the house. Aunt Jacquee's put me in charge of any repairs needed inside."

"When did you become a handyman? The only thing you know how to operate is a hockey stick."

"Do you wake up complaining?"

"Maybe. Let's see how you feel being woken up at ten o'clock in the morning to a bunch of drilling and banging."

"I've got a special drill you can borrow for get back. Whenever you need it, just let me know."

"Will you ever grow up?" Her eyes narrowed and I couldn't help but flash all thirty-two of my teeth.

"Probably not. Now hand over the keys or put them in my mailbox when you get a chance."

"You have got to be kidding me?"

"I'm not. And I think we need to get together to discuss plans for the opening in two weeks."

"I can't believe this. Ughhh!" she growled, clenching her tiny fists together. "Can you at least call before you come by?"

"I mean...I could. But I don't have your cell number."

"And I'm not giving it to you." She rolled her eyes, and I threw my head back and chortled.

"Call the landline." She took off towards the porch again where that rambunctious dog sat patiently waiting for her inside the door.

"I'm headed to Arly's. You need anything?!" I yelled after her across the lawn.

"What could I possibly need from a hardware store?"

"Are you sure you want me to answer that?"

"Your mind is permanently in the gutter." She slumped her shoulders and glared at me before spinning around and slamming the front door. The 'Closed' sign swung back and forth with the motion.

"I'm one call away!" I picked the box up at my feet and carried it over to the top of my porch step, then headed over to the 1970 Chevy blue pickup truck parked in front.

The chance of someone recognizing me in a beat-up truck with rusted rims and a poor paint job was slim to none. So for now, it works. Arly's hardware store was only a few miles away, and the only one in this small town, located right on the corner of Buzz Street.

Riding around my old neighborhood brought a sense of calm over me. I almost forgot how much I enjoyed small-town living where expectations for success were low, family and marriage came first, and money wasn't an idol.

Slow days like this are what I miss the most. Cattle stood idly behind wooden fences as tractors blazed across bright green pastures. And traffic was an afterthought, because I could travel for miles without seeing another car on the road.

A break from the hustle and bustle of cities is why I made Sunflower Falls my final destination. I hung up my skates, hockey stick, and puck for good to get back to my roots. If only I could find a soul mate to spend the rest of my life with, then everything would be good.

As soon as I pulled into the empty, gritty parking lot, my phone rang. I held my foot steady on the brake, put it in park, and removed the keys from the ignition. The number didn't look familiar. I hesitated to answer after having an anonymous caller blow up my phone last night. My lips pressed together as I clicked on the green button to accept.

"You're hard to get a hold of these days!"

Russell Foute's husky voice boomed over the speakerphone. Two white butterflies fluttered their wings around my rearview mirror and I suddenly wanted to be anywhere but here. The lawsuit I filed against Gangsley had become a looming dark cloud that I couldn't seem to shake. I woke up with it in the back of my mind while the risks and unpredictable outcomes rocked me to sleep at night.

My cramped body caused my head to curve over the tattered, leather steering wheel in the driver's seat. I released a deep breath and relaxed my shoulders before responding, "Been busy. How's everything, Mr. Foute?"

"Everything is as good as it gets. Can't really complain. I wanted to do a brief check-in on the items we discussed last month. Is this a good time?"

"I'm all ears." I braced myself for what I was about to hear from my attorney on the other end. Mr. Foute was just as slimy as the rest of the sports attorneys in the league. He would do anything to grease his palms, even if it meant throwing his own client under the bus.

He spent less than fifteen hours a week on my case after realizing he wouldn't be able to bleed me dry. One look at my bank statements and he was ready to take a bow. He only agreed to move forward with representation after I provided enough evidence on my previous agency to take to trial. But my teammates offering to cover the cost of my legal fees in the event I lost all of my collateral in this uphill battle is what sealed the deal.

By the time I discovered Mr. Foute only cared about *Mr. Foute*, it was too late to dissolve my contract with his firm. Getting rid of him would have cost me six months' worth of investigations, requests for mediation, and dismissed cases by every judge in Hammatauk County.

Gangsley had us by the balls. There has been little to no movement in my case since I filed a public civil suit back in June against their agency instead. Some news outlets have picked up the story, but we haven't ruffled any feathers yet. As quiet as it's kept, I'm not sure that Mr. Foute wants to.

"Atta' boy! Now I've got some good news and...some bad news."

"Can't have one without the other, can we?" I said in a dry tone, drumming my fingers on the dashboard. For a second, I imagined Mr. Foute's bloated face, beady eyes, and crooked smile on a hockey puck as I swung at it hard enough to break the glass.

"Sure doesn't seem like it. Now I've had some talks offline with a few of the defendant's attorneys and their goal is to settle all of this outside of court. They haven't decided on a definitive figure just yet, but I'm confident it's a sweet number."

"Did you let them know I'm willing to sue for extortion and defamation too? Because I've settled plenty of times when I got served with paternity suits and accused of fraud. Lost a lot of money doing so under their guidance, too."

"I fully understand where you're coming from. Believe me, I do. But that iron clad contract has them covered on every base. There's not much you can do once you sign on the dotted line."

How ironic? Mr. Foute recited his favorite line. It never fails. He says the same bullshit on every call when he doesn't get the answer he's looking for out of me. I'm not bowing out to take a number much lower than I deserve. I don't want hush money. I'm demanding to be made whole.

"So, hit me with the bad news then. How long do they plan on dragging this out, because I've got nothing but time?"

"We would need to build a stronger case that would hold up in court."

"So, that's what's holding us up? More evidence?"

"My team has crossed every 'T' and dotted every 'I'. We need to find more holes—"

"Then look harder! For as much as I'm paying your firm, this shouldn't even have to go to trial. They owe me triple double on top of the pennies they've offered."

"I don't mean to bring this up at the wrong time, but there are several invoices we billed that are unpaid."

"I haven't seen any bills. Are they being sent to my old address?"

"Possibly. I'll have my secretary reach out to update your information. There's something else that recently came across my desk that's a cause for concern."

I grimaced at the phone, then put it back up to my ear. "Great, what else is new? Who do I owe now?"

"There's a potential paternity suit from a Jane Doe that's threatening to go public."

"A what? ... A Jane Doe? You can't be serious."

This was a new low. Before I got a reversible vasectomy procedure at the end of last year, women were coming out of the woodwork, claiming I'm the father of their newborn child when it was the furthest from the truth.

To avoid the bad press and getting put on my team's radar as an easy trade, I paid the women off without contest. My management thought it would be best to get rid of the bad press. I never traced where that money went, and I regret it to this day.

"I'm not letting another woman get a red dime out of me. How can you threaten to file a paternity suit and not allow me to put a face with a name?"

Mr. Foute remained silent on the other end.

"Are you still there or am I talking to the air?"

"I'm still here, and you have every right to feel frustrated. Is there any chance that these allegations against you are true?"

"Mr. Foute, I got a vasectomy last year. There's no way any of this could be true."

"Well, we've already reviewed the timeline of your procedure with the date of conception this Jane Doe provided, and there's a fifty percent chance—"

"There's actually zero percent chance. I haven't been intimate with anyone in months."

"This woman claims to have been several weeks along in February."

"Then she's lying because I was in physical therapy and traveling around Europe over winter break." I wasn't stateside for two weeks during the holidays, but this sounded better. I squeezed my temple, trying to recount the rendezvous I had overseas and in the States, but no one came to mind.

Mr. Foute is trying to get me to doubt myself, but I'm certain I took extra precaution. Besides, I required every woman I slept with to sign NDAs. They wouldn't be asking for mediation with full anonymity. This "Jane Doe" just wants an easy pay out.

Jokes on her though, because I'm strapped for cash.

I've been through this rodeo with blood thirsty women many times before. Unlike my exes over the years, my flings only wanted one thing. A hockey jersey symbolized nothing more than a dollar sign. Too bad my wayward dick has a mind of its own. A nice ass and the perfect pair of round tits used to be all it took for me.

On drunken nights, my standards for companionship went out the window. Now that I'm older, it'll take emotional maturity, substance, intelligence, and more than a wet mop for a personality to get my attention.

"Hey, I believe you. I just thought it was important to bring it to your attention before anyone else catches wind of it."

"Every woman I'm intimate with has to sign an NDA."

"That makes me feel a little better."

The fact that Mr. Foute continued to question my character spoke volumes. If I ever had a child on the way, I would take full responsibility. Awkward exchanges like this just reminded me he doesn't fully support my mission for retribution. He only wanted his piece of the pie and my patience with him is growing thin. "How do we move forward from here?"

"I'll file another motion for an extension."

"Please stop with the legalese talk and explain to me what that means."

"We need more time to gather evidence, talk to more people. Speaking of which, the personal assistant you hired..."

"Yeah, Lala. What about her?"

"We can't seem to get a hold of her. Do you have any new contact information for her?"

"I don't. Plus, we didn't separate on the best terms. She's likely just not responding to your calls."

"Mmm. I see."

There he goes again. Judging. I flicked my eyes up at the cloth peeling off the roof of my truck.

"Any chance she would know where we can find more original bank statements or balance sheets?"

"She wouldn't know any of that. I hired her on as a favor for a close friend. Only my management and personal accountants were privy to that type of information. Her responsibilities didn't exceed booking appointments and meetings on my calendar and half the time she didn't get those right."

"Another dead end." He sighed.

"Tell me about it." Mr. Foute noticed my sarcastic tone and made up an excuse to cut our call short.

"My assistant, Maggie, will reach out soon. I'm running late for my meeting, but I'll see what I can find—"

"Right. Talk later, Mr. Foute." I ended the conversation before he could spit out another excuse about why his team couldn't get the job done. The door screeched as I stepped out of my truck and shook my head. I slapped on a brown baseball cap, hoping to keep a low profile, and walked towards the entrance of Arly's. Just a few items, get in and get out. With the mood I'm in, I don't want any run-ins.

"Howdy!" The bell on the door jingled behind me as a chipper white bearded man with wire-framed glasses waved in my direction. Mr. Arly's face never changed. He always reminded me of a slimmer version of Santa Claus growing up minus the red suit, reindeers, and sleigh. He wore a heavily starched, red plaid button-up shirt, a pair of dad jeans, and a leather brown belt with an obnoxious silver buckle that kept his entire outfit in place.

"Mr. Arly, long time no see!" I cleared my voice.

"I almost thought you weren't dropping in as promised. I opened up an hour early so you could beat the locals in."

"Thanks for doing that. I got a little caught up with work around the house, among a few other things."

"Oh, pish, posh! Don't you worry about it. Mornings are slow around here on Saturdays since everyone's taking a break from the week."

Mr. Arly's store phone rang mid-sentence and I'm instantly relieved.

"I've kept a few of the items you asked for behind the counter, so just let me know when you're ready."

"Thanks, Mr. Arly, I appreciate it."

The phone ring grew incessantly louder and Mr. Arly dropped his shoulders. His light hazel eyes twinkled behind the medicated lenses, as the corners of his thin lips twitched with frustration. "I oughta be used to all the calls I get this time of year. It'll be cooling off soon, and everyone has questions about last-minute repairs."

"Don't mind me. I just need to look for a few more drills. What aisle?"

Mr. Arly tucked the old, yellow rotary phone between his neck and shoulder. "A15!"

I nodded once and searched for the aisle just to find another clean-shaven elderly man, wearing a cowboy hat, crisp white shirt, slacks, and gator shoes examining different drills in the same aisle.

His attire doesn't suggest a typical hockey fan, so there's a twenty percent chance he won't recognize me. With my chin tucked close to my chest, I walked in his direction and reached for the most common brand I saw at the fairest price.

From the corner of my eye, I could see his soft, ocean blue eyes giving me a once over.

"I'd go with Deville, if I were you. The Boxer brand is nice, but the Deville offers better value." The sound of keys jingled from the pockets of his slacks as he looked at me with an eyebrow raised.

I don't know a thing about carpentry or drill brands, but after one glance at his spotted old hands and manicured nails, he doesn't appear to know much either.

"You're in construction work?" I took a step back to examine the Deville drills on the wall.

"Not since I was about your age, but I still know a thing or two."

He must have read my mind. Rather than grabbing what he's looking for, his eyes locked in on my arm tattoos. I should have worn the hoodie.

"You've got an angel on your arm. Are you some kin to Ethel Massey?"

Lifting my baseball cap, I faced him head on. No one ever called my grandmother by her first name besides my mother. Him knowing it, let me know they must have been familiar at some point in her lifetime.

"I'm her grandson. How did you know her?"

"She and I...have history. We grew up together down in—" He removed his right hand from his pocket, revealing a timeless silver Rolex watch on his wrist.

"Abellyne?"

My grandmother always reminisced about her childhood days and often mentioned a best friend by the name of Dawson Hollie when she shared her wild childhood stories at bedtime.

She loved talking about her one true love and how their plans of being together failed when he went off to some fancy law school on the East coast.

"The one and only. Name's Dawson." I shook his hand, and it felt like I was meeting a superstar for the first time. He gripped my hand with water swelling in the rims of his eyes. I could see the genuine, kindhearted man that my grandmother admired.

Slightly choked up, he continued, "Your grandmother and I lived down the street from each other. We also went to high school together. Ethel was truly one of a kind. I learned about her passing earlier in the year when my granddaughter moved up here. My sincere condolences for your loss."

He placed his other hand on top of mine and a thunderbolt shot through my body.

"Thanks, I appreciate that. She's definitely missed around these parts."

"I bet." A wide grin spread across his face as he beamed from ear to ear. "Does she have any more grandchildren?"

"I'm afraid it's just me. Dakota Callahan by the way."

"I recognized who you were when you walked down the aisle. Are you still playing?"

I shook my head. "I'm what the league considers an old head now, so those days are behind me."

"Old is a bit of a stretch, young man, but I understand. Did Ethel still have that house over on Bananaquit Street?"

"Yep. That's my childhood home."

"Wow. It's crazy how time flies." Dawson stared at me proudly, like I was someone he knew in a past life and we were direly in need of catching up. It's funny, because for some strange reason I feel the same.

"It does, indeed." Normally, I would have found a reason to excuse myself, but the connection between us is undeniable.

"If you don't mind me asking, what do you all plan on doing with the property?"

"My plan is to keep it unless I need to sell it."

Dawson shoved his hand back in his pocket and pulled out a business card with his name and number on it.

"If you're ever in need of any buyers or legal representation, feel free."

"You're an attorney?"

"I no longer practice, but I still own a few firms. I take on cases I have special interest in, here and there."

"Cool. I'm glad I ran into you."

"Sure thing, buddy." He tapped me twice on my shoulder. "It was nice meeting you. Remember, always go with Deville."

He walked over to checkout, then tipped his hat in my direction before leaving out the door. I flipped the card over in my hands as the wheels started spinning in my head. "H-L-G. Hollie Legal Group."

Everything works in God's timing.

My grandmother's voice echoed in my ear. She's never steered me wrong.

8 / THYRI

THREE WEEKS PASSED in the blink of an eye, and I still can't remember the last time I had a full night's sleep. My brain is on autopilot, running purely on sugar and coffee. As much as I hate to admit it, there's no way I could have pulled off this grand opening alone. Business ownership is not for the faint of heart. The Raspberry buzzed with chatter from wall to wall as professional photographers blocked the entryway at varying angles to get the perfect shot of the backdrop with Dakota and his fans.

After plating nine rows of mini chocolate buttercream cupcakes with raspberry filling, I rang the silver bell on the counter twice for the servers to pick them up. Dakota and I are still giving each other the cold shoulder. Sometimes, we'll catch each other's eye, but we don't speak.

Until this week, we've avoided one another like the plague just to keep the peace. But his last-minute idea to hire extra help to serve complimentary menu samples while customers waited in line for autographs turned out to be a hit.

He also brought the women of Sunflower Falls out in droves. Before he arrived, the ladies were primping their hair, touching up their makeup, and adjusting their outfits, hoping to make a lasting impression.

Visitors poured into the bakery non-stop. I recognized some old faces, but the majority were mostly new, with a few rotten apples that arrived late this afternoon. The last people I wanted to see showed up in all their self-inflated glory, inevitably turning our opening day into a Magnolia High class reunion. High school reunions were for two types of people—the popular students who failed at life and unpopular students with something to prove.

Both were pathetic, if you asked me. I kept myself busy in the kitchen, concentrating on my pastry craft, until half of our baked goods ran out. My aunt and I underestimated how much inventory we needed and there's no way a delivery would make it here in time by closing.

My last resort was the pumpkin spice donuts that people loved so much they were putting in orders by the dozen. I had a busy work week ahead of me, but all I could think of right now was getting off of my feet. I lasted in the heels Aunt Jacquee gave me for less than an hour.

My navy-blue Crocs were a lifesaver that made it easy for me to move in between orders. The temporary staff were relieved at three o'clock, which left only me, Dakota, and Sunflower Falls' infamous 'mean girls.' Except now they were milfs, divorced, or chronically single, with tires wrapped around their waists.

The crowd dwindled down outside and only a trickle of customers were still sitting in the dining area. I cleared the racks inside the display case and placed them on the tabletop carousel to show everyone what we had left.

Two banana nut muffins, a slice of raspberry streusel pie, three cupcakes, and one lemon macaroon. I filled boxes with hot donuts for customers that agreed to wait for a fresh batch out of the oven. It's amazing how much of the town's gossip you can learn in a day simply by eavesdropping on conversations.

"Please, Deborah McKinley isn't one to talk with that glass house she's living in. Her husband dropped out of the mayoral election last year after his rumored affair with Deputy Eggleston's wife.

Then, Debbie quit her job working the front desk at the Sheriff's office to be back home with their kids, but we all know that's not why. Now the money's dried up, and she's been uploading foot pics to naughty sites just to stay afloat."

"Does her husband know?"

"He's the one that encouraged her to do it. Easy, fast money is all they know."

I chuckled at that one. They left the counter with their orders in hand, and another pair of old money cackling geese stepped forward.

"Francheska suspects Mark is back cheating again. She broke down at the township board meeting last week."

"Francheska? The deacon's wife?"

I heard the woman gasp as I turned my back.

"Yep, she's married to Ole' Blue Eyes. That's him. Everyone knows it's with the twenty-two-year-old that recently auditioned for the choir this time. She's just his type. Pencil-thin. Brunette. With a fake tan and none of the sense left that God gave her."

"I know she's heartbroken."

"Well, life has dealt her a shitty hand lately. She lost her mother not too long ago and her son's got a wrap sheet as long as the Chesapeake Bay Bridge."

I handed them their boxes of donuts, and three flashy women with southern accents dripping with honey, and copious amounts of hairspray, placed their orders next.

"Remember, I told you the Mikkelson twins go to the same Pilates studio as my daughter now?"

"Um. Hm. I saw their family estate is up for sale now, too."

"That's just it. Their parents are selling off all their properties to move the money around."

"You're shittin' me? Not Marilynn, the town snob."

"My husband told me Richie got hit with a money laundering charge from that fiasco that went down last year."

"The Bonny Chello RICO case that made the news?"

"That's it. His barber said it's only a matter of time before all their assets get seized. I bet they're trying to put everything in Marilynn's name."

"I hate to say it, but they had it comin'. All those businesses they opened were just a cover up."

Townsfolk gossip reminded me of the melodramatic telenovelas I used to watch with Aunt Jacquee growing up. Although interesting, I took everything I heard with a grain of salt. Ninety percent of the rumors stemmed from exaggerated lies, and ten percent from the truth.

I spotted Gallienne when she walked in alone earlier. She told a few other patrons she would be back, but I didn't expect it to be this soon. Dakota's high school sweetheart from hell moved closer in line to the register. She's the last person I wanted to reunite with, let alone serve. Judging by her snobby tone, not much has changed except her slim body had now turned into a fat figure eight.

Time had left the pretty green-eyed princess with crow's feet, a crooked row of bottom teeth, cheap blonde clips in, and a thinning crown of dark roots in dire need of a touch-up—but her poor attitude remained. Her frumpy sidekick appeared to be more friendly, yet clueless at the same time.

"I can't lie. This grand opening has exceeded my expectations. I just wish we made it here in time for a better selection."

"This bakery has needed a facelift for quite some time now." Gallienne tapped her olive-green suede ankle boots with tassels on the back zipper on the floor with her arms folded across her chest. "A rebrand was a step in the right direction."

"I didn't know you were into marketing, Galli?"

"Oh, I had a life before I turned into a full-time hockey mom. I was one of the top brand executives at a popular marketing agency when I lived on the East coast. I worked with six-figure budgets, the whole nine yards."

If you gave Gallienne an inch, she would take a mile complimenting herself.

"Well, I be damned, girl. I didn't know that."

"As a matter of fact, I'm going to pick Chassidy's brain about getting one of the pro hockey players from her husband's team to sign autographs on opening day."

"Chassidy?"

"Oh, she's Jett Aver's new fiancée. Big names like these seem to do wonders, numbers wise."

Hearing Jett Aver's name out loud made my skin crawl. My hands shook as I placed three boxes inside of a brown bag. *Focus, Thyri.*

"I thought you said you and Dakota have history. Why don't you ask him?"

The fluffy woman wore a solid light blue coastal linen blouse, white skinny jeans, and gray suede ankle boots identical to Gallienne's. Our complimentary eggnog left her with a milk mustache that Gallienne refused to make her aware of. I chewed on my bottom lip while squirting the last corner of whipped cream onto a steaming mug of hot chocolate. I was grateful for the turnout and the money we'd made, but I couldn't wait for this day to be over.

"We do. I mean, we've dated, but that was over fifteen years ago. I'm married—"

"You're not asking the man out, honey. He's your ex. Ask him to do it as a favor." The sidekick chuckled and winked her eye twice at Gallienne so she could take the hint.

"I'm not begging him to attend Chassidy's grand opening." Gallienne pressed her delicate fingers on her chest. "Unless he offers to do it himself. I'm sure Chassidy could easily add his meet and greet to our budget."

"Why would he be charging small businesses to sign autographs? I always thought of this stuff as charity work for athletes. They're loaded, for heaven's sake." The sidekick's ginger curls bounced on her shoulders every time she spoke. Unimpressed with her animations, Gallienne stood there with a stoic expression.

"That's not entirely true for all of them. Besides, I heard his money is a little funny these days." Gallienne rubbed her fingers together like she had a few Benjamin Franklins folded in between them.

Now she's spreading blatant lies. I prepped orders for the customers waiting in front of her, purposely moving closer to the front register to listen.

"Who told you that? His team just won the championship."

"I'm on the leadership board for event planning at the Legacy Arena. Word spreads like the common cold around here." Gallienne pursed her artificially plumped lips. "And I still run his name through Google from time to time."

She snorted and the disgust I've always felt towards her came tumbling back.

"I'm surprised it hasn't made the news."

"Some smaller outlets have picked it up, but nothing mainstream. There's this civil lawsuit case against some big shot NHL agency flying under the radar right now. My husband is friends with a few of the referees and coaches from the league, and they're saying Dakota's name is all over it."

"Wait, I thought you said your husband was a welder and part-time car salesman. He played hockey too?"

Gallienne looked around to make sure no one she deemed important stood near. "Chris is a Senior Welder and he owns a car lot," she replied through gritted teeth. "He's also a stockbroker and aggressive real estate investor. He tried to make it to the pros, but it wasn't in his callin'. Chris still keeps in touch with a lot of his old teammates from college, though. His connections helped my oldest son, Gunther, get accepted on the junior varsity team."

"Really? What varsity team is that?"

"The *Firebirds*. Anywho, my husband said that the well has run dry for Mr. Callahan."

"Wow, I wonder how that happened? His career seems like such a success from the outside looking in. You can't turn a corner around this town without seeing his face plastered on billboards, light posts, and posters in store windows."

"Poor money management on top of some legal issues. All the hype around the championship win will die down, you just wait and see."

"I'm so sorry to hear that." The sidekick kissed the roof of her mouth. At least she appeared to have some ounce of sympathy. "He just seems sooo..."

"Happy?"

The sidekick nodded, her expression pinched with concern.

"If I remember nothing else about Kota, it's that he knows how to put on the perfect facade. He's bright eyed and bushy tailed whenever those cameras turn on, but a completely different person off the ice."

Tell us you're the bitter ex-girlfriend of a famous hockey player without telling us, Gallienne. Sure, Dakota could be a real jackass sometimes, but she's painting him out to be Mr.Hyde. All these lies must help her sleep better at night. Judging from the tacky outfit and big box store hair-dye, Gallienne appeared to be experiencing some financial hardships herself.

That polyester cropped sweater, faded high waisted jeans to cover her mommy pouch, fake costume jewelry, and the cracker jack Cubic Zirconia ring on her finger were the telltale signs of an NHL *WAG* dream deferred.

I sighed after returning to the register from the oven. Dealing with the likes of Gallienne wasn't exactly at the top of my Sunflower Falls bucket list, yet here we are.

"Good afternoon, thanks for coming in. Before I take your order, the only items we have left are what you see on the carousel and a dozen donuts in the oven, which may be a thirty-minute wait. We're also taking orders for pickup next week." I kept my eyes on the kiosk, awaiting their response. Luckily for me, Gallienne got distracted by a phone call.

"We'll take the dozen and split them in half." The sidekick stepped forward as Gallienne gabbed away on her cell phone. "And whatever you have left to go."

"Great, that will be sixty-nine dollars and fifty cents for your total." She placed a crisp one-hundred-dollar bill on the counter.

"Keep the change. The samples and eggnog were chef's kisses. My name's Aryn, by the way, I'm new to town."

"Thanks, Aryn, and welcome, I appreciate your support."

"Treats on me, Galli!" she yelled over her shoulder, excited to grub on more sweets. Gallienne put her thumb up and I rolled my eyes while walking away.

Out of all the years I had to share the same hallways with Gallienne 'the wicked witch,' she never stopped pretending.

The Gallienne I knew would never step foot in public with a jolly woman like Aryn unless she possessed something that she wanted. I took one glance at the three-carat rock sitting on Aryn's pudgy, freckled finger drumming on the countertop and only one thing came to mind.

Money.

Gallienne was obsessed with being in proximity to wealth. If you were attractive, fit, vapid, and ego driven, like a moth to a flame, she drew near. Aryn's head was a little in the clouds, but she seemed to be the total opposite. *How long before this friendship ends in a dumpster fire?* Life does have a way of humbling you. Aunt Jacquee was right.

Aryn munched on the assorted sweets, licking her fingers and thumbs.

"I don't get the hype about this place." Gallienne started with a contorted expression.

"I do. Everything tastes delicious."

"How do you run out of food on your opening day? I have to let Chassidy know that her competition isn't steep."

"Competition?"

"Oh, I keep forgetting you just moved here."

That explains it.

"Whisk It To Win It is our annual baking contest. The Raspberry won for ten years straight, but now that the owner has finally thrown in the towel there's an opportunity for someone else to win the pool."

"All you get is a pool?"

"A pool of money, Aryn." Gallienne's response was curt.

"Oh." Aryn nodded. "I was wondering what all these awards were on the wall. Impressive."

"Never mind those. The pool is supposed to double this year for the competition's thirtieth anniversary. Last year, the pot grew to almost thirty thousand dollars in cash. I'm thinking about throwing my hat in the ring."

"Do you keep the cash, or is it for charity?"

"It's yours to do what you will with it, and anyone can enter this year since the pickings are slim." Gallienne smiled like a Cheshire Cat. "I think *Chassidy's Choc-O-Lattes* has a shot. If I won, I'd use the money to create a custom walk-in closet. The one we have now is way too small."

Great. Gallienne and her self-absorbed cronies want to take over Aunt Jacquee's reign to fund their superficial Barbie doll house dreams.

Just as I grabbed the broom, Dakota filled the kitchen with his larger-than-life personality. Gallienne shoved his overzealous fans out of the way to make her presence known again.

"The man of the hour." Gallienne's vocal fry voice sounded like nails on a chalkboard.

"The hour? Try the decade." Dakota signed an autograph without looking up.

"You know what I mean. Long time no see."

She walked around the counter with her arms outstretched for a hug. If I could blend in with the floral wallpaper, I would.

He gave her a friendly side hug while looking back at me reluctantly. I watched her laminated brows scrunch together like hairy caterpillars over Dakota's shoulders.

"Casper? Is that you?"

It's the first time she recognized me. Dakota watched me wilt like a flower right before his eyes and immediately corrected her. "The name's Thyri, Galli, and she's the new owner of The Raspberry."

"Oh. Fitting." She gave me the infamous once over before returning her attention to the one that got away.

I shook my head, tempted to hand her the broom in my hand, so she could ride it all the way to the moon

"Did you come in for an order or an autograph?" Dakota stepped in front of me after watching my grip on the handle tighten.

"Well, my sons probably wouldn't mind if I returned home with your autograph."

"Okay, just tell me where to sign."

"Gosh, you're even more handsome in person," Gallienne teased by slightly reaching for her shirt. I got secondhand embarrassment just witnessing their interaction. Her looks have faded, but for some odd reason, the confidence is still there.

"I was thinking more along the lines of a jersey, or T-shirt..."

"Koty, you know I'm only kiddin'."

"Not the sex kitten voice." My inside voice spoke aloud by accident, and Dakota snorted while smirking in my direction.

The smell of smoke from the top oven alerted me to the donuts that were likely as black as tar from the high temperature setting. I should've used the bottom oven. "Dammit."

"I know those aren't the donuts we've been waiting almost an hour for," Galli snapped.

"I'm sorry. I completely lost track of time." I placed the pan on the stove, waving away the smoke with my oven mitten.

"Casper, did you burn our batch on purpose?" Gallienne's eyes turned into slits.

"Galli, calm down. Mistakes happen." Dakota rebutted on my behalf.

99

"Mistake?! If she wasn't so busy meddling her nose in other people's conversations, she would have removed them on time."

"I can send over a complimentary batch once we restock next week." I offered a peace treaty in haste.

"Oh, I'd like that. That would be just fine." Aryn ripped off an order sheet to jot down her address, but Gallienne snatched the notepad.

"No, she owes us a refund."

"Gallienne, you didn't even pay." I spat back in contempt.

"Doesn't matter. I need a refund for my time." She shot daggers in my direction, and I started towards her.

"Woah, woah! Ladies, there's no need to fuss about this."

Dakota hopped in between us both. Two lionesses prepared to rip each other's eyes out.

"Galli, shit happens every day. We'll make sure you and your friend here receive a special home delivery come Monday."

The shipment doesn't arrive until next Wednesday, but I'm not telling her that.

"I don't even want the donuts. It's not my problem this twit can't tell time. Full refund."

"Are you really this hard up for seventy bucks?" I continued to fan the flames.

"No, it's actually the principle I'm concerned with. Aryn, get your refund for this poor customer service so we can go."

"Are you serious?" Dakota stepped in again and it caught me off guard.

"As a heart attack. And since when did you start taking up for... *her?*"

Gallienne still refused to show me any ounce of respect. She still treated me like a stubborn glob of gum you couldn't remove from the bottom of your shoe. I prevented her from cashing in on her golden meal ticket. *If I were her, I would hate me too.*

"When rude, uncouth customers like you walk through the door. Take the offer or leave, Galli."

Watching Gallienne's complexion turn crimson brought back old memories. She wore the same grimace outside of this kitchen window when I watched Dakota break up with her for cheating with his teammate.

"You all never have to worry about me knocking on these doors again and I'll see that no one else will either."

I stepped in front of Dakota to address Aryn. "Do you want a refund? It's not a problem if you do."

"I'll take the donuts." She slid the order sheet with her number on it in my direction while mouthing 'I'm sorry' before scurrying after Gallienne through the front door.

"She's such a—" Dakota caught himself in front of our remaining guests, who slowly packed up to go.

"Something that rhymes with witch?"

Dakota hated losing his composure in public. "Sorry for the scene. I know you and your aunt are trying to maintain your reputation."

"Don't worry about it." I walked towards the front door to thank everyone for stopping by while also apologizing for Gallienne's behavior.

The 'buy one pastry, get one free' coupons came in clutch just in time. I watched their eyes light up as they exited the bakery. They left me with nothing but praise, well wishes to Aunt Jacquee, and heartfelt waves from the sidewalk letting me know that they'll be back soon.

They will spread the word about the bakery reopening, but I could forget about receiving any support from Gallienne's troops on the Magnolia PTA board, Township Community Council, or the junior hockey league's mommy club. Fifty percent of our potential revenue flushed right down the drain in a matter of minutes. I swear some things never change.

After locking the door, I leaned my back against it, rotating my neck from side to side. "What a day!"

"I thought it went well." Dakota's loud crunching on the living room couch startled me.

"What are you still doing here?"

"I figured I'd stick around and help clean up."

"No need. I've got everything covered."

Dakota looked around at the dirty dishes, soiled tablecloths, and crumbs littering the dining room floor with an eyebrow arched.

"I said I can handle it."

"I've heard that line before." He crossed his legs on the couch with his sneakers on until I smacked them down. I snatched the bag of chips out of his hand and took a seat on the edge of the couch.

I'm glad he's keeping me company, but I'm not letting him know that. "Thanks for sticking up for me back there." I focused on the cheddar ruffle chips now staining my fingertips.

"Eh, she had it coming. I can't believe after all these years she's still the same."

"Now that's something we can agree on. I never understood what you saw in her, anyway."

He looked up at me with those charming brown eyes, and I suppressed the urge to straddle him.

"Ya' know, I felt the same way about all of your crushes too."

"Here we go."

"Especially that weird kid who swore he was hot shit with that wavy slick back hair, coke-bottle glasses, and gothic outfits." Dakota shuddered at the visual.

"Danielson *Scorbees*." I chuckled. "Geeks were my thing. I could listen to Danny talk about Dungeons and Dragons for days. I was smitten."

Dakota shook his head. "What about that other prick with the cloak that used to visit you every freakin' day of the summer? What's his name? Chad-A-Berry?"

"Chaddha Burrey. Now he was actually cute...aside from the bad acne."

"Yeah, if your type is Steve Urkel."

"If you were jealous, just say that," I teased, and his upper lip quirked.

"You wish."

"Do you want me to get on your taste in women?"

"I don't have any preferences."

"Exactly. That's the problem."

He folded his hands behind his head and squinted back at me.

"Now make yourself useful. You're on dish duty."

"I'd rather sweep."

"Nope. That's my chore, remember?"

"How could I forget?" He stretched, rolled up the sleeves of his black button up, and followed me into the kitchen. His woody cologne hit me the moment he walked to the sink. The notes of tonka bean and vanilla pulled me in as he yapped a mile a minute. I piled more dirty dishes into the sink, using the excuse to breathe in his musky scent. I closed my eyes, inching closer, only to jerk back the moment he turned around.

"You mean to tell me you honestly believe that Juarez is a better MMA fighter than O'Connor?" Dakota froze with a plate and dish rag in his hand.

"Three consecutive championships. Knockouts in the third round. A second-degree black belt. What else needs to be said?"

This was our first time engaging in a conversation that didn't end in a shouting match.

"Oh, my god."

"What?"

"You're serious with those stats?"

"Dead ass." Kick boxing is the only sport I watched faithfully since I was a kid. Our back-and-forth banter about the best fighters was nothing new.

"Juarez is a chump that picks weak fighters."

"He can't help that he's a heavyweight and all his opponents are small."

"So, you don't think that's strategic?"

I placed a hand on my hip. "If it is, it's a pretty good strategy."

"That's cheating." Dakota's lips spread into a thin line.

"You're one to talk. As many times as you've pinned players against the glass to get the upper hand."

"Hey, that's just a part of hockey."

"I've also seen you use a few of Juarez's moves a time or two on the ice."

"How would you know? You don't even watch hockey."

"The few times I've watched you play on television, you definitely have." My eyes bulged as I talked with my hands.

"Okay, which one's then?"

"Seriously, Kota? Arm wrapped around the neck from behind with your opponent on the ground and a knee on his back. That's a signature Juarez move. You ain't come up with that on your own."

"What?! That's a basic fighting move."

"They wouldn't have ejected you from that playoff game if it was." I took a wet rag and wiped it in circular motions on the cutting board kitchen counter, knowing I've revealed my hand.

"So, you've recently watched me play? What happened to 'I hate hockey. It's just a bunch of cavemen fighting on ice. Meh. Meh. Meh.'" Dakota mocked me and I frowned.

"Don't make that face again. I still hate it, but..." I averted my gaze. "Noah used to watch it."

I could feel Dakota watching me as if I were prey stuck in his territory. He leaned against the sink, leering at my body like it was a piece of meat dangling from a stick in a lion's den.

"What?!" Both of my brows bent.

"So, you're not gonna share why you're divorced?"

"There's nothing to share."

"Did he really cheat?"

Those words rolled so casually off his tongue you would have thought he asked me how was the weather? My mouth formed the shape of an 'O' as I pressed a hand against my cheek. Noah's slap of infidelity during our separation still stung anytime someone asked me for the reason.

"Not how you think."

"What does that mean?" Dakota yanked his head back in a way that I despise. It was his nonverbal way of communicating that I was acting obtuse. Now I remember why I used to hate our serious discussions. Dakota towered over me and never skated around sensitive subjects. Every word was direct and tinged with condescension. He either had to be right or get the last word in every time.

"He didn't have an affair...at least not while we were together." To distract myself, I turned around to put the clean pots and pans away in cabinets.

Dakota shoved his hand into his pocket while the other palm rested on the top of the kitchen island. "Was it a man?"

"Did anyone ever tell you your jokes aren't funny?" I stopped stumbling all over the kitchen and stormed through the arched doorway into the living room.

"Nope. I never get that."

"They're not funny." I returned an icy stare and began picking up the living room.

Dakota followed me to each table, refusing to give me any space. When I stopped and turned around, my face bumped into his chest.

"Watch where you're going." I could smell his minty fresh breath from the gum he was chewing.

The sexual tension in the room was thick enough to slice with a knife. I placed my hand on his stomach to put distance in between us, but all I could feel were the steel cuts of his abs.

My fingertips brushed the top of his brass belt buckle. He allowed my hand to linger until I met his gaze. His face burned with temptation as lust seeped into the folds of his seductive smile and the curve of his square jawline. Dakota's intense gaze rendered me speechless.

He dared me to make the first move, to give him permission. I stumbled back against a table, knocking a silver platter onto the hardwood floor. The loud metallic clatter was a force field disrupting our magnetic energy. A sly grin crawled across Dakota's lips as I crouched down to pick it up. I wiped my clammy hands on my apron so he couldn't see the sweat dripping from my palms.

Why does it feel like the thermostat is on hell?

"Come on, Tee," he teased. "I asked a simple question."

"Why do you wanna know?! It's none of your business." Dakota carrying on like he just wasn't about to strip me of my clothing made my voice raise an octave higher. I was a bottle of sexual frustration, one touch away from imploding. I swept the loose crumbs off the tablecloth, then removed it for laundering.

"Because I don't understand how a man could be foolish enough to lose you?"

"You're reciting lines from '80s rom-coms now?"

"Maybe I shouldn't have picked your favorite one, huh?"

"Maybe not. But since you're so curious, my ex-husband did cheat on me."

Dakota's eyes bulged.

He's amused that I'm single and miserable. There's that stupid smirk again. Now he's sitting on the back of our couch, blocking my way with those tree trunk legs. He leaned forward and I'm instantly tempted to slap him.

"With?"

I poked my tongue into the inside of my cheek and sighed. "... With video games."

My resting bitch face remained on full display as I waited for him to double over with laughter.

"Now, was that so hard to admit?"

"You already knew, didn't you?" My eyes slitted with contempt.

"Maybe." He shrugged.

"My aunt can't hold water, I swear."

"I think you're the only one who cares."

"It was my marriage...my divorce. Of course I care!"

Dakota folded his arms again, cocking his head to the side while chewing on his bottom lip to reflect his apathy and I hate it.

"Don't look at me like that." I scolded while removing the rest of the white tablecloths from each table until both of my hands were full.

"You need some help with that?"

"No! You're getting on my nerves."

"If it's worth anything, Noah seemed like a clown."

He was a clown. "You never even met him."

"I didn't have to. Meemaw told me more than enough. He's obviously still a child."

"And you're not?"

"Not at all. You want me to show you?"

"Is there ever any time of the day when you're not a creep?"

His flirting was weaning on me. And my desire for physical touch didn't make our exchanges any better.

"I would say when I'm sleeping at night, but my dreams can get a little filthy, too." He rubbed his hand back and forth, scratching the five o'clock stubbly shadow on his chin.

"I bet they do..." I kept a safe distance by leaning against one of the wooden chairs, studying his wide, down-turned lips and the way they glistened each time he licked them. "So, what about you? Why aren't you married...or divorced?"

"I had a few close calls, proposals I never pulled the trigger on."

"Still the ladies' man, I see."

"I know it's hard to believe a stallion like me has dating problems, but—"

"Don't flatter yourself. You're a lot to deal with."

"How so?" His eyebrow shot up.

"Ummm, your harems for one?"

"That just comes with being in the league."

"Yeah, and it keeps the woman worth waiting for at bay."

"She can have a slot on the roster and move her way up the ranks."

A wave of disgust washed over my face, which prompted him to clean it up.

"I'm kidding, Thyri."

"You're not." I shook my head. "Forever a bachelor...like I've always said."

"I'm not a playboy anymore, if that's what you're getting at." Dakota's eyes shifted to the floor before he looked up again. "That lifestyle no longer serves me. When you're famous, it's hard to tell the real from the fake. Most women are only concerned with what they can get out of being attached to you."

I placed the laundry on the table and pulled out a chair to make myself comfortable. Now it's his turn in the hot seat. "What are they expecting to get?"

"Is that a serious question? Hockey players are walking dollar signs."

"I mean, that's nothing new."

"No, Tee. The schemes I've seen. You wouldn't believe the half."

"Oh, I'm sure I wouldn't flinch."

"How would you know?"

"You know how many athlete groupies flock to online forums and social media outlets to strategize and tell on themselves? I'm well-versed in *WAG-ology* because of it."

"Really? Tell me what you know about dating athletes then."

"Turn a blind eye to the cheating, count the contract money, ask for real estate, diamonds, and cash. Have everything put in your name until you secure the ring. Oh, and make sure you're seen by other players as a backup in case you're kicked to the curb. Use a turkey baster as a last resort."

Dakota's mouth fell open. "A turkey baster?"

I held up my hands to surrender. "Hey, I don't make the rules."

"Wait, so women sit around and discuss this stuff?"

"I don't, but I've been around plenty of women that do."

"So, you all are worse than the guys?"

"That's a stretch." I held up my finger.

"No, I think it's fair. A lot of athletes can be morally bankrupt too."

"Yeah, but trapping men... It's never that serious."

"Tell me about it. Heck, half of my public relationships were fake."

"You're joking, right?"

He shook his head. "Another public figure or celebrity brings in more publicity. And a healthy relationship and clean image means more brand deals, which essentially brings in..."

"More money." My lips pinched.

"Yeah, if only that were true." His voice trailed off.

Dakota's solemn demeanor spoke volumes. Miss Massey was a grave loss for him, but his resentment for the hockey league was very telling. As much as I want to rat Gallienne out for the rumor she's spreading, it's not my place. Personal finances are a touchy subject for most. Dakota never struck me as a person who measured his worth in dollar signs, but over time, things change.

"Are you happy about retiring?"

"It could've been under better circumstances."

"I get that," I replied in a faint whisper.

After turning around for a quick glance out of the window, I noticed a strange woman standing across the street next to a stroller. Give or take a few inches, she was around the same height as me. She wore a black athleisure set with a red puffer vest that made her resemble a stop sign.

I spun my head around at Dakota. "Is that Gallienne outside gaping at us?"

"What? Where?" He jumped to his feet.

"The woman looking over here from across the street."

"She's not that bold. I doubt it's her."

"That's definitely her standing over there, looking like a maniac." I removed my apron, and switched out my slippers for my track shoes, prepared to give her a piece of my mind.

"What're you doing?"

"I'm going out there."

"To do what?" He chuckled. If we were younger, he would have asked for more time to grab some popcorn and a front-row seat.

"What do you think?" I slapped my hand down on my thigh and opened the door.

"Don't forget the Vaseline!"

Dakota watched from inside the doorway as I walked onto the front porch with my fists balled. The woman appeared to be fixated on him.

"Hey!" When she saw me jump down the stairs and sprint in her direction, she grabbed the handlebar of the oddly shaped stroller and took off. I've never seen someone power walk that fast in my life. By the time I caught up with her, we were at the entrance of the cul-de-sac.

"Excuse me?! Hey!" I tapped her shoulder and hopped back when I saw her face.

A dejected woman with strained eyeballs, dry and cracked lips, thinning platinum blonde hair, prominent cheekbones, and freckles glowered at me. The blunt bangs hid her forehead, shortening the length of her heart-shaped face. But those dilated, molten-honey eyes made it hard to look away.

Her lips parted, but no sound escaped. She used her frail body to shield the stroller. Except the seat held no baby, only a blue waffle knit receiving blanket, but a swollen bump under her shirt revealed she was pregnant or had recently given birth.

"I'm so sorry. I mistook you for someone else."

"It's okay." She avoided eye contact with me, slowly turning around while rolling her shoulders into her puny chest. Seconds later, she disappeared around the corner. Instead of making my way back to the house where Dakota stood on the sidewalk waiting, I didn't move.

The morose expression etched into her face looked dangerously familiar. I've seen her before. I just can't remember where.

110

"Hey, track star, did you get your lick back?" Dakota tossed Bean-bug's chew toy across the lawn, and he snarled back at him.

"No. False alarm." Out of breath, I rubbed Beanbug to calm him down.

"I told you it wasn't her."

"Yeah, but I feel like I've seen her somewhere before."

"That's not surprising. It's only like five people in this town."

"Maybe you're right."

Dakota tossed another chew toy off the porch, but this time Beanbug was rolled onto his back with four paws in the air with one half eye open.

"What's up with this weird dog?"

"He does that sometimes."

"Rollover and play dead?"

"He has narcolepsy...among other things." I made my way back up the steps.

"Serious question?"

I turned around. "I'm listening."

"When did you start liking pets?"

"He wasn't my dog. I stole him."

"From who?!" Dakota shuddered just looking at Beanbug drooling with his tongue out.

"My ex."

Dakota shook his head. "Are you still taking me up on that offer to help you clean up?"

He wanted to stick around, so I gave him the green light. "I could use the help."

"Well, I be damned. Thyri is accepting some 'help' for once. The world must be ending."

"People do change, you know."

"Oh, I can see that." His eyebrows raised suggestively as I rubbed my arms from the chilly breeze.

"You can come back inside, but only under one condition."

"What's that?"

"Behave."

Dakota was cute, but he would have to do much more than flirt and make me laugh to knock down the wall between us.

"Yes, ma'am."

I clapped three times, and Beanbug jumped to his feet. "Let's go, Bug!"

———

Dakota blabbered nonstop for the rest of the night. He seemed happy about our reconnection. It's almost as if he enjoyed my company.

We reminisced about our childhood. From the neighbors we hated, epic summer pranks we pulled, and all the petty squabbles we got into with the McClains.

It's funny how time heals. Things that seemed irreparable back then. We couldn't stop laughing at now. Dakota opened up to me like a peony in bloom. He revealed his vulnerable side by sharing some heartfelt private moments with Miss Massey that left me teary-eyed.

The mature version of Dakota was winning me over, but I couldn't let him see me sweat.

By the time we made it back to the couch, I made sure we kept a comfortable distance.

Some of his tales of living life in the fast lane as a famous hockey player had me on edge. They were wild, scary, and a little taboo, but interesting nonetheless.

My boring married life with Noah didn't hold a candle to Dakota's adventures, so I was reluctant to share. It made me think about all the years I had wasted, not chasing my own dreams but trying to turn a house I never truly owned into a home.

Surprisingly enough, Dakota's regrets are my mistakes. That's where we collide.

"The grass isn't always greener on the other side, that's for sure," I reassured him.

"Yeah, but if I had settled down while I was in the league, I'd at least have someone to come home to."

"But at least you created some crazy memories to look back on."

"That's just it. If you keep looking back, you can't move forward."

"Look at you! Being all profound and shit." I grabbed the remote controller off the coffee table, closed off as usual.

"Do you have any regrets?"

Many. "I wish I was more of a risk taker, and I married way too soon."

"Meemaw always talked about fate..."

"What about it?" With my back against the arm of the couch and my legs folded Indian style, I turned on the television.

"She said sometimes two people can have the same destination, but—"

"They may have to take different routes to get there..." I added, as a flashback of Miss Massey pulling my hair into two Dutch braids on their front porch tip toed across my mind. "And even if the timing isn't right..."

"The only thing that matters is that they do."

An awkward silence befell us.

"How did you know that?"

"I spent a lot of time with her, too. You were always traveling with the Falcons, or somewhere hooking up with girls, remember?"

"I was a teenager. Sounds pretty normal to me."

"Of course, it does." I forced a fake smile. "Now, are we going to watch a movie or what? It's late." The sentimental moments between us had reached their peak for the evening.

"Yeah, your pick. As long as it has some action, none of that fantasy apocalyptic crap that you used to watch."

"Let me guess, you're still obsessed with the Fast and The Furious? Does Vin Diesel still tickle your fancy?" I shimmied my shoulders, and Dakota stifled his laughter.

"No, The Rock was my favorite. Just put something on, doofus. You're still annoying."

Satisfied, I snuggled up with my knees tucked into my chest under a throw blanket.

As much as I wanted to ask him if he'd like to share, I didn't. We were getting to know the new adult versions of ourselves, and I didn't want to send any mixed signals.

Thirty minutes into the movie and we were both out for the count. When I woke, birds were chirping beneath the window, and the chimes danced to the gusty wind. Sunlight streamed in, making my eyelids flutter. I peeled back the blankets, hoping to find Dakota still snoring beside me, but I was alone.

9 / DAKOTA

FOR OLD TIMES' sake, I sat high in the stands, bundled up in a hooded duck jacket to combat the frigid temperature inside. Rings of smoke escaped my mouth every time I yawned.

The Legacy Arena was almost too quiet; the only thing I could hear was the swish-swoosh of Bear's hockey stick blade gliding across the ice like he owned it. He resembled a giant, even from the nose-bleeds, as he rehearsed every move as if he were leading a hockey clinic.

Body fakes. Spin aways. Toe drags and a slick fake shot to back-hand; I couldn't help but smirk at his talent. Same Bear, always showing off, even with no one around. I shifted in my seat, my left knee grinding in its socket as I put on my hockey gear.

Legacy's management allowed us to have the arena to ourselves with no promise of any heat. The cold was biting, but it felt good in a way. Familiar. I missed this old building more than I cared to admit.

I made my way down the old steps with filthy blue ratty carpet lifting from its corners. The lingering stench of bleach, popcorn, and bromodosis slapped me in the face as I walked through the bench.

Stepping onto the ice felt like slipping into an old skin, though I could tell right away I wasn't as nimble as I used to be. Bear slid towards me with that cocky grin of his, one that would've sent me to the moon back when we played together.

"Thought you were gonna chicken out and sit up there all night," he said, twirling his stick lazily.

I chuckled, shaking my head. "Save the trash talk for the game."

"You know I can back it up."

He dropped the puck between us, and we took off, scraping skates, jabbing sticks, and a whirlwind of vicious tight turns. I pushed myself harder than I should've, trying to keep up with him. And for a minute, I did. But damn, he was relentless. Bear's passion for winning the game was unmatched.

I played dirty when I needed to, but crushing bones and slamming opponents against the wall was his love language. I called several timeouts just to catch my breath. No one can convince me that youth isn't an advantage.

In the last stretch of the scrimmage, Bear came barreling in, and I thought I had him locked down, but to my surprise he used my signature move. A slick little slip of the puck right through my legs before sending it past me into the hockey net. On my knees, I growled as he released a haughty laugh, skating a slow circle around me.

"Rusty already, brother? It's only been a few weeks," Bear teased, his warm breath visible in the freezing air.

I shook my head, half scowling. "You lost our last two games, remember? And who are you trying to impress? There's no one here."

I whipped my head around for emphasis. I tried to laugh it off, but I felt his deep-set, protruding eyes on me.

"Everything cool?" I looked up at him, skeptical, pushing my intrusive thoughts about Thyri to the back of my mind.

"You've been acting weird lately," Bear said, slightly annoyed, leaning on his stick. "We've barely hung out all off-season aside from doing home repairs. The only time I get you to myself is out here, and even now, you're not *really* here."

"You sound like a nagging woman." I wanted to brush him off, but his words hit too close to home.

Bear's intuition never steered him wrong. I exhaled slowly, watching my breath vanish into the cold. He skated over and helped me to my feet, the weight of my gear pressing me down. "I got it. I got it."

"What's up, dude?"

I glanced down at my skates, then back at him. "I have a lot going on. The judge is about to toss my case out again."

"Why would they do that?" Bear's eyes pinched.

"Not enough evidence to go to trial, they say." I tried to keep my voice steady, but it was tough.

Bear straightened up, frowning. "That's what's eating you?" he asked. "That's why you've been dodging me?" He placed an over-sized hand on his chest mockingly.

I nodded, a weary chuckle escaping my lips. "Not just that," I admitted, hesitating. "There's this girl who used to live next door..."

Bear's eyebrows shot up as the raucous laughter echoed throughout the stadium. "I knew it. I fuckin' knew it, dude! You ditched me for some chick."

I glared at him, though I couldn't help smirking a little. "It's not like that. She's not just any woman... She's different. Intelligent. Funny. Hard to read and a bit of an ice queen when she wants to be."

"She sounds normal to me. So, how long have you two been hanging out?" Bear scissored two of his fat fingers together, implying that we've hooked up.

"No, it's nothing like that. I'm too chicken shit to even ask this one out."

"You're afraid? Well, that's new." Bear leaned on his stick, studying me with a proud grin.

"Tell me about it. I don't want to scare her off. And honestly? I'm not sure if she still hates me or not from when we were kids—" I stopped, the weight of my own words settling over me.

"Oh, there's bad blood?"

"Enough to fill a well."

"Everyone's been telling me about the crazy history of this town, but every time I hear a story, I'm underwhelmed. Nothing tops the crazy shit I've seen growing up."

"*Underwhelmed?* What have you been reading lately?"

"I've got a few locked and loaded in my vocab arsenal. Don't worry about it. Just keep going."

"Thyri's never been a town favorite."

"But she's obviously yours, so why does it matter?"

He had a point. "We haven't talked in ages. I scared off her senior prom date, and she burned our high school gymnasium down for it. She never forgave me after that."

"Alright, here we go; now I'm all ears. Who was her date?!"

"Take one guess." I flashed a sinister look in his direction.

"You've gotta be shittin' me."

"Nope. None other than Jett Avers."

"That creep? She ought to be thanking you."

"That's what I said, but I'm still not sure if that's what actually sent her over the edge. I asked her about it countless times, but always ended up with doors slammed in my face."

"Sounds ridiculous to me."

"It's the same way between us now. Some days, she'll open up to me like we're old buddies, and the next day she's giving me the cold shoulder." I shrugged, unable to put the pieces of the puzzle back together.

"Maybe she's just playing hard to get?"

"Thyri doesn't play games. She's the most serious, unserious person I know."

"I don't mean to burst any bubbles here." Bear swiftly skated around me, etching a circle in the ice with the front of his skate. "But buddy, while I know you may not be used to the friend zone, it appears you're in it."

"Nah, I'm not accepting that. At least not yet. There's gotta be some way to remove that shield of armor she has up."

"What have you been doing to break it?"

"I don't know. Hanging around."

"Just casually hanging out..."

"Yeah. What else am I supposed to do? Grovel at her feet?" My eyebrows stitched together.

"If that's what it takes."

"Uh, I don't know about that. I don't have to chase women. They chase me."

"Hate to break it to ya', pal, but there's a first time for everything."

"Eh, she's not the mushy type. And she can be really standoffish when she's in one of her moods."

"Maybe she's been hurt before and doesn't want to be put through the wringer again."

"Why do you know so much about women, Bear?" I shook my head, visibly annoyed. He had an answer for everything, good ones at that.

"Bro, you've seen my family. All I listened to growing up was girl talk. That's why my dad and I stayed on the ice day and night. It nearly drove us insane."

"Yeah, well, maybe you're onto something. The ink on her divorce papers hasn't even dried yet. Dating is probably the last thing on her mind right now."

"That'll do it. One of my exes was a divorcee. She was the easiest one to crack. Sure, there was emotional baggage, but with her, there were no strings attached."

"You never told me you were in a relationship with a divorced woman. How old was she?"

"I was twenty-two, and she was like..." Bear struggled with counting the fingers on his hands.

"Ten years older?"

"About twenty." He scratched his unruly beard. "What? I like 'em seasoned."

"I know. Spare me the details."

"So, what are you gonna do, Prince Charming? Asking her on a date would be a step in the right direction."

"A date? Seems a little weird to ask the girl you once lived next door to on a formal date. Thyri was like my bratty kid sister back then."

"If you don't ask, then the next man will. And if she's as special as you say she is, it's only a matter of time before they are lined up at her door." Bear slowly skated backwards. "Next time you see her, ask her if she prefers her men with a bit of meat on their bones who get buck wild in the bedroom."

"Bear." I shot him a stern look for him to proceed with caution.

"Then stop being a wuss and ask her out. Women like to be swooned, it doesn't matter what age. I don't know why, they just do. Classic red, long-stemmed roses. They go a long way. Trust me."

Never in a million years would I have imagined I'd be taking dating advice from my protégé.

Thyri wasn't a fifteen-year-old girl anymore. She was a grown woman and expected to be courted as one.

But could I provide her with the finer things in life? Dazzle her with a lifestyle that she's not accustomed to?

I'm not sure what anchored Thyri's interest in men, but I'm the direct opposite of her type.

A former hockey jock with fleeting fame, who had all his riches cunningly swiped away within the blink of an eye. I sighed.

The rink suddenly felt colder, quieter, and heavier, like even the ice could sense I was skating on thin ground.

If only she could accept me for who I am now.

It's worth a shot.

10 / THYRI

I EXAMINED my outfit in the full-length mirror, contemplating my decision to have dinner with Dakota tonight.

He asked me for seven days straight until I finally gave in accidentally.

My lips twisted to the side as I posed. I placed one foot in front of the other, with a hand on my hip. Hopefully, Aunt Jacquee's marshmallow bodycon dress and these gold padlock, metallic leather stiletto sandals don't send the wrong message. A miniature gold clasp the size of a brioche cinched my waist, securing the subtle cut-out above my hipbone.

Everything about it screamed 'undress me.' One slip-up would send my dress pooling around my ankles on the floor. My black lace thong gave the illusion that my ass was bare, and this adhesive tape had my perky C-cups standing at attention on my chest.

For once, it felt good to play dress-up and feel confident about my appearance. I even took a few minutes to put some flat curls in my hair for a wavy style. Makeup wasn't my expertise, but Kels taught me how to create a mean smokey eye with faux wispy lashes.

"Aww, Beans, it's just me." Beanbug twisted his head from side to side as I put down a fresh bowl of water. Even he couldn't recognize me. I left out an extra bowl of treats at the bottom of the staircase just in case I didn't return home until the morning.

He'll be curled up on the bottom step, waiting to greet me. As soon as the cuckoo clock struck seven at the end of the hall, a pair of headlights turned down my street. I flipped on the porch light and grabbed my fur shawl to combat the biting chill.

"Don't wait up, Beans!" I slammed the door shut behind me and ignored his scratches and whimpering behind the wood.

The redwood and fir trees grew smaller in density an hour out from the countryside. When Dakota invited me out to eat at The Rowe, I assumed he meant a bourgeois authentic Italian restaurant, but the driver parked in front of the Topanga Hotel.

"Are you sure he gave you the right address?"

"Yes, Too-panga."

English wasn't my driver's first language, so I didn't bother to inquire any further. Seconds later, my door flung open and two members of the concierge team helped me out of the back seat. My aunt's brown chinchilla fur shawl may have been overkill for the season, but it did the job. I pinched it closed with my YSL clutch in hand until I made it through the revolving doors. Growing up, I used to dream of lodging here without wincing at the nightly cost.

What does Dakota have up his sleeve?

Notes of apricot and eucalyptus wafting from the hotel lobby engulfed guests in a luxurious spa-like oasis as soon as their shoes hit the bamboo floors.

Handmade embroidered rugs with Indonesian-inspired designs and plush loveseats provided a warm and romantic ambiance. Gold accents with hand-carved Buddha art adorned the towers surrounding the indoor garden and elephant fountain statue in its center. My long-awaited trip to Ubud, Bali, was no longer needed after stepping foot in here.

"Welcome to Topanga Hotel. With whom do I have the pleasure of meeting this evening?"

"Thyri Richards? I may be on the reservation list under Callahan."

"Of course, give me a second. I'll get you checked in. We'll also need to make a copy of your photo I.D. for security."

"...What do you need?"

"Your license, please."

What is this, Fort Knox?

"If you insist." I pulled out my license from my aunt's classic YSL crossbody quilted leather handbag. He handed it back to me, and I sighed while he took his precious time scrolling through a screen embedded in the front desk. The crease in my forehead deepened the longer I waited for further instructions. His thick handlebar mustache twitched as he pushed up his square-framed, matte black Prada glasses on the bridge of his ski-slope nose. The dim, recessed lighting shone a spotlight on the top of his close-shaven head.

I whipped my head around at the other guests walking back and forth enjoying their evening while mine was off to a slow start.

"I'm sorry, is there something wrong?"

"Pardon my silence, I'm browsing our reservation list, and I'm afraid we don't have a booking for anyone under that name tonight."

My mouth fell open as my mind raced to the worst-case scenario. There was no way this man had stood me up. Beads of sweat slid down the back of my neck as I scrolled through my text messages. I chewed my bottom lip. "You know what, I'll just call Dakota."

I was a ball of nerves, digging through my clutch to distract myself. *A tiger never loses its stripes. How could I let this asshole embarrass me again?*

"Something told me—" I grumbled aloud.

"Sorry to interrupt, but did you say Dakota? As in Dakota Callahan?" His beady eyes grew smaller and smaller the longer he stared at me.

"Yes, unfortunately. The pompous ex-hockey star."

He cleared his throat while pulling on a pair of white gloves. He took a few brisk steps around the counter. "My apologies, right this way."

He snapped his fingers at two bellhops while I followed him into a hall with various sets of elevators until we stopped at the one at the very end with smoky black doors. "I'm sorry for the inconvenience. We'll be heading up to Mr. Callahan's penthouse suite on the forty-eighth floor?"

"Penthouse suite?!"

"Yes, Ms. Richards. Bobby Magnamara is the alias you can use with the concierge for any requests. We like to protect the identities and safety of our high-profile residents."

Residents? Dakota owns a penthouse? I didn't know he was living this large.

"May we check your coat and offer some light refreshments on your way up?"

"Of course." I removed the cape from my shoulders and instantly felt ten pounds lighter. I tucked the gold chain inside my oversized clutch.

"Cristal, madam?" A cherry bobbed around the rim of the champagne flute the bellhop offered me in a French accent. The elevator doors flew open, and Mr. Prada glasses and I stepped inside.

"Is the temperature and music selection to your liking?"

The plush carpet, sprawling city lights, and small aquarium embedded in the ceiling had me too stunned to speak. A curated experience on an elevator ride was top-tier.

"I'm comfortable..." I said with my back turned, enamored by the view of the galaxy beneath me.

He gave my scantily clad outfit a once-over and added, "I'll turn up the heat just in case."

On the opposite side of the elevator were tiny bites of fresh shrimp scampi, fried asparagus, steamed oysters, sushi and chocolate candy with caramel filling and specs of gold.

"Feels like I'm being teleported to Abu Dhabi right now. May I?"

The colorful touch screen with endless music selections caught my eye.

He nodded once with his hands behind his back, pleased by my compliment. I could tell that running this hotel consumed his entire life.

A picture of Marvin Gaye singing into a silver vintage microphone popped up under the Rhythm and Blues selection, and I pressed play.

"I've been really tryinnnn' baby. Tryin' to hold back this feeling for so long.

And if you feel like I feel, baby. Then come on, oh, come on, woo!" Swaying to the music, I sang along, holding out my champagne flute for a refill.

As a lightweight, it only took a few rounds for me to feel a slight buzz. My ride up to the forty-eighth floor was uninterrupted and rectified the underwhelming start to my night.

Now I can only hope that Dakota doesn't say or do anything that will kill my vibe.

"Ms. Richards, we'll be reaching our destination in approximately sixty-seconds."

"I've never been up this high." I held on to the railing, smiling from ear to ear.

Marvin's crisp, swoon-worthy vocals made me feel sexier than I looked. "I wanna get it onnnn. You don't have to worry that it's wronggg. If the spirit moves ya. Let me groove ya, good. Let your love come down!"

The doors opened, but I remained in my zone. I dropped my hips to the side just like my mother used to at her house parties when the liquid courage in her cup had her feeling right.

Now that I'm older, I understand.

After a two-step and slow body roll with one hand on the rail, I turned around to find Dakota with his arms crossed, leaning against the elevator doors.

"Let's get it on, babbyyy. This minute, oh yeah..." His irresistibly charming smile was on full display, twinkling like a shooting star. "When did you get some rhythm?" His eyes didn't break away from the high slit in my dress.

"Okay, keep it cute, Kota." I brushed past him with a smirk to find the hotel manager standing in the cozy hallway, looking straight ahead at a rodeo Western abstract painting hanging on the eggshell wall. He kept one hand behind his back while the other arm remained in front.

Is this a five-star hotel or the Marines?

"Thanks for the champagne."

"You're welcome." His thin lips pulled into a smile, humanizing him again.

"I'll take it from here, Davis, thanks."

Dakota walked through the door at the end of the hall shortly after me as I struggled to unstrap my heels.

"Let me help you with those."

"No, I got it."

"C'mon, Thyri. Relax...sit down."

I hobbled over to the sheepskin rug and took a seat on the curved contemporary sofa.

"Why do I feel like I'm on an episode of Selling Sunset?" I lifted my head, amazed by the floor to ceiling windows, skylight and the moon tap dancing on the rooftop.

"Breathtaking, isn't it?" Dakota knelt down, gently unstrapping my shoes to allow my feet to breathe. His firm grip on my feet sent tingles down my spine. I bit down on my lip to stop myself from moaning. For a moment I watched him freeze. He examined my legs as if they weren't the only parts of my body he wanted to explore.

"So." I placed my feet back on the rug, scrunching my white pedicured toes to bring myself back down to Earth. "Are we still going out to eat? It's getting late, and you haven't gotten dressed."

My eyes rolled over his sun-kissed, sculpted chest. I licked my lips and massaged my neck after miscounting the number of thick, muscular veins tracing his broad shoulders and forearms. *When did he get this ripped?* My eyes trailed the V-shape leading down to his groin that stopped at the top of his Hanes briefs. There wasn't a prick of pubic hair in sight.

I forgot Dakota was the same guy who used to shave his leg hair and armpits. If he's bald down there, it wouldn't be shocking.

"No, I said we'll have dinner together. I didn't tell you where... and what's wrong with my attire?"

He flicked his eyes up, flashing that sexy-ass smile again that's going to make me lose all sense of control.

"Then you should have said that. Now I feel overdressed."

"I think you look amazing."

I frowned while tilting my head to the side, waiting for the backhanded compliment to land. "But—"

"No buts, except I feel honored you got all dolled up for me." He clutched his chest playfully.

"Don't flatter yourself. I dressed up because I was expecting fine dining at a Michelin-star restaurant tonight."

"Well, aren't you fancy?" He nodded with his lips turned down.

"As a matter of fact, I am..." I scoffed. "I've never eaten at one before, but I wouldn't mind trying it."

"Interesting..."

"What's so interesting about it, Kota?" It's been less than five minutes and I'm this close to wringing his neck.

"I don't know. Most of the items on their menus come with an acquired taste."

"I have an...acquired taste." Whatever that means. I sat on the edge of the sofa, squeezing my hands on the cushion, looking everywhere but at his delectable upper body.

He folded his arms unconvinced. "Huh. So you no longer ditch restaurants that don't have chicken fingers or pizza on the menu?"

"I'm grown now. My palate has changed."

"Your palate?"

I nodded vigorously, knowing damn well I tried nothing new outside of Italian or Mexican food.

"I can have Davis make a few calls for last-minute reservations. You can order some squid, foie gras, and a little sea urchin on the side."

I swallowed hard at the thought of something slimy slithering down the back of my throat. "Okay, you got me. What are we eating then? Take out?" If I had known any better, I would have worn one of my favorite sweatsuits. Now I'll be re-adjusting this dress all night.

"Dinner's still heating up in the oven. It's a home-cooked meal with every basic thing that you like."

"Are you calling me basic?" My eyebrow jumped.

"Does the shoe fit?"

"Just shut up and give me a tour."

Dakota chuckled, holding both his hands out to help me off of the couch that I had sunk into. Lately, he seemed to find every opportunity to stand closer or touch me in any way he could. As much as I wanted to give in, the timing never felt right.

Both of us are navigating the stages of grief because of personal losses. He's looking for a crutch, and I want something real, something long term that I can rely on. Why can't men tell us what they want so we can rightfully tell them to go to hell? I'd rather they were upfront, so we can stop wasting each other's precious time. Inviting me over for dinner and a potential nightcap is the oldest trick in the book. *Was he embarrassed to be seen out with me in public?* I wish he would just tell me his intentions rather than pulling fast ones like this.

"I think I can lift myself off the couch." The wagon I'm dragging is heavy, but not that damn heavy.

"Do you have to push back on everything that I do?"

"Do you have to touch me every chance that you get?"

"Thyri, I'm not trying to touch you." He rolled his eyes back into his head. "Can't men be gentlemen anymore?"

"You can...I just don't like to be touched." I twisted my lips to the side while his hands remained steady in front of me. "And I don't trust you...yet."

"I'm not asking you to. You promised me you would go with the flow tonight, remember?"

I glanced up at the pillars towering over us before responding. After sucking my teeth, I placed my small hands inside of his, and said, "Okay, alright."

I promised Aunt Jacquee that I would try my best to have a good time, but my concern isn't Dakota. He's harmless for the most part. Giving in to my wanton desires is what I'm afraid of. The way the defined muscles in his back flexed and contracted while leading me across the living room caused my mouth to water. My nether regions had been dry as the Sahara Desert for months, but watching him maneuver around the mini-mansion in the sky broke the dam between my thighs.

I counted the tiny specks of birthmarks, freckles, and moles all over his smooth olive skin. He smelled as though he had just stepped out of the shower. The fresh aroma of Irish Spring soap and Garnier Fructis shampoo on his slicked-back hair clung to the air. I listened to him ramble on about his art decor and the inspiration behind the porcelain pebble stone tile floors in the powder room. But the architectural history behind this museum's design didn't intrigue me at all.

All I know is that I could get used to this. Dakota led me up the spiral stairs to see the movie theatre and game room. The king-size mattress in his master bedroom was custom-fitted to his headboard and circular frame. He could wrestle me into the pretzel-dip right now and I wouldn't protest. He led me over to the master bathroom and showed how it doubled as a sauna. As the mirror fogged, Dakota increased the temperature on the heated floors. I stared back at him with a deadpan expression, pretending to be unimpressed. Dakota twisted the knobs on the freestanding whirlpool clawfoot tub to show how strong the jets were.

I could soak my body in this tub for hours. This bathroom was the sanctuary every woman dreamed of. When Dakota lit up for my reaction, I shrugged with a lopsided grin. "Cool, I guess."

Earlier I contemplated bringing an overnight bag; too bad I didn't. By the time we made it back downstairs to the main kitchen, I could smell the food heating in the oven. "What's on the menu? It smells good."

"You'll see soon enough. Ignore the mess."

He made a mess indeed. Chopping boards with remnants of tomatoes, red onions, and parsley covered the obnoxiously long island, large enough to fit a family of ten. Half-eaten bags of tortilla chips, limes and avocados that were cut and peeled the wrong way littered its edge.

"I'm guessing Mexican. Tacos? Guacamole?"

Dakota scurried around the luxury modern kitchen, throwing empty takeout containers into brown bags while running water over dirty dishes in the stainless-steel farmhouse sink. "Not quite. But I'm sure you'll be pleased once we sit down to eat."

"I can help plate if you like."

"Nooo, nope. You're my guest, just relax. Tell the Smart Assistant to put on some more jazz, anything you like. I'm going to finish tidying up in here and then run upstairs to throw on some clothes more fitting for the occasion."

"A nice button-down would be nice."

I had never seen Dakota this jumpy before. His upper lip curled into a half smile while the tail tucked in between his legs wagged uncontrollably. The more we hang out, the fonder we grow of each other's company. He must enjoy having me around.

It's a stark contrast to our usual cat-and-mouse dynamic. If I didn't know any better, I'd think Mr. Callahan has a schoolyard crush on me. All the signs were there, but he'll never admit it.

No situationships.

No one-night stands.

Those were the top two items I planned to honor on my list of things *not* to do after returning to Sunflower Falls. But I might as well scratch jumping into a new relationship headfirst off the list. Dakota anchored his boat on the shores of my heart, and I'm afraid I've already fallen in too deep.

It's only a matter of time before he dives in to rescue me.

11 / DAKOTA

"TEN MINUTES of mansplaining Balinese culture from a boring-ass canvas painting... Really, dude?" I stared at my reflection in the mirror, perturbed, removing any residue of the aftershave left on my chin with a white cloth.

I need to calm down.

"You need to calm down!" I looked down and shouted at my other brain, zipping up my pants.

Thyri looked good enough to serve on a platter tonight. The revealing white dress had my mind doing backflips and somersaults right into the gutter. When she placed her soft, bare feet in my hands, the temptation to appease my sexual appetite intensified. I would have spread her spindly legs from coast to coast and eaten her petal for breakfast, lunch, and dinner, if she had let me.

Greeting her at the elevator with my shirt off wasn't a chess move but completely unplanned. She arrived earlier than I expected, and I was running downstairs to grab a takeout order I had called in at the last minute. I kept her occupied long enough for Davis to sneak the food into the oven downstairs.

Close call, but at least our evening is off to a decent start. Thyri can't keep her eyes off me, which is a good sign. Our physical attraction is mutual, except that a woman like Thyri requires a much deeper connection—if only she would let me in. I pulled on a dressy long-sleeve chiffon shirt, purposely leaving a few buttons undone at the very top.

The tailored taupe pants and shiny brown and black Ferragamo Angiolo lace-up shoes raised my aura. I examined my outfit while raking my hands through my slick hair in the closet mirror.

"Just a little more mousse will do." I released a piece that dropped an inch above my thick brows, placed my hands in my pockets, squinted, then posed.

Debonair.

Satisfied, I doused on more cologne. I didn't prefer the woody scent, but I've never had a woman turn me down with Tom Ford OUD on. I glanced at all the moving boxes stacked along the closet wall. Thyri has no clue I'll be moving out of here soon, and I'm not sure if this is the right time to tell her. She'll notice I've permanently moved in next door sooner than later. My funds are all tied up with legal fees.

As much as I wanted to take her out on an elegant date with hundred-dollar plates, I couldn't. My financial advisors are keeping a close watch on my spending habits. I sued Gangsley, yet I'm the one being punished for fiscal irresponsibility. I can't wait for this nightmare I'm living to end.

When I'm rich again, I can spoil Thyri with all the Michelin-star restaurants, trips overseas, and designer labels that she desires. She deserves to be carried in a relationship, and I'm willing to sweep her off her feet. A low vibration from my phone on top of the antique wardrobe whipped me back into reality.

"Eighty missed calls? Now this is getting out of hand." I positioned my face in front of the phone screen to be granted access to my homepage. Eighty missed calls filled my call log; five are from prospective attorneys I contacted, and one is from Bear. The rest of my call log list are 'unknown' callers. *Another incoming call.* This time I swiped left to answer it, gripping the phone so hard my knuckles turned red.

"Who is this?!"

Heavy breathing.

"Who are you? Tell me what you want!"

I heard a sniff on the other end, but I can't decipher whether this person simply has a cold or is crying. Either way, I don't care. I just want whoever it is to get a life and stop calling my phone. I've changed my number five times in three months because of this. "Seventy-four missed calls, and I'm keeping every record, just so you know!" I barked into the phone. "This is harassment and borderline stalking in case you don't understand the law—"

Click.

The call dropped, and my phone went dark again. Why do I constantly feel like I'm spiraling out of control? Ever since I parted ways with the league, my life has gone to shit. I have no privacy. No assets. Extortion schemes are popping up every time I turn my head. I can't even access the money I worked fifteen grueling years to make. And now, I have a stalker I can't do anything about, because I have no clue who the hell it is. I picked up the small plastic trash bin in my path and tossed it across the walk-in closet.

After taking a seat on the olive-green velvet bench, I massaged my temple to regain my composure. At least I don't look like the hell I'm going through. *How much longer will I be able to keep up this ruse for Thyri?* When I'm around her, all my worries flutter in the wind. I feel at home just being in her orbit; my only hope is that she allows me to stay.

I walked out of the master bedroom to catch the bright moonlight bouncing off of Thyri's gilded skin. She peered out the window as if she were in outer space, captivated by the glowing lights below. The glass of Chatteaux Margaux red blend she held stained her pillowy lips, making them even more beguiling to kiss. My heavy footsteps disturbed her fleeting trance. When she glanced up at me, I grinned.

"How did I do?" I held out my arms and spun around.

"You clean up well."

I took the leap and wrapped my arm around her neck, almost landing a peck on her forehead until I remembered we weren't there yet. "Let's eat."

"Let's."

We walked around the corner into the dining room, where a romantic candlelit dinner table awaited us.

"All of this for moi?!" Thyri beamed.

I pulled out her seat, gently placing my hands on her delicate shoulders. "I thought I'd make a good impression. Is it working?"

"Mmmm." Thyri cocked her head to the side, twiddling her fingers. "A little." I can tell she was tipsy by how low her eyelids hung.

"Why don't we lay off the drinks until dessert, shall we?"

"Are you calling me a lightweight?"

"If you get too drunk, I'm not letting you walk out that door alone tonight, so unless you want this to turn into a sleepover, be my guest."

Embarrassed, Thyri lowered the glass onto the solid wood dining table with a rich golden-grain finish, long enough to seat a hockey team. Thyri naturally sat at the head of the table, a throne fit for a queen. Lampshades crafted from handwoven rattan hanging from the ceiling cast a diffused glow over us. Framed contemporary art in warm tones of navy blue, rust, and burnt sienna covered the back wall, which blended in seamlessly with the coastal luxury and contemporary design theme. I removed the plates and escaped to the kitchen to retrieve the first serving of our three-course meal.

For advertisers—tiger prawns, Tasmanian oysters, Bok choy salad, and sesame almond crunch. Our main course—veal chops, crispy potatoes with cherry pepper sauce. To top it off, we had Thyri's favorite, coconut cream pie.

Thyri used her fork to pick up the very last crumb on her plate. "Oh my God, everything was so delicious. But I think my eyes were bigger than my stomach. I'm stuffed. How did you know about the coconut cream pie?"

135

"Didn't think I remembered, huh? So, what's my cooking grade?"

Thyri pressed her lips together after dabbing the corners of her small mouth with the cloth napkin. "I'll say 'E' for effort."

"I know you're kidding me. Forget the food; my plating skills are A1."

"Okay, I'll give you that, but Dakota, I wasn't born last night. There's no way you cooked this food. You don't even know your way around the kitchen."

"And you're one to talk? You may know how to bake, but you don't know how to burn." I snaked my neck and rolled my eyes.

Thyri snorted. "Don't ever make that face again."

"You know I'm tellin' the truth."

"You're not. But after all these years, Rooby's is still the best restaurant in Sunflower. I'd call them up to cater any event."

I returned a blank stare from across the table with my tongue in cheek. "What gave it away?"

"Dakota, you don't know how to boil oysters, let alone clean prongs. The chef cooked the veal to perfection, and their staple is the cherry pepper sauce. Your grandmother treated me to this same coconut cream pie every time I visited during the summer. There's no way in hell you could fool me about it."

"Alright, alright. You got me." The mention of my grandmother reminded me of the heaviness still lingering in my heart. "I still don't remember you two having pow-wows."

"The summers after you left for college, we were thick as thieves."

"At least you have those memories. Sometimes I wish I had come home to visit more often." I leaned back in the plush velvet chair.

"I know how you feel. I regret having stayed away from here as long as I did. It's not so bad after all."

"Would you feel the same way if I weren't here?" I didn't break eye contact with her on purpose. Thyri skipped her way through serious conversations all the time, so I kept my following questions direct. "How do you feel about me now compared to when we were younger?"

"What's with the sudden barrage of questions?"

"Simple questions require simple answers." I fixed her with an unwavering glare.

"Give me some time to think about it."

"Really, Thyri?" I threw the cloth napkin onto my scrap-ridden plate.

Her eyes widened at the base in my voice.

She exhaled, allowing her eyes to fall to her lap before she had enough courage to look me in the eye.

"...Okay, fine. Am I physically attracted to you? Yes. Who wouldn't be?"

"Thanks for the compliment, babe, but that wasn't the question." I refused to wipe the arrogant smirk off my face. I wanted Thyri to tell me something I didn't know. I wanted her to bend under pressure, but I needed to see where her head was at more than anything. We were clearly reading from the same damn book, albeit on different chapters, but I'm tired of feeling like I'm a thousand pages ahead. *Why can't we get on the same damn page?*

"Do you still hate me?"

"Hate you?!" Thyri reached for the solace glass of water and took a swig.

She's uncomfortable. This time, I don't care.

She swallowed hard. "That's such a strong word to use. I don't hate anyone."

"Why didn't you give me a chance back then? You let the entire world know how much you despised me."

"As if you didn't do the same?" she snapped back with a wrinkle in her nose, and I struggled with stifling my laughter.

"Not without reason." I folded my hands and leaned forward.

"You really want to get into this? Right now?!"

"Shall we? I'd like to know what exactly made me the villain in your story."

"You're so cocky…"

"Tell me, go on." My nonchalant, smug expression always made Thyri blow a gasket, so I turned it up a notch.

"You're giving yourself way too much credit, bud."

"You can't tell me without sounding crazy, can you?"

"What do you think I'm doing? Just pulling shit out of my ass?"

"I'm still waiting for an explanation." I looked around in search of someone who could give me one.

"You got all the attention and then some from every girl that looked your way. But you're upset about little ole me?" Her eyes locked onto mine.

"I genuinely liked you, Thyri." *Fuck that, I loved you.*

"I don't believe that one bit. You never even talked to me."

"We lived right next door to each other, how could I not talk to you?!" I could feel the vein in the middle of my forehead throbbing.

"Only when we were engaging in shouting matches like this!" Thyri didn't hold back, my emotional fit didn't intimidate her in the slightest. "I'm talking about at school."

"Why would I talk to you in public? You were a freshman when I was a senior. Everyone knows it's uncool to talk with Freshies."

"Fair…but you never stuck up for me."

"That's a lie, and you know it." The ripples on my forehead were creating rip currents.

"Keeping all the boys away from me and spreading nasty rumors was not protecting me."

"Rumors?!" Flabbergasted, my head ticked in every direction as I wracked my brain for a clue. "What rumors?!"

"Come on, Kota. Be honest for once in your life!" She hit her hand on the table.

Thyri's veiny eyes and stiff neck forced me to pull back and lower my tone. "I would…if you would just tell me what I did wrong."

"I don't find it a coincidence that every boy who avoided me like the plague didn't come around until you left."

"Because it's not. I told those jerk-offs things about you so they could stay away." I shrugged. "I don't know why you keep making a big deal of it."

"Do you know the hell I went through growing up? All of those girls were whispering about me, taunting me when I passed by."

"Okay, so maybe I told them..." I hesitated with my mouth propped open. "That you watched The Hobbit every night."

"That's it?" She frowned.

"...And that your breath smelled like hot dog water...and you were flat-chested, but it could've been worse than that."

Thyri's sour expression was justified. "You told everyone that?"

"Yeah. Well, only to the guys that brought your name up in the locker room. Eventually, I had to show a few that you were off limits." I cracked my knuckles.

"Kota...what did you do?"

"Punched a few faces in. Gave one guy a broken rib. I still regret that one...a little. Maybe not." I cracked my neck, completely unfazed by this awkward walk down memory lane.

"And all this time I thought I was the ugly duckling until my junior year."

"Who told you that?"

"I'll let you take a guess." She frowned.

I shook my head. "Gallienne and Company."

"Even the one friend I thought I had in middle school ditched me for them."

"What's her name again? Wise or something like that?"

"Wisdom, they called her 'Wise' for short. There was a time we kept things cordial, but by senior year she acted like I hit her dog with a six-wheeler Mack truck. I still don't know what I did."

I raised my hand. "Can I ask a question?"

"What, Kota?"

"Why do you care?" I pushed away from the table, leaning forward with my elbows on my knees with both brows bent. Discussing people from high school at my age was like watching paint dry on the walls. The only person who mattered was sitting right across from me in this room.

"Because treating me like I didn't exist never made sense to me."

"They were jealous of you, Thyri." I cradled my chin in the palm of my hand and sighed.

"Nah..." She wagged her head in disbelief.

"You were cute, mysterious, athletic. How many girls around Sunflower Falls could you find with big fluffy hair who were smart, funny, loved boxing and skateboarding, with sexy tattoos down their arms and legs? What's not to like? You blossomed like a butterfly, and every guy I knew wanted you on his arm."

"But that makes little sense, though. Wisdom and Gallienne had all the boys wrapped around their fingers, and I looked nothing like them."

"Boys chase after anything that's easy to catch. Some girls hated you because they knew I cared about you."

"You said something to them about me?" Thyri leaned back, skeptical.

"I told them to knock it off a time or two."

"So, I was collateral damage because I lived next to you?" A light bulb illuminated in her head.

"It's not that deep."

"I mean, now it makes sense. I snitched on you to a lot of them, too."

"Wait, what?" My head tilted with a puzzled expression.

"I only told them I couldn't keep track of all the girls you had over when they asked about your relationship status."

"I figured that much. Hope it helped you sleep better at night."

An awkward silence filled the void between us, and I could still feel the tension brewing. "Thyri, that was a joke, ya' know? *Ha-ha.*"

"I got that... I'm just thinking." Her brows furrowed as she drummed her marshmallow fingernails on the arm of the chair.

If I had known how much the taunting affected her confidence back then, I would have put an end to it sooner. "About?"

"If you knew all the boys were only after one thing...then why did you tell Jett that filthy lie about me?"

"I lied about you? To Jett?!"

"Uh, yeah, you did." Her voice cracked as she unravelled.

"What the hell did that dickwad say?!" My voice boomed.

"Never mind. Just forget it..." Her eyes glistened with tears.

I rose from my seat, walked over and lowered myself on bended knee next to Thyri until we were at eye level. I had never seen her this emotional.

"If you don't tell me right now, I'm going to find that asshole and make him tell me himself." I gently grabbed her chin and turned it towards me.

"...He said you told him I was an easy lay, so I blamed you for everything without knowing the truth—"

Jett Avers has been a thorn in my side throughout my entire hockey career. Learning the disgusting rumor he accused me of spreading, made my blood boil.

"I can't believe that son of a bitch! I said nothing like that about you to him or anyone else! Why are you just now telling me this?!"

"It's okay, Dakota. Calm down."

Livid, I stood up and paced back and forth, ready to rip the picture frames and sconces off the wall.

Thyri had seen me black out plenty of times on and off the ice, but that's when I was younger. I'm much stronger and relentless now. Life has a way of bringing out the worst in you, and these days, I'm working with a short fuse. I gripped the edge of the table with adrenaline soaring through my veins. All it'll take is one flick of my wrist to send this table flying against the wall.

Thyri's calming touch from behind instantly curtailed my anger. It's the lighthearted hug I didn't know I needed.

"Maybe we shouldn't talk about our childhood in Sunflower anymore. It never ends well."

I released a long-winded sigh before turning around, and like putty in her hands, I obliged. Without heels on, Thyri was several inches shorter than me. I made the first move and pulled her towards me, my hands effortlessly slipping around her waist. I went in for the kill until she pressed two fingers against my lips.

"Wait. I didn't answer your question."

"I don't care how you felt about me two decades ago. All I care about is now."

"I used to hate you..." she started.

Those words rolled off her tongue, and I still didn't believe her. She's not getting rid of me that easily. "And now?"

This time, she held my gaze without looking away. "I'm in *like* with you now."

"Bullshit." I glided my hand above her chest, slowly wrapping my fingers around her neck while she tilted her head backwards like she already knew the drill. I'm the ventriloquist, and she's my puppet. In full control, I parted her lips with my tongue, massaging her throat.

Minutes later, I allowed her to come up for air.

A soft moan escaped her lips, and it's like music to my ears. This is the kiss I've been dreaming of for years, and it was well worth the wait.

Fireworks exploding at Iron Finch Field served as the perfect backdrop for when our worlds collided. I rested my forehead against hers, eyes closed, and squeezed her hands, silently asking for her permission.

"Can I experience you?" I whispered. I pecked her on the lips once more, biting her bottom lip until it quivered. She jumped into my arms and wrapped her legs around my back, anticipating the ride.

Breathless, she panted, "In more ways than one."

A handful of her flesh between my palms caused blood to rush to the tip of my member. Standing at attention, I walked out of the dining room towards the steel spiral staircase. Before we could reach the second floor, I ripped away her thong as my barrier to entry. Thyri felt light as a feather in my arms. By the time we reached my bedroom, I could feel her pulsating mound.

12 / THYRI

I'VE NEVER SCREAMED this loudly in my life. My body trembled with pleasure several times before we made it through the door. I clawed at Dakota's back, arching my back as he drilled into my canal. Dakota had pulled his clothes off, leaving them scattered on the dark cherry-wood floor. Pinned against the wall, he slowly pushed his wood further inside of me. The euphoric feeling suppressed my moans to a low hum.

"Ah!" A tear rolled down my cheek as my legs spread further and further against the back of the bedroom door. He unhooked the dress sticking to the sweat on my back, allowing it to collapse around my hips.

"Want me to stop?" Dakota's warm, minty breath blew on my ear. I was in pain, but I refused to tap out.

"Nooo," I whimpered, unable to keep my composure. Dakota wrapped his hand around my neck again, but this time he applied pressure. Dakota choked me—a kink I've always been curious about. My eyes rolled to the back of my head as his thrusts picked up speed. He hammered into me, sucking and biting the thin skin between my neck and shoulder like I was a meal he couldn't wait to devour.

I threw my hips forward, breaking his concentration, so he

punished me for it. My legs shook as he closed the two-inch gap between us. Our bellies collided on impact. Fully stimulated, my twins hardened with both of my nipples saluting from the erection. Dakota pinched my thighs every time I attempted to break free.

"...Oh. My. Fuckin'... Ah!"

He pulled out right before I climaxed. My body felt like rubber as he carried me over to his gigantic bed. In a daze, I flipped over from exhaustion. The lips between my thighs were throbbing and dripping with cum. My flower was numb yet still yearning for more. After tossing my dress across the room, Dakota cupped my breast with his right hand while taking a mouthful of the other.

"Mmmm."

His brick-hard cock poked my inner thighs, aroused and ready for the second round. The way Dakota navigated every curve of my body made me feel like a virgin all over again.

My ex-husband... What's his face?

Dakota fucked me so good I couldn't even remember that man's name. He never made my kitty purr like this. He pulled both my legs onto his shoulders. Lowering his head to lick my clit, swirling his tongue around my pearl until I erupted. After years of longing to taste me, he finally had his chance. Just when I thought it was over, he got up and stood at the foot of the bed. The juicy head of his member winked at me.

"Come here," he demanded.

On all fours, I crawled over to him and returned the favor. I wrapped my full lips around the top of its head and went to work.

"Ugh... Umm." The more he grunted, the faster I bobbed up and down.

My head game was rusty, but I aimed to please. With his mouth open wide and his head tilted back, I took one glimpse at his curled toes and knew that he was about to blow. I massaged his shaft with my free hand, moving my tongue around the sac and back to the tip again before he exploded.

For an hour, we explored each other's bodies with minimal breaks in between. Dakota took intimacy to another level, or maybe he's just this way with me. Our wild night ended with him hunched over my back in the middle of a disheveled bed with my face buried in a pillow and my wet ass in the air. We collapsed onto each other, out of breath. I fell asleep in his arms, and he kissed me on the forehead, careful not to stir.

The next morning, I awakened to natural light blinding my face and a beautiful sunrise and clouds peppering the sky. Mummified in stone-grey sheets, I turned my head to find Dakota still lying next to me.

So this isn't all a dream?

I wiggled my body closer to his, leaning back against his bare chest as he instinctively wrapped his arm around me. His body heat combatted the chill in the room. I felt his lips press against the back of my neck, and my lips curled into a smile.

"How did you sleep?" He yawned.

"Like a newborn baby."

Dakota cradled me in his arms until I sat up.

"Where are you going?"

"I'll be back; I have to pee." He relaxed his grip and rolled onto his back.

I peeked at the modern alarm clock on the nightstand. *A quarter after ten.*

Dakota's usually a morning person. On weekdays, he's usually up at the ass crack of dawn. Wrapping on the door at The Raspberry, bright-eyed and bushy-tailed. As soon as I open the door, he's filled with a case of the zoomies from the coffee in his cup, talking nonstop. But his lack of energy this morning means I wore him out.

Proud, I pushed my fluffy hair back behind my ears, dreading the painful walk of shame when I spotted a sticky Trojan condom on the bathroom floor. I picked it up between my forefinger and thumb and pitched it. At least we attempted to be responsible for most of the night. I brushed all the negative possibilities to the back of my head while washing my hands. One look in the mirror and I nearly scared myself to death.

There's no way I'm letting Dakota see me like this again. Smudged mascara. Dry lips. Bed head. I cupped my hands over my mouth and nose. "And morning breath?! Hell no." Dakota's bigfoot hung over the bed as I crept over to his closet where I found a pair of oversized slippers, white washcloths, and an unused terry-cloth robe. I hopped into the steamy shower, and the heat brought me back to my senses.

Dakota got exactly what he wanted.

I should have held out longer.

What's the next step after this?

Dammit. I usually think things through.

Flustered, I scrubbed my skin until it turned red. I know Dakota is a lady's man, but after that labor of love last night, there's no way I'm not staking claim to what's mine.

I molded my hair down in the front with a bit of mousse left on his double-basin, floating marble sink. My overnight bag would have come in handy right about now. After squeezing some Colgate whitening toothpaste on my finger, I swiped it all over my teeth, swishing it with water so my breath could smell a little fresher.

"Tee!" Dakota called out, and I trotted back into the room and stopped at the entry.

"Hey gorgeous, I thought you dipped on me."

"Why would I do that?" I walked over, and he wrapped his arms around my back, laying his head on my chest like it was his new pillow.

I raked my fingers through his sandy blonde hair, realizing I could hug him like this forever. *Thyri, don't move too fast. Don't get ahead of yourself.* There's my conscience, always the voice of reason.

"I'm hungry. You want me to cook you breakfast in bed?" he muttered with his eyes closed.

"Kota. We've discussed this before. I don't want any overcooked eggs or burnt toast."

Dakota squeezed me tighter, lifting me off of my feet and back onto the bed until he was back on top of me. His piercing, alluring eyes made me squirm underneath his weight.

"Dakota...no." The bulge in the boxers he had pulled on alerted me to his morning wood. He tried to untie the belt around my waist while dropping his face closer to mine, but I pressed two fingers against his lips instead. "We need to talk."

"Great, the awkward morning after." He let me up as he flopped back down on the pillow, patting the spot beside him.

"It doesn't have to be awkward." I crawled over, snuggling in the crevice of his shoulder with a giddy grin. "Why do you think it's awkward?"

"It's not, Thyri. But you're starting already..."

"Starting? What am I doing?" I fidgeted with the snagged nail on my pinky finger with both of my brows bent.

"Overthinking."

Is that a line? Wait. Does he say that to all of his women? My eyes raced, and I could tell he's staring at the top of my head. He pinched the bridge of his nose, and like clockwork, I sat upright in the bed to face him.

"So, what are we doing here?"

"I don't know. Taking in the view."

I picked up the throw pillow behind me and smacked him with it. "You know what I mean."

"Do we have to talk about this right now?"

"Simple questions deserve simple answers, remember?" I mocked him.

"Oh, come on, Thyri. Don't go all postal on me."

"I asked you a reasonable question, Dakota. What are we? Is this serious or just some...casual thing?" My temperature was rising, and I could feel my face getting hot. I'm over thirty, divorced, and having a fling with the boy I once hated next door. The thought alone made me depressed.

"It's whatever you want it to be."

147

The cocky Grinch resurfaced. *Why is he acting like this?* "Are you twelve? What does that even mean?"

He chuckled. "Look, I already know I don't have a leg in this fight. If I say we're serious, you'll say the opposite. If I say we're just F-W-B, you'll have a fit. So, no, I'm letting you call the shots. What's it gonna be?"

I swiped my tongue across my teeth, bit my lip and nodded my head. "You think you know me."

"Probably more than yourself."

"That's a stretch, and just for that, I'm not talking about this..." I pursed my lips together, hating that he looked even hotter right out of bed. Unruly hair and black Hanes boxers. Ugh, it's so unfair. "Not now anyway."

He shrugged one shoulder. "That's what I thought." He pulled me back over, kissing my cheek, like I'm a prized possession he wanted to protect at all costs.

I sighed and rested my thigh on his, as if it had always belonged there. Letting my fingertips trace his washboard abs and smooth chest, I became painfully aware of what I'd been missing.

"I could wake up to you like this every day." He closed his eyes.

You would think those words would give me some reassurance, but I know life isn't a fairytale. Dakota's track record with women isn't the best, so I'll need more than just words. Instead of responding, I turned the page.

"Remember when the *Big Hockey Four* was a thing?"

Dakota squinted with one eye fully open. "Yeah, what about it?"

"You couldn't go anywhere in Sunflower Falls without seeing y'all's faces."

"Oh-kay. But that came out of nowhere..."

"Are you still friends with Logan and Xander?"

"Logan. Xander, not so much. He's still a rookie."

"I know. Xander was only what? Eleven?"

"Yeah. Something like that."

"How's Logan?"

"He hit a rough patch some odd years ago, but he's back on the right track."

"You guys talk often?"

"Nah. He's not stateside right now, but only one call away. I owed him a favor as payback for what he did for me in the past."

"Are you talking about that fight with the Evans boys?" I rolled my eyes, still remembering the big brawl that had happened at Millstone Creek. The Evans family took a scrimmage loss way too far.

"Yeah, I'm sure the nepo baby set me up." Dakota's surly expression made me aware of the malice he still held in his heart for Jett. It's nice to know I'm not the only one who feels the same. "Logan's the only one who had my back that day."

"It was a pretty nasty fight. They were jealous of everyone. My aunt used to call their entire family Sunflower's rust."

"That sounds like something she would say." He grinned.

"To know you're going to be rich and famous, and scouted that young into the NHL is insane."

Dakota didn't respond but looked off into space.

"Hey, you...what's wrong?"

"Just thinking."

"Well, I'm not used to being the one that's doing all the talking." I squeezed a chuckle out of him this time.

"...I'm not sure that I would take the same route again."

"What do you mean?" My expression pinched. "Going pro?"

"I probably would've just stuck around and coached...or done something else."

"And give up all of this?" I frowned back at him like he was crazy, placing the back of my hand on his forehead to check his temperature. "You don't have a fever."

"Everything isn't as it seems."

"Was it really that bad?" My antennae shot up.

Any other time, Dakota's an open book. Lately, whenever I ask him about life in the NHL, he speaks in tongues. This is the same person who lacks a filter and demands attention in every crowded room he walks into.

"It had its ups and downs."

"So, what did you hate about the league?"

"The politics. The owners. The scavengers."

"Why do you keep talking in code?"

"Why do you keep pressing me about it?"

I'm taken aback by his tone. "Let's see. There were millions of guys who would have done anything to trade places with you. I'm just curious. Every time I ask you about your career or retirement plans, you blow me off."

"Listen...the only thing I miss about the league is the game. That's it. My body took one too many hits, leaving me with a shattered kneecap, torn ligaments, and two bone fractures in my foot that I'm still struggling with today."

"Fair." I changed the subject. The more he remains tight-lipped about his retirement, the more I believe Gallienne's southern sweet tea may have a tinge of truth to it. Her gossip is usually dirty dishwater. There's definitely more to Dakota's story. I just need more time to peel all of his layers back. "Are you stopping by the bakery later?"

"You're already leaving me?"

"We open at noon. And if I'm a minute late, Aunt Jacquee will blow up my phone. Plus, I have to prep and bake before the line wraps around the corner."

"Okay, big time." Dakota glanced at his watch on the nightstand, and I hopped off the bed, scouring the floor for my belongings.

"Beanbug is probably losing his mind right about now too."

"That's nothing new."

I cut my eyes at Dakota, and he lifted his hands to surrender. By the time I found my dress in the hallway, I noticed Dakota was following me around like a lost puppy. Talk about a stage-five clinger. I need my space, but it's kind of cute in a way.

"I think you forgot something."

"What...?"

Dakota blocked the stairs, leaning on the railing with his slab of abs and winker on full display. I licked my lips, unable to resist as he walked towards me.

"One more for the road?" His tone was firm, like there was no room for negotiation. And that's when I realized it's more of a demand than a question. Dakota untied the belt on my robe, allowing it to fall to the floor before he bent me over the balcony in front of the master bedroom. I gripped the rail, bracing myself for the pressure.

"Just one...more," I moaned, unaware that I'm no longer in control. Little did I know, this was only the calm before the storm.

13 / DAKOTA

EXCEPT FOR A MOTHER and her babbling toddler, no one else was inside of *Patti-Cakes* but me. The little girl, who didn't look over the age of two, banged her sticky hand on the display case with a mouth-watering assortment of confetti cake, coconut cake, different bundt cakes and cupcakes inside.

She wore brown strappy sandals, a white ruffle jumper, and a baby bucket hat strapped to her chin. Her curious green eyes blinked up at me while she slobbered on a pacifier and swung her foot back and forth. The mother gaped at me after scolding her daughter for leaving prints on the glass.

The gig is up. There's no way in hell the townspeople didn't know who I was when I stuck out like a sore thumb. The black and white checkerboard floor, weathered chalkboard menu, and giant gumball machine in the corner remained exactly as I remembered them. I stepped forward, hitting the countertop bell for service. A subtle hint of vanilla flavor and nutmeg lingered in the background, instantly wrapping my senses in a state of nostalgia.

"Hey there, Kota. We weren't expectin' ya' this early."

"Morning, Patti, hope I didn't stop by too soon. I just left Grace's flower shop and figured I'd stop by to pick up the cake."

152

"Darlin', you're right on time. I put the final touches on it last night. Let me go grab it from the refrigerator. I hope you like it." Her Southern drawl dripped like honey from her tongue.

Patti was a homegrown Southern woman with silver and blonde hair, flabby arms, a double chin, a busty chest, and legs that looked like twigs on a pear. I've never seen her without an apron on or some sort of satin ribbons or barrettes in her hair. Age spots covered her hands and arms, and I'm positive she's still blind as a bat without her prescription glasses on.

Her style has changed little since I was a little boy. Floral crew neck sweaters, linen blouses, corduroy pants or loose-fitting denim jeans. When the weather gets warm, she shows off her pale, spider-veined legs in frayed shorts and graphic tees. She possessed a creative, quirky personality fitting for a baker.

"Here you are, darlin'. White chocolate frosting, vanilla raspberry cake layers, and pure raspberry filling. Getting the layers just right on this baby almost broke my back, but we made it."

I looked inside the box, more than satisfied. In the middle of the decorative piping was the message, 'Congratulations, Thyri!' It matched the 10k balloon design and pink tulip bouquet I bought for her perfectly. Aunt Jacquee wasn't here to celebrate the ten thousand dollars in sales milestone Thyri surpassed in record time, so I figured I'd do it with her instead.

"How do you like it, hon?"

"I couldn't ask for anything better."

"Alrigh' now!" She clapped and rubbed her hands together.

"What's my damage?"

"That'll be one hundred and fifty even, sweetie."

I pulled my debit card out of my wallet and slid it over the counter.

"I'll ring you up in just a second. I want to make sure the lid on this is nice and tight." She pulled a brown bag over the cake after taping the box down at each corner. "Okay, now."

She adjusted her glasses and slid the card through the reader.

153

"That one didn't go through. Maybe I slid it too fast." She examined the card with pinched eyebrows before swiping it through the reader several times. "Well, that's strange. It keeps declining. I know it's this old machine. I'm so sorry, Kota, do you have another form of payment by any chance?"

"Sure." I reached back into my wallet and placed another credit card on the counter.

She shook her head, frustrated. "I'm sorry that one didn't go through either."

I pulled out another card, then another. All five declined. Patti's lips formed a thin line out of sympathy as other customers poured in. They interrupted our exchange by requesting pictures and autographs.

I returned to the counter, talking in a half-whisper. "Are you sure there's nothing wrong with the system?"

"I'm afraid not. Their credit card payments are processing just fine."

"I'm sure it's just some issues with my bank. Do you mind if I come back a little later?"

"You know what, hon, give me a second." Patti walked through an open door of her old office. She came out, and a familiar face followed her through it.

"Mr. Choi?! What are you doing here?"

"Patti's my wife. We tied the knot almost eight years ago." A chipper smile spread across his rugged face. He still looked the same even with the thin mustache and slicked-back stringy gray hair. Mr. Choi loved a pair of crisp slacks, boat shoes, and white button-down shirts.

What an odd pair? Mr. Choi was my stern tenth grade physics teacher, who took pleasure in kicking me out of class and calling my grandmother any chance that he could get. We shook hands and hugged.

"You know I never missed a game." He wagged his finger like a proud father.

Patti allowed us to have our moment while greeting and serving other customers.

"My wife told me about your grandmother and how loyal she was to Patti-Cakes when it first opened back then. Don't worry about the cake today. It's on us." A wave of fine lines washed over the corners of Mr. Choi's hooded brown eyes.

Talk about a quick turn of events. My humiliation subsided in a matter of seconds as I rubbed the back of my neck. I was a cocky, unruly teenager and undeserving of Mr. Choi's grace.

"I can't do that. I've got some extra cash out in the car; I'll just go back and get it."

"No, no. I can't let you do that. Take the cake." He picked up the bag and pressed it gently against my chest. "You're playing at the Icebreaker Classic, I take it?"

"I plan to."

"We've already got tickets. Can't wait to see you there." He prodded me forward like a little boy again out of the door.

"But how can I repay you?"

"You brought the cup home to Sunflower. You already did."

He held two thumbs up and waved as I returned to my truck.

How can I deny that my meemaw's covering follows me wherever I go?

I shoved the keys in the ignition and sped out of the parking lot kicking up dust as I put it in reverse. A few miles down was the only bank in our old town.

West Bird Bank.

I needed to speak with a private banker as soon as possible. Two days ago, I checked my bank account. After several withdrawals for attorney fees months ago, miscellaneous purchases, home repair expenses and utilities, there was a little over thirteen thousand dollars still left in my checking. None of the credit cards I handed over to Patti worked because my assets are frozen, but it was worth a try.

Has it really come to this? I pulled into the dusty parking lot, tempted to call Bear.

But how much of a man would I be relying on another man for financial help? Asking Thyri is out of the question. My bruised ego won't even allow me to tell her that I'm broke. I couldn't get a commentator job or become a coach in the league if I wanted to. This public legal battle has branded me with a Scarlet letter. Who in their right mind would hire me now?

I sat in one of the black cushioned chairs inside the compact old banking office. They've painted over the paneling on the walls and are in the process of pulling up the hunter green carpet. A petite woman with a sleek bun and glints of gray and copper strands around her crown closed the door behind her with a clipboard in hand. She took a seat in the swivel chair before looking up at me.

"What can I help you with today? Mr. ..." She squinted at the clipboard once more while unwrapping a piece of hard candy. "Callahan."

"I think there may be some fraudulent activity on my account."

"Okay, let's see." There was a velvet rhythm to her words. Each syllable kissed with her native Spanish tongue, like a purr caught in mid-sentence.

She placed the thick framed glasses on her face, wiping remnants of her lunch out of her lap. Raised moles were pocked across her flushed cheeks where she used too much rouge. What's left of her lipstick is on a half-eaten sandwich on the other side of her mousepad. I sat in an uncomfortable silence looking at the computer monitor as she tapped on the keys.

"Do you know your account number?"

"I'm sorry, I don't—"

"Don't worry about it. I'll look it up." She fired back as if she had no time to waste.

"When was the last time you said you checked your balance?"

"Umm. Two or three days ago."

She looked over her glasses at me and then back at the screen.

"It says right here that you closed this account last night online."

156

"I didn't do that at all." I remembered exactly where I was and what I was doing with Thyri.

The rapid tapping on the keyboard made me uneasy. "Is there a way you all can track what account the withdrawal was made to?"

Without looking up, she responded with a short, "Mmm. Hmm."

Next thing I heard was the loud printer, spitting out several sheets of paper into a tray. She grabbed the documents and placed them in front of me. She's a wisp of a woman, but her energy is loud. I took note of a metal name tag pinned on her cream silky blouse. A bit of formality may earn me some points here.

"These two accounts look familiar to you?" Aurora Dominguez's thick East coast accent pinned me to the wall.

She's not from Sunflower at all and her bold brown eyes, with several coats of black eyeliner are hard to break away from.

Why do I feel like I'm back in high school sitting across from the principal attempting to explain myself?

Speechless, I run my finger across the last four digits of each account number on the paper in front of me. "Yes, they are my—"

"Do they belong to you?" she interrupted.

"Yes, ma'am, but—"

"It says right here that you withdrew the total amount of thirteen thousand two hundred and forty-eight dollars yesterday at eleven ten."

"I see that. I understand what you're saying, Aurora, but I'm telling you, I did not withdraw any money from my account at West Bird Bank."

"But you did."

Oh. My. God. I massaged the ingrown hair on my chin.

"This account right here." She shuffled the papers and tapped on the sheet like she was in a rush to go absolutely nowhere. "It belongs to you, correct?"

"...Yes."

She held up a finger. "Is this your electronic signature?"

157

I peered at the picture of scribbles from a digital pen and shook my head. "No. It's chicken scratch. Anyone could have signed this."

"Mr. Callahan, there are several security measures you would need to pass to authenticate your identity. Did you receive a text message, phone call, or email from West Bird yesterday?"

"That's what I'm trying to tell you—I didn't."

"Is there anyone close to you that may have access to any of your personal or sensitive information like a social security number?"

Aurora's rapid-fire questions are killing me. Is this an interrogation room? There's one hidden camera in the light above us and I'm sure it's there to ensure her safety, not mine.

"No. No one that I can think of. I moved recently, but I made sure all my personal information was shredded."

"I know it's unfortunate to hear, but thieves will dig through the trash and tape every piece of your information together like a puzzle if you have something that they desire."

"So, what's my next step? I haven't used the offshore account where they deposited the money for over a year. I thought it was closed, but I had accountants and personal assistants handling my funds for me."

"That's never a good idea, Mr. Callahan. If I can offer you a bit of advice moving forward..."

I wasn't in the mood for a lecture, but I nodded without saying a word.

"Review everything that's coming in and out of your accounts. Pay attention to your bank statements. Allow no one to have access to your personal account information." She spun back around and frowned at me before tapping on her keys. "Ever."

We sat in silence for the next few minutes as she answered a few calls and printed out more sheets of paper.

"We'll need to open up a case to investigate the fraudulent transaction of funds."

"What about bank insurance?"

"We're a small bank in the middle of nowhere, Mr. Callahan. We insure only up to ten thousand dollars per account to protect ourselves, and even that may take a few weeks to deposit." She waved her hand dismissively.

So much for my rebuttal. I sighed and signed the stack of papers she placed in front of me, seemingly at a dead end.

Selling meemaw's house is my last resort. And a positive outcome for my lawsuit didn't look very promising.

What the hell am I going to do now?

Bear would wire me twenty thousand dollars without hesitation, no questions asked about repayment. Chewing my lip, I sent Bear a code red text message. My attorney fees were already overdue.

14 / THYRI

"Koᴛᴀ, ʏᴏᴜ ᴅɪᴅɴ'ᴛ?!" I paused at the foot of the stairs in awe of the humongous balloons and tulips Dakota greeted me with.

"Congratulations, babe!"

"Thank you!" My eyes moistened from the gesture. It's the nicest thing anyone has done for me in a while.

"I also got you a cake to celebrate but forgot the champagne for our toast."

"Shut up. You didn't..."

"I did. It's on the table. You've been working your ass off for the past couple of weeks. I think you did a damn good job for a one-man show."

"Eeeee!" I jumped up and down, wrapping my arms around his neck, and smelling the flowers. He led me into the kitchen, where the cake with specks of gold and pink piping was on full display. He sparked the number ten and the letter 'K' with a lighter for me to blow out the candles.

"Dakota, this is so sweet."

"Wait until you taste it." He beamed, grinning from ear to ear like a star student proud of his work and waiting for praise.

I swiped my finger along the piping detail at the bottom.

"Mmmm. White chocolate. Whoever baked this is a pro!" I took another sample and swiped it on Dakota's nose.

"Alright, now you're doing too much. Blow out the candles and let me and Beanbug here know what you wish for." Dakota cradled Beanbug in his arms, no longer repulsed by his lopsided tongue. Lately, Beanbug has been loving Dakota's daily belly rubs but still snaps at him when he's not in the mood. He's such a user.

For many more moments like this to share with you. I closed my eyes and blew softly.

"Hey, you didn't tell us the wish."

"I'm not telling you, nosey. You'll just have to wait and see if it comes true."

Dakota placed Beanbug on the floor. "I've got a wish of my own."

"Oh, yeah?!"

He nodded, roaming his eyes over my loungewear. A waffle knit long sleeve T-shirt and leggings to match with berry pies and neon spatula graphics.

"What is it then?"

"To taste you."

"Nope!" I teased.

He ran his hands up and down my waist, underneath my shirt, threading his fingers between my untamed breasts. I turned around, and he placed both his hands on the counter, trapping me in so I had nowhere to run. "We can't, not here. There's a camera."

"Where?" His sexy lips twisted into a sinister grin.

I glanced over at the entrance. "I'm sure it can see us from over there."

"I don't mind being recorded."

"Well, I do. You're such a freak... But I kind of like it." I bit my lip.

"I know you do."

"I've got a better idea. Let's eat some cake and play 'Kiss and Tell.'" I passed him two small plates and grabbed the cake spatula, ready to dig in.

"Fine. You better be glad I like the sound of this game." Shot down, he removed his hoodie and threw it on a stool while I cut us two large pieces of cake.

A few knocks on the door broke my focus. "Did I forget to put the 'we're closed' sign up again?"

"It said closed before I came in. Stay here. I'll see who it is."

The knocks grew more incessant as I followed Dakota back into the foyer. I took a bite of the cake, and it instantly melted in my mouth. He opened the door, and my eyes bulged from the giant that stepped inside. He's wider and almost twice Dakota's size with a shaggy mahogany beard that could use a good trim.

I couldn't hear Dakota's muffled words, so I interrupted to make them aware that I'm standing on the other side of the door.

"Hi!" I waved with my fork in hand. "Dakota, are you going to introduce me to your friend?"

Dakota looked embarrassed about what, I'm not sure, but the giant appeared to be in a chipper mood even though his face was glistening with sweat. Dakota stumbled back as his friend approached with a beefy, hairy arm outstretched. "Bromine, but I go by Brody or Bear."

Fitting, to say the least. He's all muscle except for the belly hanging over his sweatpants. He's wearing an authentic hockey jersey and a pair of athletic shoes that resemble ships on his feet. I'm not very keen on warming up to strangers; I need more time for that. But this guy has a light about him. Like he's someone you can sit and talk with into the wee hours of the morning about everything under the sun.

"Thyri." I slid my miniature palm into his hand, and his mouth dropped.

"You're..." He whipped his head back at Dakota, who hid his frustration behind a facepalm. "This is the..."

"Thyri, this is my pal and former teammate, Bear. Bear, this is... Thyri," Dakota said dryly.

"Wow. You *are* stunning." Bear clutched a hand to his wide chest, and I could already tell why they were buddies. They have the same silly sense of humor.

"Nice to meet you, Bear. Thanks for the compliment."

"Anytime," he replied as though it was a given.

"We were just about to have some cake. Would you like some?"

"That actually looks delicious. Don't mind if I do."

"Eh—erm!" Dakota cleared his throat, placing his hand back on the doorknob hoping Bear would take the hint.

"Or... Or maybe I'll just take a few pieces to go."

Each word grinded out of Bear's mouth like the slow rev of a motor, thick with an underlying growl as if his vocal cords had been laced with steel and sandpaper.

My eyebrows jumped, intrigued to learn more about him. His scruffy face and size may intimidate, but his energy was bright and as vibrant as a hummingbird.

"You've got it."

"We'll just step outside for a quick chat."

Bear looked between the two of us.

"Okay." I shrugged and returned to the kitchen to cut and pack up a few slices of cake.

I'm not sure what those two are trying to keep under wraps, but they aren't doing a good job of it. Curious to know what Dakota couldn't speak about with Bear without me within earshot, I unlocked and cracked open the window above the tarnished metal radiator in the dining room. The brisk air bit my chest as I crouched down to listen in.

"I drove over as soon as I left the game."

"Did you forget the address?!" Dakota whispered.

"Dude, you weren't next door. And your truck's parked right there. Where else would you be?"

"Never mind. I just don't want Thyri anywhere near my problems. I have to resolve this on my own."

Problems? I turned my head to place my ear closer to the screen.

Of course, Beanbug found the perfect time to yap because I'm encroaching on his territory.

"Shhh!" I slid his chew toy into the living room for him to fetch it, knowing he wouldn't bring it back.

"There's no way I can get it back in time. I'm two months behind."

"What's the full amount?"

"I can't ask you to do that."

"I mean, how much will it take for them just to do their damn job?"

"Questions that still need answers." Dakota paced back and forth on the porch with both of his hands dug deep in his denim pockets. He's worried about something. At one point, he found a pebble in one of Aunt Jacquee's hanging plants and skipped it across the grass.

"Do you have any clue who may have done it?"

"That's what's upsetting me the most. I don't. The accountants know I'm in a legal battle. It wouldn't make any sense for them to touch my money."

"Unless they were trying to set you up."

"But what would they get out of that? To prove that I'm frivolous and careless with money? To prove that everything I'm accusing them of is a lie?"

"I guess you're right." Bear pressed a few keys on his cell phone, and the notification on Dakota's phone on the table lit up. "I've sent enough to hold you over."

My eyes shifted from the window back to the dining table above me.

What on earth is this man hiding from me?

Bear and Dakota exchanged a handshake and a lighthearted hug. No longer afraid to take my chance, I grabbed his phone and pressed on the screen. I've advised Dakota time and time again to lock his phone, but he insisted on asking why when he has nothing to hide.

"Let's see if today is your lucky day." I swiped downward to reveal the text notifications, and there's a message that reads:

$cashapp - $35,000.00 received from
Pulkovich, Bromine

My eyes narrowed. Apparently, I need to watch television more, because who the hell is Bromine Pulkovich? And why is he wiring Dakota half of my old salary with only the press of a button?

I don't know how long Dakota plans to keep me in the dark about this, but I'm not letting this go tonight.

With the phone glued to my hand, I snatched the door open and stepped out onto the porch. No shoes, just waffle knit pajamas and purple fuzzy socks on a welcome mat. I looked like a fairy gnome standing between them.

"Sorry to interrupt your powwow, boys." My cheeks lifted as I cut them a frosty glare. I held up the Cash App notification to Dakota's face. "But do either of you mind cluing me in on what the hell is going on?"

———

Dakota walked in front of the flat-screen television mounted above the fireplace in the living room while I sat on the sofa with my arms folded.

"What are all these problems you're having Dakota?"

He pointed the controller at the television, and two podcasters wearing synthetic wigs came into view. "I can show you better than I can tell you."

"Good evening, Donald. What do you have for us tonight?"

"It's been a slow news week, but I've got an update on the Dakota Callahan vs. Gangsley lawsuit, hot off the press." Donald's copper-red toupee didn't move. It was stiff as straw. The wrinkles on his forehead rippled as he paused for the host's snarky response.

"Ah, yes, Sunflower's hero." The host's wet n' wavy lace front wig was practically kissing her eyebrows. She went overboard with the banana powder that was five shades brighter than her toffee skin.

Who are these people?

"I'm not so sure we can hand over that title to him just yet. He may have brought the Glory cup home, but we've just confirmed that he's wrapped up in a nasty legal battle with his former agency. The NHL has seen nothing like this before. There are all types of bones jumping out of the hockey closet."

"That's uh...quite a way to go out on the tail end of your career. I'm surprised it's gotten this far."

"I agree, Monica, he's definitely ending things with a bang. We're talking about some serious allegations here." The co-host in the light gray suit and striped navy blue tie adjusted his earpiece. "From what I've gathered so far, this may be the case of the century, unless they can come to an agreement."

"Tell us more, Don." Monica leaned forward and winked.

Oh, brother. I rolled my eyes.

"It's got everything from defamation, fraud, extortion, and multiple counts of theft."

"Ouch! He must have a whole legal team."

"According to this, I'm not sure if he can afford it."

My heart sank into my lap. I guess the rumors are true. Whose bright idea was it to make this public?

"Come on, Donny. Dakota spent almost twenty years in the league and is a soon-to-be Hall of Famer. Most people won't get to see that many zeros on a paycheck in their lifetime."

"And unless Callahan wins this legal battle against Gangsley, he won't either. At least not anymore. The case documents are thick! I was up all night reading it. Let me tell you..." He leaned on the desk, talking with his tanned hands. "They examined everything. His agency left no stone unturned. They investigated how frivolous Callahan was with his finances during his first stretch in the league."

"That's every rookie's mistake when they enter the NHL." Monica flicked her eyes up at the blinding studio lights, unconvinced. "What else are we talking about here?"

Donald flipped through the pages on his desk on the split screen.

"Over the course of eighteen months, Callahan depleted all the funds from his first contract with the Pittsburgh Crows. Big purchases like Lamborghinis, multi-million-dollar homes, escorts, lavish weekend trips, and lofty bets in gambling rings."

Monica shook her head in disappointment. "A tale as old as time, Don."

"Seems like this guy's eyes were bigger than his plate if you ask me." Donald sounded like an animated character. I wonder how he really talks offline.

"He definitely bit off more than he could chew. So, what's the status of the lawsuit right now?"

"Right now...it's in limbo. But let's say Callahan gets lucky, and he pulls off a win against one of the top agencies with managers who rub shoulders with executives in the owner's suite. It'll go down as one of the most iconic lawsuits in NHL history."

"It'll shed some light on what goes on behind closed doors, that's for sure." Monica shuffled the papers on top of the oversized desk into a neat stack. "How much is he suing for?"

"With damages, it might be a seven-figure settlement."

"Whew! I can't wait to see how this unfolds." A wry smile spread across her juicy red lips. "Keep us posted, Don."

"You got it! Have a good night."

"Alright, well...you heard it here first on the *News Worthy Hockey League* podcast. Dakota Callahan may have his assets frozen, but we all know he performs best under pressure. Only time will tell if he can pull off yet another win? Until next time, pucks down."

The lights dimmed in the podcast studio as a cheesy outro song played. I was too stunned to speak. "Is this a joke?"

"My life? I'd like to think so, but it's not." Dakota hung his head, with both hands hidden in his pockets.

I slapped my thigh with my head twisted towards him on the couch. "No! All of this." I pointed at the television, frustrated. Not at the fact that he was financially struggling, but because this is how I found out about it. "What happened to transparency? And being an open book?"

"I didn't feel we were at the point where I needed to share it."

"So, you just planned on keeping everything under wraps? Until when?"

The arguments I used to have with Noah came crashing back in waves. I squeezed my eyes shut. I had no plans of reliving that nightmare. All the snooping around, listening in on phone calls, being kept in the dark.

"My plan was to wait and see if it all blew over."

"Then I wouldn't need to know in that case at all?" I scrunched my shoulders with both eyebrows pinched as I peered up at him.

Dakota's eyes shifted from right to left, unsure if it was a rhetorical question. "Rigghhhtt."

"Wrong!" I hopped off of the couch to stand in front of him.

"Something told me that was a trick question."

"I can't do this." I walked around him towards the kitchen.

"Do what?" Dakota's eyebrow lifted as if what I said was unacceptable. He followed me with his eyes until I turned back around.

"This! The dishonesty—"

"You guys, I don't mean to interrupt, but this cake is absolutely delectable. From the texture, fresh filling..." Bear pressed his long, pudgy finger on each crumb.

Dakota and I turned our heads. We forgot he was still in the room, stuffed in the corner, licking his plate.

"If you want more, you can help yourself. It's on the kitchen counter." My forehead throbbed from the sudden migraine.

Dakota frowned at Bear, signaling for him to give us some privacy.

Bear lifted from his seat and whistled. "Will do." The floorboards creaked under his weight.

I shook my head, and Dakota did the same.

"Maybe all of this was a mistake." I blinked back tears.

"Wait. What's a mistake?" Dakota's sleepy eyes raced.

"Me... You... *Us*." I threw my hands in the air. I freed myself from one shit show just to join the next. "I came back here to focus solely on me. To find something that made me breathe again. A small business that I could build from the ground up, one I'm passionate about for once. Something I can be proud of."

"I'm not following. How does my lawsuit affect you?"

"Okay, now. Let me take a step back, because maybe I'm confused. I thought we..." I gestured from myself to him, "...were going to make this work?"

"We are."

"Then Dakota, I need you to be upfront with me about everything. Scandals, financial problems, illnesses. I want to support you, but I can't do that in the dark."

He folded his arms across his chest. I knew what that meant. "You don't think you're overreacting?"

"Coming out of a divorce from a ten-year marriage? No, not at all! Why can't you see how this can be a major problem in a relationship? I need to see how you're moving so I can step with you. Who else knows about this?"

"Likely everyone in Sunflower by now. The NWHL podcast alone has millions of viewers, so there's your answer. And since we're being honest, I really don't care."

"Mmm." Bear returned to the living room with an oversized metal spoon and my homemade bucket of toffee pudding ice cream.

"Is this for sale? I've tasted nothing like it in my life." Melted ice cream dripped from the corner of his mouth. Several bits of icing and crumbs were stuck in his beard. "It's the perfect pairing—"

"Bear, take it all. It's yours." I spoke loudly enough for him to hear me.

"Say less." Bear saluted Dakota with two fingers and left out the front door with the bucket of ice cream under his arm. Two seconds later, he returned to retrieve the rest of my raspberry cake, then left right back out the door without shame.

I scowled at Dakota. "Is he always this hungry?"

"That's just Bear. You'll learn to love him."

"Tell me we're not making a mistake."

"After all this time, it has to be fate."

"I don't think I have it in me to be anyone else's ride or die. I tried that crap with Noah just to receive no reward, and look where it got me."

Dakota's eyes softened as he sighed, grabbing both of my hands.

"I don't know everything you went through with Noah, but I don't require any woman to keep up with me. As a man, it's my job to lead and protect you. I didn't tell you about the lawsuit, because taking care of you was a given either way. Providing for my wife and family is a requirement, not an option."

Wife? Provider? Hearing those words made my cheeks flush. But even though Dakota talks a good game, his words are merely chicken scratch on a page. I'll believe it when I see it.

"I want to believe you, I really do. But I've been burned before."

"He's not me." Dakota pulled me close enough for our foreheads to touch.

"Don't lie to me. Don't gaslight me." I outlined the rules and weakened at the knees as soon as he sucked a purple bruise onto my neck.

"I would do none of those things to you. You...just...have to trust me." He kissed my collarbone between each pause.

I kept my eyes closed. The perfect dream life I envisioned with Dakota over the past couple of weeks slowly slipped away. "I need some time...and space."

Dakota squeezed my hands. "Don't push me away...not yet. Let me make it up to you." He grabbed my neck. I listened to his hurried breath as he rushed to peck me on the lips.

"How are you going to do that?"

"I can show you better than I can tell you."

Just whispering those words in my ear made the river between my legs flow. He swept me off my feet and carried me upstairs to my bedroom. Dakota didn't expect me to clean up his mess. I was dealing with a different breed of man this go-round.

Next to him, I could finally take a backseat and let him steer the wheel. Dakota dropped me on the bed, and I opened my eyes to a black cloth napkin dangling in front of my face.

"What the hell do you plan on doing with that?"

"Close your eyes again."

"No sir. I'm not letting anyone blindfold me."

"It's either this or handcuffs?"

"I'm getting worried. This is not the type of foreplay I'm into."

"Relax, baby. I'm only kidding."

He grabbed both of my wrists, pinning them to the bed while planting kisses on my neck. I allowed his hands to caress my body in places you would only imagine. He pulled down my pajama pants until they bunched around my knees.

Caught up in the moment, I didn't reject his second attempt at blindfolding me. Now it's dark, and all I can feel are Dakota's fingers moving inside of me. I released an orgasmic sigh as my nectar slid down my inner thighs. My pouty lips parted every time he played with my clit.

"Do you want me to stop?" I felt his warm breath on the tip of my earlobe. Now he's putting in overtime like we're in the third quarter, forcing me to ride his fingers. "Shit!"

"Don't cum," he instructed.

I tried to clamp my knees together, but he wouldn't allow it. Just when I thought nothing could top the rock-hard eight-inch eggplant in his pants. Dakota knew exactly which buttons to push with his hands.

In sync, I moved my hips up and down. His middle and pointer fingers slipped in and out of me.

"Ahh-ah-ahhh!" My thighs shook as he granted me release. I squirted and Dakota licked my vulva like the assignment was quenching your thirst on the hottest day of summer.

I tried to scoot back, afraid of the impending eruption from my fountain. But Dakota locked his muscular arms around my thighs and pushed all the right buttons with his hurricane tongue.

Seconds later, my eyes rolled to the back of my head. Then I levitated off of the bed. My mistake, it's just Dakota lifting me onto his face. He buried his face deep enough to see my birth canal. I removed my top, determined to put on a stellar performance.

Dakota licked my pearl with no complaints of drowning while I rode his face like a mechanical bull. My inability to see made me feel more animalistic and free. Dakota's mouth was my first shot at winning first place in a rodeo. When he loosened his hands on my waist, I froze and asked, "Dakota? Are you still breathing?"

He stopped sucking like his life depended on it, flipped me over, and smacked me on the ass. I collapsed before he straddled me.

"I don't hear you talking now." He removed his shirt and unbuckled the top of his denim jeans.

I shouldn't have challenged him and kept my mouth shut. Now he has that hungry look in his eyes again. He's about to ravage me. Two more reverberating smacks on my cheeks and I reluctantly got into position. Doggy style. I grabbed my feather down pillow to bury my screams so the entire neighborhood wouldn't hear me.

Punishing me for fifteen minutes straight with no breaks in between should be a crime. I couldn't stop moaning as I rubbed my sore pussy to soothe it. My numb lips were dripping with cum. Dakota moved as fast as a jackhammer drilling into me.

"Fuck...meee." On the brink of tears, I passed out before he abruptly pulled out.

The sound of shattered glass and a loud bang at the front door downstairs broke us out of our euphoric daze.

15 / THYRI

THE NEXT MORNING, I awoke to Dakota taping more cardboard over the front door. He swept a pile of propane glass into the dustpan I left in the corner a few hours before.

"What's up, sleepyhead?"

Groggy, I waddled down the stairs and into Dakota's arms. We hugged, then he kissed me on the forehead.

"Your iced triple espresso's on the counter."

"Two pumps of—"

"Brown sugar syrup, caramel syrup, almond milk, and caramel drizzle. I've got it memorized."

"I appreciate you...Mmm. This is the pick-me-up I needed. I'm still recovering from last night." The last part I didn't mean to say out loud. My eyes fluttered from embarrassment. "You put on quite a performance."

Dakota flashed a cool smile, satisfied with my compliment. "Guess I was making up for lost time."

Our wild night overshadowed the red flags blinking right in front of us. Someone threw a brick through The Raspberry's front door and left without a trace.

My aunt and uncle installed cameras inside the house but

neglected the perimeter. Home invasions, car theft, and armed robberies are just unheard of on this side of town.

Destructing property in Sunflower Falls was equivalent to a bank heist. There was only a matter of time before word spread about the break-in attempt. If I can't count on anything else, I can count on Sunflowerians blowing this out of proportion.

Aunt Jacquee blew up my phone all night until I put it on vibrate. The silent burglar alarm alerted her to the incident at two o'clock this morning. No matter how many times I assured her I had everything under control, she called non-stop with more concerns. With the plastic tumbler in my hand, I glanced up at the camera.

"Maybe now Aunt Jacquee will let me add security cameras to the budget."

"Yeah. She might need a camera on the doorbell or one on the porch." Dakota cut off another strip of masking tape. "... Then we could have at least gotten a license plate number or glimpse of their face."

"You mean *her* face?"

"I'm telling you, Gallienne would never get her hands this dirty."

"She could have easily gotten some young boys around here to do it for her."

"And what reason would she have to destroy property at The Raspberry?"

"I don't know. Let's see... She hates my guts."

"True, but this would be a new low, even for her. Are you sure you didn't ruffle anyone's feathers in the past few weeks? Maybe a disgruntled customer did it."

"A brick, Dakota. A brick? Why would an unsatisfied customer return and do something like this? This screams personal."

"We can still call up the sheriff and have him look around."

"No. I don't want the sheriff's five-man department crawling around our front lawn like it's a crime scene. We were just gaining momentum these past few weeks with lines wrapped around the corner. I don't need their unnecessary caution tape scaring customers away."

"Everyone will know something is up when they find out their favorite local bakery is closed on a Saturday morning."

"You're right...all the gossip girls will send owls to deliver messages to every household that fits their narrative either way."

I took another sip of my drink, tapping my slipper on the floor a mile a minute. "How long is the wait for the new window?"

"Arly said he could try to expedite the order, but he didn't make any promises. Tee, it's just a window. It won't stop people from coming in. Your food is irresistible."

"I guess you're right." My anxiety crept up on me like a thief in the night. I was on a mission to reopen our doors as soon as possible. "After all, it could have been an accident or a harmless prank?"

Dakota's lips twisted. "Maybe." The skepticism that washed over his face said otherwise.

I scanned the kitchen and let out a sigh. Bags of unopened flour sat on the stools, and two mixing stands held unfinished icing. My plan to polish the floors and launder the tablecloths kept getting postponed because of the beautiful distraction standing in front of me. The past two weeks were mind-blowing, to say the least.

I've had some of the best sex of my life, and I haven't laughed this much in ages. Dakota's presence swept me away from the countless eighty-hour workweeks I spent getting The Raspberry off the ground alone.

But now I understand why Aunt Jacquee was seeking extra help. A baking business isn't for the weak. Custom orders were flooding in daily, demanding more of my time and creativity. Some special ingredients were back-ordered or too expensive, so I swapped them out for substitutes that often affected quality control.

Not to mention all the late nights and early mornings I've spent with Dakota. It's hard to balance it all. During the week, I wake up hungover and grumpy, struggling to prepare for the morning rush. The only thing that keeps me going is that I have something to prove

—to myself and Aunt Jacquee. I can start a project and see it through. The Raspberry provided me with a sense of purpose and a reason to get up every day without a frown on my face. For once in my life, I genuinely enjoy what I do.

Dakota leaned his face towards mine, gently lifting my chin. "Hey, are you alright?"

"Yeah. Yeah. I'm fine. Just a lot on my mind."

"Don't worry about this. If anything else strange happens around here, we'll take things a step further. I don't think it's a good idea for you to stay here alone."

I opened up my arms and wrapped them around his torso since I couldn't reach his neck without heels on. "Thanks. I appreciate that." I pressed my lips together until they pulled into a grin. I considered asking him about his lawsuit with Gangsley and if I could help, but I didn't.

Was I really in the headspace to accept an application for another grueling relationship? The ink on my divorce papers wasn't even dry yet. My PTSD with Noah had me in a chokehold. Anything Dakota did that mirrored my previous relationship made me keep one foot outside of the door. And if I'm being honest with myself, I'm not interested in claiming someone else's baggage that they can hardly manage themselves. Exchanging worry for worry with me doing the brunt of the work is not what I wanted to sign up for again.

I deserve a life of ease, and I know Dakota can provide that for me and more. But this time around, I want to take credit for doing it on my own. We need to sit down and have a heart-to-heart about what we'll be to each other. Dakota's anxious attachment style and my tendency to detach didn't exactly mesh.

Personality-wise, we're at two opposite ends of the spectrum. Learning this new information about his dire financial situation last night just reaffirmed that he was still careless with his responsibilities. Unless it involved a helmet, puck, or hockey stick, he didn't take it seriously.

I mean, what's the plan if things don't work out in his favor? Why isn't he panicking? If I were him, I'd be losing my shit right now.

Calm down, Thyri. This battle isn't yours to fight.

I massaged the back of my neck and watched as Dakota tried his best to bribe Beanbug out from under his favorite table next to the heater in the dining room with a strip of beef jerky. This man legit has no worries and no cares. Dakota wore exactly two emotions on his sleeve. Either he was happy or mad as hell.

"C'mon, dude. It's time to eat." Dakota reached his hand under the chair, and Beanbug snapped at him. "Where was all this attitude last night when we needed you?"

"Don't come for my dog." I chuckled.

"It's not teasing when it's the truth. Beanbug was in the basement on his back with four paws in the air. Not a bark out of him then."

"So what? He was playing dead. It's exactly what we taught him to do in case of an emergency."

"All that yapping, but not when it counts." As soon as Dakota stood up, Beanbug crept out of the corner to taste the gourmet dog food I had put in his bowl earlier.

"This dog hates me."

"He doesn't hate you." I rubbed Beanbug while he ate to soothe him.

"Can we replace him with a bird or a cat?"

"Buddy, we're a package deal. If you want me, you'll learn to love him." I winked.

The loud ringtone on my phone interrupted our tiff. Dakota picked it up off the counter before I could get to it.

"It's probably our new vendor calling me back."

"It's a FaceTime call." Dakota smirked and swiped right. "Good morning!"

"Who is it? Aunt Jacquee?" *A few romps in the sack and we're already screening each other's calls?*

"Oh my, well aren't you handsome?" My mouth dropped at the sound of Sebastion's voice. I missed the last three weekly check-ins but promised that I would be available for this one. Hoping to protect my well-kept secret, I stormed over.

"Dakota?! Sebastion, this is the neighbor that Thyri said she hated." Kels never missed a beat.

"Give me that!" I snatched the phone out of Dakota's grip. He loved this type of stuff for his own personal amusement. Instead of moving from behind me, he stood there looking over my shoulder at the split screen of my two best friends in different settings.

"Would you mind?!" I looked up with my eyebrows knitted together.

"Aren't you going to introduce me?" He laughed, and I nudged him in the stomach.

"Don't mind Thyri, she's always been a little rude. I'm Sebastion. We've heard a lot about you." Sebastion winked, sporting a plush baby pink floral headband around his head while sitting inside of a bustling cafe.

"Nice to meet you. I hope it wasn't too harsh." Dakota pinched my side to get me back. "She talks about you two all the time. Kels, is it?" Dakota turned on his charm, and I could already see them both melting on screen.

Dreamy-eyed, Kels cradled her chin in her hand with a cup of steaming coffee sitting in front of her. With the orange kitchen countertop and outdated cabinets serving as her backdrop, she replied cooly, "Yeah. I think that's me."

I rolled my eyes. "Alright. Now you've introduced yourself, are you happy?" I slapped my hand on my thigh. Dakota bent further down and kissed me on my cheek. "You all take it easy."

He threw up a peace sign and headed for the door. As much as I wanted to throw my phone at his back for ruining my privacy, I hit the mute button instead.

"You're such a chaos agent. I didn't want them to know."

"I will not be your little secret, Thyri."

Maybe he knows me better than I thought. "Wait. Where are you going?"

"To the old creek."

"Again? Is Bear meeting you there?"

"Nah. I go alone sometimes for my morning routine."

"Fine, but we still need to talk."

"Whenever you're ready." He smirked.

"Stop by later?" He bugged me while he was here, but whenever he leaves my side, I can't wait to see him again.

"You've got it." He saluted and then turned the knob.

I pressed unmute to eavesdrop on Thelma and Louise throwing a hissy fit.

"I can't believe this whore muted us. I need to talk to *our* new man."

"He's not my man, Sebastion. He was just being facetious."

"Tee, usually I have your back, but there wasn't anything facetious about that kiss or the way he looks at you."

"It was sensual, wasn't it?" Sebastion admired his coffin-shaped Gel-X nails.

Kels nodded. "So, Mr. Hockey Stick is the reason you've been dodging my calls? Here I am, trying to get my flight booked in time for Friendsgiving."

"Friendsgiving?" My eyes shifted. It was the furthest thing from my mind.

"Uh, yeah, hello? You told us you had changed your mind and would host our dinner this year. Don't tell me you forgot?"

"No, of course not." I lied. Dakota had me so enraptured in his world I could barely remember my last name. "Umm. Just let me get back to you on that date. I'm not sure if I want to host it here or someplace a little fancier."

"Damn all of that. Fill us in on the fine hockey star that has your head in the clouds." Sebastion's eyes narrowed before they widened to the size of silver dollars. "Hold up, bitch!" He pointed a half-eaten cake pop at his phone.

I walked into the messy kitchen and propped the phone up on a glass cookie jar. By the time I was back in view, both of them were examining me on the split screen silently.

"Do you see what I see, Kels?" Sebastion's perfect smile mimicked the Grinch's.

"You're glowing, babes," Kels added.

"That's a given. My skincare routine is top-tier." I tried to play it off, but I knew exactly what they meant.

"Girl! You're sleeping with him?! Already?!" Sebastion's voice boomed over the speaker, nearly scaring both me and the patrons behind him half to death. He jumped up from his seat, spun around, and danced like he'd caught the Holy Ghost down a church aisle. "Now that's what I'm talking about!"

I shook my head. "We are not—"

Kels drummed her fingers on her puffy cheeks. "If I were you, I wouldn't be ashamed."

"I'm not ashamed. And, Sebastion, can you calm down?" I tried to sound firm, but his theatrics made me chuckle. He held onto the side of his chair, twitching as if he were experiencing a seizure. "See, that's why I didn't want to say anything until the timing was right. We're not even serious yet."

"Who cares, Tee? A little sex therapy never hurt anyone."

"Kels, you're supposed to have my back. Now you sound like Sebastion."

"I'm not mad at an F-W-B situation. If things don't work out with the state of Dakota, put in a good word for me. My momma always said we looked alike." Sebastion scrunched his face up at a passerby minding his business.

"Sebastion, please," Kels retorted while he pushed his imaginary hair back behind his ears.

"I've missed you guys. Things have been hectic around here since the grand opening, and I'm afraid I'm a little in over my head."

"Well, we know you hate to ask for help. I plan to be there for a week. I'll stay longer if you need me. Anything to get away from

Tony's lazy ass and these gremlins, so if you need an assistant, I'm there."

"That would actually help me tremendously. Aunt Jacquee won't be back until after the holidays, so I'm trying to show her I can run this place on my own."

"And judging by the look of that kitchen behind you, you should have hired help like yesterday." Sebastion's lips pursed from disgust.

"I...had a long night."

"I bet you did. What's Dakota's last name again?"

"Callahan," Kels responded.

I could hear Sebastion's fake nails tapping away on the keyboard to conduct his infamous background check. "There's no need to run a report on him, Sebastion. I practically know everything about him."

Sebastion's head dipped into the screen. "Did you know he filed for bankruptcy in 2018?" The tapping continued. "And a paternity suit settlement... Several."

"When? A long time ago?" Maybe I don't know Dakota as well as I think. Sebastion ignored me and continued reading.

"The current lawsuit states that they froze his assets, and that he is suing his former agency for millions! Oh no, ma'am, spill the Lipton! Hold on, let me pour another drink before my lunch break is over."

Hesitantly, I sighed and filled them in on everything. It felt good to get my feelings off my chest, except I didn't receive the response I expected. Just two pairs of doe eyes blinking back at me.

"That's...it?" Kels frowned while Sebastion peered at the arches on the cafe's ceiling with his arms folded across his chest.

"Did you skip something?" Sebastion leaned forward.

"What? Am I tripping?"

"Tee, you're always trippin'. You're mad at him for not telling you about the lawsuit he filed before you all reunited, and he doesn't even know the outcome."

"You're not even married to this man. Why is what's in his bank account any of your business?" Sebastion's word vomit came as no

181

surprise. "See, ya'll ask too many of the wrong questions. The only thing you need to be concerned about is how he plans to spend a bag, not keep it."

"He's my friend, Sebastion. I care...about him." I peered down and then back up again.

"It's only been a few weeks. Loosen up, boo." Kels shimmied her shoulders.

"I'm saying. And then you've been upset with him for years over a rumor he never started in the first place. What the hell is wrong with ya'll?"

I paid Sebastion no mind. "I'm still not sure if I can trust him, and it's possible he may struggle financially if this lawsuit doesn't work out."

"But what if it does?" Kels reassured me.

"Then good for him. I've never been with a man solely for money. I just know that I'm tired of being the ride or die for someone's son."

"You and Noah weren't necessarily Bonnie and Clyde."

"Kels, you know what I mean. I held him down since college."

"He was a mama's boy when you met him. Which role did you think you were going to take?" she continued.

"That's true, but Dakota's also a big kid at heart."

"Maybe you should stop comparing him to Noah."

"Thank you, Kels! Thyri, he's led a full life with an accomplished career in the national hockey league. He's a household name, but you're talking like he was in the D-League." Sebastion patted his imaginary wig and shook his head. "Hand Dakota's sexy ass over to me. I'll know exactly what to do with him. Look at that." He brushed his fingers over his laptop screen.

"Are you looking at his picture?" I asked.

"Mmm. He looks even better in uniform. I'd take him in, rich or not. As good as he looks, I wouldn't care if he was homeless collecting tin cans on Bryar Street." Sebastion had the best one-liners to break the ice in every room.

We burst into laughter, and our round-robin check-in began.

Talking with them made me remember how much I missed and needed them around. "So, ya'll think I'm doing too much, huh?"

"What else is new? At least give the man a chance to knock on your door first before you slam it in his face. Damn girlie."

Kels had a point.

"Yeah. Don't overthink it. I may try to make it down there with Kels if I can get off work. But I'm over my break and money calls. Toodles, bitches." Sebastion waved and then disappeared from the screen, leaving only Kels and me on the phone.

"Call us if you need anything. I mean it! Ditching us these past few weeks had us worried."

"Ahhh! It's sooo good lovin' somebody when somebody loves you back! Yeahh." I broke into my rendition of Teddy Pendergrass' song, and Kels shook her head with a gleeful smile.

"Then let that man love up on you as much as he wants. You never know. He might be the one."

"Now you're pushing it." I stopped dancing and pointed at the screen.

"Alright, get some rest, chica."

"I'll try." I turned the phone off to prevent any further distractions.

The next twenty-four hours were mine to get this place back in order. Beanbug clung to my heels as I maneuvered around the house. I turned on the oven to three-hundred and fifty degrees to make a fresh batch of Dakota's favorite pumpkin spice donuts.

There's not a second that goes by that I don't think of him. And that's what scares me the most.

What if we are meant to be?

16 / DAKOTA

MILLSTONE CREEK IS STILL my place of peace. I inhaled the kiss of the wind, circling my blades around the frozen stony brook in search of the red-tailed hawk diving in and out of the tops of the eastern white pine trees. Everything felt much smaller now. A mixed forest surrounded the bank, closing it in.

It's shaped like the Little Dipper, narrowing at the tail end before its mouth opens into the nearest lake ten miles north of here. This used to be our go-to spot for hockey scrimmages off the record. There were no refs, no rules, and no repercussions for dirty moves or illegal hits. We left everything on the ice. All of our blood, sweat, and tears.

Amid reminiscing, I glanced up at the blue sky stamped with clouds, and there it was.

"Kee-eeeee-arr."

The infamous red-tailed hawk, coasting, playing hide and seek between the trees, unfazed by the powerful gusts of wind opposing it. Leaves rustling and the sound of sticks splitting in the distance compelled me to take a closer listen.

I wasn't a stranger to nature. Squirrels. Deer. Chipmunks. On one rare occasion, I witnessed a family of bears fishing as they crossed the stream when I lived in the mountains on the upper west coast. Except they weren't the culprits this time.

Crack. CRACK! Those were the footsteps of a human.

"Thyri!" I spun around, wondering why she would be on the opposite side of the frozen water brook. "Thyri, is that you?!" My voice echoed into the hush of the trees.

"Who else would it be?" Thyri emerged from behind a tall brush with a pair of ice skates dangling over her shoulder. Snowflakes crystallized on her double-breasted navy blue pea coat, contrasted by her wool multi-colored striped scarf and pom-pom hat to match. "I had to turn back around to grab my winter essentials."

"You look like a ten-year-old."

"Gee, thanks." She leaned on the three enormous logs stacked on top of each other to put on her skates. "I got lost only twice looking for this entrance again. Everything looks so different."

"Why didn't you call me?"

"Because I didn't know if I was going to drive back out here or not."

I shook my head and skated over, trying my best to conceal my elation. "So, you were just going to bail on me?"

"I'd rather be dry inside." She pouted. "Are you sure you don't want to go home?" Thyri swiped the wet snowflakes off of her curly eyelashes. "Of all days, you invited me out here on the first day of snowfall."

"This is my home. I figured we could do something that I enjoy for a change." I crouched to the ground to take over lacing up her skates.

"I'm here, aren't I?"

Her crass tone made me smile. "You're something else."

After I finished tying up her skates, I grabbed her hands.

"Dakota, wait. I haven't gone ice-skating in years."

"Remember, it's just like riding a bike."

"No, don't let me go."

"I'll carry you if I have to."

"I could get used to this side of you." She smiled with her eyes.

"You say that as if it's an act."

"That's because you were a dick to me when we were young—"

"Hey, I thought we'd let bygones be bygones?" I slowly let go of her hands while she kept them outstretched to balance herself. I skated backwards with my hands folded behind my back.

"We did." She almost stumbled over, but I caught her just in time. "I got you." Thyri squeezed the back of my jacket, laying her head on my chest.

"Let's start with a bit of a warm up, shall we?"

"Warm up? Dakota, I'm not about to do laps with you. It's freezing and—"

"Shh. Shh. You hear that?"

"Hear what?!"

"Close your eyes."

"No, not this again."

"Just...trust me. What do you hear?"

The crease between Thyri's furrowed brows let me know she was listening. "The faint whispers of the wind...Ducks squawking overhead."

I nodded and added, "The distant caw of crows, dry leaves rustling."

"A soft flutter of wings and creak of tree trunks..."

"Tell me that doesn't sound like home?"

"It does," Thyri breathed. "I needed this."

"Follow my lead." I wrapped both of my bare hands around her mittens. "One step forward at a time. Listen to my voice."

"Don't let me go."

"Glide right. Left... Right. Left. You got it."

"I don't think so."

"Skating is all about muscle memory, Tee. We're just reactivating them. You used to be a brilliant skater."

"Yeah, fifteen years ago."

When Thyri's legs stopped scissoring on the ice, I gently pushed away. "Listen to my voice."

"Dakota...I'm opening my eyes."

"Open them! You're skating."

"Huh! That wasn't so bad."

"See." I continued skating around her in circles until she got comfortable enough to branch out on her own. Half an hour later, she was showing her infamous skater spin and jumps that I'm pretty sure she was executing wrong. I applauded her efforts, pretending to be impressed while she carried on like a giddy teenage girl in a talent show.

"Alright, let's take a break from the tricks before you're whining about a sprained ankle later." I chuckled, wrapping my arm around her neck and landing a kiss on her forehead.

"This was actually fun. I need to come out here more often." Thyri struggled to catch her breath while taking a seat on the log beside me. I took her hand in mine.

"About our talk," I started.

"You don't want to wait for this?"

"This is as good a time as any."

She paused, clapping the soft snow off of her mittens. "Dakota, there are some things from your past that I need clarity on."

"I've been an open book this entire time, I swear."

Her head canted to the side. "Then why did you wait to tell me about the lawsuit?"

"I don't want you to think that I'm incapable of taking care of you because I can...and I will."

The light in her eyes made my heart sink to my stomach. *How could I disappoint a face this angelic?* Hopefully, the sincerity in my tone lets her know I mean every word.

"What about all those old paternity suits?" She cut her eyes at me.

I smirked. "Apparently, I have a five-year-old in Minnesota. A newborn in Switzerland, and a bun that's still in the oven. We don't know its gender yet. All three are with women I've never met."

"I'm serious." She searched my eyes for a hint of doubt.

"Listen, welcome to my world. I don't have any children, at least none that I'm aware of. Eighty percent of what's written about me online is false."

She gently grabbed my chin. "And the other twenty percent?" I winced as she pinched my lower jaw until it turned red. "Be honest with me...about everything from now on, I mean it."

"You've got my word."

"Don't embarrass me, Kota."

"I won't." I reached into the backpack I had left next to an oversized rock within arm's reach. My water bottle, Swiss Army knife, house keys, and a wireless speaker are all that I needed. I pulled out the Bluetooth speaker and opened up the music application on my phone.

"What's that for?"

"Relax, I'll show you in a minute." I reached out my hands, pulling Thyri to her feet once more as the snow blanketed the surrounding forest. Ed Sheeran's voice instantly made her perk up with joy.

"Not my favorite song?!"

"*Thinking Out Loud*. I told you I listen... Dance with me." I extended my arm and spun Thyri around. She guffawed when I dipped her upper body down and brought it back up to mine.

"Where'd you learn that?!"

I ignored her inquiry and continued grooving to the song, reciting the lyrics while skating away with my arms open wide. "So honey nowwww! Take me into your loving arms. Kiss me under the light of a thousand stars." Snapping my fingers, I kept my moves on the ice slow yet suave, skating off one foot before landing the other.

Thyri fanned herself before bursting into laughter again. I circled around her like a shark does its prey. "Your turn, baby." I held out my hand for her to grab, and she spun into my chest, releasing a hearty laugh before I turned her loose again.

She skated backwards, swaying her hips while she sang her favorite part. "I'm thinking about how people fall in love in mysterious ways. Maybe it's all part of a plan."

Impressed, I stroked my beard as she showcased her seductive moves. Thyri dipped low to my ankles, her delicate hands gliding up my legs as she rose. She spun around, rolling her body in front of me, and I wrapped my arms around her waist. We swayed back and forth together as she closed her eyes.

Slow dancing on skates wasn't the easiest thing to do, but with Thyri in my arms I could conquer the world.

"I want to be your protector...lover...and your best friend."

Thyri clasped her hands over her mouth as I dropped on one knee. "What are you doing?"

"Something I should have done when I was seventeen."

Puzzled, deep lines inched across her forehead. "I'm not following."

I pulled a small red velvet jewelry box from my coat pocket. "Thyri, will you be my plus one at the Icebreaker Classic...as my girlfriend?"

"You bought the earrings I've been saving up for?! You didn't have to do this. Oh my, they're even more stunning in person." She took no time twisting the two-carat princess-cut earrings in her earlobes.

"Glad you like the earrings, babe, but what about my girlfriend proposal?"

"Are you sure it's the right time to go public with a relationship?" Apprehension coated her voice.

"I don't care. No time will ever be perfect, but you're perfect for me."

Bewildered, Thyri took in the scene before looking back down at me. "All the fans, media..."

I smiled and pulled myself back up to my feet. How could I forget? She hates attention.

"I will reserve a box. There's only a select few on the VIP list that can be in there at a time."

Thyri's shoulders slumped with relief. "Of course, I'll be your girl." Her teeth sparkled as the sun broke through the clouds again.

"That's all I wanted to hear." I picked Thyri off of her feet and spun her around, kissing her pillowy lips as they melted into mine.

17 / THYRI

THE NEXT MORNING, Dakota took me to every designer store on King Street I never imagined stepping foot inside of since I was a little girl. Bottega Veneta. Loro Piana. Yves Saint Laurent. Chanel. Dior. Hermes. Cartier. I left one store with two handfuls of bags, unloaded them into the back of the UberXL, and entered another store just to do it all over again.

"Babe, this dress is to die for, but the price is out of this world." I slipped the tag back into the sleeve.

"Don't look at the price tags." Dakota didn't bother looking up from his phone. Witnessing him in business mode put him in a different light. He's given orders, accepted and declined interviews, and virtually agreed to a new sponsorship and two brand deals for tonight's hockey game.

If this is what it feels like to be led and carried the 'right way,' I could get used to this.

I don't have a care in the world when I'm with him, and that's the way it should be. Eighteen-carat solid gold Cartier bangles adorned my wrists as I strolled down a marble hallway into a large dressing room concealed by heavy black velvet curtains in the back of the Vérité Atelier boutique.

Private luxury shopping was quite an experience. I've never had a store salesman show me all of their exclusive items in a backroom while offering premium dark chocolate truffles, hors d'oeuvres, caviar, and Dom Perignon Brut. My personal shopper, Etisé, provided me with pointers on how to pair bold prints, basics, and high-quality textures cohesively.

The wise Parisian woman's intense hazel eyes hid behind a pair of cat-eye glasses. Her impeccable style was 1980s chic with a hint of sophistication. She schooled me on the importance of fabric. Apparently, you can't go wrong with mulberry silk, vicuna wool, mohair, cashmere, linen, zibeline, and some other materials I couldn't pronounce. When Dakota and I returned to The Raspberry, he got suited up for the pre-game conferences and met me at the bottom of the staircase.

"This is what you're going with?" He rubbed his hands together, the corners of his mouth tugging at a cheeky smile.

"You said to be myself." I hopped off the last step in a pair of high-top sneakers, a pair of distressed high-waisted denim jeans, and his fitted jersey tied into a knot behind my back.

"Best choice you could have made." He cupped my face with both hands, and kissed me all over my face.

"Okay, that's enough. You're messing up my makeup. Let's go, or you're going to be late." I grabbed my jacket, and he locked the door behind us. On the way to the Legacy arena, we passed hockey tailgating parties, live band performances, and endless lines around the arena that went on for miles.

Dakota pulled my hand onto his lap, squeezing it for additional comfort as we pulled into the back of the building to enter the underground parking lot. Even while occupied, Dakota still made sure that I felt safe.

The garage door of the private entry was lifted after security screened our driver's ID. We drove down the pavement to parking level one, filled with Bentleys, Bugattis, Ferraris, Lamborghinis, and a matte black Rolls Royce.

Dakota tucked my arm under his after security helped me out of the truck. I glimpsed the team locker rooms and tunnels before we took a private elevator up to a restricted floor at the very top that I never knew existed.

"So, this is how you get up to the box seats?" I smirked, and Dakota wrapped his arm around my neck, planting a soft kiss on my cheek.

"Just make sure you don't wander off during the game."

"I'll sit tight and pay attention as long as you promise not to be too rough out there."

I shuddered at the memory of referees skating out of the way with their whistles in hand. The players pummeled each other to the ground until they bruised each other in hues of black and blue, and bled from their faces. Dakota toyed with the idea before responding. "I won't make any promises."

I shook my head as we stepped out into a narrow hallway where three brolic security guards adjusted their earpieces, media teams flashed their badges for entry while their camera crew lugged equipment not too far behind.

The skybox featured new carpet, colorful murals, framed black and white photographs, and a chef's kitchen with an all-you-can-eat buffet. This was nothing like the cramped nosebleeds I experienced, where a sea of heads blocked my view, and the only thing guaranteed was stale popcorn and chewing gum stuck to the bottom of my shoe.

"You're in Box 37." Dakota struggled with keeping his attention on me after being pulled in every direction.

He introduced me to a few of his former teammates. The team wore jerseys of metallic silver, electric blue, and emerald green, each emblazoned on the chest with a ferocious raven. Its sharp, curved beak revealed a menacing snarl, ready to strike.

Every other minute, someone forced Dakota into an impromptu conversation or asked him to say a few more words to the press about his upcoming Hall of Fame induction.

It didn't take long before several media teams from different local news stations flooded the place. Dakota stood in the middle of his all-star scrimmage team holding the Glory Cup. Bear stood in the back, so he wouldn't take up the entire frame. Watching and supporting Dakota in his natural element made my heart melt.

We parted ways, him reassuring me that he'd see me later and instructing me to stay in the box until the game ended to avoid the crowds. But by halftime, I already felt suffocated by the disgruntled chatter all around me.

"These games are rigged, if you ask me."

"I've been saying that for years. It doesn't matter what city you're in. Whichever team has the hottest in-demand player at the moment, that's who you bet on."

"I'm surprised number seventeen has all of this recognition. The stats at the end of his career were at an all-time low. And the guy's got Rice Krispies for knees, how is he the goalie?"

Several times I've stopped myself from dumping the platter of hors d'oeuvres over the balding heads of the two jerks sitting in front of me. Peering out of the glass at the sea of white and red jerseys roaring and chanting the last name of the player I despised the most didn't make me feel any better.

"Avers! Avers! Avers! Avers! Woohhh! Woo-woo-wooo!!"

The Ravens were now down by two after the Phoenixes led a ten-minute scoring streak in the second quarter. Their defense was unmatched. They officially turned the Legacy Arena into a blood-bath with complicit referees who were apparently indifferent to illegal hits.

In true Sunflower Falls fashion, all the odds were in the favor of the infamous Jett Avers. I grabbed my badge and walked out of the plush theatre-style room to get some fresh air.

Just when I thought I'd escaped what seemed like yet another of Jett's victories, I discovered there were multiple screens on every wall televising the game. Against my better judgment, I left the private skybox.

My chest stopped tightening, but I found myself lost in the

tunnels. No one stopped me because of my wristbands and the VIP badge of honor around my neck.

Minutes later I reached the main entrance of the arena and instantly recognized the old black and blue concession stand. Letter magnets on a blackboard to list menu items and the vintage cotton candy machine were still in use.

A loud commotion and thundering crowd compelled me to turn around.

"Jett! Jett! Over here, can we get your autograph?"

And there he was, in all his mesmerizing, cocky glory, standing between two burly bodyguards dressed like secret agents, wearing aviator sunglasses to match. With a smug grin, he reluctantly took the pen out of the boy's hand and scribbled his initials on a sheet of paper.

My mind urged me to turn away, to flee in the other direction, but I couldn't get my legs to move. He lifted his head, and those unforgettable moss green eyes pierced right through me.

A sinister smile crept across his striking face; all sharp angles and wicked intent. The same expression that made me buckle at the knee when the fallen angel knocked on my doorstep.

————

Magnolia High School
Senior Prom
May 12th, 2009

"Hey, gorgeous," he drawled, his southern twang slow and heavy, like honey sliding off a spoon.

The mere sight of Jett stole my breath away. His green eyes sparkled under the moonlight as he looked me over with a gleam I've only ever imagined, like I'm a piece of tender meat falling off the bone and he can't wait to take a bite out of me.

My stomach fluttered, but there's a strange tightness in my chest, like I forgot the rules of how this was supposed to go. The Jett Avers is taking me to prom, and he's standing right here on my porch?! I can't speak. Can't move. I think I'm supposed to be flattered. Thyri, girl, just relax and make sure you don't say anything stupid.

Jett leaned against the doorway, crossing one foot over the other, wearing a custom red and white suede leather jersey jacket, an oversized graphic t-shirt, straight-leg jeans, and white Converse sneakers. It was a far cry from the tuxedo we discussed weeks prior, but Jett was so handsome I refused to make a fuss about it.

Who am I kidding?

He could make a potato sack look good. Jett's casual outfit surprisingly complemented my satin pink skater dress with matching fluffy tulle wrapped around the bubble hem. He styled his strawberry-blond hair in a high-top comb over fade. I preferred the clean-shaven look, but the stubble on the perimeter of his square chin gave him a bit of an edge. I inhaled the scent of my aunt's freshly baked butter cookies mixed with the earthy warmth of the humid air.

"Wha... What're you doing here? I thought we agreed to meet up at the dance. I don't know when Dakota will be back—"

"Don't worry. Someone spotted him over at the new outdoor ice-skating rink on Fox Grove."

"Okay, then...I guess we better get going." I stumbled over my words; a nervous wreck. "We're already late. I'll go grab my sweater—just wait right here." I attempted to close the door, but Jett's foot blocked it.

"Wait. Aren't you going to invite me in?" He glanced up the stairs suggestively.

"Oh, I would, but my aunt's number one rule is no boys. She'd kill me if she found out I had company over without supervision."

Jett's reptilian-like eyes scanned the living room and foyer behind me. "How's that gonna happen? You said they were out for the night."

"Well, they are—" I didn't have time to finish my sentence before Jett shoved his way inside. Miss Massey's screen door slammed behind her as she walked onto her front porch, a metal flowerpot in hand.

196

Why is she watering her plants at night? As much as I loved and respected Miss Massey, she was the last person I needed as a witness. She had my aunt's number on speed dial although they both hated each other.

"Loosen up. It's okay if we bend a few rules." Jett turned around, admiring the personal touches Aunt Jacquee added to each wall with her hand-drawn art pieces.

"We're not bending them. We're breaking them."

"This isn't what I expected it to look like in here."

"Not all of us can afford fountains and chandeliers, but we make do with what we have."

"No judgement here." Jett faced me and grabbed both of my hands, bringing me closer into his orbit. With one sensual kiss on the cheek, I became putty in his hands. My cheeks heated as he hypnotized me by whispering sweet nothings in my ear.

Did I forget to mention that he smelled divine? He led me up the stairs, and I almost forgot where I was. I'm not sure what gave my room away—the pink paint covering the walls or the illusion of a purple universe on the ceiling, complete with white stars glowing in the dark.

"Want to see something cool?"

"Sure, why not?"

Too innocent to see through Jett's intentions, I flicked on the second light switch that triggered the lava lamp and light show on the walls. Jett removed his jacket and made himself comfortable on my bed.

"Don't be shy. Come sit next to me." He patted the glittery comforter.

"—Alrightttt." My voice cracked as I swiped my tongue across my braces. "But only for a minute, we should be on our way to the dance..."

I dreamed of Jett being the first boy I let into my bedroom for a make-out session many times, but I'm not sure if first base is all he has in mind.

"Relax." He touched the side of my cheek, pulled my mouth closer to his and parted my lips with his tongue. Completely inexperienced, I thrust my tongue forward and chomped down on his lip, causing it to bleed.

"Sorry..." I recoiled.

"It's okay." He pressed on, placing his muscular hand on my thigh. Seconds later, it made its way up my dress.

First base, I thought to myself. When Jett removed my dress strap, a red light went off in my head, and I hopped up in protest.

"Okay. I think we're moving a little too fast." I walked over and turned the light switch on.

"Come on, Thyri. We were just getting started." He removed his shirt.

"Jett, we're missing the dance." I gritted my teeth, praying this isn't what he pursued me for. I blinked back tears and quickly wiped one away before I let it fall.

He stood up to grab my hand, leading me back over to my bed. I tried to pull away, but his grip tightened around my wrist.

"Why are you acting like you don't want it?"

"Want what?"

Jett cut his eyes at me and scrunched his nose up like I'd turned into a question mark. "I've heard all the rumors. You don't need to play hard to get."

"Hard to get?" My eyes narrowed.

"Yeah. Dakota said I had you wide open." He stood up, swiping his thumb across his bottom lip.

"He just chased you out of here less than a few hours ago. That doesn't make any sense."

"He's just upset you're with me tonight." Jett grabbed my wrist again. There were no longer tingles on my spine, just worms crawling underneath my dewy skin from the sudden onset of disgust.

"Not anymore." I snatched away.

Jett let his mask slip. His tantalizing eyes darkened as the wiry veins running down his neck and arms throbbed.

"You need to leave." I spun around, rushed to the doorway and flicked the light switch, unaware that Jett Avers always gets his way.

I stepped aside, attempting to move out of his line of fire. I couldn't stomach looking at him any longer. Then, my feet levitated off the floor after he grabbed me from behind. His hand silenced my screams as the door slammed shut and the lights turned off. Consumed by darkness, I kicked relentlessly until a sharp pain shot up my side. He slammed me down on the bed, bruising the inside of my thighs with his knees.

I clawed at his face, hollering into the moonlit sky on the ceiling, praying to God that someone outside would hear me.

"Shut up!" Spittle fell from Jett's lips. He transformed into a monster, and all the blood that rushed to his face caused me to panic even more. I writhed beneath his weight while he hog-tied my wrists with his hands. I could hear his rapid, shallow breathing near my ear. Exhausted from my resistance, his wanton stare dissolved into pure rage. My rejection sent him over the edge.

This can't be happening. This can't be happening. God, please help me!

Panick-stricken, my internal cries turned into verbal pleas.

"Please! You don't have to do this!" I cried out loud while tears streamed down my face, burning my cheeks as fear gripped me. He covered my mouth again, and my eyes bulged when his hand slithered up my chest to my small neck.

"Stay still!" he ordered, but I didn't listen. I waffled my legs in the opposite direction, making it a struggle for him to take full advantage of me. He unbuttoned the top of his jeans with one hand and, like a record screeching, the light turned on.

Hope showed up as a petite old lady with feathered white hair, hot pink capris, a floral blouse, a pair of reading glasses, and a black cast-iron skillet she held over Jett's head.

"One bold move and the medics will be dragging your scrawny ass out of here." Miss Massey kept one hand hidden, which led me to believe she was concealing a much more powerful weapon behind her back.

Jett released my wrists as I kicked him off of me. My heart drummed inside my chest. The pillow served as my only barrier of protection while Jett faced off with Miss Massey. Nervous, I massaged my wrist, which was sore from his grip.

"We were just tussling around."

Miss Massey frowned, glancing at me out of the corner of her eye. Speechless, I shook my head with my eyebrows furrowed.

Jett's anger switched to agitation. "Thyri, tell this old lady we were just playing a game."

"I oughta shoot you for calling me old. Or better yet, I'll make a quick call to Sheriff McClain's office to let them know that Sunflower's hero, Jett Avers, likes to force himself on young girls and refuses to understand that no means no. I'll include Coach Kind on the call, too." She winked.

"Where do you get off meddling in my business, huh?" Venom laced Jett's tone. He snatched his shirt off the floor as his mouth set in a hard line. By the time he stood upright, he was staring down the barrel of a .44 Colt Magnum handgun.

"Thyri is my business. Now you've got one second to haul your rotten tail out of here before I make you leak."

The click of Miss Massey's revolver was deafening. A wave of fear washed over Jett's face as he seized his one and only opportunity to escape. She trotted behind him, shooting a warning shot through the open front door. I jumped back at the loud bang, trembling from the turn of events.

"Thyri! Thyri, baby."

I still couldn't bring myself to speak, it was as if my mouth had been sealed shut with cement. How had I been so naive? Jett had turned what should've been the prom night of my dreams into a living nightmare.

The steps creaked underneath Miss Massey's weight as she made it to the top of the stairs.

"Wha... What? What happened? Is everything okay?" My eyes raced.

"I missed that asshole by an inch." Miss Massey examined her chipped nail, shaking her head. "I take it you've learned that the Avers don't like to take no for an answer. After all these years, their rotten apples still don't fall too far from the tree."

My brows bent. I tried to decode the message Miss Massey was trying to convey but came up short. "You know Jett's family?"

"Unfortunately, more than I care to. My mother used to work for them growing up."

"Really? Doing what?"

"Believe it or not. She was the groundskeeper. Managed all the landscapers and gardeners for their old mansion in Roswell Hills."

"I didn't know women could be groundskeepers?"

Miss Massey peered at me, perturbed. She took a seat next to me and lifted my chin. "We can be anything that we put our minds to. A little less, softer muscle than men never stopped no show."

I struggled to grin, still shaken up by Jett's aggression. "Jett didn't seem like a bad guy. I don't know what I said—"

"Oh, ain't no sense in reasoning with the devil. Those Avers boys have always been bad news. Nothing but a family full of rich, handsome, ginger-headed fools. They may be powerful in Sunflower Falls now, but I've got stories for days. A lot of them could easily put their fake, squeaky-clean image to shame."

Tears rolled down my face, but Miss Massey's warm hug instantly made me release a comforted breath. She rocked me back and forth. "Now. Now. Let it all out so we can get ready to go."

I sniffed. "Go where?"

"To the dance, where else, honey?"

I shook my head. "I'm never showing my face at that school again."

"Thyri, I know you feel wronged and violated. I get it, but burying your head in the sand won't right his wrongs. Life is going to come at *you hard, and many people will not be very kind, but win or lose, sometimes you have to fight fire with fire."*

"Fire with fire?" I lifted my head off her shoulder.

She glanced over at Jett's jacket draped across my computer chair. "Looks like that Avers boy left something. Why don't we take it back?" Miss Massey's squinted eyes and wry smile almost appeared evil.

My nose scrunched up in confusion until a light bulb went on in my head.

Miss Massey tapped me on the leg twice. "I'll be waiting outside in Old Betty. Don't take too long getting dressed."

Old Betty was a 1990 ice blue Cutlass Ciera with rusted rims and a muffler that was hanging on for dear life. I threw on a pair of tattered black skinny jeans, a red KISS T-shirt, and a pair of red and white Converse with Jett's jacket clutched in my hand.

The scent of it tainted the air—an unwelcoming, foul, cruel reminder that made bile rise in my throat. Before I turned off the light, I grabbed my uncle's lighter with just enough fluid to get the job done. Minutes later, Miss Massey and I pulled up to the front of Magnolia High School.

"Thanks for the pep talk." I reached over and hugged Miss Massey in the driver's seat.

"Oh, anytime."

Before opening the door to step out, I turned back around. "Miss Massey?"

"Yes, dear?"

"Do you mind if we keep what happened tonight between you and me? I don't want my aunt overreacting."

Hesitantly, Miss Massey agreed. "Your secret's safe with me."

I intertwined my pinky finger with hers and exited the vehicle. I walked towards the entrance with confidence, unperturbed by the loud music blasting over the speakers inside.

"And Thyri..."

I spun around; shielding myself against whatever she might say to change my mind.

"Don't do anything that I wouldn't do."

She winked to give me the green light. I walked through the hallway, ignoring every single person standing in it, and made my way to the gym.

Wisdom greeted me with a scowl while standing outside of the girl's restroom. I'm sure it's because I'm holding Jett's jacket. The only boy she'd been in love with since the ninth grade who wouldn't give her the time of day—no matter how much she marveled at his feet. Wait until she finds out he's the king of all jackasses.

I walked into the smaller gym, ignoring the nerdy couple kissing under the bleachers in their prom attire. I found the boy's locker room and pulled out as many hockey uniforms and equipment that I could find and threw them in the center of the pristine gymnasium floor. One spark of a flame to a hockey mitt is all it took to set the pile ablaze.

The flames flickered, glowing on my face until it doubled in size, triggering the alarm and sprinklers. I followed the steps for the fire drill and took the nearest emergency exit onto the football field. The screams and wails of all my classmates were like music to my ears. Sirens cried out from a distance as I marched my way up to the last row of the metal bleachers. Jett Avers. Number 8.

My thumb rolled backwards on the fluid lighter, instantaneously melting the leather trim on the sleeve. I pulled the chains counterclockwise on the flagpole, lifting his jacket into the air where everyone could see it. My cryptic message was clear.

18 / DAKOTA

"I never planned on retelling that story. At least not in this lifetime." Thyri held an ice pack on her forehead, outstretched on the examination table in the nurse's office of our locker room. "I should have told you sooner."

Choking on a ball of tears, I swallowed hard and turned my head away to control my temper. I remember that day more vividly now than I ever did before.

———

Meemaw rushed in from outside, forcing me to see what brought an Avers' boy to our neighborhood. From the window, I spotted his flaming red hair ablaze as he approached our side of the street, too preoccupied with his phone to see me coming.

"Lost?"

"What's it matter to you?"

"If you know what's good for you, you'll turn back around." I intimidated him with my size and the hockey stick in my hand.

"We've got a date," he said with a glint in his eye.

"Who is we?" I pressed him until we were chest to chest.

"Kota, leave him alone. He's here for me!" Thyri yelled from her front porch, but I could feel my meemaw's eyes burning a hole in the back of my head.

Jett's mischievous grin was the only confirmation I needed to snatch him up. Thyri's contest fell on deaf ears as we rumbled in the grass. Within seconds, I had the upper hand. Jett tapped out when I twisted his arm behind his back and made him eat dirt.

I offered him mercy until he stood up and snipped me on the chin. I ran him down, tripped him up with my hockey stick, and delivered several body shots and a final blow to his jaw.

He retreated into a shell like a tortoise on Mr. Fisher's front lawn. I ignored Thyri's cries as I went back inside. Meemaw sat at the head of our dining room table, sipping brandy while smoke from the cigarette teetering between her fingers evaporated in thin air, satisfied.

———

"Eh-umm." I cleared my throat, and an exasperated breath left my mouth before I spoke again. "Everyone knew you started the fire that night; I just didn't understand why—but now everything makes sense. I'm just upset that we wasted so much time hating each other over a lie."

Thyri shook her head, overwhelmed with emotion.

"Why didn't you tell me sooner? I would have protected you." I needed answers to suppress the guilt.

"I was seventeen. I didn't know who to believe. After graduation, I moved away with no intention of ever coming back. I locked the horrific memory behind a door in my mind, then bolted it shut with locks and chains. That's where it lived until I saw his face..."

"Well, I'm not surprised my grandmother is the one that put the battery in your back. She was always a bit of a rebel."

"She knows how to keep a secret, that's for sure."

My mouth twisted to the side, skeptical. "That or she knew how to use it as leverage to make sure you walked across the stage."

Thyri propped herself up on her elbows. "What do you mean?"

"I remember all the mayhem from that night, but I didn't find out you were behind the fire until days later. I overheard my meemaw and Aunt Jacquee talking on the front porch. There was a lot of back-and-forth chatter between them I couldn't follow.

Meemaw was threatening to get the police and lawyers involved about information she's been wanting to share for years. I remember stepping out to ask what was going on, but she refused to tell me, and now all the pieces are falling into place. That's probably why she made me do it."

"Do what?"

"Chase Jett away. She didn't even want to look at him back then. When she saw him walking down our street, she almost lost it."

"Must've been some pretty bad blood she had with the Avers growing up."

"I wouldn't know. She never indulged, just told me the entire family was scum. That was enough for me, and Jett never proved her wrong."

"Hell would have frozen over if my aunt knew."

"Maybe it's a good thing that it all blew over. I still can't believe he did that to you. I should've stuck around longer; I would have slept outside all night to protect you from him."

"It isn't your fault. If Miss Massey hadn't interrupted us when she did, I would have suffered even deeper scars than I already have. Things could've been much worse."

"Thyri, it shouldn't have happened in the first place!" I threw my helmet so hard against the wall it cracked. The more I thought about it, the angrier I got. "I promise you'll never have to see him again. When I reconstruct his face, you won't be able to recognize it." I stormed towards the door on a mission to incite revenge.

Thyri sat up with a start. "Dakota, don't go out there and do something that you'll end up regretting."

"I'm not. I'm just going to teach him a lesson."

Watching Thyri laid out on the examination table in pain with a knot on the side of her forehead, made my heart burst at the seams. Nothing she said would deter me.

"Just make sure you win the game for me. I'm tired of everyone talking shit."

My upper lip quirked. That one line alone lifted my spirit. She knew just what to say to keep me in stitches. "You want to go back upstairs to watch this epic ass-whooping?"

"I'd rather not. Can they just bring a television in here?"

"We'll work something out." I kissed Thyri on the hand, handling her with care like the delicate flower she is. I heard disturbing stories about Jett Avers' egregious acts toward women behind closed doors, but this one hit too close to home.

Back on the player's bench, I struggled to focus on the coach's clipboard and his strategic plays. I had one thing on my mind and the perfect secret weapon to do it. Bear skated up to the bench, howled, and amped everyone up for his return after the referees ejected him for unsportsmanlike conduct in the first half.

I'm sure his management had a long talk with the refs to retract the call. After all, this industry wasn't about following the rules, but making a profit. Entertainment meant more viewership, which meant they needed Bear on the ice at all times.

"Alright, girls! Which of those clowns out there can use a little more lovin'?" Bear rubbed his huge hands together.

In the zone, I removed my new helmet and shook the sweat out of my hair.

"Let's go with Avers. *Number eight...*" My jaw muscles twitched with anger. "Crush his bones."

"You got it, boss!"

One by one, we hopped out of the player's box. The lights turned down low, and the crowd erupted into cheers.

"Time to finish what I started."

19 / DAKOTA

MY UPPER LIP curled as I watched Bear smother Thyri's signature 'Berry Blast'n' pancakes with maple and honey syrup. This was his second serving of a full stack of pancakes, drizzled with blueberries and raspberry puree. Thyri kept spinning the whipped cream on top until Bear gestured for her to stop.

She placed a cherry on top, and Bear picked up the stem between his pointer finger and thumb. He had already soiled the old sheet tucked into his shirt collar.

"You need a bib." My nostrils flared as I chewed on the savory, tender bacon, annoyed I didn't have Thyri all to myself. I had gotten used to our morning rituals. A cup of coffee served with a side of morning wood in the shower. Ten-minute debates over hot takes from the news we watched together on social media. I'm still trying to figure out how they became best friends overnight. They're carrying on like I'm not even sitting here.

"I actually prefer using three shampoos instead of one. A clarifier is a staple in my routine. Gotta make sure I get all the gunk." Bear removed the hair tie to reveal his shiny wavy hair. "It grows like a weed. Every few months I have to cut it."

Thyri ran her fingers through his thick head of hair as if she were prepping it for a new style. "I wish I had those kinds of problems. Three shampoos, huh?"

I stirred in my seat and huffed like a dog protecting its bone.

"Does the trick...every time," Bear talked between mouthfuls.

"Okay, I'll have to try that. What's your favorite brand?"

"Alright, Bear, enough of the beauty salon talk." I peeked at my watch. "Don't you have a flight to catch at noon?"

"The jet's not taking off without me on it."

I frowned while my eyes studied the ceiling.

"Babe, don't be rude. After that performance last night, he's an honorable guest at The Raspberry from now on. Show him some hospitality."

"Thanks, Tee. I was just doing my job."

Tee?

Bear rolled his eyes to the back of his head and stuck his tongue out the side of his mouth to tease. I reached over and smacked him on the back of the neck.

"Ouch, dude! What was that for?" Bear winced from the sting.

"You're six foot three and three hundred pounds—you'll survive."

Thyri returned with a glass pitcher of orange juice to refill both of our glasses. "You both did a phenomenal job. My voice is hoarse from shouting so loud."

"Yeah. I bet their doctors are still counting fractures." Bear boasted, chugging down his juice in one gulp.

"Seeing Jett being carried out on a stretcher was the highlight of my night." Thyri lit up, over the moon we served her redemption on a silver platter.

"It was a blowout they never saw coming." I pushed away from the table and brushed the streusel crumbs off my pants.

Thyri stood over the stove, bouncing from side to side in gray leggings and an oversized sweatshirt, still in a celebratory mood. "Bear, are you up for another round?"

I surveyed the table, realizing Bear and I had devoured the breakfast feast. The basket of biscuits had been overturned, and we licked the plates of hash, fried green tomatoes, ham, and scrambled eggs clean.

"I could—"

I pierced Bear with the daggers in my eyes.

"Take another stack for the road."

I shook my head. "I can't believe you're still hungry."

"You see all of this belly? I've got plenty of room."

"You've got conditioning in two weeks. Shouldn't you be laying off the carbs?"

"You're one to talk. I didn't even get a whiff of those donuts. You ate the entire batch all by yourself."

Thyri smirked, amused by our tiff. "Boys, there's more than enough to go around."

I stretched my arms and cracked my neck.

My one-on-one time with Thyri would have to wait. My phone vibrated, and the number I'd been dreading to see scrolled across the screen. Robert Foute. I'm over half an hour late.

Why does it feel like I'm the one on trial?

The firm claims they have some important information to share and think it's best to discuss it in person. More bad news, but what else is new? Little do they know, I have an agenda of my own. I pushed back my chair and slipped on my jacket.

Thyri walked up behind me, wrapping her small arms around my stomach. "And just where do you think you're going, mister?"

"Headed out..." I sighed, knowing that if I didn't share more, she would become suspicious. "To meet with Foute."

Thyri's mouth propped open. "Oh. Do you want me to come with you?"

"No, I'm sure things will get a little busier around here this afternoon."

"I sure hope so."

"Bear." He and I pounded fists with a brief shake. "Safe travels, brother."

"Good luck. I'm one call away." Bear's sympathy shone through a nod and toothless grin.

Hot on my heels, Thyri followed me to the door. "You sure you don't want me to shut the bakery down for the day?"

"And have your aunt kill both of us? I'll pass." Before exiting through the door, I left Thyri with a sensual kiss to hold her over while I'm gone. She's been clinging to me a lot more lately, and I can't deny that I'm all for it. Affection from Thyri felt like a warm blanket on a brisk winter night. I'd rather she wrapped me up in her love than give me the cold shoulder. "Wear something nice tonight."

"Okay, now you two need a room." Bear eavesdropped while scrolling through his phone.

I put on my boots and then tied them before shutting the door.

"Hey, Tee. You've got any cute friends you can introduce me to? My phone's been pretty dry."

"Oh, Bear." Thyri chuckled light heartedly. "You'll learn soon enough that I'm not that popular around here."

I shook my head while listening to their conversation.

"Cuffing season is around the corner. I need someone I can come home to after my games this winter."

"Now, what do you know about cuffing season?"

"I'm a homegrown, southern boy from Baton Rouge. What? They call it something else here?"

I closed the door behind me, sifting through my thoughts. What else could go wrong that hasn't happened already?

"Call me when it's over!" Thyri yelled after me as I walked down the cobblestoned pathway.

"Sure thing, baby." I lied. I planned to keep Thyri as far away from my dumpster fire of a past as possible.

———

"Mr. Callahan, we weren't sure if you were going to grace us with your presence today." Robert opened the door of the conference room, and I followed him inside. To my surprise, we weren't alone. Foute's team wore their finest A-line dresses, gold brooches pinned to silk blouses, designer heels, tailored slacks, and striped bow ties. Astute demeanors with a subtle twinge of arrogance. They certainly knew how to play the part. Foute's attorney dream team had absolutely no work ethic and were only concerned with getting their palms greased.

"I didn't plan on attending until you agreed not to charge me by the hour."

"Yes, yes. I see. We'll discuss the past-due invoices another day."

"I'm a little pressed for time." I scanned the room, uninterested in exchanging pleasantries. "So, if we skip the introductions, that's fine by me."

"But of course, time is money and—"

"Money is time. Yeah. What do you have for me?"

"Jill, would you mind doing the honors?" Robert's paper-thin lips pressed together as he took a seat at the head of the glass conference table. The black ergonomic chair leaned backwards from his weight as he averted my gaze.

The woman with blunt bangs and a bowl-shaped haircut shoved a manila envelope across the table. The tab displayed only my legal name.

"What's this?" I looked up at Robert, who appeared to be at a loss for words.

"We received this information by mail two weeks ago. I figured it would lessen the blow if we discussed it in person."

"You've been withholding information from me for two weeks?" Skeptical, I opened up the front of the folder to find a one-page letter. I skimmed it. Quickly distracted by the photos hidden underneath. "What the hell?"

"It's what we refer to as a shakedown."

"A what?"

My eyes widened at the graphic photos, each one filled with memories I couldn't place. I saw my legs sprawled across my old luxury platform bed, with the nude upper half of a woman straddling me. Another shot captured me passed out on the modular couch, my arm draped around her slim waist.

But every photo showed her from the neck down. I spread out the pictures of us in various settings in search of a feature, a hair color, or a body mark that would allow me to identify the woman on top of me.

"A shakedown is an illegal way of extorting money from someone through threats or deception."

"Like blackmail? I'm getting blackmailed by a Jane Doe who refuses to reveal her identity? Unbelievable."

"According to this letter, it's definitely extortion. She's threatening to release these photos to the media if she doesn't receive the amount shown."

"Two million dollars?! For what?"

"If you read here, she's claiming to be with child."

He pointed to a line of words. "Eight months pregnant."

"And let me guess, she believes I'm the father? A tale as old as damn time."

"We can resort to mediation like the others. Make this all go away with a flash."

"Mediation? You're kidding, right? How many times do I have to say it? I'm done paying these women hush money. There's no more honey left in the pot. I've lost a fortune over false claims like these." Infuriated, my eyes narrowed as I looked around the table and emphasized, "Lawsuits that should have been easy wins for this firm in the past."

The lawyers readjusted in their seats, fidgeting with their clothes and notepads, discomforted by my venom-laced tone.

"I mean...our only other option at this point is to countersue for defamation and damages once, or if, these photographs ever hit the media outlets."

"Rob, there should be no ifs. You should have resolved this issue the moment you received it. Your team has a fiduciary responsibility to protect me against any allegations."

"The best we can do is send a cease and desist, but it'll cost—" Robert avoided my glare.

"Cost me?! Is this why you all invited me here today? Is this the urgent matter? To discuss this bullshit letter, which looks like a toddler wrote it. Misspelled words all over the place." I picked up the paper again and then flicked it away. "Who is her legal representation?"

Robert picked up the paper again with his porous nose scrunched to the high heavens. He slid the paper to the left for his other pair of eyes to read it.

"I don't see an attorney listed."

"There's no way any of this is true. It's physiologically impossible. I didn't reverse my vasectomy until this spring and, to be quite frank, I've been unlucky all summer."

Some lawyers coughed and scoffed at my candor.

Robert leaned back, clasping his chubby fingers together. "Alright, I've laid all the options on the table. She's got another couple of weeks before she can file a paternity suit and for you to decide how you would like to proceed." Robert's southern drawl sounded like nails on a chalkboard.

"Do you have any other pertinent information regarding the lawsuit against Gangsley? Any new discoveries? Updates?" I bit my lip to prevent any unsavory words from escaping my mouth.

"I'm afraid we don't have...uh...any recent developments. You see, there's not much more we can look into until those invoices get paid." His scraggly white eyebrows twitched on his wrinkled forehead.

A knock came at the door, and Robert gestured for a petite old woman to enter. As if his protruding belly wasn't already bursting at the seams, he couldn't miss an opportunity to stuff his face. A large order of takeout from Rooby's rolled in on a silver tray.

"Rob, it's been over two months since I paid those invoices."

"And we haven't worked on your case since you paid the last

one." Emboldened, he sputtered back. "Mr. Callahan, even though this may be a small town, we seldom have time to work on cases without full compensation."

"Your team received a handsome payment upfront for subpar work, and we've been in litigation for over a year. Now you're requesting more money on top of what I owe for this shot in the dark extortion attempt?" I pushed away from the table, gathering all the pictures, one on top of the other.

"I'm sorry to hear that you have been unsatisfied with our services."

Robert's low and choppy voice turned into a hum of mindless drivel as I picked up the last picture on the table. The Jane Doe in question had positioned herself on top of me. Both our bodies were imprinted on my old velvet couch.

Her hand was on my chest, with her bare leg hitched above my Hanes boxer shorts. Of all the women I invited into my space, there was only one with a tattoo of three black birds flying on the corner of her ankle. The piece of the missing puzzle had been glaring right in my face.

I tuned into Robert's long-winded spill about his firm's accolades.

"Robert, thank you, but no thanks. I'll have my full balance wired to your account tonight. I'll be seeking counsel elsewhere."

"Are-are you sure this is the right move? What if we give you a discount? Is a retainer on the table?"

"Robert, I'm afraid the table is quite empty at this point. I've spent eighteen months on this merry-go-round with your firm just to land absolutely nowhere." I added all the contents back into the manila folder and tucked it under my arm. "Enjoy your lunch."

A weight lifted off my shoulders as a powerful gust of wind whipped across my face. One minor detail was all it took for everything to click.

The dead flowers. Anonymous calls. Stolen funds.

Lala.

Why didn't I think of her sooner?

One Year Before

I stepped inside my home, which looked completely different from the way I left it.

Three months ago, I hired my best friend's sister, Lala, as my fake part-time assistant. I came up with a bullshit title and job description so she would believe her role was legit. She had a Trello account and full access to my personal calendar.

From time to time, I threw her a few things to schedule, like date nights and business lunches. Every single date, time, and location ended up wrong. After her tenth mistake, I gave up. Had I known babysitting a skittish twenty-six-year-old woman with bipolar disorder was part of Logan and I's agreement, I would have happily declined.

"Oh, you're back sooner than I expected."

"I just told you I was ten minutes away on the phone... You know what? Never mind."

I dropped my duffel bag by the door, noticing the remnants of the tornado that ripped through my kitchen. I pulled the drawstrings of a trash bag overflowing with empty beer cans, takeout boxes, and smelly food scraps. Waving my hand in front of my nose, I set it outside of the door.

"Did the cleaners come yesterday?"

"They did, but I turned them away."

I walked further into the open-concept condo. "Was there a reason?"

"Because I planned on cleaning up, silly. But I couldn't remember your flight arrival time. I wanted to surprise you." Lala punched her tiny freckled fist into a ball of sticky dough.

"Right." Lala's fingertips were stained red from crushing cranberries with her hands instead of using the mixer on the far right of the counter. There's so much flour on the floor that my shoes left footprints

in it. I swallowed hard, raking my fingers through my hair at the disaster she had made. Sticky residue from the cranberry filling covered the refrigerator door. I reached for a bottle of water but ended up choosing the half-empty bottle of Van Winkle Bourbon instead.

Lala burped and then giggled. "I'm making what used to be my mom's favorite dessert."

"Yeah? What's that?" I asked in search of the nearest escape route.

"Cranberry Christmas Cake." She pretended to bite her nails that were already nubs. "See, I've got one that's already done." She removed the piece of parchment paper to reveal a misshapen pie with a burnt crust that looked like it belonged on a crime scene.

"You don't think that's a little too much texture for the cranberries?"

Her eyebrows bent, and I immediately regretted saying anything. Her bow-shaped lips twitched at the corners. "Guess I could have crushed them a little while longer in the sink."

I plucked out what appeared to be a chicken bone and held it up to my face for further examination.

"Whoops!" She snorted, holding up her hand to her mouth. "How did my lunch get in there?" Lala spoke in a high pitch tone; the silky cadence of her voice reminded me of a whistling flute.

I sighed, observing Lala's frail frame. A spray of natural freckles decorated her pale olive skin with warm tones. Freckles also speckled the bridge of her button nose, which upturned at the tip. She pushed her long bangs behind her small, protruding ears. Sweat caused strands of her brunette hair to stick to her nape while she gathered the rest of her hair into a messy bun.

One of Lala's most striking features was her copper-kissed eyes. They were rich and reflective, holding unspoken sorrows and quiet questions. She appeared smaller than the last time we stood in the same room together. I counted the empty wine glasses in the living room area. A flask on the couch. Several champagne flutes sat in the sink.

Too bad Logan is spending the next two years overseas. The NHL suspended the only anchor left in their family halfway through the season. Punished with unpaid leave and a mandatory stint in rehab for steroid usage and a pain pill addiction.

I chewed on my bottom lip while leaning against the counter, watching her flip and knead the dough while chattering her teeth. It's clear Lala has developed a habit of her own. Or maybe it was there all along? She reached for the bottle of Bourbon, and I politely removed it from within her reach.

"Ah-ah-ah. The last corner's mine," I teased while walking away.

"Are you going to stick around for dinner? I made our favorite."

"Our favorite...?"

Words ran off her tongue a mile a minute. "Chicken pot pies! And my infamous—" Lala walked over to the freezer. "Frozen lemon drops!" Lala brought me a glass of pink slush, with white crystals crushed around the glass, and a lime stuck on the rim.

"Hm. I can't say it doesn't look refreshing. What's that? Sugar or salt?"

"A bit of both." She flashed a gappy smile, but I couldn't tell if she was excited or suffering from jarring pain.

I removed the glass from her hand. "Sure, I'll try it."

"Yes! Yes! Yes! Yes! Yes!" She bounced back into the kitchen and opened the oven door. "I think these are just about done."

I took several sips of her Lemon Drop concoction, impressed by the perfect proportions. A third of Tito's Vodka and the rest, off brand strawberry lemonade.

"This doesn't taste bad at all." I took one sip after another until I heard the thud of what sounded like stones being dropped into a metal bucket. I turned around and saw that both sides of the chicken pot pies had charred. "I think I'll pass on dinner."

"Noooo." She whined. "You can't!"

"I can." I learned that assertion was much better than giving in to Lala's meltdowns.

"But these are your favorite."

"Pot pies are Logan's favorite. Not mine, Lala."

218

"We all used to eat them growing up, or were those mud pies?" She looked upwards and paused, as if she were hearing voices.

My eyes narrowed as I sighed. "It's been a long flight. I'll probably just order in."

"Okay, I can help you feel more relaxed." She wrapped her icy fingers around my arm, and I lifted her hand away.

"You know what would make me feel more relaxed?"

Lala jumped up and down like an excited Chihuahua eager to please.

"Waking up to a clean kitchen after my nap." I turned around, walked into the living room, and plopped down on the couch from exhaustion, ignoring her pouty lips and down-turned eyes.

Lala has tried to make a pass at me several times since she's moved in. She's invaded my privacy and crossed all of my boundaries. One night, I returned home wasted and found her passed out in racy lingerie in my bed. I must admit.

There were a few occasions where I almost caved in, but the vision of her small face as a little girl never erased from my memory. I kicked my feet up on the ottoman and turned on the framed television. Lala made her way over to the couch with a notepad and pen in hand.

"What would you like me to order?" I gave her a simple task that she couldn't mess up. "One large pepperoni pizza from Francheska's Pizzeria. Nothing else. Here's the number."

"Got it!" Before she scurried back into the kitchen, she reached over to grab my empty glass. "I'll order the pizza, then clean up the dishes, the bathrooms, your office, and all the bedrooms tonight." She panted out of breath. I can't imagine what it looks like upstairs right now, and I don't want to.

I welcomed Lala into my world with open arms, and I regret every single second of it. She returned with another lemon drop in hand, and I accepted it without protest. I looked over my shoulder after she stood there for minutes watching me down the fuzzy, cloudy substance.

"Is there something wrong?" I asked with an eyebrow of volition lifted.

She shook her head, grinning from ear to ear, twiddling her fingers together.

If only I could tell when she's acting weird.

Lala's always weird. I frowned, closed my eyes, and drifted to sleep. When I woke up, I was shirtless, my denim jeans were unbuckled, and Lala was kissing me.

———

I drove down the road, noting the storm clouds gathering up ahead. The smell of fresh rain calmed my senses as I approached Old Eden's Farm. Farmhands summoned horses back into their stables while the cows chomped on grass for a midday snack.

Everything made sense now. Lala was the only one who had access to all of my personal information. But why steal money when she could have just asked Logan for it?

Lala wants my attention; that's obvious, but she's the least of my worries right now. I need to get my life back on track. Not only for me, but for Thyri. She deserves the world, and I intend on giving it to her. I pulled the glove compartment open to retrieve the bent business card Dawson gave me at Arly's.

20 / THYRI

"Oн, Beans! You look so cute with your new haircut bubs. Look at the wittle mohawk and your rockstar vest." I picked Beanbug up while I locked the front door. Business has been getting slower and slower to the point I can make afternoon runs and not miss a beat.

Last week I went through the camera footage to see if any patrons stopped by while I was gallivanting around town with Dakota, and not a peep. I've got eight more weeks until Aunt Jacquee returns for Christmas. Hopefully, business will pick back up closer to the holiday season.

I tucked Beanbug into his car seat before making my way over to the driver's seat. A cardstock jammed under my windshield wiper caught my attention. I turned it over, realizing it was an advertisement for another new bakery in town.

"*Chassidy's Choc-O-Latte?* How creative?" I rolled my eyes, looking around to see if the culprit was near. After hopping back into my car, I examined the glossy finish. Their menu items were vivid stock photo images, and a hand-drawn coffee cup with chocolate bubbling over the top was their custom logo. I turned the cardstock back over, browsing their offerings typed in script with dotted lines to their ridiculous price list.

Gimme Some Sugar Donuts
Sweet Talkin' Tarts
Butter Me Up Brownies
Hush Your Mouth Eclairs
Fried and Fabulous Pies
Bless Your Heart Fudge Cake
Fix Your Face Beignets
Chewy Chocolate Cookie Munsters

I can't lie. The clever titles alone were enough to reel anyone in. But a closer look at the description of each item in small print made my heart skip a beat.

"Beanbug, can you believe this shit?"

Every single ingredient mimicked Aunt Jacquee's original recipes.

Her fried apple pies, tarts, old-fashioned donuts, down to her eclairs and crumbly brown butter brownies. Many could argue that it's a coincidence, but who else in Sunflower Falls is using Valrhona chocolate, crème de marrons, pear brandy, and Tonka beans? My eyes dropped to the location. Someone got their filthy hands on Aunt Jacquee's family recipe book, and I already have an inkling of who it is.

"Strap in, Beans. I've gotta pay our favorite drama queen a visit." I turned the key in the ignition and skirted away from the curb. In a matter of minutes, I pulled up to Chassidy's Choc-O-Latte, barely able to enter the parking lot of our local strip mall at Harper's Court. My patience ran thin just sitting and waiting, so I double-parked my car, and hopped out like a madwoman on a mission.

Two lines of people wrapped around the corners from the main entrance in opposite directions. I shoved my way through the double doors, pretending I needed to make a return. Some huffed about it while others continued guffawing and smiling from the experience.

What made me even more upset was that the customers seemed

pleased with their purchases. Groups of influencers took selfies with chocolate mustaches, sharing their humongous chocolate glazed donuts with gold edible glitter on their social media platforms. All items came packaged in small hot pink gift boxes with pink and white stripes on the inside and the logo on the top.

The checkered pink and white flooring with a mini chocolate factory in its center was a unique addition. It was a great photo op and drew the attention of toddlers, but the 90s pop music and bubbles blowing everywhere made it a short-lived gimmick. By the time I reached the pink glossy countertops with a pair of teenage cashiers adorned in silly chocolate eclair hats standing behind it, I had no more colorfully profane words left in me.

"Welcome to Chassidy's Choc-O-Latte, where you can get your chocolate fix—sweet, Southern, and made with love!" The teenage girl with long, sandy brown flat curls cascading down her back sang confidently, swiping her tongue across the silver train tracks on her teeth.

"I need to speak with your manager immediately."

"Sure, one second, let me go grab her."

A mousy woman emerged from the back of the kitchen with a flour-stained apron, white polo shirt, beige pants, a hairnet, and electric blue Crocs with anime buttons on them.

Maybe I should have asked for the owner. I palmed my face.

This young lady appeared to be only a few years removed from high school. She sported a nervous grin, rocking back and forth on the balls of her feet before resting her hand on the counter.

"Good afternoon, I'm the manager. How can I assist you today?"

"I'll need to speak with you in private regarding this."

"Sure, I'll step out."

I spent several minutes explaining my dilemma. To my surprise, she didn't look upset, but empathetic towards my revelation. She shook her head, bringing her hand to her mouth as if I had rung a bell. Something tells me she knows more than she's letting on.

"I'm so sorry, ma'am. This is devastating news. I've only been with this bakery for a little over a month now. The owner is Chassidy Brown, but there's another co-owner who can help you."

"So, you don't have a clue where these recipes came from? You don't create them? This isn't a chain."

"I understand why you're upset. Honestly, I do, but I accepted this position not knowing much about the brand or the bakery. My fiancé and I just moved here. I'm fresh out of culinary arts school, and I was quite desperate when I accepted this position. They looked at my portfolio and hired me on the spot." Teary-eyed, she touched her pale cheek with her left hand; the modest heirloom ring reflecting off the streaks of sunlight peeking in from the windows above us.

"What about training? Did any consultants come in to create a customized menu?"

"We didn't have formal training. My manager instructed us to stick to a specific list of recipes that they gave us. I learned how to bake everything from scratch without skimping on the ingredients."

"I know this may be too much to ask, but would you mind letting me see those recipes?"

Her head wagged with worry. "Listen, I don't want any trouble. I really need this job since I'm in the family way. I'm already on probation for showing up late."

I looked down, finally noticing the basketball-sized stomach hidden beneath her apron.

"Alright, okay." I backed off. Here I am stressing this young lady out as if she doesn't have enough on her plate. I extended my hand. "I'm Thyri, the owner of The Raspberry over on Bananaquit Street. If you're ever back on the market and looking for a new baking home, just drop in and let me know."

"I'm Blythe." Her rose-colored cheeks jumped. "And thanks, I certainly will... Oh look, there's Galli! She's the other owner I was talking about. She should be able to help."

I turned around, and there she was. Dressed like a Cuban queen pen in a winter white monochromatic ensemble. Wide leg trousers. A turtleneck, black patent leather ankle booties and a dainty black YSL belt.

All the gold costume jewelry and the wool ankle-length trench coat made her resemble Cruella De Vil. Gallienne made her rounds around the bakery. She wasted no time adopting the old money aesthetic now that she has a fraction of the funds to match. Watching her greet familiar faces with double air kisses on each cheek made bile rise in my throat.

How are you a terrible actor and a thief?

Gallienne stopped in her tracks as soon as she spotted me across the way. I twiddled my fingers, and her face screwed up like a cat plunged into water. With her infamous poker face, she glided over, keeping up airs as usual.

"We cross paths yet again. I actually wasn't expecting to see you this soon."

"What's that supposed to mean?" I crossed my arms over my chest, kicking out my right foot like a kickstand.

"Not much foot traffic your way lately, I presume?"

"Are you spying on me?" I inched forward, and she clutched her imaginary pearls.

"Oh, Casper, I'd hate for you to make another scene."

"I'm certain you know my government name."

"If you're looking for employment, I'm afraid we're not hiring at the moment. And when we do, it's only by referral." She looked me up and down. "Part-time hours. We max out at twenty per week."

I gritted my teeth. "I'm not looking for a goddamn job, Galli!"

"Then why on earth are you here?"

"Can we talk somewhere in private...please?" My scathing tone let her know I meant business.

After a long pause, she spoke again. "I suppose we can chat in my office. But I must warn you, we have cameras in every room." Gallienne's bright eyes turned into slits.

"Wouldn't want to get caught stealing premium ingredients for the customers we don't have." I hurled a snarky remark, and she caught it with a sullen smile.

"Let's take a step back here, shall we?" She increased her volume with a fake smile for customers within earshot.

Gallienne led me to a bright room, past the kitchen, down a hallway on the right. Navy blue tufted wool carpet covered the floor. Built-in bookshelves with everything but books lined the walls. Sconces and floral wallpaper filled the gaps in between.

An unwrapped walking pad was in front of a fireplace next to the oversized antique wooden desk that still looked brand new. Gallienne walked around it, removing the sunglasses from her head. She took a seat and tapped the spacebar on the hot pink keyboard, illuminating the desktop.

"So, what brings you here today?" Gallienne folded her hands together with a puzzled expression.

Before I spoke, I noted the family photos and fake certifications framed behind her. "Who gave you a culinary arts degree? Heh."

Gallienne parted her lips to lie, turning her eyes down to her lap before peering back up at me again. "I don't believe we're on good enough terms to discuss my professional or personal background."

"I couldn't agree more. Let's discuss why I dropped in." Sarcasm seeped through my fake grin.

"Let's." Her upper lip quirked as her shoulders slumped onto her chest. She clicked the ballpoint pen while drumming her nails on the mouse pad.

She already knows why I'm here. I can tell by her grimace.

"Do you mind telling me how the hell you came up with this menu?" I flung the cardstock onto the desk.

Her lemur-like eyes scanned the empty room and then landed back on me.

"We updated our menu since we printed those. What's it to you anyway?"

"Galli, you and I both know these are my aunt Jacquee's recipes. Every single one of them on that board out there."

"I'm a co-owner. I don't create menus."

"Then who the hell does?"

"I'd have to consult with my partner."

"Partner?! Galli, I swear, if you don't hand over my family's recipe book right now, I'll have this entire bakery shut down."

Gallienne happily accepted my bluff. "On what grounds? You have no proof, and why would we need to steal from you of all people?" She dismissed me like a piece of stubborn lint she couldn't roll off her clothing.

"After all these years, you still feel that you're a step above me, why?"

"I'm sure you already know the answer to that, but today I have time. Everywhere you go, you're rejected."

"By whom?" I chortled. "I'm loved day in and day out by those who matter. I wake up with a smile on my face every freakin' morning." A sly grin crept across my lips, hinting at the obvious. "I'm sure you've already heard about me and... Kota."

"Glad to hear you're enjoying my leftovers." Gallienne rose out of her chair and leaned on the desk. "Newly divorced, no children of your own, and you couldn't wait to hop in Dakota's lap out of all the single men in this town, you chose him. How convenient?"

"You and Kota haven't dated since the *days of Yor*. Get over it."

"I wouldn't expect you to understand. You've always wanted my spot. But guess what? I had the best of him. He's old, washed, and on his last leg financially."

I cut my eyes up at the tray ceiling. "That's the difference between you and me, Galli. I don't chase after a man's riches, and I sure as hell don't desire fame. Maybe you should stop projecting so much."

"Honey, you ain't got nothin' I want!" Gallienne's face cracked. Her syrup-thick drawl made a comeback, each syllable dragging like the toke of a cigarette on a hot and dreary summer day.

"Unfortunately, I can't say the same. Hand over my aunt's recipe book and I'll leave." I stuck out my hand, and she opened a drawer.

"Are you talking about this?" She turned a white three-ring binder around, with tattered pages of articles, and old recipe notes hanging out of it.

"You've had it all along?" My eyes narrowed. "You're the one who tried to break into The Raspberry that night, aren't you?"

"I'm a mother of two, for heaven's sake. Breaking and entering your bakery for what? My husband fulfills all that my pretty heart desires, and to be quite honest, stealing sounds more up your alley than mine." Galli's bane of existence was being somebody's *wife*, somebody's *mom*, or somebody's *boss*. She didn't have an identity outside of that. "I purchased this gem a while back at a garage sale."

"A garage sale that was my aunt's, who lived next door to Dakota. You know what, none of that even matters—just hand it over or—"

"Or what?"

"Prepare to be sued out the ass, Galli!" Veins were practically popping out of the side of my neck.

"We searched for all these recipes, but no one has published them online," she replied coolly.

"Because old newspapers and magazines published them, genius. My aunt still has copies of those same articles framed in her house from before we were even born!"

Galli bit her lip and leaned back, still holding the binder against her chest. "I'm sure there's a statute of limitations or whatever it's called."

"Galli, grow up. Chaos follows you wherever you go. Do you ever wonder why?"

She gasped. "You're one to talk. I'm set up nicely here in Sunflower Falls, and my reputation speaks for itself. No one knows who the hell you are except for the girl who—"

Don't say it. My upper lip curled as my hands rested on my hips. "The girl who what? Which high school rumor? I don't know if you know this, Galli, but we graduated from Magnolia High almost two decades ago, yet you're still stuck there."

"Say what you want, at least I'm not known as a firestarter."

As much as I'd like to take the high road, I can't. This woman deserves no mercy from me, and the fact that she's clutching my aunt's recipe book like her life depends on it makes me even less empathetic. "I would tread lightly if I were you."

"I knew that would strike a chord." She gazed at me, satisfied she was crawling under my skin. "You think getting your hands back on this recipe book will save The Raspberry? What type of name is that for a bakery, anyway?" Her shoulders rose slightly as she contained her laughter.

"Maybe you should ask your husband."

"Pardon me?"

I nodded at the picture above her head. As small as this town is, it's hard to forget a face.

He came in on his lunch break every other weekend with a different woman on his arm and his car salesman uniform on full display. The rotund potbelly, gray slacks, and a pair of black leather loafers with scuffs on the back. He didn't even care enough to remove his nametag or wedding band before he came in.

"Mr. Chris O'Malley sure fancies our specialty deli sandwiches we make every Tuesday. One thing I noticed is that he never dines alone. He has a different woman clinging to his arm every time."

"You're lyin'. Girl, you don't know a damn thang about my husband!"

That did it. That broke the camel's back. I eyed the recipe book she had dropped on the desk. Seconds later, we were back where we left off at The Raspberry, inches away from each other's faces. I held my hands up as we stood off.

"Galli, I'm only going to tell you once. Back the hell up!" The smell of old black coffee and liquor on her tongue forced me to step back.

"Say you made it up!"

"I'm not saying anything. You know it's true. He's unfaithful to you. That's why you're miserable and always starting shit. Hell, that's why you're still obsessed with your high school ex!"

Galli held up a ten-carat solitaire diamond ring she recently upgraded. "You're just upset because I have the perfect family, the perfect husband, the perfect life. I'm everything you're not."

"Have you ever considered taking a seat across from a shrink? Apparently, it's long overdue."

"Imagine that. An arsonist with parents who didn't feel she was worthy enough to keep accusing me of being crazy." Galli's strained eyeballs bulged out of her head as she released a wicked laugh. "Dakota's life trajectory will continue to spiral downhill if he stays connected to you... Everything you touch turns to ash."

That one hurt.

"You know, Galli. It's a shame we never became friends. You and I have a lot more in common than you think."

"What could you and I possibly have in common?"

"My parents may not have been prepared to raise me, but neither were yours."

"What are you getting at now?"

"Your last name used to be , right?" I kept my foot on her neck without letting up. "Before the Hawthornes adopted you when you were a toddler..." I paced the office, roaming my eyes over the wall art and out-of-place figurines used for office decor.

"Who told you that?!" Her erratic breathing let me know that I finally had the upper hand.

"Funny thing is, you never knew they weren't your parents until you asked to see your birth certificate for a fifth-grade history project."

"Dakota swore he would never tell."

"We can keep it a secret between the three of us if you hand over what belongs to my family."

"And who do you suppose will believe you?"

"I have my sources. The ushers and choir members at the church would be a start."

"You wouldn't dare."

"Why are you so ashamed of being an Evans? I can smell their rotten backwoods stench on you from over here. You all have quite a reputation in this town, that's for sure."

"Don't talk about—" Gallienne's knuckles turned red from the two fists she balled at her side.

I cut her off. "Let's see. Three brothers incarcerated, your father's in rehab, and your mom auctioned you off to the highest bidder."

"Get the hell out of my office, Thyri!" She shrieked as knocking came at the door.

"Is everything okay in there?" A woman's voice barked through the door.

"No!" Gallienne screamed, trembling all over.

"Fine, I'll go. Just give me the book and I'll never tell a soul."

"Tell who you please. The only way you're getting this back is over my dead body."

"You asked for it." I started taking off my earrings, and Gallienne held up her cell phone like it was her shield.

"You take one step over here and I'm callin' the sheriff's office."

"Call em'."

"I ain't kidding!" Within a matter of seconds, streaks of mascara stained Gallienne's cheeks as she ripped her turtleneck from the shoulder down.

"What are you doing?"

"You attacked me."

"I haven't touched you." Perplexed, I stepped back.

"They don't know that." Gallienne gave a horrible rendition of a damsel in distress. "Officer, a woman just fled on foot with all my precious belongings. She's five foot seven, brown-skinned, with her hair pulled into a topknot bun. She's wearing a cheap black tracksuit and sepia-colored sneakers. Help me, please! I don't know what to do!"

"You're sick. And to think, just a minute ago I actually felt sorry for you."

"I don't need your sympathy." Gallienne tossed the phone onto the desk to end the scene.

"You know what? Keep it. You'll be hearing from our lawyers soon."

"I look forward to it. Just worry about closing The Raspberry's doors for good."

"That'll never happen. Because unlike you, we're actually passionate about what we do. It's not a get rich quick scheme for us, but a legacy that we'll continue to build with or without our recipe book. There are centuries worth of handwritten recipes with our family history woven into every page."

"Nice try at pulling at my heartstrings there, but does it look like I care?" Her blank stare remained devoid of any emotion.

"Doesn't matter." I shrugged. "You're already reaping what you've sown."

Ignoring my insidious message, she placed the recipe book back in the desk drawer and locked it.

Wiping her hands clean, she exhaled. "All I need to determine is which one of those recipes we'll use in the Whisk It To Win It competition next weekend."

She walked back around her desk over to an empty floating shelf. "I think our first-place trophy will look amazing right here. What do you think?"

"Keep dreaming." I turned around to give her my ass to kiss.

"One more thing..." she yelled out with a finger raised.

Hesitantly, I glanced over my shoulder.

"The next time, you and Dakota are pillow talking about my past."

"No one is talking about—" I tried interrupting, but she talked over me instead.

"Tell him to paint the full picture. When I said I had the best part of Dakota...I wasn't talking about him."

"Whatever, Gallienne."

"There's a reason my brothers cornered him at Millstone Creek that day. I was sixteen...and pregnant."

I slammed the door as her words clung to the air.

On my way back to the car, I could hear Beanbug yapping and frightening passersby in the parking lot.

The moment I opened the door, he slid into the passenger seat beside me. For an hour I drove around aimlessly in silence, wondering why the hell Dakota shared every unimportant detail about his life with me, but conveniently skipped the part about expecting a child with Gallienne in their teens?

21 / DAKOTA

THE PAST TWENTY-FOUR hours Thyri has given me the cold shoulder. She keeps telling me she's fine and to let it go, but I know I'll feel the brunt of her anger sooner than later. Right now it's boiling at the surface, and I'm trying my best to keep the lid on.

We drove for three hours straight to meet with Dawson at his family ranch up in Ironwood Acres. She spoke barely two words to me on the way over. Now she's all smiles with Rhett, the equestrian trainer. I stepped down off the porch to get a closer look.

"Watch your hands, man." *Why didn't she ask me to help her into the saddle?*

Thyri followed his instructions for proper posture.

"Sit tall, relax. Shoulders back." Thyri made adjustments and used her calves to cue the horse to walk. The small trot began, and I walked closer to ensure her safety.

"Close your fingers on the reins, and say, whoa to halt, Thyri!" She glared back at me over her shoulder, and I shrugged. She's still pissed.

"Dakota!" Dawson's jolly voice called out from the modern farmhouse door. He waved me over. "I'm ready for ya'!" I jogged back over to the porch, but not without one more peek at Thyri now practicing the walk and trot.

"She seems like a natural." Dawson chimed in as I made my way up the stairs. "Girlfriend?"

"Yeah," I replied in a somber tone.

"Don't worry, she's in excellent hands. Rhett's been on staff here since he was a teen."

"She's enjoying herself. That's all that matters."

Dawson smirked. Even he could tell I was head over heels.

"Come on in. Don't bother taking off your shoes. Our cleaning lady, Lourdes, will be here tomorrow."

"Thanks for having us over at such short notice." Dawson welcomed me into his humble abode. A staircase with a tribal carpet runner led to the second floor. There was a stretch of hallway with cherry-wood floors that opened up to a kitchen. On the left, there's a bright dining room with tufted carpet that matches the dated decor and china cabinet along the wall. To the right, I see a dark office with blue walls hidden behind a pair of French doors.

"You're always welcome. In this big house, I can use the extra company." Dawson led the way into the kitchen, where he set up shop for the day. "I got your call earlier in the week and couldn't wait to hop on your case."

Stacks of paper covered the black marble countertops and the round wooden table over by the breakfast nook with the dangling chandelier above it.

"Nice pad you've got here."

"It's been in my late wife's family for years."

"Sorry, I didn't know—"

"Don't worry about it. She left it to my daughter along with the ranch. I come up here every so often because she used to love it up here."

"I know that feeling." I walked over to the patio doors, taking in the scenery. There's a dock by the small lake, cobblestone steps that lead to a garden encased by a wooden security gate, and an outdoor kitchen. I turned around, surveying the double ovens and oversized hood with golden pot fillers on the mixed finished ceramic tiles. The crackling from the fireplace and the smell of cinnamon and cedarwood from the scented candle on the table were relaxing.

"Coffee?" Dawson poured himself a mug full before turning to me.

"Please."

"The ride up here is a bit of a stretch from Sunflower Falls. If I had known sooner, we could have made it a weekend trip. Would have prevented me from blowing up your phone."

"Oh no, I appreciate it. I finally have someone who's willing to do the work and keep me in the loop, so I don't think I could ask for anything more." That quickly, I almost forgot about the envelope of cash inside my flannel jacket. "I also wanted to drop off my payment in person. I'm sorting out some bank security issues. Figured it would be best to pay you up front."

"I appreciate the gesture, but I'm doing this as a favor." He sipped the coffee while handing me a fresh brew of my own.

"A favor?"

"For your grandmother. I owe her that much."

"She mentioned your name a lot when I was growing up."

"Good things, I hope." His bushy grey eyebrows raised over the black coffee cup with colorful calligraphy that read *The World's Greatest Dad.*

"From what I can remember...funny childhood stories here and there."

"We shared a lot of great memories. They say distance makes the heart grow fonder, but I'm sad that wasn't the case for Ethel and me. Things went south when we got older."

"Do you mind sharing what happened between the both of you?"

"Long story short—I was a fool. It wasn't until later in life that I learned you only get a few shots at love. Lord knows I've had my fair share of chances, but there's nothing like your first."

"Tell me about it."

I've grown so attached to Thyri it pains me to even think about not having her in my life. Sometimes, I teeter on whether she feels the same about me. At any minute, it feels like she's about to jump out the window, especially when she hits me with the infamous silent treatment.

"Your grandmother never wore her emotions on her sleeve. I think she prided herself on being hard to read. I spent nights, sometimes weeks, wondering how the hell I got on her bad side, then she would eventually come around and we were no longer at odds."

"So, you all were a couple?"

"Not officially."

I read between the lines and held up my hand. "I understand."

"We loved each other dearly. I know that for sure. Our spats always ended in laughter except for when I told her I was moving across the country for good for my career and my newly found wife." Dawson's eyes moistened as he cast down his gaze at the table. "To this day, I regret my decision."

"I'm sorry things didn't work out. I would have loved getting to know you."

"Just don't make the same mistake I made—searching for love out there in a world when it's staring you right in your face."

"Honestly, I couldn't agree more."

"Atta' boy." Dawson squeezed my shoulder. "Let's get to work."

"Are these documents for me, or do you have other cases?" I scanned the kitchen once more.

"I've got a few other clients who keep me on retainer, but all of this is for you."

"In that case, Dawson, you've gotta take this payment. I don't know how else to thank you."

The corners of his mouth twitched before he spoke again. "If I had to ask you for anything in return, it would be not to sell Ethel's home."

"Believe me, that's the last thing I want to do, but it's all the collateral I have in case..." I sighed. "All this falls through."

"I'll tell you what. Let's stick a pin in it and revisit this conversation later. Hold on to your money. We've got a lot to cover in a few hours. It gets pretty dark on the roads by nightfall. I want to make sure you two make it back home before nightfall."

"Alright, where do we get started?"

Although overwhelmed with the mountains of files and mail in front of me, I tried to sound as optimistic as I could. I didn't speak or understand legalese. By the time Dawson stopped explaining the litigation process, risks, contractual terms, and accountant jargon, my head was spinning.

"Does any of this make sense?" Dawson peered at me over his rimless reading glasses while I nodded slowly.

"How common is it for agents to siphon money from their players? And how could we even prove something like that?"

"I'll tell ya'. After all the research I've done on this, it's more common than you think. Some big-time players, like yourself, were unfortunately too trusting. Once you give managers or agents power of attorney, they've got enough access to do as they please."

I looked down at the table and then back up again. Dawson blinked a few times before his mouth formed a hard, thin line. He took my silence as the answer to his impending question.

"It's alright, buddy. This is actually a good start."

Instead of sulking with me, Dawson took a different approach. "Let's start off with your first contract." He grabbed a sheet of paper in his hand. "Three years for your entry-level contract. Base salary five million dollars. Signing bonus of fifty thousand dollars."

I observed as Dawson's fingers, blotted with age spots and a gold wedding band, went to work on a handheld calculator. "Any performance bonuses? A-level...B-level?"

I stretched my neck to peek at the paper. "They told me at the beginning of my first year that I was eligible for both. Are they not listed there?"

"I mean, they should write everything in the contract. It doesn't matter if they disburse those funds at the end of the season. No two-way clause, not that you needed that." He skimmed more documents before addressing me again.

"Gangsley doesn't have the best reputation."

"I know. Too bad I found out ten years in."

"That's a good thing, though. We've got an angle."

My eyes shifted. "I'm not following."

"Legal work is like putting on a show. I'm not a criminal attorney by any means, but I approach many of my cases that way. Think about it. There's always a picture being painted on both sides. There's the defendant's story. In your case, that's Gangsley, and then there's you, the plaintiff. While they may have the perfect image to the public eye, my job as your attorney is to sling mud on the canvas." Dawson used his arms to reenact a digging motion. "Now, two things are always constant in civil cases." He counted on his fingers. "That's the motive and history. Are you following?"

"I'm following." I smirked, happy to have someone in my corner who's passionate about their work and not only concerned with emptying my pockets.

"What we want to do is mold and shape the jury's perspective to be in favor of our story." He used his wrinkled hands to mimic the motion.

"And how is that accomplished?"

"We find as much dirt as we can." He held up a finger. "As long as it's rooted in facts. I don't mind embellishing, but one thing I don't do is *lie*."

"I can respect that."

"We'll dig until we can't dig anymore, so knowing previous clients with similar suits to yours is important. Sometimes, a small slingshot will do as a secret weapon if your shotgun gets jammed."

His use of analogies reminded me of my grandmother's. No wonder these two hit it off so well.

"I'll have one of my buddies look up those old client names, and we'll keep that in our back pocket for now."

"Okay." I nodded more confidently. "I see where you're going with this."

"Right now, we want to focus on making your picture look better than there's. I want to make sure we have every single piece of the missing puzzle before I meet up with my team."

"You've got a team?"

"*We* have a team," Dawson corrected. "I asked my attorney buddies if they were interested in returning to the courtroom just one more time. At first, they weren't very enthusiastic about it...then I mentioned you. They are retired ranchers now, just like me. Good solid men and Big Time Callahan fans."

"I'm honored. Seriously."

"We're here with you every step of the way."

"I appreciate that."

"Happy to be at your service. Now..." He clapped and then rubbed his hands together. "These bridge deals and long-term contracts over the past couple of years. Do you have the original copies?"

I shook my head. "If they weren't in any of the delivered boxes, I might not have them, or they were misplaced."

"Don't worry about it. They should be easy to get with a demand letter."

"Why do you need the originals?"

"To ensure they weren't tampered with."

"Oh. That never crossed my mind."

"Everything you think they wouldn't have the gumption to do. Consider it a possibility."

"Got it." My jaw clenched.

"Let me ask you this."

Dawson hit me with the attorney stare, and I straightened up my posture. "Yes, sir."

"Did you at any point in your career ever handle your day-to-day finances?"

"Like...phone bills, rent?"

"Any bills. Taxes. Investments..."

My life as a twenty-something flashed before my eyes. Fast cars. Women. Clubs. Jets.

"During my first year in the league, but I can't say that I have until now... Does that set us back?"

"Not at all. I'll just need the names of every agent, accountant, and finance manager that ever touched your bank accounts, online or in-person. You think you can handle that?"

"Yeah. I can do that."

"Good. We also want to investigate whether there were ever any shell companies or accounts. Once we have all of this information, we'll comb through all your expenses with a fine-tooth comb."

"Okay." I picked up a notepad and began taking notes myself.

"Did Gangsley ever approach you or your manager at the time with any complex investment deals?"

"All the time."

Dawson paused. "So, what happened with those?"

"Well, they were performing well until they weren't."

Dawson's brows bent as he started scribbling back on his paper. "Falsified performance reports."

"What's that?"

"Another way for sleazy agencies like Gangsley to pocket or divert money. Athletes think their investments in real estate or private equity are getting a large return when they're performing poorly. Meanwhile, all this money you're investing is going else-where. How often did you review your accounts?"

I'm too ashamed to admit that I can count on one hand the times I actually checked where my money was going. Seeing the long string

241

of zeros gave me a false sense of security, despite my complete lack of financial literacy.

"Here and there..." I replied.

"Did you sign all of your checks?"

"Only when they presented them to me."

Dawson's eyes dimmed with dismay before he returned his focus back to his notes.

"Is that the missing puzzle piece?"

Dawson put down the pen, leaned against the plush backrest and folded his arms. "It's a start."

———

Thyri and I argued the entire car ride back to Sunflower Falls. When we arrived back at The Raspberry, she slammed the door in my face. I gathered my bearings before twisting the knob.

"Did that make you feel better?" I removed my boots at the entryway.

"Get out, Kota! I don't want you staying with me tonight."

I shook my head. This wasn't one of our petty disagreements that ended with us ripping each other's clothes off with an intense love-making session to follow.

We've had our issues, but I never imagined that our first real argument would be about Gallienne.

"I can't believe that you're taking her word over mine." I followed Thyri into the kitchen.

"That's just it. How can I believe you when you're never fully honest with me?"

"To be fair, Tee. You haven't disclosed every single detail of your past to me either. There are still things I'm learning about you."

"Really?! Like what?"

"All the shit that went down at your senior prom, for one. So, if you ask me, we're on the same playing field now, baby."

Thyri's glassy, red-rimmed eyes darted away from mine. "You

should have let me know about Gallienne before she had the chance to sling mud in my face!"

"How was I supposed to know you were going over there? I'm still stumped on how any of this applies to the relationship we're building with each other, right here, right now!" I leaned against the sink as she whipped around the kitchen like a brimming storm. She slammed cabinets and drawers while pointing spatulas and knives in my direction.

"I don't understand how you don't get it. You got her pregnant at sixteen. No one wants to get rid of their child."

"Do I need to spell it out on paper for you? The baby wasn't mine!" My voice raised an octave higher, and I instantly knew I had made the wrong turn.

"And how do you know that for sure?"

"You know better than anyone else! You're the one who revealed she was messing around!"

"That was your senior year." Thyri pressed her palms on the island with the cutting board counter, canting her head to the side.

"It wasn't only my senior year, Thyri." I lowered my eyes to the floor. As much as I chastised Thyri about being more open with me, vulnerability wasn't my strong suit either. "Gallienne stepped out on me several times when we were dating back then."

Thyri's mouth propped open as she seared a hole into me. "Then why would you stay with someone like that?"

I shrugged. "I don't know. Because I would be a hypocrite if I didn't..."

"So, it had nothing to do with your ego?" Thyri threw another jab, but I stopped defending myself. "I don't know how we're going to make it if you keep telling me half-truths."

"Why do the mistakes I made in my past matter so much?"

"Because when you live in small towns like this." Thyri moved her finger in a circular motion. "It's only a matter of time before all the bullshit, secrets, and lies come back to haunt you."

My eyebrow lifted as she continued pouring flour into a mixing bowl. "It's almost midnight. Why are you baking chocolate chip cookies?"

"Because I have a craving for them." Thyri rolled her eyes. "Why do you care?!"

The *luteal phase*. How could I forget? There's nothing I can say to win her over. It's best for me to keep my mouth shut until this all blows over. I retreated onto the couch and turned on the television. Twenty minutes later, a velvet throw pillow slapped me in the face, jolting me awake.

"Dakota, wake up!" Thyri pointed the remote controller at the flat screen television on the wall. The volume increased, but the screen was still a blur. Her pink bunny slippers were the only things I could see as I sat up, wiping my eyes, groggy from my short-lived cat nap.

"That's her!"

"That's who?!" I yawned.

"Remember the night that strange woman was standing across the street looking into our window?"

"Awh. Yeah." I scratched my head, uninterested.

"Look at her face. Doesn't she look oddly familiar?!"

I squinted to zoom in on the woman's face obstructed by the mic on the NWHL's live studio set.

"Today, we're catching up with none other than Logan McDermott's sister, Laila McDermott."

Thyri snapped her fingers. "That's where I remember her from. She's Logan's sister!" Thyri's excitement melted away after Monica introduced the topic of the podcast episode. I jumped to my feet and walked around the ottoman for a closer look. The jet-black wig and septum piercing prevented me from recognizing her.

"Now, Lala, you contacted us a few weeks ago with some exclusive news that you'd like to share with the people about Logan's former teammate, and your former boss, Dakota Callahan." Monica's eyes glinted at the camera.

I ran my hand down my face, throwing my head back. "Thyri,

listen to me. Whatever she says, I'm telling you right now. It's not true."

Thyri refused to look in my direction. She cocked a brow as Lala stood up on screen to showcase her pregnant belly under a black sweater dress with a cowl's neck and cropped black leather jacket over it.

"Dakota and I are expecting our first child together, but he won't return any of my calls. I recently discovered he's in a relationship with another woman, but I'm willing to look past that if it means having a present father for my daughter."

"Her daughter?! What the fuck?"

"Dakota, shut up! Shut up!" Thyri's cheeks heated. I could see the smoke blowing out of her nose, but hearing the strain in her voice made my entire world stop spinning.

"Thyri, believe me. This...This isn't what it seems." I panicked, unable to find the right words to sway her.

Everything Lala is spewing about me on air right now is a lie, but how can I convince the love of my life otherwise?

The timeline is adding up. We definitely blurred the line between boss and assistant. We were roommates for almost a year. I can see how people could misconstrue that as a relationship and believe that we were intimate. Lala's in her third trimester with a gut full of baby, except it isn't mine.

"Dakota," Thyri whispered my name as she closed her eyes.

Watching the tears fall down her cheekbones felt like a punch to my gut.

"I can't even look at you right now."

I could feel the steam radiating off her skin as I stepped closer. She muffled her sobs into her hands, and it made my heart sink deep into my chest. Thyri shifted her weight from one foot to another to prevent her legs from collapsing. She possessed the strength of a raging river, but this is the first time I've watched her come undone.

"When was the last time you all saw each other?" Monica adjusted her microphone.

"At the Vipers championship game." Lala sniffed and spoke in a somber tone, but there were no tears in sight.

"Did you all ever solidify the relationship?" Monica smirked.

Lala hesitated before answering. "We were getting there at one point, but he said he didn't want to mix business with pleasure."

"Thyri, I swear I've never said that. We weren't ever together."

"Welp!" Monica chuckled. "Looks like it's a little too late for that. When did Dakota stop communicating with you?"

"After he ended my employment contract earlier this year. I tried to tell him about the pregnancy, but he blocked me on everything."

"Wow, cut you off cold turkey."

"I sent a card with a note inside admitting my frustration and how I didn't—" Lala dabbed the inner corners of her eyes. "I didn't want to raise our child alone."

"She's not even crying. Can't you see? It's all an act." I moved closer to close the gap between us.

"Dakota, please!" Thyri hissed at me, and I retreated. She didn't want to miss a word, and my only option was to let her hear it.

"How far along are you? I mean, you look like you're six, maybe seven months, if I had to guess," Monica continued.

I clenched my jaw as the number of live watchers grew by the minute.

"I'll be eight months next week, and I'm struggling with preeclampsia...alone." Lala stared at the camera to garner sympathy, with her glossy lips angled downwards.

Monica shook her head. "You poor thing. Now I'm wondering whether all those other allegations about Dakota dodging paternity suits are true."

"I don't know." Lala lowered her head. "I just want our family back together again."

"Family?!" I threw my hands above my head. "Oh my God, she's officially off her rocker."

Thyri paced as I pulled out my phone.

"I've got to end this. I love Logan, but this is slander. She's getting a cease and desist."

"Why?" Thyri paused and turned her head. "Is it because you're caught?"

My mouth fell open. "What—"

"You know I've had doubts. Deep down, I knew something was off."

"Come on, Thyri. I don't need this woman's intuition bullshit right now."

"Excuse me, mister! Your privilege to tell me what you want and don't need has officially been revoked, especially under this roof."

The spring in Thyri's neck, furrowed brows, and the wag of her finger in my face reminded me my back was against a wall. I tucked my tail between my legs as she lit into me.

"You never even told me about her! And here I am, stuck on stupid, thinking it was one of Gallienne's minions this entire time."

She had a point. *Did Lala break the window?* "Listen, just give me five minutes to explain."

"And how the hell did Lala become your assistant, anyway?" Thyri's head swiveled around.

One wrong move and she'll burn me to a crisp. "I was doing Logan a favor."

"By what?! Knocking up his little sister?! You know what, Dakota..." Thyri pressed praying hands against her lips. A clear indicator that her patience was wearing thin.

"Right hand on the Bible, I never slept with that woman."

"Dakota, you love women. Love em' to death."

"Okay...and?"

"So, you mean to tell me Lala lived with you for almost a year and you all never touched each other?"

"No! I didn't. Why is that so hard to believe?"

Thyri looked at the television and then back at me. "Maybe I'm suddenly hard of hearing, because she said you kissed her."

My eyes bounced around in my head before I responded.

"Is she lying or telling the truth?" Thyri placed a hand on her hip.

"...Both."

"Dakota, just go. Go!"

"No, I'm not letting you snip me out of your life just because you're upset." I took a seat back on the couch. "Not over this. I lost you once; I'm not losing you again. I'm staying put until we talk things out."

"Where was all this talking two months ago? For one—" Thyri counted on her fingers. "You never mentioned a personal assistant, or that she was your roommate, and now, somehow, she's miraculously turned up pregnant eight months later. And to add insult to injury it's Logan's little sister!"

"I don't know whose child that is! Hell, I don't even know if she's really pregnant. Either way, it's not mine. You don't know, Lala." I shook my head. "She's not an innocent little girl anymore that just needs saving."

"What are you talking about?"

"She's...not all there in the head."

"I don't care if she's clinically insane. My concern is that you and I are supposed to be in a relationship, the entire world knows, and now you're this father-to-be. What happened to being on the same page?"

I hung my head. "You're killing me here, baby. What do I have to do to prove it to you? I recently learned that Lala was putting me in compromising situations when we lived together."

Thyri snorted. "That's your excuse? Lala's a hundred pounds soaking wet, and I'm supposed to believe that she took advantage of you? You can't make this up."

"I don't know how she did it. One minute we're on the couch watching television, and then hours later I wake up with half my clothes off."

"Were you all drinking?"

"Is that a trick question? Because I can tell you right now, it was more than just booze."

Or was it? I bit my lip, perplexed. I couldn't walk through the door most nights without Lala shoving one of her new alcoholic beverages in my face. How else would she have taken those pictures without my permission?

"Things can go far when you're under the influence. Mistakes that require a lifetime of commitment." Thyri blinked back tears, swiping a lonely tear off her upper lip with her tongue. The light disappeared from her eyes as she longed for what could have been.

"Thyri, the only person I'm committed to is you."

"Well, don't be. Because you and I..." She gestured to us both barely able to speak. "Are done."

"Never." I shook my head. "I'm not going anywhere."

"Dakota. Please, just leave. Give me some space to think."

"I'm sorry, I can't do that. You've been looking for a way out this entire time, and now that you've got it, logic and reasoning are out the window."

"Looking for a way out?! What does that even mean?"

"There aren't any second chances with you. Good people walk into your life, and your first instinct is to slam the door, don't even give a man a chance to knock on it first. You sabotage every opportunity that's given to you."

"No.No.No.No." She disagreed. "You will not gaslight me. Your dishonesty is what got you here! Your bones are popping out of the closet, and you don't want to be held accountable for it. This has nothing to do with me. Keeping your relationship with Lala a secret is as good enough reason as any to cut you out of my life and you know it. What did I say when you asked me to be exclusive?"

I stood up and turned my back to her with a sudden urge to rearrange the living room. Monica and Lala were still rambling on the screen, and Thyri's chastising sounded like nails on a chalkboard.

"Hellooo?! I told you not to lie or embarrass me, but you've already checked those off your to-do list."

I could feel the blood boiling underneath my skin. From Thyri's rapid foot tapping and the women's non-stop yapping, I couldn't concentrate.

"You're such a liar, Kota. I thought you changed..."

"How many times do I have to tell you? I did not sleep with her!" I shouted loud enough to wake the neighborhood and Thyri jumped back.

"Oh no, I will not allow you to disrespect me in my home."

"Look, I didn't mean to frighten you. I just—" I outstretched my hand, but pulled back when she recoiled. I shrunk myself to make her feel safe again. Raking my fingers through my hair, I sat on the edge of the couch, doubled over. "Arrghh! Thyri, just tell me what I have to do!"

I held my fists to my burning eyes. My Adam's apple bobbed up and down inside my throat as I choked back tears. We writhed from the emotional anguish. And although we're only standing several feet apart, somehow the distance between us feels permanent.

Thyri shut off the television, waving her face to prevent the tears from stinging her eyes.

"There's so much you don't know about her. I wanted to keep you in the dark until I came out on the other side. The lawsuit. The blackmailing. Stalking. I didn't want you to question your future with me. You've already got enough on your plate with the bakery. You're my calm amid every storm, Tee."

"Dakota, you're expecting a child...and it's not...with me." Thyri's voice cracked as she wept into the palms of her hands. I walked over to console her. Thyri broke down in my arms and a wave of guilt overcame me for her inability to breathe.

"It's not true. I promise you it's not true." I buried my face in the top of her head, planting kisses while I inhaled her signature scent of white freesias, pear and amber. I never wanted my poor decisions to be the reason for her pain.

She's the one for me. No other woman walking this planet will ever take her spot. I cupped her face in my hands, intertwining her lips with mine. When she didn't resist, I got a sliver of hope that we could move past this. But without warning, she unlocked her mouth from our earth-shattering kiss and opened the front door.

Her decision was final.

Winded from our tangle in the ring, I grabbed my cell phone and put on my coat. Little does she know, I'm not straying very far. She'll change her mind by morning.

"Goodbye, Dakota."

"See you later." I stepped outside, slowly turning around to see if I could squeeze in one last hug, but from the sound of the locks clicking, that's out of the question. Whisps of snow mixed with rain snapped at my back, propelling me forward. Seconds later, I had Logan on my speakerphone.

"Bruv!" Logan answered more chipper than I expected.

"Lo! Are you free? It's important."

"Give me a second, will ya'? I've got company."

Company? I frowned at the phone screen. How is he in rehab and still surrounded by women?

"Okay, I'm alone. It's been a minute, innit?"

"What's with the British accent?" I cocked an eyebrow.

"Sorry. I've been in character all night."

"You're still pretending you're from East London? You know what, never mind." I sighed. "Did you know Lala moved back to Sunflower?"

"Last time we talked, she didn't mention it. What the hell has she gotten herself into now?"

"Besides wreaking havoc and ruining my life? Do you have computer access there?"

"Not without supervision. What are you sayin'?"

"I think Lala's back off her medication again. I know this may sound crazy, but I think at one point she was giving them to me."

"Oh shit! Does she need another evaluation?"

"I don't know, dude, but it's not looking good. She made up this entire story that I abandoned her while she was pregnant, and something tells me she actually believes it."

"Pregnant?!"

"That's the same thing I said."

"Wait until she hears from me." Logan rasped on the other end.

"Do you have any bottles of her old medication on hand? I'm trying to see something'."

"Uhhh. Hold on, let me check my old receipts. We used to order her prescriptions through my pharmacy."

"Were any of them sleeping pills by chance?" My ears perked up.

"Possibly. Ah... Here one is. *Seroquel* and...*Benzodiazepines.*"

"Has she ever tried to get rid of her meds?"

"Hell yeah, bro. I used to get on her about doing that shit all the time. But how would she have given them to you?"

I shook my head. "It's a long story. How much time do you have?"

"As much as you need."

"Hold on." I turned the ignition on, increasing the heat. When I peeked at the second-floor window of The Raspberry, Thyri moved away from the sheer curtains. I waited until she turned off all the lights before pulling away from the curb. "I think Lala may have been slipping medication pills into my drinks."

"You let...my sister make you a drink?"

"I mean, yeah, why not?"

"Lala's sense of humor is different, bro. It's cruel. It's taboo. When I signed my first contract with the NHL, I did everything in my power to get her more help. All of her psychotherapy specialists said her behavior was due to a trauma response not uncommon for patients with bipolar disorder."

"Gee, well, thanks for telling me at the tenth hour."

Had he told me any of this information up front, I never would have hired her on as my assistant. I spent almost two hours filling him in as I put every puzzle piece in its rightful place.

"Then, somehow, she got a hold of my bank account information overseas, wired it, and withdrew the money under my name. Now everyone thinks I'm the one that's lying and going insane."

"I told Lala to stay put until my time was up in rehab, and she did everything but that. I'll have all your money back in your account by sunup."

"Don't worry about it."

"I'm a man of my word, you know that. Lala knows when she's wrong. I'll get all of this sorted. Would you be willing to hash things out or?"

"As long as she agrees not to let those photos hit the internet. If Thyri sees those fake pictures, I'm a goner."

"Would she believe Lala if she confessed the truth?"

"I don't know if it'll make a difference." I rubbed the back of neck. Thyri's stubborn and I'm confident she's already replaced the bricks I tore down trying to get her to trust me.

"If you say so, hearing it straight from the horse's mouth may rectify things."

"You know how Thyri gets. She's convinced I'm still the guy she hated years ago. Ain't no changing that. I still can't believe Lala was drugging me for months."

"I should have given you a heads up."

"I mean, don't get me wrong, the drinks were fire. I'll at least give her that."

Logan snorted on the other end.

"It didn't matter if they were super sweet, tangy, or hot. I started looking forward to em' after practice every night. I couldn't detect a damn thing."

"Damn, she had your ass hooked," Logan joked, uplifting my mood.

I missed the days when we were kids playing hockey at Comisskey Park and horsing around in meemaw's backyard.

"The last time I accepted a drink from my sister was after I cut up her concert tickets to see *The Gemstones*. We got into it about her dropping out of college. Hours later, she apologized and offered me a vodka tonic. Dude, I took a few sips and was out of it for twenty-four hours straight."

"Now you're just being extra. I don't believe you." I chuckled as we continued to reminisce, but for some reason I couldn't take my mind off Thyri.

"Lala should have gone to bartending school instead of having me waste money on three semesters of college."

"She's definitely a mixologist." I yawned, rolling my palm down my face. Block letters outlined the numbers on the glowing radio clock.

One o'clock. I bet Thyri's knocked out sleep. That's where I should be right now— next to her. I tuned back into our conversation just in time for Logan to drop a detail that confirmed it all.

"Yeah, man, Lala can make one mean Lemon Drop."

Damn.

22 / DAKOTA

THE WIPERS BRUSHED AWAY the light splatter of rain on my window. I looked in the rearview mirror just in time to glimpse a woman waddling up the pathway to the gazebo at Fox Park.

"Why am I doing this?" I kept checking my phone for missed calls from Thyri, hoping she had a change of heart.

Logan convinced me to hash things out with Lala, and against my better judgment, I agreed to meet her. I hopped out of the car and pulled my coat over my head until I reached the gazebo.

Electric blue ribbons spiraled down from two space buns on the top of her head. The jet-black hair and black lipstick made her resemble an emo anime character.

Which version of Lala am I getting tonight?

Judging from her poker face, something tells me this conversation will not work out in my favor.

"Lala, all I want to know is why?" My warm breath turned into frost in the brisk air.

"Now you want to talk?"

She slowly faced me, a malicious scowl spreading across her lips. Ignoring her disposition, my attention immediately fell to her lopsided stomach.

Lala concealed her baby bump under one of my old gray Vipers sweatshirts. She must have taken it when she moved out. All the extra weight had gone right to her belly, nowhere else. Lala pulled her cotton-white joggers above her navel and tied the drawstring into a perfect bow under her unzipped jacket.

The knee-length electric blue down jacket swallowed her up like a sleeping bag. Up close, she had more piercings down her earlobes and face than I could count. Her pale complexion reminded me of a blood-sucking vampire. To top it off, she looked sleep-deprived from the dark stamps around her pink, veiny eyes.

"I just don't understand what all this is about." I spread my arms as wide as her stomach, stepping backward.

"If you didn't want to be with me, then why did you sleep with me?"

"Lala, listen to me carefully. This one-sided relationship you're in with me stops right now, and I mean it."

"You're only saying that to me because Thyri's in the picture. We grew so close last year. I cooked. I cleaned for you. We watched movies together. I obeyed every command you gave me in the bedroom."

Lala came closer, rolling her bony fingers down my chest. I grabbed her wrist and moved her hand away.

"I hired you as a favor to Logan. You and I both know we never slept together. And all of those other things you did on your own."

"You're sadly mistaken because I've got proof right here." Lala reached into the pocket inside of her coat to retrieve an ultrasound photo. "Do you believe me now? He's ours."

She rubbed her belly while raising her eyebrows, expecting me to reconsider. I examined the grainy black-and-white photo, turning it over on the back to examine its authenticity.

"LaBelle Studios?" My jaw clenched as my shoulders slumped. A light gray script formed the tiny signature on the back. "Lala, this is fake."

"It's not." She snatched it back. "I mailed you the original when I sent you those flowers. I've been trying to reach you for months."

She flashed a crooked smile, slowly inching her way back over to me.

"Those flowers were dead, and you've been calling me from an unknown number non-stop. When I answered, you just breathed on the phone."

"I wanted to say something, but I was too nervous. I came to see you face to face, but then I discovered you were cheating on me with another woman."

"Lala, we are not together!" I don't know what was pissing me off more, her insisting that we were a couple or the mere fact that she was wasting my time? Just as I expected, this conversation is going absolutely nowhere. My only concern is returning to Thyri and making everything right.

"Ughhhh!" Lala's hands shook as she transformed from Little Red Riding Hood into a werewolf. "What is it about her you love so much?!"

The vitriol in her tone made me aware of the actual issue. She thinks Thyri is an obstacle in her way.

"I'm the better catch." She circled around me like a shark, shaking her head. "Dakota, I'm willing to forgive you. We can—" Lala licked her black lips and swallowed hard. "We can put all this behind us, but you have to promise you won't ever speak to her again."

Lala tried to grab my hands, but I snatched them away.

"It was you, wasn't it?"

Lala rolled her eyes.

"You broke the window at The Raspberry that night. Have you been watching us this entire time?"

"I've been trying to get you alone."

"You're sick, Lala. You seriously need help."

Lala covered both of her ears and then screamed at the top of her lungs. "Argh! Don't tell me that! You don't mean it."

She turned on the fireworks, and I flicked the fake ultrasound in her direction. Her eyes glistened with tears as it dropped to the icy concrete.

"Stay away from Thyri. Stay away from me," I said sternly, exasperation coiled beneath my controlled fury.

"Dakota, wait! I wasn't going to spend the money. I planned to give it back. Listen to me!" Lala followed me down the walkway, reaching for my arm, but I kept snatching it away. "There's a place on the other side of the country. We can buy a small cottage together and forget this ever happened. Just us! We don't have to worry about anyone else...not anymore."

The smell of smoke in the air and sirens singing from first responders a few blocks over compelled me to stop. I felt my phone vibrate in my pocket, and the first person who came to mind was none other than Thyri. When I opened it, Aunt Jacquee's number glowed on the screen. Hair stood up on the back of my neck from the eerie magnetic field.

Something's wrong.

"Aunt Jacquee, what's going on?"

"It's Thyri, Dakota! I can't reach her. I got an alert. There's a fire at the house." Aunt Jacquee's panic and wails made her message hard to follow. "Is she with you?!"

"No, I'm on my way back over there now."

"Dakota, please! I can't lose her!"

"Don't worry; everything will be fine. I'll call you in ten." I tried to keep calm for her, but my palms were already sweating. Lala kept her distance, returning a blank stare while biting her nubby fingernails.

My eyes squinted in her direction, and a wicked grin rested on her face.

"What have you done?!" I charged over, pointing my finger at her temple to make myself clear.

"You stay the hell away from my family, do you understand?" I could feel my face burning red as she wilted in front of me.

I hopped back in my truck, burning rubber in reverse to take the shortcut that would get me back to The Raspberry in record time.

The smell of burnt metal and wood suffocated the air as ghostly coils billowed above the bakery's rooftop. A subtle glow flickered in the distance through the dense hickory trees. Neighbors walked stealthily onto their porches while flames danced outside the windows on the first floor.

An ambulance blocked the entrance to Bannaquit Street, forcing me to park several houses down. Numbed by the sight of the blaze, I couldn't feel my feet carry me to my meemaw's front lawn. Waves of shimmering heat rippled through the air as my heart drummed inside my chest.

What if she's already gone?

My body turned to stone.

23 / THYRI

THE SCENT of burnt plastic and fried wiring assaulted my nose. I stirred underneath the duvet, still reeling from the events that had happened hours before. I couldn't get Dakota off my mind. Finding out about his unborn child on a podcast still had me in shambles. He had been hiding it all this time.

I tried to retrace my steps from the past eight weeks, kicking myself for driving past all the red lights. Dakota kept me at arm's length regarding his future, because fatherhood and financial ruin were looming around the corner.

How could I let a little charm, a pair of muscular pecs, and a dreamy smile lead me astray?

Just when I thought I found the *Neo* to my *Trinity*, now I'm back at square one. Unable to delve into a deep sleep, I'm jolted awake by the whooping sound outside my window.

In all my years of living in this sleepy town, I've only seen a fire truck once. I snatched the sleeping mask off my eyes, scrunching my nose to see if I had left one of my bedroom windows ajar. That's when I realized there's another alarm going off downstairs; now it's jumped to the second floor.

"Fire! Fire!"

An automated woman's voice echoed through the room. I shot out of bed in my flannel pajamas, slipping on my runners without hesitation. I didn't even bother turning on the lights until smoke seeped from under my bedroom door, freezing me in place.

A loud gasp escaped from my mouth, and for a second I forgot to breathe. The sound of cracking wood came from the other side of the wall. My hand trembled as I reached for the tarnished doorknob. It's too hot to touch, so I jumped back to avoid a potential explosion.

Quick on my feet, I searched for my phone on the bedside table, then under the sheets. All my bedding was on the floor before I remembered I had turned my cell phone off and left it on the counter downstairs, so Dakota had no way to reach me. The 34-oz water bottle on my nightstand ended up being a godsend.

I removed a dirty towel from my hamper and doused it with water, placing it underneath the door to buy me some more time. I opened all of my windows to prevent the exhaust from entering my lungs. I poked my head out and yelled into the darkness. "Help! Help!"

I ran to the other side of the room near Dakota's old window, screaming and coughing from the haze of black smoke.

"Kota! Someone, anyone...Please! Help me!" I sank to the floor, praying help would arrive before the walls collapsed with me inside. "This is officially the worst day of my life." I wept into my hands, wondering why everything I work hard for keeps falling apart. I shook my head.

What have I done to deserve this?

Down on all fours, with wisps of smoke curling around me, I felt the temperature on the floor get hotter. Suddenly, my body kicked into 'fight or flight' mode.

Would I rather suffer two broken legs or draw my last breath? Think, Thyri.

My eyes shifted from the pile of sheets on the floor to the four wooden posts on my queen-size bed. I'm confident it can hold my weight. I jumped up and poked my head outside of my window, startled by the sound of shattered glass from blown-out windows in the stock room down the hall. I closed my eyes, distraught as I envisioned Aunt Jacquee's brand-new equipment succumbing to the inferno.

The flames hungrily consumed everything in their path. Pots and pans blackened with soot. Cabinets cracked and splintered as the refrigerator's sleek metal exterior blackened and warped, melting into dripping molten streams.

Everything you touch turns to ash!... You sabotage every opportunity that's given to you.

Gallienne and Dakota's voices echoed in my head. The acrid smell of scorched metal and charred wood made my bedroom spin. I held my head steady to get rid of the dizziness. After making the sign of the cross, I began tying every piece of clothing and bedsheet I could find into figure-eight knots.

Wrapping the last sheet around my waist, I moved to the window. Just as I had one leg outside, I glanced down and saw Dakota below, his arms stretched out wide.

"Thyri, I've got you down here, baby. Just jump to me."

Although we were at odds right now, hearing Dakota's voice was the calm I needed in the midst of this raging storm.

"We don't have much time left. You've got to trust me and let go!"

I held onto the ledge, my core strength working overtime as I pinched my eyes and loosened my grip. "It's now or never."

The jacket slipped out of the knot as soon as I landed in Dakota's arms. He carried me away from the flames as firefighters and EMTs rushed over to throw thermal blankets over me. I inhaled the gas through the oxygen mask. A river of tears rolled down my face as I watched the fire devour the heart of my childhood home.

Two fire trucks took up half the street, obstructing my view. Firefighters ran back and forth to keep the fire contained as paramedics hung back on standby. Blue, yellow, and red flashing lights blurred my vision—I felt like the star talent in a scripted movie scene. Dakota lamented to my aunt over the phone.

A handful of neighbors gathered in the street for a front-row seat while others watched the chaos unfold from the comfort of their homes. One medic bent over me, pointing towards the house. The woman's mouth moved in slow motion. She's yelling, but I can't hear a word coming out of her mouth. A moment later, she's no longer mute.

"Ma'am, is there anyone else inside?!"

I shook my head until I remembered Beanbug.

"He's in the basement! Oh my God, my dog. Beans, he's still in there." The woman in charge exchanged a glance with her partner, and in that instant, I knew. They didn't think he was worth saving.

"Anyone else?" The woman with thinning brown hair and broad shoulders chewed on her bottom lip. Her black and red polo shirt and khaki pants didn't have a wrinkle in sight. She hiked one leg up on the curb near me, rocking her foot back and forth, before scrunching up her nose to signal to her partner that their job was done.

I removed the blanket from my shoulders and the IV from my arm. There's a chance Beans may still be alive. I shoved past onlookers, snatching away from firemen who instructed me to keep my distance. The glass-block windows were still dark.

"Miss, it's dangerous. We need everyone out of this area."

"It's my home. My dog..." I threw my hands over my head. "My dog is still in there!"

"Miss, we need you off the premises immediately." A stern man with a walkie-talkie, wearing a white polo shirt, black pants, and rubber boots, blocked my path. If only I could make it to the sloped cellar doors to let Beanbug out.

"My dog—he's probably still alive! I just need to open the cellar." A man grabbed my arm and pulled me back with all his might.

"Hey, don't touch her!" Dakota intervened without question, causing the man to stumble backward on his feet.

"Dakota, Beans is in the basement. I keep telling them to open the cellar doors. He's trapped; he needs a way out."

Hesitant, Dakota, sighed. "Okay, we won't be able to get past them over here, but there's an old window on the other side. I'll see if I can remove the screen."

"Good idea. That's big enough for me to slip through."

"I'm not letting you go back in there."

"He's my dog, and I'm willing to do whatever to save him."

"It's been a long time. I doubt I can still fit inside, but if Beanbug comes close enough, I can grab him."

"Okay... Okay. My aunt has boxes stacked against the walls. If he hears my voice, he'll come. Wait, how did you know about this window?"

Dakota shrugged. "I used to sneak in sometimes."

"How?... And when?!"

"After school when you used to lock me out, sometimes at night."

"Without us knowing?" I looked him up and down.

Dakota flicked his eyes up. "Does it really matter?"

"You're such a creep."

"Would you come on? We're wasting time." Dakota grabbed my hand, and he led the way. We trudged across the lawn on a mission, slipping through the rickety gate into Aunt Jacquee's weathered garden.

"Stay on the lookout."

I stretched my neck like an ostrich ducking from the flashing lights as more ladders leaned on the opposite side of the house. Dakota quickly unscrewed the last nail left in the screen's corner with his fingers.

"Beans!" I whistled. "Beanie man!"

Dakota slipped his arm down and tapped on the brick wall. "I'm surprised it's still cool."

Neither of us could see through the darkness.

"This would have been the perfect time for a treat." I scratched my hair, anxious and running out of options. "You think he inhaled too much of the smoke?"

I dropped to my knees and yelled. "Bugs! C'mon, Bugs!"

Another whistle but no Beanbug.

"I can't believe this." I stood up with both my hands clasped over my head. "I've lost everything in one freakin' night."

Dakota dug into his pocket to retrieve a crumpled butter cookie I had baked a few days ago. "I forgot I had this in my jacket." Dakota laid down, stretching his arm back into the window. He made the paper wrapping crinkle, but I had already given up.

Unable to come to terms with the events of the night, I started walking towards the front in a daze until I heard a faint snarl and yap. I glanced back to find Beanbug's teeth clenched to the sleeve of Dakota's jacket.

I covered my mouth and squatted. "Beans!" He detached from the sound of my voice and scurried in my direction. He jumped into my arms and licked my face. I bounced him up and down in my arms like a baby while he rubbed his head against my chin.

I mouthed, "Thank you."

Dakota nodded and said, "My pleasure."

As much as I wanted to include him in our reunion, I couldn't. Despite what Dakota says, I still need more proof that he's telling the truth. This was the longest night of my life. The Raspberry is burnt to a crisp. Soon, only our family's memories and a charred skeletal frame will remain. Dakota walked over to further explain his where-abouts tonight, and I'm floored when Lala's name rolls off his tongue.

"You left me to go see her?"

"Yes, after I spoke with Logan. Lala's been harassing me for months. She's the one who broke the window a week ago. Apparently, she's been following us around."

"Lala admitted all of this to you?" I asked skeptically.

"Yes! As crazy as it sounds. Lala has been blowing up my phone, threatening to blackmail me with fake photos, now this pregnancy—"

I held up my hand and stepped back. "Wait, so Lala's been stalking you for months?"

"Yes! And I'm pretty sure she's responsible for this fire, too."

"Dakota, I can't do this. I'm not sure if she's the crazy one or you. A stalker and an arsonist? Why would she do something like that?"

Dakota looked taken aback. "You think I'm making all of this up? For what? To win you over?"

I shrugged with a frown. "I don't know what's fact or fiction at this point, to be honest."

"Thyri, I just saved you from a burning house. Why are you always finding an excuse to punish me? Why can't you just trust me?"

"Oh, like it's so easy. You don't have the best track record!"

"If you keep holding my past against me, how are we ever going to make this work?"

The crease in Dakota's forehead let me know that our exchange wasn't just another tiff. I kept him on the fence and at arm's length to guard my heart.

"I have to feel safe with you. I need you to have both feet in."

"That's rich. You're asking me to be all in while you've got one foot permanently out the door and prepared to sprint anytime life gets too tough."

I'm a track star. He's not wrong about that. I run away when things get hard and when people I care deeply about get too close. "I'm tired of being disappointed."

"We're human, Thyri. I can't guarantee that things between us won't get hard. Look at this." Black smoke floated above our heads, with flashing red lights reflecting off of the brick wall onto our faces. "We can't plan and prepare for our misfortunes."

"But we can avoid distractions." I avoided his steely glare.

"So, that's what I am now? A distraction?"

"Your situation is distracting," I corrected him. "I'm not saying that I believe her, and I don't believe you. Hearing that Lala is carrying your child tonight just...ripped me to shreds."

"And yet none of it is true. Loving someone is trusting them."

My eyes bounced around my head. "That's debatable."

"Maybe if you fully let me in instead of putting me on ice whenever you're in one of your moods, your apprehension about us would change."

"Mmm. I don't know about that. We've only been dating... hooking up for two months. I prefer to test the waters first."

"Thyri, we aren't strangers in the getting to know you phase with some ninety-day rule in place."

"I get that, but we certainly skipped a few stages."

Dakota threw his head back. "No."

"No?"

"You're just telling me that to keep the ball in your court."

"It is in my court, Kota. Look, just because we have a history and great chemistry in bed." His eyebrows lifted at the compliment, and I rolled my eyes. "Doesn't mean that we're ready to skip off into the sunset."

"You act like I'm asking for your hand in marriage. I just want you to leave the door open instead of bolting the locks as soon as we're at odds."

"What do you think I've been trying to do? We take two steps forward and ten steps back, because of you!" I bellowed, and Dakota backed down as usual.

"Alright, alright." Dakota waved his hand. "It's late; it's been a long night. And I don't want to argue."

"No, don't bow out now. Clearly, you've felt this way for a while. Lay it all out on the table."

"Fine. I will." Dakota took the gloves off. "You've got me on this never-ending hamster wheel to prove that I'm not the boy you used to hate."

"That's...not true." *Now I'm the liar.*

"You've got me jumping through hoops all because of your inability to trust people."

"It's been two months." My voice was barely a whisper as I returned a blank stare. He's calling me out on my shit, and I don't like it one bit.

"Please, we've been inseparable since I moved back in next door."

"And that's likely the problem." I looked down, and Beanbug was snoring in my arms.

"Why can't you just let me love you? Huh?" Dakota surveyed our surroundings, pinching the bridge of his nose.

Ambulances put their trucks in reverse as townspeople retreated into their homes.

"Without conditions, despite our flaws. I could take a bullet for you, Tee, and I'm convinced you still wouldn't appreciate it."

"I didn't ask for this. I came home to discover myself again, not to find love. And if I had a crystal ball in my past, you're the last person I expected to see in my future. But—"

We gazed into each other's eyes with questions neither of us had the answers to.

"But...you've developed feelings for me. Why is it so hard to admit?"

"Dakota, you love hard. And as much as I'd like to return the gesture, I just don't have the capacity anymore. You don't have to be my everything, it's not a requirement."

"Who said I needed your permission? Listen, I can't control my heart. It wants what it wants, and I know the timing is right. You don't think our returning to Sunflower Falls is more than a coincidence?"

"We found our way back to each other, that's for damn sure..." I sighed. "Tell me, how am I supposed to know that I'm not just another notch on your belt?" I extended an olive branch to lighten the mood.

Dakota chuckled. "Whether you believe me or not, those days are behind me, and I never considered you a conquest. You meant more to me back then, and even more to me now."

My bottom lip quivered as I struggled to keep my emotions under control. "These past few weeks have been a roller coaster."

"You're telling me?" Dakota pressed his hands into his pockets to combat the chill and rocked back and forth on the balls of his feet.

My eyebrows threaded together, and he smiled. "One you couldn't pay me to get off of, Tee."

"It's been fun. I'll give you that."

"You love me, just say it."

I rubbed Beanbug's stomach as he snored. "I need some time... and space."

"I can respect that." Dakota's shoulders rolled into his chest as he walked closer. My request stung like a thousand bee stings to his chest, and I felt guilty for it. "I've already called you an Uber. There's a suite waiting for you at the Topanga Hotel."

"Thanks...but what about you? Your grandmother's house will need at least a day or two to air out."

"I'm gonna stick around for a bit and make sure everything's okay."

An Uber driver pulled up to the sidewalk, missing the fire hydrant by an inch. After opening the car door, I spun around to get Dakota's attention.

"Hey—" I looked down at the soiled runners on my feet and dirty pajamas, then back at him. "I appreciate you, too."

"I'm still waiting for those three special words, Thyri."

"Then don't hold your breath." I hopped into the backseat and closed the door of the black Toyota Camry.

"What about the fire? Do you want to file a report for damages or press charges?"

"Not unless you plan on bailing me out of jail tonight."

Dakota's puzzled expression let me know he didn't have a clue.

"The fudge for the chocolate chip cookies..." I said solemnly. "I left it on the left burner."

24 / THYRI

"THYRI...THYRIIII." My aunt's soothing voice sang from the computer screen.

She doesn't sound upset; I'm just not ready to face her yet. Not the morning after my disaster. Dakota's been keeping me updated since I've been dodging her calls left and right. There's no way I'm lowering my head into this computer screen for a virtual meeting.

She texted me a link to join with the caption:

> Hop on here right now.

I cried all night, and my eyes are bloodshot red and swollen. I took down my faux locs at two in the morning just to keep myself occupied. Sleep deprived, I drummed my fingers on the fluffy pillow I used to prop up the laptop. Aunt Jacquee can only see me from the neck down, and I prefer it that way.

I destroyed everything she and my uncle had built with years of blood, sweat, and tears in less than twenty-four hours, leaving them with nothing but memories, a year of battling insurance claims, and resentment for taking me in.

"Thyri! Girl! If you don't put your face where I can see you...I'm not gonna call your name again." Aunt Jacquee's voice shared a shocking resemblance to my mother's. High-pitched yet rough around the edges, like wind whistling through a cracked window. It's etched with emotion, yet carries a natural vibrato that adds a soulful, bluesy depth to it.

You would think the chance to hear her voice again would suffice after what could have been a tragic night. But my pride won't allow me to face my problems. For the umpteenth time in my life, I allowed my emotions to get the best of me. It's easier to place blame on someone else than to take accountability. All night long, I've mulled over the 'what ifs' and how I should have reacted to Dakota.

At my big age, I'm still emotionally immature, and I need to stand in it. What's even funnier is everyone thinks I have the skin of brass, and that I can let negativity roll off my back. That couldn't be further from the truth. My silver lining in chaos is the option to remove myself from it.

Sniffing, I crossed my legs, leaning the laptop screen backwards, so Aunt Jacquee could see my puffy face in clear view.

"Oh, Thyri." A mixture of disappointment and sympathy coated her tone.

The dam of tears broke again as my chest heaved up and down. Ashamed, I hid my face behind my hands. My chest stung from the whooping cough I developed from crying so much.

Aunt Jacquee winced at the reverberating sound. "Why are you so upset about this?"

"Because...I..." I swiped my tears away with the back of my hands, reverting to the little girl inside of me crying out for help. "I feel like... I...I let you down." Words stumbled out of my mouth in hiccups, and I eventually gave up.

"Thyri, I'm proud of you. Losing things is a part of life. Keep living and you'll see. Baby, I'm just glad you made it out okay."

"But The Raspberry is gone."

"And you're still here; that's all that matters to me. I couldn't stop thanking Dakota yesterday. Your uncle and I almost booked a flight

271

until Dakota calmed us down. I watched the camera footage of you two arguing before the screen went black from the fire. It was so eerie it sent chills down my spine. You had me worried sick...in there acting a damn fool, but what else is new with you two. I couldn't hear a sound, so I didn't know what was going on. Then you had me on the edge of my seat in stitches when I couldn't reach you."

"Dakota had the concierge send me up a new phone last night." I peered at the breathtaking vast blue sky hovering over a cluster of buildings, stretching over rolling hills and mountains. Aunt Jacquee's words were stern yet soothing, but I still couldn't come to grips with the mistakes I had made.

"Then why didn't you call me first thing this morning?"

I shook my head, unable to find the words. "I don't know. Maybe I should never have returned home. You'd still have The Raspberry at least."

"But not you. Thyri, you've gotta stop running away when life gets hard. Sometimes, you need to just be still and sit in it until God shows you the way out."

"How am I supposed to right this wrong? You're out of the country for the next three months... After the grand opening, everything was going great, then I couldn't keep up with the inventory, I didn't have enough time in the day to come up with more marketing strategies, then I got all wrapped up with Dakota and—"

Shit. Did I just say that?

A slight quirk surfaced around Aunt Jacquee's mouth. She knew way more than she let on. I know she watched that camera footage day in and out like it was a soap opera. "Don't get shy about it now. I knew something was going on between you two; I just wasn't sure how serious."

"We're not...together anymore."

"Mmm. Hmm." Aunt Jacquee frowned. "You know I'm not one to meddle..."

I frowned back at the screen, skeptical. Meddling was her first, middle, and last name.

"Why didn't you let me know you needed help?"

"Because I wanted to show you I could run the bakery on my own. I didn't know how much work went into it."

Aunt Jacquee chuckled. "Congratulations, honey! Welcome to entrepreneurship, where everything falls on you."

"I guess I'm not cut out for it."

"And what's that supposed to mean, missy?" Aunt Jacquee's eyebrow lifted.

I shrugged. "I've been looking at flights back out West. Maybe I need to put some feelers out for another job."

"You're applying for jobs outside of the one you already have?"

My lips parted. "But The Raspberry is—"

"Temporarily shut down because of renovations."

"Huh?" My face twisted.

"Did you think you were about to get out of this that easily? You made a commitment when you signed that contract. The bakery is your responsibility as much as it is mine, co-owner. We cleaned up your mess when you were a teen; you're a grown woman now."

"But I don't know—"

"Ah. Ah. Figure it out." Aunt Jacquee pointed her electric-red fingernail at the screen that matched her bold glasses, and I sighed. "Life is about solving problems every single day. You can't just run off and cry in the corner whenever obstacles get in your way."

"What am I supposed to do? The Raspberry is nothing more than soot and ash."

"Then go find a brick and lay it."

Now this is the Aunt Jacquee I knew. No nonsense, a stern tone, rolling of the eyes, and the slither of her neck. The apple doesn't fall far from the tree in our family. She served me a dose of my medicine. The gemstones on her hands, golden cuffs and sterling silver bracelets complemented her black blazer, silk white blouse, and the striped two-toned tie around her neck perfectly.

"What about the Whisk It To Win It competition next week? This will be the first year The Raspberry can't compete."

My aunt took pride in her winning streak, and I flushed it all down the drain from overreacting. A growl erupted from my stomach. There's so much going on I forgot to eat.

"What do we say about the word *can't?*" Aunt Jacquee asked me that question, and all I could think about was my mother scolding me when I was younger. Anytime I reached my hand out for help, she slapped it away. She never assisted me with grooming, preparing my food, or homework.

It took years for me to learn how to tie my shoes, let alone put them on the right foot. Eventually, I stopped asking and whining about the things that I couldn't do. I carried that same mentality with me into adulthood. I played Robin to every Batman and never sought help when I needed it.

Who would show up for me when my own mother wouldn't?

"That it should never be in a Black woman's vocabulary," I answered her question.

"And what else?" Aunt Jacquee continued, and I realized her correction didn't come from a place of resentment or malice.

"We need to use our resources and lean on the support systems that we've nurtured around us."

I grinned, grateful to have such a pillar of strength in my corner.

"Learn to outstretch your hand, Thyri. I applied to take part in the competition over the summer. I don't intend to withdraw our candidacy. Borrow someone's kitchen, I don't know."

As much as I wanted to tussle, I didn't put up a fight. After all that transpired, I owed her that much to win it. "Do you think the kitchen at the church is an option?"

"That's actually a great idea. Go down there to Pastor Driggs this Sunday and ask. Tell him I sent you."

"It's just that I haven't been to church in so long."

"That's okay, you probably need a touch of the holy spirit on you, anyway."

My eyes narrowed as she peeked at her watch.

"My art show is starting soon." She hopped off the stool, only a few inches taller than the pristine marble counter, and blew air kisses at the screen. "Call me later."

"I will. Send Uncle Kai my love and tell him...I'm sorry for everything."

"Chin up, Thyri." After one last wave, her face turned black.

Now what excuse can I give to Sebastion and Kels for cancelling this year's Friendsgiving?

———

In Sunflower Falls, nothing is ever what it seems. We have one chapel, but three different pastors held church services throughout the week. Without enough land to build on, the mayor and towns-people compromised on a fair schedule. Pastor Walter Driggs preached the eleven o'clock service on Sundays since he had the largest congregation.

People traveled for hours to listen to him speak every week, and from the looks of the packed parking lot, nothing has changed. On any weekday, people were welcome to worship their religion under one roof. Christianity, Islam, Judaism, Confucianism—you name it.

By the time I arrived, Pastor Driggs was halfway through his sermon. I could hear his familiar voice bellowing from behind the stained-glass windows. The front doors of the chapel locked after a fifteen-minute grace period, so I knocked and entered through the side.

"Good morning, welcome to Greater Hope!" A middle-aged woman with weathered hands embraced me with open arms as soon as I stepped through the door.

Heat hissed from the old radiators, filling the air with humidity. With winter a sneeze away, it's not uncommon for building mainte-nance to put the thermostat on hell. She handed me an offering enve-lope and the Sunday bulletin, and one of the younger ushers dressed in all white led me to the end of a polished wooden pew.

Churchgoers sat shoulder to shoulder, including children,

couples, and elderly women in whimsical, feathered church hats rocking back and forth, obstructing everyone's view.

Ceiling fans whirled lazily, doing little to cool the swaying congregation. Their hand-held church fans fluttered like the wings of doves. Anointing oil, old wood, and the scent of vanilla intertwined with delicate florals and white musk perfumed the room.

Choir members faced the congregation in robes of lavender and gold. With their spirits high, and their voices warm, they stood in unison to perform the next song. Men in crisp, casket-ready suits leaned forward on stage, elbows on knees, with their eyes locked on the pulpit.

Pastor Driggs moved across the stage under the bright lights, an elderly Black man with a voice like rolling thunder. His oration captivated the audience as beads of sweat trickled down his grey brows and temples. He clutched a Bible in one hand and a handkerchief in the other. Gripping both sides of the podium, he leaned forward into the mic, with a steady yet resonant voice, oozing with wisdom.

"Saints, I'm almost finished...but before I close, I need to tell you one thing! Stop looking back."

The congregation erupted with a resounding "Amen!" and "Yes, Lord!"

A few church mothers waved their hands midair, with their eyes closed, rocking in their seats.

"Too many of us spend our days stuck and dwelling on the past, cryin' over what we lost, what we messed up, and what we can't fix. But let me tell you something. God ain't in your past! So, whatever it is, you can leave that right there. Lay it down... He's in your future!"

"Hallelujah!" A woman sitting in the third pew from the front row jumped to her feet. "Thank ya', Jesus!"

"Now turn with me to *Genesis 19:26*. When you've got it, say, Amen."

"Amen!"

"Now read it with me... But Lot's wife looked back, and she

became a pillar of salt. Stop there." Pastor Driggs flicked the back of his blazer, crossing his size twelve feet, one foot over the other.

Leaning against the side of the podium, he stood at an average height of five foot eleven, with a double chin and a belly that hung over his black leather belt. Holding up a finger, he spoke into the mic. "The Bible says Lot's wife looked back..." Pastor Driggs turned around to dramatize the passage. "And what happened to her?"

"She turned into a pillar of salt!" the audience shouted out like obedient children in an elementary classroom.

"And you know why?!" He held the mic and took several steps down from the pulpit, dabbing the handkerchief across his glistening face. "It's because she longed for what was behind her! You can't keep your eyes on sin, on destruction, and on what's already dead and expect to progress forward! You see, God was tryin' to bring her out, but she was too busy lookin' back at her sin." He scurried up the stairs. The organist struck a chord, and the audience shifted on cue.

"My God!" a woman repeated as other churchgoers clapped and nodded while the Holy Spirit moved throughout the chapel.

"Some of y'all are still looking back at that addiction...that heart-break...and the abuse that left you abandoned, broken, and confused!"

Tears rolled down the cheeks of everyone around me. There wasn't a dry eye in sight.

"I don't know who this message is for, but God put it on my heart. There's a few of you in here...that still can't forgive yourselves for the things God has already forgotten!" Pastor Driggs held up his hands like a magician.

An old lady in a toffee-colored pencil skirt and black long-sleeved shirt jumped into the aisle with tears streaming down her face. "Thank you, Jesus! Thank you, Jesus!" she chanted as her body jerked. Kicking off her heels, she moved with a force beyond herself. Two ushers wearing white gloves rushed to her aid, fanning and steadying her with one arm outstretched and the other hidden behind their backs.

Pastor Driggs' thunderous voice trembled with power. "Hear me today, saints! If you don't leave here with nothing else, remember this!"

He wiped his forehead with the handkerchief again. "The reason the rearview mirror is so small is because where you're going is *bigger* than where you've been! Look ahead!" he shouted, and everyone stood on their feet at once. He stomped across the stage. "I said God has a promised land waiting for you, but you gotta trust Him! You've gotta move forward! Say it with me one more time!" Pastor Driggs extended the microphone to the audience.

"Forward!" we shouted back, and before I knew it, I was wiping away tears of my own. Pastor Driggs closed his Bible, then stepped back with his chest rising and then falling. I'm surrounded by clapping, shouting, and hands lifted to the heavens.

"Hallelujah!"

"Glory to God!"

"Thank you, Jesus!"

My eyes roamed over the cushioned lavender seats, white walls, and hand-painted murals on the ceiling. Pastor Driggs sipped from a cool glass of water, resting on the side of the pulpit while deacons rushed over to whisper in his ear. The choir sang an old gospel hymn that caused an overwhelming feeling of peace to wash over me. Ushers took their rightful places in front of the stage as a deacon opened the doors of the church, inviting new souls to come forth.

Praise dancers moved gracefully down the aisle in flowing white skirts and leotards, swaying to the music with their arms stretching toward the sky. The Holy Ghost gripped my spirit as my feet moved without my instruction. An usher grabbed both of my hands and prayed profusely over me. I couldn't stop my tears from flowing.

Everyone rejoiced as they led us to the back of the church, and downstairs to the communion room. Instead of making introductions, I wandered through the old halls with violet walls.

Everything looked exactly the same. The aroma of soul food wafted into my nose, and before I knew it, I was standing at the entrance of a stainless steel, state-of-the-art kitchen; industrial-grade appliances, including a double-door smart refrigerator, a six-burner gas range and a built-in convection oven. The massive center island with a soft metallic sheen was everything I needed and more.

Trays of fried chicken and catfish, smothered pork chops, collard greens, black-eyed peas, and sweet cornbread made my mouth water. Two stumpy, elderly women moved with grace around the kitchen. Their soft, flabby arms jiggled as they stirred pots and kneaded dough. Fine-mesh cooking nets held their wigs in place on top of their heads.

Their smooth mahogany skin, rich with history, glowed under the recessed ceiling lights. Their expressions twisted as they kept their voices low. They looked up with sharp glances at the door every so often. I stepped behind it to eavesdrop and test the temperature of the room.

"I don't know why Pastor agreed to share parking spaces with Mr. Cunningham's family."

"Your guess is as good as mine, Cora Jean. He's cunning, just like his last name."

"They ain't gon' give it back. Walter's been the head pastor of Greater Hope for almost twenty years. You would think he has more authority around here by now."

One of the women whispered like her life depended on it.

"Mmm.Hmm. I know it. Seems like all they want to do is take over. Did you know they cut choir practice from two hours down to one? And only on Wednesdays before Bible study?"

"I wonder what made them do that?"

"Somethin' about having to heat the church and a high electricity bill. But as soon as Ramadan hits, the building is open til' midnight."

"Now how is Sister Taylor ever gonna hit that C-note?" Cora Jean snorted.

"She's only been practicing for the past two years, just to sing flat on *Amazing* every single time."

279

They cackled together while removing more pans from the double ovens.

"Oh, that's what I forgot to tell you. So, you know we just reopened the Sunday Dinner program to feed the homeless five months ago, right?"

"Yeah." Cora's brows knitted together.

"Tell me why I went to the executive committee meeting last Friday, and they're already voting to shut it down."

"Delores, now you know all they care about is money. If the costs are too high with no profits, that program will be the first to go. It's been that way forever."

"It wasn't like that back in the day. Churches were there to help people in need; now they're run like Fortune 500 companies."

"Last I heard, Mr.Cunningham's brother made a hefty donation. That's how we got that new nursery next door and this kitchen."

"See there. I know what I'm talking about. We tithe the most and always end up with the short end of the stick."

"Speaking of Mr. Cunningham's brother, you know he remarried that trifling woman, Alabama. The who abandoned her children..."

"Naw. Who is that?"

"It happened a long time ago during my pledging years. Alabama's abusive husband went to prison, and then she took off with a new man shortly afterwards. She ought to be ashamed of how she left those kids."

"The McDermott's?!"

"Yeah. That's them. The kids got separated in foster care, but her son ended up becoming a famous hockey player."

"I bet she was kicking herself when she found out."

"They say she tried to walk back into their lives, but her son cut her off."

"And that poor Lala."

My ears perked up.

"She's been in and out of group homes since she was a baby.

Pastor Shaw was like a father figure to Lala back then. She was such a troubled teenager."

And that's when it hit me. Lala's familiar face. Those round, hazel brown eyes, sticky fingers, half-eaten bag of marshmallows, and freckles checkered across her murky chipmunk cheeks. I found Lala hiding in a broken deep freezer in Logan's basement. I can still smell the musty scent of mildew and old concrete.

Logan tried to raise his sister alone until teachers noticed signs of neglect. Dakota kept Logan's secret the longest until authorities popped up one Saturday afternoon unexpectedly. Logan thought Lala had run away, but she was playing hide-and-seek. He gathered a group of kids from around the neighborhood to help find her, and I won the game.

"She might have turned out okay if her mother had stayed in the picture."

"You might be right, Cora. But Alabama's too busy trotting around here in linen suits and Chanel frames whenever they visit."

"When were they here?"

"The beginning of summer, right around Pastor Shaw's Independence Day retreat. Maybe next time she'll come looking for her daughter. Someone needs to douse some holy water on Lala quick."

"Dang, my new job has me missing everything. What's going on with Lala? I haven't seen her in ages."

"Word around town is her brother is in rehab, so she's free to roam as she pleases. She appeared to be in the family way the last time I saw her."

"Really? How far along?"

"It's funny you ask that, because the first time I saw her, she looked ready to pop, and that was two months ago. Last Sunday she had a manic episode at the front desk until Pastor Shaw called her inside his office. There was nothing more than a pudge, and now she's all belly again."

"That's strange. Well, where's the father?"

281

"Nowhere to be found. Either that, or she doesn't know who the hell he is. Sound familiar?"

"Just like Alabama. She probably doesn't have anyone. What did she come to see Pastor Shaw about?"

"Chile, who knows? When it comes to them, I try my best just to mind my business."

I frowned, but continued to listen.

"Is her mental state any better now that she's older? People used to say that she's got a few loose screws, like her daddy."

"I can believe it. I tried not to look her in the eyes upstairs. The lights are on, but no one's home."

"Excuse me! Ma'am! Can we help you?" Cora snapped.

It took a moment for me to realize she was talking to me. My coat sleeve gave me away. I stepped forward, pretending to be lost. "Oh, I'm here to see a deacon."

"All of them are upstairs, baby, not down here."

"Okay, because my aunt Jacquee sent me here."

They exchanged glances. "The owner of The Raspberry, Jacquee?!"

"Yeah..." I hesitated and nodded slowly. "She's my aunt."

"Girl, get your tail in here then. We're all family then."

"She looks just like Jacquee, doesn't she?" They welcomed me in, hung up my jacket, and sat me down in a folding chair like we were in the middle of their living room.

"You hungry? We've got plenty to eat."

The food in front of me looked delicious, but I declined. "No, I'm fine—I wouldn't want to deprive anyone of a plate."

"Chile, please, there's more than enough to go around." The ladies talked with their hands, piling samples of food onto plastic plates while carrying on about their relationship with my aunt.

"We heard about what happened the other night at the bakery. You alright?" They genuinely seemed concerned.

"Because if you all need help with anything, just say the word."

"As a matter of fact...we do."

It felt good to accept a helping hand for once.

25 / DAKOTA

CLIMBING the stairs of the Circuit Court of Sioux County felt like the longest trek of my life. It feels like I'm falling into quicksand with each step. I gazed up at the pillars holding up the structure of the old white building that resembled the Pentagon and its equally intimidating.

Today is my first court hearing that Dawson scheduled at the last minute. I asked him to expedite the process, but I didn't expect things to escalate this quickly.

Thyri and I are back on good terms. I'm not sure what changed, but I accepted her apology for not trusting me. I learned a long time ago not to unlock a woman's *Pandora's Box* if I didn't have to, so I asked no questions. Yesterday she asked to tag along, but she's got enough on her plate.

She's been pulling all-nighters at the church for the Whisk It To Win It competition with Aunt Jacquee virtually holding her hand every step of the way. It's in less than three days, and I've been encouraging Thyri to assemble a team. She's got the right recipes and ingredients, but not enough hands to feed a crowd of three hundred people.

Thyri's not a fan of hiring overhead, or working with anyone who doesn't follow baking instructions to a tee. Thank goodness Aunt Jacquee and I have been chatting when she's not around. We've got something up our sleeves.

I offered Thyri my five-star Michelin skills in the kitchen, but she abruptly declined. Watching her stress over dessert options and taste testing made me concerned. It took all of me not to stick around this week, but Dawson's phone call shifted my priorities.

I spent the past two months pouring into Thyri's cup while neglecting my own. I needed to lock in like I was back on the ice, and Thyri agreed. For the past few days, I stayed over at Dawson's ranch, preparing for cross-examinations.

During our time together, we've bonded over local sport rivalries, barrel racing, and old Westerns like *The Dukes of Hazzard* and *Bonanza*. He told me about the first pickup truck he purchased to impress my meemaw and shared a core memory about their first date, which ended with them dancing under the stars.

Dawson showed me statues, paintings, and other family lore that got passed down through generations. We even reminisced about the greasy smash burgers with beer-battered caramelized onions served at *Sue's*; an old diner that hasn't been open in over a decade.

I shared some of my wildest hockey moments and the places I loved to visit while traveling overseas. Talking to Dawson felt easy, like two chums catching up after years missed.

I opened up the courthouse's heavy doors to freshly waxed luxury vinyl floors, and polished wood moldings adorning the ten-foot walls and ceiling. Long hallways from the entryway ran in every direction, with wooden benches nailed to the flooring. The old wood creaked as frantic conversations echoed throughout the hall.

Arched windows invited natural light to illuminate the vast space at every angle. Sunrays created a sheer sheen that reflected off of attorneys huddling outside of courtrooms to deliberate. I passed by several men engaged in an intense debate about the jury. Incessant whispers, squeaky patent leather loafers, and the click-clack of heels on stone floors surrounded me.

Some families held hands in prayer, while others hugged each other, burying their faces in their palms in disappointment over the final verdict. Everyone adhered to the unspoken dress code, carefully choosing their outfits to make an impression. Three-piece suits. Slacks. Ties. Trench coats. Blouses and knee-length skirts for women.

I climbed five flights of wide-cased stairs. My sweaty palms slipped down the railings. As planned, Dawson greeted me outside of Courtroom C on the fifth floor at a quarter past nine. We had fifteen minutes to debrief before the start of the hearing.

I struggled to catch my breath as I rested my hands on my knees. My stomach churned at the thought of taking the stand for cross-examination. I'm an excellent public speaker when I'm not being grilled. Winded, I interlocked my fingers over my head.

"Guess I should have warned you about the stairs?" Dawson stared back at me, puzzled.

My shirt is stuck to my skin from the sweat rolling down my back. "I'm nervous."

"Good news is, you shouldn't be."

Skeptical, I frowned. "So, what's the bad news?"

"Gangsley has decided to settle."

"You're joking?"

Dawson's lips turned down. "I'm not much of a jokester when it comes to my cases. We presented our findings to their team, and they're scared shitless." He chuckled. "The potential damages your lawsuit will do to their agency's brand and current partnerships with high-profile athletes wasn't worth the risk. So they would rather settle out of court...with your blessing of course."

Speechless, my mouth propped open. "How? I've been mulling over what we rehearsed for hours."

"One of our attorney's sons, Jamie, is a tech geek. He detected that the bank statement copies you gave us were fake. All the unauthorized transfers for the last seven years of your contract weren't a good look either." Dawson jingled the loose change in his pants pockets.

"We handed over every piece of incriminating evidence that we could find to the judge. One of my buddies even put a colorful presentation together to examine the documents on screen in front of the jury with a clicker. That would've been fun."

"Unbelievable." I'm astonished and tempted to drop to my knees.

"Congratulations, buddy." Dawson double-tapped me on the back of my shoulder and extended his hand. I pulled him into a hug, patting his back out of gratitude. Overwhelmed with joy, I stepped back, pinching the inner corners of my eyes to stop the waterworks from flowing.

"Ready to meet the All-Stars?"

"Yes, please." I blinked my eyes. "Wooh! Now that's what I call good news."

Dawson opened a door to a narrow hallway filled with empty conference rooms and tufted carpet. "Sorry for the noise. I think the libations are flowing already."

"I'm glad, I could use some myself."

Fumes from the fresh coating of white paint on the walls and what smelled like lasagna drifted into my nose. Chatter and laughter at the end of the hallway led me to a long table of ranchers sitting in leather ergonomic chairs, each donning wide-brimmed cowboy hats, blazers, patterned shirts, and custom-made belt buckles. Two liters of soda, plates with breadsticks, a pan of beef lasagna, and a half-eaten Greek salad covered the table.

"Is there enough Rooby's for me?!" I joked as I stepped through the door. Their eyes lit up, and the next thing I knew, they were all on their feet clapping for me.

"There he is! The man of the hour." A man with a southern accent, slicked-back ponytail, and a bushy gray handlebar mustache walked over to greet me. "I'm Jonnie. Next to me is Herrold. We're brothers. Dawson took us under his wing almost thirty years ago."

"It's a pleasure. You all deserve the standing ovation, not me." I shook hands left and right as we made introductions around the room. "I'm sorry if I'm a little tongue-tied; I'm still in shock. It's been a long time comin'."

"Hey, Dawson, you tell him what he's looking at for the settlement package yet?"

Dawson stopped talking mid-conversation. "I haven't. I didn't want to take all the credit."

Everyone laughed light-heartedly around the room.

"You're right, Jamie deserves it!" Another lawyer chimed in, with fine lines around his eyes and a roadmap of wrinkles etched across his face. He wore a blue plaid shirt, black jeans, and a pair of snakeskin cowboy boots.

"Is Jamie coming? I'd love to meet him."

Jonnie spoke up. "I tried to get him a flight out, but he's got finals."

"He's a college student?"

"Senior year in pre-law at Tennessee State." He tipped his hat proudly.

"Wow. I'll have to send him something, or maybe we can hang out once he's back in town?"

"Man, he probably wouldn't even believe me if I told him that. It would surely make his day."

"It's the least I can do. I can't stop thanking all of you. My heart is full, honestly." I pressed a hand against my chest, noticing Dawson had disappeared from the room.

We took pictures, talked about hockey, and horse riding. I signed hats, T-shirts, and hockey paraphernalia that they brought along with them. I even spoke to family members on FaceTime calls. Dawson returned with a brown envelope in hand and placed it on the table in front of me.

"What's this?"

"Open it up. Just promise us not to faint."

I pulled out several sheets of documents, and my eyes immediately landed on the bolded amount—*twenty-two million dollars.*

Blood rushed to my face as I stood up and hugged Dawson, tight-lipped. I put my pride aside and allowed the tears to fall freely.

"Thank you. Thank you." My voice was nearly inaudible as I whispered into Dawson's ear. He held me up to prevent me from breaking down.

"You deserve it, buddy."

Leaning on the back of the chair to steady myself, I stood still for a moment, squeezing my eyes shut. The angelic face winking back at me was none other than my grandmother.

26 / DAKOTA

HOURS AGO, I received what felt like the best news of my life until I realized I had no one to share it with. I've been calling Thyri nonstop, but she hasn't answered all day. Text messages left on read. No returned calls. I even called up Aunt Jacquee to make sure she still had a pulse.

Just when I thought we were back on good terms, she's ignoring me again. I've never chased a woman in all my thirty-six years of living on God's green Earth. But Thyri has me running marathons to keep her attention. If my teammates ever found out how hard I've fallen for her, I wouldn't hear the end of it.

I've invested my blood, sweat, and tears in our budding relationship. But I can't lie, sometimes, Thyri makes me feel like I'm in this by myself. She constantly reminds me that her career comes first. Before a husband, before children. Anytime I bring up starting a family, she just stares off into space and says, "Someday in the near future."

Family. It's the first and last thing on my mind when I wake up in the morning and go to bed at night. I'm trying my best to remain understanding, to see her side of things. I've reached the height of my career, but for her, this is only the beginning. I peered at my watch.

My arms were still glistening from the fresh coat of body oil I'd rubbed all over.

Eleven o'clock.

She has to be in this suite; there's no way she's still over at Greater Hope.

I raised my hand to knock on the door, and there's music blasting through the speakers, which is strange because Thyri hates noise. I blinked, wondering if there's something amiss. *Does she have company over? And why wouldn't she tell me this?* I knocked on the door hard enough to make sure that she could hear me.

After calling her phone, I pulled out the extra card key I had taken without her knowledge and slipped it into the slot. The executive suite is pitch dark except for the red candles illuminating the path to the living room. Usher's voice crooned over the stereo system; rose petals covered the stairs to the second floor.

Now that you're here
I got somethin' to say baby
I think that you should know
You're doin' the most, sugar
So don't worry 'bout the situation
I'd never let you go

"Thyri!" My eyes narrowed as I placed the bag of Chinese takeout on the plush five-piece sectional couch. As soon as I turned around, I spotted Thyri leaning against the glass balcony. Legs. Ass. Tits. They're on full display, and I can't look away. Her back is lit by the soft glow of the bedroom hallway, and she's wearing a silk robe, loosely tied at the waist.

"Damn." I uttered, following her every move as the fabric slipped over her curves like a whisper. Lingerie straps run up her juicy thighs, and I get aroused from the mere thought of sinking my teeth into them.

Lace panties rode low on her hips, delicate and sheer. Thyri took her time walking down the marble stairs in six-inch pumps with stiletto heels. Light from the flames flickered across her stunning face in sync with the music.

She offered me temptation on a platter, and I'm ready to sin. Before she took the last step down, she pulled open her robe, exposing every inch of her dewy sienna skin to tease.

"Hey handsome, I haven't seen you all day..." She glided towards me, moving like a cheetah hunting its prey.

Every step she took was slow and deliberate. Her thighs flexed as the garter straps climbed up like secrets waiting to be revealed. I licked my lips in anticipation, eager to satiate my ravenous appetite.

Her twins sat up high, jiggling in a satin, strapless bralette, fighting for freedom. I moved closer. My member stood at attention. He's ready to get down to business. Inches above her waist is where my hands landed.

"All of this? For me?" I kissed her forehead, then her cheeks, down to her neck, stepping back to see the entire package.

She nodded. "You like what you see?"

"You've been ignoring my calls. Then I walked into this, I thought you were stepping out on me."

"Seriously? With who?"

"You're right. I'm as good as it gets."

"Shut up. I knew you would come looking for me."

I exhaled as she melted in my arms. "I've been waiting to hold you in my arms like this forever."

"It's only been a week."

"Yeah. The longest one of my life."

"How did things go today?" She searched my eyes, bracing herself for a hit that wouldn't come. "Never mind. Don't tell me. Not til' after tomorrow."

"Fine with me." I licked my lips to stop myself from drooling.

"Good. Now let me get back in character."

Thyri dropped the robe off her shoulders, instructing Siri to play 'Seduction.' She led me over to the couch, where crackling wood and notes of sandalwood and patchouli from burning incense saturated the living room.

Whipped cream, pink furry handcuffs, and a bowl of chocolate-covered strawberries and champagne flutes filled to the brim were on the coffee table. She pushed me into a cushioned chair in front of the fireplace, and I smirked at the performance. Thyri could never walk in heels, but it looks like she's been practicing. I rubbed my hands together, reaching out to grab a handful, but she smacked my hand away.

"Rule number one..." She leaned forward with both hands on my knees. "Hands off the private dancers." She slowly turned around, allowing me a clear view of her rotund cheeks with a black G-string down the middle as she walked upstage.

"Okay. I see where we're going with this."

Thyri bent over, grabbed her ankles and then rocked her wagon from side to side. I bit down on my fist, leaning in to give her my undivided attention. Her long, boho goddess braids cascaded down her shoulders as she unsnapped her bra.

"Woo! Take it off, baby!"

Thyri paid me no mind as she performed the sultry choreography to 'Seduction'. Every step was in sync. She followed Usher's instructions to a tee. Thyri rolled her body around, poked out her ass before she dropped into a squat with her legs spread eagle. Her breasts bounced under her hair as she got down on all fours, scooping her back up and down while moving her juicy ass in a circular motion.

My imagination ran wild thinking of all the dirty positions that I could put her in. A few back shots, from the side, and her ankles pulled back far enough to touch her ears. Thyri danced seductively around my chair, lightly lifting my chin, and brushing her fingers down my torso.

She threw one leg over me, positioning herself in my lap while leaning back to the music. Thyri bounced her ass on top of me, and my lips parted. I tugged at her panties, but she wagged her finger in return. Sexually frustrated, I couldn't resist breaking her rules. I squeezed her perky, tender breasts, brushing my thumb over her nipples to make her wet.

I palmed her ass every time she came close enough for me to touch it. Thyri continued dancing in my lap as I moved her hair over her shoulder. She bent over, discreetly unsnapping the garters around her thighs. I planted a wet one on her left cheek and smacked it until it reverberated off the right. She stood before me, then glanced back, fluttering her lashes like butterfly wings. Her curves cast a silhouette on the wall behind her.

Sliding her foot between my legs, I removed the straps and slipped each heel off her delicate feet. I'd suck every single one of her toes right now, if she'd let me. With only one piece of clothing left, I can only assume we're headed for the grand finale.

My face heated with arousal as she stretched her long brown legs into a split.

"Mmm." I grunted, my temperature rising by the minute. Back on her hands and knees, she moved her body back and forth like she was riding an imaginary bull.

"You're such a tease!" I yelled over the music.

Thyri crawled over to me, and I gazed into those mesmerizing pools of chocolate, tempted to rip her panties away. She rolled her flexible body backward like a gymnast. Using her core strength to lift her body upside down, she slowly scissored her legs until she moved and isolated her thighs in waves. When she clapped her cheeks in the air, I lost my composure.

"Where's the real Thyri at? You're an imposter."

Thyri lowered herself back down onto the shaggy rug, stifling her laughter.

"Where did you learn all this stuff?"

"Pole dancing classes."

"You took a pole dancing class?"

"Is that so hard to believe?" The music faded to soft jazz as Thyri caught her breath. "I learned this routine at an old cabaret class. I've been practicing and setting up all day." Thyri stood up to grab the bowl of chocolate strawberries and then sat on my lap to feed me.

"So this is what royalty feels like?"

"Yes, King."

I folded my hands behind my head and allowed her to serve me. "I could get used to this."

"Oh, I bet. This is my thank you for all that you've done for me."

"True." I winked, and she cut her eyes at me playfully. "And what about my apology?"

"What about it?" Thyri quipped, and my expression required no answer. "Okay, fine. I'm sorry for not believing you when told me about Lala and not trusting you more."

Satisfied, I said, "Apology accepted."

"Now put these on." She took a page out of my book and dangled a black sleep mask in front of me.

"Are you blindfolding me?"

She nodded with a mischievous grin, and I shook my head. "I don't think so...I've got a better idea. Let's take these off." I pulled her in between my legs and tugged at her panties with my teeth.

"Not yet. I've got one more surprise."

My eyebrow lifted. "What's that?"

"No questions, just do as I say." Her kitten voice turned me on. She pressed her finger against my lips to silence me, and I licked it. "Undress."

I did as I was told. First my shoes, then I peeled off my sweater and undershirt. The warmth of the fire made the room feel cozier than normal. I sat back down in a pair of white and grey crew socks and jersey knit boxers.

"What are you doing?" She turned back around after pulling out glass bowls filled with nuts, sprinkles, cherries, and hot fudge. "I said get undressed."

"Are you making dessert?"

"As a matter of fact, I am." She dropped to her knees in front of me with a fresh coat of lip gloss on her lips. "Now drop em'."

My eyes widened as I peered down at her. A naturally gorgeous face prepared to serve without request. What else could a man ask for?

"Are you sure you're ready for this?" My boxers fell to my ankles, and I stood proudly in the nude. Clean shaven. Well endowed. And from the sparkle in her eye, I could tell she liked it, too.

"I'm in control tonight. Sit down." Her persona returned, but I was ready to get to it. I didn't want dessert. I wanted a full-course meal.

Her.

Thyri walked behind me and slipped the sleep mask over my head. The entire room went dark, and I felt vulnerable. "Thyri! If you don't hurry and sit on top of me, I'm taking this off."

"Stop whining. I'm making a banana cream sundae."

"A banana what?!"

I felt her soft hands brush against my inner thighs. Then, a cooling sensation on the tip of my rod compelled me to jerk back. I could hear her giggling in the background.

"Did you just squeeze whipped cream on my dick?"

Drizzles of a thicker substance and particles fell down my sac. "Thyri, what the hell?" I lifted the blindfold over one of my eyes for a quick peek to catch her placing a cherry on the head.

"All done. Here's the banana." She pointed to my erection, then swirled her tongue around the cherry, dropping the stem onto the floor.

Thyri started at the base, licking up every drop of fudge on my sac before she wrapped her lips around my cock. She swallowed the whipped cream, and I counted the sprinkles on her tongue, letting the sleep mask fall to the floor.

I threw my head back instead of guiding her neck. She didn't need any direction from me as she performed magic on my shaft. Within seconds, it vanished down her throat.

"Fuck." I uttered as my toes curled. I flexed my feet as she bobbed faster and faster. I wasn't ready to cum. I wrapped her hair around my hand to slow her motion.

Listening to her moans turned me on. Giving head made Thyri even wetter. I envisioned the swollen lips between her thighs, dripping with sweet nectar.

"Damn, I wasn't expecting this." I struggled to keep my breathing steady.

Thyri looked up at me with tantalizing eyes, proud of her blowjob. She glided her pouty lips up and down my pole, circling the tip with her creamy tongue as I exploded. My face turned crimson red. By the time I came to, she was using a damp towel to wipe me clean. I exhaled, and she licked her lips. Her nipples were both aimed at me. I stood up, ready to switch gears, but she pushed me back down.

"Awh. Come on, Thyri. Look at me." I glanced down at my wood: locked, loaded, and prepared to empty another chamber of seeds into her pulsating peach.

"Not until you put these on." Two pink furry handcuffs swung from her fingers.

"Nope, not doing it." I smacked her on the ass and pulled down her panties. While kissing her stomach, she gently pulled my head back. "I'm not letting you inside me until you put them on."

I slowly grabbed the cuffs and slapped them on my wrists. "Are you happy now? I don't know why you're handcuffing me, anyway?"

"I'm still in charge tonight, remember?"

She turned around and picked up the bottle of whipped cream again.

"Babe, what are you doin'? I'm getting blue balls waiting."

"Now it's your turn to eat." She trotted back over to me, both of her breasts bouncing with whipped cream, toppings, and a cherry. "Lift your arms."

Thyri sat on top of me, purring as soon as she positioned my head inside of her clit.

"Ahhh!" Her walls tightened, molding to the curve of my rock-hard dick. She moved up and down in a counterclockwise motion, and I rode the waves. I lowered my arms back down around her waist, savoring the whipped cream as I suckled her breasts.

"Mmmm. Ah!"

Pleasing her felt like music to my ears. I palmed her cheeks, jack hammering her juicy well. Thyri attempted to move, but my muscular arms pinned down her thighs.

"Don't run," I whispered as she murmured in my ear.

"Mmm. Mmm. Ah. Ah. Ahhhh."

I drilled harder until her ass slapped down on my dick. She screamed, and I politely asked, "You want me to stop?"

A lonely tear rolled down her cheek. She set herself up for this, handcuffing me. Thyri's tight canal turned me into the energizer bunny. It felt so good I could go until morning.

"...Nooo." She wept in my ear, catching her breath as I intentionally slowed down my rhythm.

"Now who's in control?"

Thyri's lips tightened as she closed her eyes. I inched further inside of her, hitting her G-Spot.

"Shit!" She gasped.

"Thyri..." I growled. "Who's in control?"

"Ahhh! Youuu." She sang, licking her lips as I pressed my hand against her stomach. She folded under the pressure. We went round for round in the same position. Our bodies melted on top of each other like wax from the candles surrounding us. Shadows on the wall outlined our lovemaking session. When the subtle glow from the fireplace fizzled into smoke, we called it a draw.

Thyri provided the perfect balance between the best of both worlds. A classy princess in public and a freak behind closed doors. But more importantly, she's my best friend, and the only woman I'll ever wife.

27 / THYRI

"Dakota, where did you find all these people at the last minute?"

"Don't look at me. Patti, Mr. Choi, and your best friends are the only ones I can take credit for. Everyone else is here for Aunt Jacquee."

"Wow." I rested my hands on my hips, taking in the scene. Cora Jean and Delores made sure I had full access to the kitchen in Greater Hope's basement to operate out of while we rebuild.

Business would continue as planned to recuperate our losses, but I didn't expect to see so many volunteers the night before the Whisk It To Win It competition. Delores taught Kels and Sebastion how to roll, pinch, and knead dough. Patti gave me several tips on how to elevate my glaze and pastry decor. Mr. Choi wrangled a group of artsy teenagers around the neighborhood to create a banner for my booth and tie-dye table skirts.

More familiar faces walked through the door. Some hugged like they were long-lost friends, although everyone lived within a five-mile radius of each other. Even Mr. Henry made an appearance. Dapper in a three-piece suit, he flaunted a toothless grin to veil the weariness furrowed in his expression.

A stout, elderly woman wearing glasses, a floral dress, and a silver up-do with rosy cheeks held his hand. It's the first time I've ever seen him interact with the public. He's quite a charmer. When he looked my way, he held up a hand. I waved back, happy to see that he's found someone that at least makes him smile again.

Starstruck fans ran up to Dakota, jumping up and down on their tiptoes, tugging and wrapping their arms around his shoulders for selfies. We exchanged flirty glances before I snuck out to take a breather from the lively crowd. Just as I turned the corner, I bumped into Jace.

"Jace, what are you doing here?"

"Hey, Tee. My mom and me come here—"

"For church. We're members at Greater Hope," Jace's mother interjected, squeezing her hands on his shoulders. "Long time no see, Thyri."

I didn't recognize the woman standing before me. She and Jace didn't share similar features other than their chubby bellies, round faces, and their wide-set eyes. Maybe. Her thick lips tugged upwards, revealing a subtle gap between her front teeth.

That's when it hit me. My partner in crime from elementary school, she sported the same smile when we used to rollerblade and practice the latest dance moves.

"Wisdom?"

She looked completely different from what I expected of Magnolia High's four-time Homecoming Queen.

She shrugged. "That's me."

"Wow!" I opened my arms to embrace her. Our weak hug exchanged fifteen years of awkwardness and pent-up aggression. "It's been years."

"I didn't know you'd moved back."

"My aunt never told me she was babysitting your handsome son here." I pinched Jace's cheeks out of nervousness, and his eyes squinted up at me, skeptical of my odd behavior.

"Is Beanbug here?"

"No, we left him at home, buddy."

"Ohhh, mannn. Can I have a donut?"

"You sure can."

"Jace, what do you say?"

"Thank you, Tee!"

"Now go wash your hands." Wisdom's silky voice didn't match her appearance. Her black, loose, wavy hair no longer flowed down her back. It barely scraped past her shoulders. Her ends, chewed and split by blonde highlights, and her edges, thinned around the crown.

She wore an oversized black hoodie and bellbottom denim jeans that were faded at the knees from too many washes. The hem hid a pair of sneakers with worn rubber soles. "Sorry. I know he can be a handful."

My lips parted as I pointed over my shoulder with my thumb. "Is his father... Umm?" I blurted out for confirmation.

She pressed her heart-shaped lips together, peered down at the floor, and sighed. "I'd rather not talk about it."

I nodded, embarrassed that I had asked such an intrusive question. "It's none of my business."

"Miss Jade's been a blessing in disguise. We connected through my godmother. They were roommates back in college." She quickly changed the subject.

"I remember."

"She offered to watch Jace for a couple of months while I was out looking for work. I tried to pay her, but she wouldn't accept any money. She even sent back the small birthday gifts we tried to give her."

A sympathetic grin crawled across my face. I had no clue this is what my aunt meant when she said Jace's mom needed a little help. I feel like such a brat; whining about my pitiable problems that pale in comparison. "That sounds about right for her."

"I heard about the incident at the bakery and figured we could lend a helping hand to show our appreciation." She attempted to sound chipper, but it didn't erase the exhaustion on her face and emptiness behind her eyes.

"Yeah, she would be happy you came out to support her. I mean, I appreciate it too. God, I keep forgetting that I'm the one competing tomorrow. I'm so nervous."

"Congrats..." Her voice tapered off. Once again, she averted my gaze, fearful of being judged. "Listen..." She started before taking a deep breath. "I know our friendship didn't end on the best of terms... I..." Wisdom stopped talking, and I put a hand on her shoulder.

"Don't worry about it. It happened, and it's in the past."

Back then, I wanted closure. I wanted to know why my best friend since the third grade woke up one day and gave me the cold shoulder. Now it didn't matter either way.

"It's been a minute, you're right." The subtle chin dimple she used to complain about was still there.

Aside from the bloated face and hair, Wisdom was still a stunner. Her flawless coffee-bean complexion didn't require artificial coverage. Every time she blinked, her naturally long lashes swooshed, accentuating her almond-shaped eyes. Wisdom's nose was the perfect size with an upturned tip, proportionate to her full lips. The lamination of her thick brows made them appear painted on.

But the one feature she obsessed over when we were younger hasn't changed. Wisdom never left the house without freshly polished nails and toes. She once said it was the only thing she could control in her life. I didn't understand back then, but now I do.

Speechless, I chewed on my bottom lip, staring at the woman I once thought would be my maid of honor. We were both humbled by life and still nursing old wounds left by Jett Avers.

Wisdom may not know it, but we have more in common now than we did before. A struggling single mother is the last 'most likely to' caption I would've put next to Wisdom's senior yearbook picture.

"Welp! I'm all yours for the next hour." She scanned the kitchen, noting the different stations. "I'd stay longer, but Jace has hockey practice in the morning. Put me wherever you need me."

I spotted Sebastion using cake decorations for face makeup and shook my head. "We need all the help we can get at table seven."

"You've got it." She shimmied over, removing the strap of her green faux-leather purse from her shoulder. And for the first time in a long time, I missed my ex-best friend.

————

Before Cora Jean and Delores left for the night, I asked if they would do me a favor and taste test my samples. They happily agreed, sharing which icings needed more vanilla, butter and less sugar. Kels and Sebastion loved every single item on the menu. I usually take their opinions with a grain of salt, but I needed all the feedback I could get to boost my confidence.

"So, what's everyone's favorite item besides Kota's?" I rolled my eyes while he scraped the paper plate clean of every crumb left over from sampling a slice of my key lime pie. He frowned afterwards.

"The pumpkin spiced donuts are unmatched. It's the best dessert in the lineup, hands down." His eyes were pink from exhaustion, but he still got the first word in. With his sexy, cocky ass.

"I don't know, Tee. Your man might be right." Sebastion wore a handmade headband made of dandelions on his head to match the floral decorations on his apron.

"It was the apple butter pound cake for me." Cora Jean chimed in, pulling her jacket onto her shoulders. "Baby, that one ate down, you hear me?"

"Yeah, I'd pay top dollar for that and those cupcakes, especially around the holidays. My grandbabies would love em'," Delores added.

Dakota smiled with his eyes at me from across the table. I felt elated about all the compliments raining in.

"And I heard the money pot for the competition almost tripled overnight." Cora Jean turned to Delores. There wasn't a conversation between these two that didn't end in gossip.

"Mmm. Hmm. Now they're sifting through all those new applications at the last minute."

"With the sale of those raffle tickets, it might be up to six figures."

"I know you lyin'?"

"No, ma'am, and they said the organizers received some anonymous donations yesterday."

"It's probably one of those rich hockey players sponsoring the event. I should've thrown my hat in the ring."

Delores and Cora Jean carried on, and I inched my way around the stainless steel counter bidding farewells. Dakota slipped out the door before I could catch him. I exchanged goodbyes with everyone and thanked all the volunteers for their help. As soon as I found a moment to track down Dakota, Sebastion stopped me in my tracks.

"What do you think I should wear to the competition tomorrow?"

"Ummm. Comfortable, loose-fitting clothing. It's not a fashion show, Sebastion."

"I know, but I need to look good while I'm in the kitchen."

"You're supposed to be helping me prep and pass out plates, not look for dates."

"But what if Dakota's friends are there?" Sebastion smacked his gum.

"The NHL season just started; none of them are in town. Trust me."

He nodded in contemplation. "I'll bring my heels just in case."

"I doubt you're their type, boo."

"Don't be a hater, Tee. You don't know that. Besides, I've already asked Dakota to hook me up."

"With who?" I huffed, my eyes half-lidded from sleepless nights.

"Eww, why are you so nosey?" Sebastion stalked off to annoy Kels, and I walked up the stairs of the church and out the back door to the gated parking lot.

The chalky white moon played hide and seek behind smoky clouds. It was the only light on my path as I made my way to Dakota's ratty, blue pickup truck. I'm not sure why he thinks it's a Batmobile that makes him disappear when he wants.

No one else drives a 1970 Chevy C10 truck around here.

Everyone knows it's his because he's had it since high school. I knocked on the window, disturbing Dakota's doom-scrolling session on the ESPN app. He's thumbing through the latest hockey stats with numbers and abbreviations I don't understand.

"I've been looking for you."

He reached over to unlock the passenger door, and I hopped in. "I stepped out to make a few calls."

"What was that back there?"

Dakota's eyes shifted. "Did I miss something?"

"The donations for the competition tomorrow? Please tell me you didn't have your teammates triple the pot?"

"What if...I did?"

I sighed. "Come on, Dakota, why would you do something like that?"

"Why not? They're only trying to help."

"That's great and all, but there's no guarantee that I will win."

"You need more faith in yourself. Your competition isn't that steep."

"What's that supposed to mean?"

"I'm talking about Gallienne. She wouldn't know her way around a kitchen if you locked her in it."

"Gallienne isn't the problem. It's Blythe I'm worried about."

"Blythe? Who the hell is Blythe?"

"The reason The Raspberry may lose its title tomorrow."

28 / THYRI

A LIVE BAND of middle-aged men with rockstar dreams was on stage performing a cover of 'Ho Hey' by *The Lumineers*. A few strummed guitars and banjos while the others played harmonicas, keyboards, and drums for entertainment. Cowboy hats tipped in every direction as women sang along to the lyrics with their arms wrapped around the waist of their partners.

Jugs of beer fizzled over the top while children chased each other around, dropping cotton candy and cookie crumbs on the artificial turf. Folding tables under tents formed booths for all the Whisk It To Win It contestants. Six judges sat in front of the gymnasium bleachers, tasting decadent sweets and deliberating after each bite.

I wouldn't mind trading places.

"What do you mean we've run out of food? We stayed up all night prepping, so there should be plenty."

"Kels, you see all these boxes, right?" Sebastion lifted the pink cardboard in his hand.

"Yeah, your point?"

"They're empty because we have nothing left to put in them."

I walked over to Curly and Mo to break up their bickering. "I have to let Aunt Jacquee know that things didn't go as planned."

"Oh, c'mon, Tee. Don't tell us you're bowing out?" Sebastion frowned.

"What else am I supposed to do?" I shrugged. "The warmer broke. We only prepped for three hundred people. It's double that in here. Chassidy's Choc-O-Latte's line is damn near wrapped around the corner."

"What a dumb name?" Sebastion glanced upward in annoyance.

"We don't have a chance. I'm going to call my aunt." I walked a few feet away but remained close enough to overhear my best friends talking.

"How is Miss Jade going to help when she's all the way overseas?" Sebastion couldn't whisper to save his life.

"I don't know. Maybe she can give Thyri some more direction and reassurance. She trusts her aunt's word more than anything."

"But we're a part of this team too. She needs to trust all of us."

"Why are you so invested in this competition?" Kels' sharp eyes cut into Sebastion.

"If that pot is big enough, I want my cut. Even if they just shave a little something for me off the top."

"I should have known. You are something else, you know that?"

"What? We stayed up all night working too."

"Look, this is Thyri's business. It's her decision at the end of the day."

"And the day's gotta end. All I'm sayin' is Tee needs to put her big girl panties on and figure it out."

"Remember, we're here to support. She just lost her family bakery in a fire. Just have her back."

My friends were right. I shouldn't be so quick to throw in the towel. In three brief hours, everything that could go wrong came to fruition. Our equipment malfunctioned. Competition is steep. And we've sold out of pumpkin-spiced donuts, our most popular menu item.

Why didn't I listen to Dakota?

I've gotten so used to running away from my problems over the years, it's turned into my go-to option. I dialed Aunt Jacquee's number. Four rings later, I heard her raspy voice on the other end.

"Everything alright?"

"I forgot it's nighttime in Japan."

"You know I'm still up working. What's going on?"

"There are way more guests here than I expected, Auntie. We didn't prep enough food."

"What time is it there?"

"Noon...why?" As soon as I turned around, I caught Gallienne smirking at me from behind her booth. I turned around and walked into the hallway for more privacy.

"Never mind. What's your plan B?"

"My *plan B*?"

"We discussed this, Thyri." Her tone remained stern.

"I prepped as much as I could. How can I plan for things that I can't foresee?"

"You can't. That's when you lean on your team."

"Team?" I sighed. "Aunt Jacquee, I've been on crunch time since the accident. I didn't have time to assemble a team."

"Who do you have there with you?"

"It's just me...Kels, Sebastion..."

"And no one else? To serve over three hundred guests. Did you ask for help?"

"Well...yeah...for prep."

"And where's Mr. Callahan? I know he's not too far away."

"I asked him to see if he could bring me some tools to fix the warmer. I don't want him involved. He draws too much attention."

Aunt Jacquee cut me off mid-sentence. "Thyri, what sense does it make to fix the warmer if you have nothing to put in it?"

"Aunt Jacquee, I didn't call you for a lecture."

"Then why did you call, Thyri?"

"I just wanted to let you know what's going on."

"No, you called for my permission."

"Permission to do what?" I moved closer to the glass windows looking out into the gymnasium parking lot.

"Permission to quit."

Dakota stepped out of his pickup truck with his favorite black corduroy baseball cap on, a grey hoodie, and his jacket collar flipped up to his chin. He's one of the tallest guys in town, yet this is his way of being inconspicuous. He spotted me through the window and raised his hand; leaning against the old truck. I waved back with a lop-sided smile.

"I didn't say I was quitting, *per se.*"

"But you're thinking about it?"

Boisterous laughter near the entrance distracted me from our phone conversation. A group of women stormed through the side doors, cracking jokes, their volume loud enough to fill a concert stadium. Except for one of their voices, it sounded distinctly familiar. Much like Aunt Jacquee's it was naturally soft and warm with a raspy, slightly smoky tone.

A woman wearing a gray jogging suit and a pair of sneakers, with braids the color of honey pulled into a large topknot bun on her head, cut the corner. Occupying her tiny arms were plastic lidded containers filled to the brim with freshly baked goods. The steam inside is thick and cloudy enough for me to trace my name on it. Listening to the short, petite woman's banter made my cheeks burn red. That's when I notice it's Cora Jean and Delores following her closely behind.

"Thyri! Thyri, can you still hear me?!" Aunt Jacquee yelled into the phone.

I put the phone back up to my ear, with both brows bent. "Did you tell my mother I was here?"

"There's no sense in getting your feathers ruffled about it. It's been years since you all saw each other. Now, whether you decide to patch things up with Trice is up to you."

"Then why force it? Why is she here?"

"She's my *Plan B*."

Before I could say anything else, I heard the dial tone. "No, she didn't." I closed my eyes, rolled up my sleeves, and braced myself for the storm. My head throbbed, and my left eye was jumping from all the stress crashing down on me like a roll tide.

Just when the walls felt like they were caving in on me, Gallienne reared her ugly head. It's bad enough that her booth is right next to ours. Her uniformed staff of ten made us look like a bunch of amateurs. But, no surprise there, Gallienne hasn't lifted a finger. She's left Blythe to do all the work.

"Did you make a call for reinforcements?" Gallienne walked past me with a devilish grin etched on her swollen face.

"Gallienne, did a beehive fall on you again?"

Shocked, she touched her puffy face.

"Yeah, maybe you should lay off the fillers for a minute."

"Ugh!" She disappeared into the crowd, and I made my way back over to our booth.

There goes one thorn in my side; now onto number two. My mother, Cora Jean, and Delores have completely taken over. Kels and Sebastion are happily taking orders and packing boxes again while I stand with my arms folded across my chest. Guarded.

Kels and Sebastion exchanged glances with each other, then went back to work. They knew the dark secrets I shared about my mother while growing up. Although tempted to, I owed it to Aunt Jacquee not to make a scene. The winner gets chosen tonight. I'll put up with my mother for the next couple of hours, and she can walk right back out of my life again.

"There's my baby girl! Long time no see." The dimples in her cheeks were deep enough to hide beads in them. Despite her alcohol addiction, she kept up her appearance. Her tawny skin was flawless, and the ridges in her full lips had deepened with age. Every time she flashed her pearly whites, lines of crow's feet danced around her chestnut almond eyes.

"Oh, get over here, you!" She pulled me into a hug, but I didn't return her embrace. "It's so good to see you in person, damn girl, you look as good as I did when I was your age." Her laughter trailed off when she saw my expression.

"You know I was invited here?"

"I know," I replied curtly.

"She called me last week to tell me about what happened. You had her worried. Hell, me too."

"Considering our past, why do I find that hard to believe, Mom?"

"I—"

"Look, let's just make it through this competition—for Aunt Jacquee. There's no need for any back and forth...okay?" I stepped around her, and her shoulders slumped.

All the anger I suppressed towards her suddenly bubbled to the surface. I joined Kels and Sebastion who immediately checked on me.

"Are you okay?" Kels placed a hand on my back.

"She just showed up out of nowhere?" Sebastion's upper lip curled.

"No, my aunt told her to come," I replied somberly. "Just do as she says."

For the next couple of hours, my tyrant mother took over.

Everyone worked on the serving line, while Sebastion and Cora Jean joined the publicity team. I'm not sure where my mother is going with this, but I kept my mouth shut to keep the peace.

"Bastiòn and Cora, I need y'all to use that gift of gab to bring more people to our booth."

"Who the hell is *Bastiòn?*" I mumbled under my breath.

"Girl, your momma doesn't seem all that bad to me. *Bah-stee-yon* is the nickname she gave me. It's French." Sebastion snapped his fingers and walked off.

"Delores, you got my samples ready yet, baby?" My mother ran a tight ship.

"I'm workin', I'm workin'." Delores gleefully waddled back and forth.

"Alright, I need them all plated in less than two minutes. The clock is ticking; let's run these numbers up."

"Kels? How you doin' with the ticketing system I showed you, hon?"

"I'm on it, Ma."

Ma?! Great, everyone likes my mother but me.

Aunt Jacquee once told me she and my mother practically ran a bakery out of Grandma's kitchen growing up. But my mother never struck me as the hardworking type. She spent so many years locking me out of her room or passed out on the couch I never saw her work ethic.

Then again, I can't remember when she was fully sober. Except for my kindergarten graduation, when she brought me home a stray kitten, so I'd have something to keep me company while she partied at night. I bit a sample of her maple pecan glazed donuts, and my knees buckled. The flavor was rich, and the dough was so moist it melted on my tongue. "Mmmm." I licked my lips and fingertips to make sure I didn't miss a crumb.

Aunt Jacquee's right. She is the better baker.

Instead of making healthy, home-cooked meals, my mother made sure our cramped apartment never went without sweets. She used to fill my lunchbox with leftover fried pound cake, scones, and butter cookies, but never slaved over a hot stove.

No fruits. No vegetables. No Sunday dinners.

I learned how to cook and bake on my own.

"Thyri, baby, what are you doing?"

Caught red-handed, I turned around with crumbs sliding down my chin. "Huh?"

"You're coming with me."

"Me?! Nuh-uh. I can't leave this booth. I have to wait until the warmer gets fixed."

"What you talking about? Mr. Fix-It is over there repairing it right now."

I stretched my neck around her shoulder to find Arly frowning at

312

a screwdriver with twisted lips. "That's strange. Arly never leaves his hardware store. It's like his second home."

"Apparently, he doesn't do house calls either, but he showed up for Dakota." My mother looked at me suggestively.

"What? Why are you looking at me like that?" My mother looked me up and down.

"Girl, you know exactly what I'm looking at. How's life with Dakota?" She placed a hand on her hip.

"How do you know about him?"

"Take one guess."

Aunt Jacquee can't hold water.

"I prefer to keep my relationships private."

"You and your secrets, Thyri. If I lucked up on a good man like that, I'd be shouting it from the rooftops."

"I'll pass on that. I've never understood why people invite others into their bedroom."

Kels and Sebastion have been requesting a "D" report ever since they've learned about Dakota, and they still can't get a peep out of me. We're no longer in college, and Dakota is actually someone I care deeply about. Call me prude, but what goes on in the sheets between us is no one else's business but ours.

"I'm not meddling. If there's a wedding, maybe this time I'll receive an invitation." She chortled, and my eyes narrowed in her direction. "Fill those bags up with donuts and put them in the warmer when he's done."

"Shouldn't I be keeping a tally of tickets and speaking with customers?"

"You wanna go out there and talk to people?" she quipped.

I sucked my teeth and sighed.

"That's what I thought." My mother shimmied over to a booth across from us to chit-chat with another bakery owner just as animated as her. It always baffled me how she effortlessly made friends.

She sparked a fire in every room she walked in with a warm smile and a contagious laugh that ignited curiosity and made everyone's mouths twitch at the corners. My mother had the energy of a hedgehog.

As a child, I imagined there was a magnetic force field surrounding her. Somehow, she always became the center of the crowd. She drew people in with her charm, wit, and down-to-earth personality. In public, she was cool and vibrant, but at home she was a shipwreck; barely able to pull the pieces of her life together and addicted to the bottle.

I did as I was told, grateful Dakota came through for us in a crunch. Sebastion and Cora pulled people to our booth left and right until our lines wrapped around the gymnasium.

"Kels, what are they requesting the most now?" I pulled the rubber gloves onto my hands to assist with serving.

"The pumpkin spiced donuts!"

"Okay." I nodded humbly. Two months ago, I knocked on Dakota's doorstep with a dozen in hand, and we've been inseparable ever since.

"Thyri Richards, please come to the Judge's table. Booth 13, please report to the Judge's table." The announcement boomed over the speakers, prompting Kels and I to stare at each other as I removed my apron.

"Wonder what that's about?"

"I don't know, but I'm about to find out." I pushed my way through the pulsating crowd. By the time I made it over to the bleachers, Gallienne's screw face was peering over at me from the opposite end of the Judge's table.

"I'm Thyri, co-owner of The Raspberry."

"Uh, nice to meet you, Ms. Richards. We received a complaint from Booth 11. The owner has stated that a few of your staff are stealing customers from her table."

I blinked rapidly, visibly annoyed. "So, Gallienne's upset people are tasting items on our menu? Technically, they are customers for all of us."

"Well, yes...and no."

"Where in the rule book does it mention that outreach is prohibited?"

"That's a good question." The balding old man wearing a Simpsons T-shirt glanced over at another judge in a three-piece suit. He shrugged his shoulders in return while flipping through a binder of rules.

"From my understanding, all guests purchase tickets to cast their votes for their favorite desserts, no?"

"That is correct but—"

"Then they are required to taste every food item in here, no? Votes aren't casted until the very end for the top three contestants anyway. I don't see the issue." I glared at Gallienne and she turned her back towards me. *Such a coward.*

"I think The Raspberry should be disqualified. You can't pull people out of line and drag them over to your booth for more ballot entries."

I overheard Gallienne talking to her sidekick, Blythe, who averted my gaze.

"Gallienne, please, save it!"

She spun around with her arms folded across her chest and her mouth propped open. "Why don't you try following the rules for once?"

"What rules am I breaking? The ones you made up!"

"Ladies, there's no need to argue." A hefty, elderly woman wearing a leather cowgirl hat, over a copper red bun, and white embroidered dress interrupted our spat. "The number of tickets are used to keep track of how many guests visited your booth. Votes for best menu items aren't cast until all dishes have been tasted. We'll select the top three contestants from there. Outreach is a marketing strategy that is allowed at Whisk It To Win It every year."

She held both her hands up like she was prepared to draw her guns if needed.

I smirked at Gallienne before she stormed off into the crowd.

"I swear she's not working with a full deck."

"Psst. Psst." One of the judges at the very end nodded for me to come over. A jolly man with rosacea on his cheeks, a wiry grey beard that curled at the tip and coffee-stained teeth pointed to his clipboard. "I don't have anything important to say... Judges aren't supposed to talk with contestants until the competition is over but..." He kept his voice low. "My wife and I's anniversary is next week, and I just tasted those chocolate donuts you all brought in and my god are they to die for."

Proud, I continued listening.

"Is there any way I can pay for two boxes to go? And place another order for next week?"

He spoke to me like we were negotiating a drug deal.

"I can't promise the two boxes today. They're a hot commodity, but I can work something out next week. We'll be operating out of Greater Hope until renovations are completed at our original location." I left him with a business card. We didn't have a blueprint let alone a contractor, but it felt good to speak my plans out loud. I needed to speak something into existence, including winning this competition. I have no collateral and insurance would take months, maybe even years to kick in.

"You've got a deal."

We shook hands and my mother was right back in my face.

"Thyri, I've been looking all over for you."

"I was—"

"Never mind that. We've gotta go."

"Go where?"

"Prepare for the bake off. Where else?"

"We don't even know if there will be a tie."

"Aunt Jacquee told me she prepares every year, just in case."

I shook my head and followed her lead. "Wait, I don't think we should both leave at the same time. I don't trust Chassidy's Choc-O-Latte over there. Gallienne loves to scheme."

"Well, *Gallentine* better tread lightly, whoever the hell she is.

Cora Jean and Delores agreed to help out at the last minute. They love them some Aunt Jacquee. Their eyes lit up when I told them we were sisters. I think they're doing a fine job manning the ship."

I observed Cora Jean and Delores giving instructions to organize the group of people gathering by our booth. They instructed everyone to split into two separate lines and they parted like the red sea.

"Let's head back over to the church now. They'll be announcing the finalists in an hour or two."

Apprehensive, I pulled my car keys out of my back pocket. The last place I wanted to be was stuck alone with my mother with no one around to referee.

———

My mother thumbed through a pile of old recipe clippings I used to create the menu. I hadn't seen her for so long, I lost track of how much time we'd lost. She's wearing readers, and her roots are fully gray.

Smile lines have become permanent dents in the textured skin on her face. The dark lines on her neck are so deep they resemble healed scars. My mother's aging, but she's still an undeniably beautiful woman.

"What do you think about German chocolate cake?"

"Cake? You looked at all those recipes, and that's what you came up with?"

"You got something better?" she shot back. "Thyri, I'm trying to be a team player here, but I can't do this alone."

"Why did Aunt Jacquee send you here? Did she feel I was incapable of competing on my own?"

"My sister didn't send me anywhere. I insisted I should come."

My expression relaxed. Maybe Aunt Jacquee had faith in me after all.

"Yesterday, I reconsidered until Jacquee called me at the ass crack of dawn to get a crew together. She wanted more batches of everything on your menu list in case of emergencies like this."

My eyes danced around the kitchen. "Oh."

"You've been through a lot. The divorce. Returning home. The fire."

"Okay, and? Did you show up out of nowhere with a cape on to save me?"

"Honey, I'm too cute to be wearing anyone's cape." She placed her hand on her hip. "I've been asking Aunt Jacquee to visit you since your teenage years until you shut me out when you got older, and rightfully so."

I pressed my palms against the counter, finally ready to address the elephant in the room.

"Remember all the times I begged you to come to my birthday parties, school plays, and track meets when I was a kid? You never showed up then."

"I wanted to attend everything you were involved in growing up Thyri, but Aunt Jacquee thought it was a bad idea."

"Don't try to place the blame on her."

"I was sick, Thyri. I was in and out of AAA. For months I'd go without a drink, then I'd lose a job or housing, and run right back to Jack Daniels to numb myself again."

My mother's somber tone compelled me to soften.

"I wasn't in any condition to walk back into your life and give you false hope that I'd remain. I struggled with having a steady income to keep a roof over my head."

"Why didn't you ask for help?"

"I did. Many times. To your aunt and uncle, people I thought were close friends."

I shook my head as my lips formed a thin line. "Aunt Jacquee would never leave you out in the cold."

"She did...to protect you."

"That doesn't make any sense."

"My sister took sole custody of you when I turned twenty-four.

She had every right to keep me out of your life. She offered me visitation with supervision, but I didn't want it. I was sixteen when I got pregnant with you. My plan was to run off into the sunset with your father, get married, and secure a decent job while he went to school. But obviously, the Lord had other plans."

"You told me my father went to the army."

"He did for a few months, then he dropped out, and when he returned, he decided he didn't want the responsibility."

"Responsibility, meaning me?" I clarified.

"He didn't want a family. No one knows what they want that young. But by then, I had already started partying and drowning my sorrows away with liquor bottles." She forced herself to crack a painful smile. "I developed a taste for it, one that even I couldn't see. It helped me cope with the present, clouding all of my judgments, and wiped away my dreams for the future and what could've been."

"So I'm the mistake you and my father made from irresponsibility, then you both resented me?" My eyebrows bent. "Got it."

"That's not what I'm saying, Thyri. We were young, and I didn't heed the warnings your grandmother and aunt gave me. I never planned on abandoning you. I wrote a letter to you every day during my sobriety journey, but Aunt Jacquee thought it was best to continue the no contact until you got older. She wanted you to have a normal childhood."

"All my classmates and friends had their parents around for support. It's not the same when you've been adopted by your uncle and aunt. I used to look out into the audience, hoping you would show up, but you never did."

My mother's eyes sweated with disappointment.

"You put my life in danger many times, and I ended up in a group home because of your negligence. If Aunt Jacquee hadn't rescued me, there's no telling where I'd be today. So, why should I let you back into my life now? I don't need you anymore. I'm no longer the little girl who cries herself to sleep at night. I've stopped wondering why my parents abandoned me and second-guessing my worth. It took me a while to curate my circle, but I'm surrounded by supportive friends and family, and loved by a man that's willing to go to the end of the Earth and back for me if I asked him to. There's no room left in my life for fickle friends and family that I can't trust."

My mother nodded vigorously. "I deserve every bit of anger that you've stored in your heart for me. But I didn't come here to rub salt in old wounds. There will come a day when we'll be able to put the past behind us. I have faith that it will happen."

"I can tell you that today is not that day."

She mustered a grin and put her glasses back on. "You remind me a lot of myself when I was your age. Very firm and direct, I can respect that. But Thyri, baby...you slammed that door in my face before I even had the chance to knock on it."

My mother guffawed, and I couldn't help but crack a smile. Joking was another coping mechanism of hers; she laughed to keep from crying.

I'm proud I said my piece. I released everything off of my chest since I was a little girl stuck in the back seat of my mother's Oldsmobile. She drove it into a tree and left me trapped inside, coughing and choking from smoke inhalation. This is the first time I've seen my mother sober in over twenty years. She doesn't deserve my forgiveness, but I forgave her a long time ago. Not for her, but for myself to move forward.

My mother rubbed her hands together. "Now let's make this mouth-watering dessert, so my sister can reclaim her throne."

"Let's," I agreed, letting my guard down, even if only for the moment.

"So, there's this lemon meringue pie that your grandmother used to make."

"I think Aunt Jacquee made it right before she left. One bite and you feel you're transported to a tropical island, sipping champagne on a yacht somewhere off the coast. It was to die for."

"Are you talking about the one with the lemon-infused pie crust, mousse, and toasted coconut on top?"

"I'm pretty sure that's it."

"I can make it just like Aunt Jacquee, maybe even better."

"Oh, I'm not denying that, but everyone doesn't like pie or lemons."

"For the final round, the only ones that matter are the judges, right? I've seen all six of them, and trust me, they're not turning away any plates."

"But bake-offs are only what? Thirty minutes long? A pie will take at least an hour."

"Not if we prepare ours now. Crust ain't nothing but a little flour, salt, water, butter, and sugar." She pushed her glasses up. We both glanced at the clock on the wall. It's a quarter past two. The winning announcements don't start until around five o'clock.

"What about elevation? I heard the judges will look for creativity, flavor, texture. Can we pull all of that off with a pie?"

My mother shot me a wry smile. "Watch me work."

An hour later, she proved me wrong. I tasted a sample of the old-fashioned lemon-raspberry Swiss meringue pie and took flight.

The toasted almond shortbread crust added a buttery texture and nutty twist to our family's classic recipe. Tart lemon-raspberry filling, pureed and strained, added a refreshing citrus punch. For appearance, I drizzled raspberry coulis over the topping and torched the Swiss meringue before serving. We clapped hands and then hugged. Win, draw, or lose, we were a winning team.

———

There's no way I would have been able to make it to the final round of the Whisk It To Win It competition without a team. I stood shoulder to shoulder with my best friends and my mother on stage as we awaited the judge's results.

When they announced Blythe's name as the runner-up pastry chef in the bake-off between *Chassidy's Choc-O-Latte* and *The Raspberry*, I felt my mother's hand squeeze my side. We were already jumping for joy and hugging to celebrate when they called my mother's name.

"Dauntrice Richards is the first-place winner for The Raspberry in our annual Whisk To Win It Competition."

They brought out the oversized check for sixty-thousand dollars, and Sebastion fainted. I stepped over him to shake hands with the organizers as Gallienne rushed over to the judges, outraged.

Blythe lingered behind to shake hands and congratulate everyone on our team. I wonder whose bright idea it was to use Aunt Jacquee's signature Olive Oil Citrus Cake with pistachios and blood oranges? Gallienne picked the same recipe Aunt Jacquee had used to compete in bake-offs for the past two years.

"Ooh-wee! That lady has quite a tude on her." My mother approached me from behind holding our golden plaque.

"Don't mind her." I pulled out my phone. "Let's FaceTime Aunt Jacquee to let her know the good news."

Aunt Jacquee sang our praises for ten minutes straight until I noticed my knight in shining armor standing in the gymnasium's entryway. This time I didn't care who saw us together. I trotted down the stairs of the stage, pushing my way across the sea of people on the floor, and into his arms. He picked me up, and I removed his cap, wrapping my lips around his as sparks exploded around us.

"We did it, babe! We won."

"I expected nothing else. Which menu item got y'all to the final round?"

"The pumpkin spiced donuts!"

We kissed as the live band played a familiar tune. I looked up on the stage and my mother was in the band's section giving them directions. Cameo's Candy played over the speaker, and everyone in the gymnasium started grooving. At the front of the stage were my mother, Delores, Cora Jean, Kels, and Sebastion starting up the Soul Train line. I peered at Dakota, and he couldn't stop grinning.

"Go ahead, get up there." He folded his arms and leaned against the doorway, turning his hat backwards as fans made their way up to him in awe.

Who knew that taking a few steps back would make way for alignment? God put me exactly where I needed to be. I found happiness in the last place I expected to find it. Right where I left it all along.

Back home.

29 / DAKOTA

"WHAT DO you think she would say if she saw us together?" Thyri's eyes squinted from the sun beating down on her brow.

I placed a bouquet of sunflowers on my meemaw's headstone, fighting back tears.

"Well, I'll be damned!" I mocked the southern twang of my grandmother's voice and chuckled to myself. With moist eyes, I broke down, and Thyri squeezed my shoulder for support. "God... I miss her so much." I sniffed, listening to the crows caw overhead in the clear blue sky.

The air was still with a bitter winter chill that lingered from the first snowstorm of the season we witnessed last night. We woke up to a fresh blanket of snow, covering every inch of Sunflower Falls from the rolling hills to the city lights. Two inches of slush crunched under my boot as I wiped off the headstone to reveal my meemaw's legal name. *Ethel Massey.* While crouching, I wiped away my tears with my coat sleeve and placed my hand over Thyri's.

"Ahh. I remember when you were the only one I let see me cry. Now Thyri's taken your spot."

"He's a big baby, Miss Massey, but I'mma stick beside him."

"Man, I wish you were still around to see us together." My lip quivered while blinking back more tears.

Thyri crouched down beside me, wrapping her arms around my neck. "She still sees us. She'll always be with you, right here." Thyri pressed her finger against my chest, and I held it there.

"You're right." I took Thyri's palm in mine and kissed the back of her hand. We stood up, overlooking the empty cemetery.

"I know she's proud of you. Proud of the man you've become."

"I guess I have matured..."

"Quite a bit."

"If that's a compliment, I'm taking it." I lifted Thyri's chin and pecked her on the lips softly. My hands slid down her waist, and I rocked her in my arms as we peered down at the grave.

"We're gonna miss you down here..." I talked into the wind whipping around me. "This is harder than I thought."

"With time, it'll get easier." Thyri rubbed my lower back to comfort me.

"She can't hear me." I wilted.

"Yes, she can. Just close your eyes and listen..."

Leaves rustled on the tree branches above us, and I imagined them waffling to the ground. The angry whistle of the wind calmed into a soft hum as sparrows fluttered their wings above us, singing a rhythmic sweet tune.

This isn't the end of the road I envisioned for my grandmother and I—at least not this soon. I spent so much time traveling with my teammates throughout the years; I didn't carve out enough time in my schedule to return home.

My meemaw encouraged me to keep going, not to worry about her living alone back home. But that wasn't the case. If only I had more time, but I know God makes no mistakes.

The last time we talked, she agreed to be my travel buddy after my retirement since I kept struggling to find a girlfriend. She didn't like planes, so we compromised on scenic train rides and cruise ships.

Thyri recently found a notebook paper filled with destinations on my grandmother's bucket list inside an old jewelry box in her bedroom closet. Construction is currently underway for The Raspberry, but once it's completed, we plan to check off every place on her list.

"What is she saying?" Thyri looked up at me.

"She's glad that I'm okay." I slipped my fingers into Thyri's hand, and we walked back onto the cemetery's pathway towards our ride. When my phone vibrated in my pocket, I believed it was another call from the contractors we hired until Herrold's name popped up on my screen.

"Hold on. I gotta take this."

Thyri made her way back over to the truck, where our driver held the door open for her to escape the biting cold.

"Hey, Herrold, everything alright?"

"Howdy, Dakota, but I'm afraid not. I've got some not so good news to share..."

"About what? Just lay it on me."

"It's Dawson. He had an accident up at the ranch."

I turned around to hide my forlorn expression, clutching the phone in my hand. "What happened? Is he alright?"

"I'm out of town right now, but folks are telling me he had a mild stroke while riding Glorie. He fell off, bumped his head pretty badly. Lost a lot of blood..."

My heart raced inside my chest, but I kept my movements rigid and steady. "Where is he now?"

"Cedar's Pointe near Andersonville. Jonnie's on his way up there now. They transferred Dawson overnight after he left the intensive care unit."

"That's a two-hour drive for me. I'll head there now."

"His granddaughter is en route too, but I just wanted to make sure you knew."

"Yeah. Yeah. Of course, I appreciate the call."

"Dawson's tough. I'm confident he'll pull through." Herrold's words felt heavy and ballooned with doubt.

326

"Me too." I ended the call, surveying headstones burrowed in the snow on either side of me. I refused to take it as a sign of foreshadowing what was to come.

Dawson served as an integral pillar in each of our lives. After working together over the past few months, I can say that he's become both a mentor and the father figure I never had.

My father wasn't present during my childhood, and when I saw him, he walked in and out of our lives like a revolving door. When my mother fell ill, he promised he would return once he got back on his feet.

Left me with a teddy bear and a sympathy card with twenty bucks inside of it on the day of her funeral. Today, I wouldn't recognize him if we passed each other on the street.

I returned to the car to let Thyri know about Dawson's riding accident. She offered to come along with me, but I needed her to stay behind in case there were any issues with the construction site.

Later that afternoon, I arrived in Andersonville with questions and a heavy heart. I walked up to the circular desk to be greeted by a nurse with long, black wavy tresses, a flat broad nose, dense fake lashes, wearing royal purple scrubs with buttons next to her name badge.

Pa'Rys S.

"Good afternoon, do you need to check in?" She didn't bother to look up from the computer screen as she typed and gave instructions to a patient's mother on the phone glued between her shoulder and right ear.

"Uh, no. I'm actually here to visit a friend—I mean, a family member of mine. The hospital admitted him last night."

The double doors at the end of another hallway swung open as ENTs rushed inside with a bloodied teenage boy in distress on a gurney.

None of the nurses at the counter blinked an eye. Two of them grabbed clipboards and followed the gruesome scene as if it were just another day in the trauma unit.

Pa'Rys chewed on her gum and released a sigh after hanging up the phone. "Teenagers don't need a license until they're twenty-five. First and last name, please?" She shook her head.

"Dakota Callahan." Captivated by the chaotic scene in the waiting room and doctors speeding by like bolts of lightning, I didn't realize Pa'Rys wasn't asking me for my name.

She stabbed the keyboard with her coffin-shaped nails, which had intricate, colorful artwork on each of them. "I don't see that name in our system. You said they brought him in yesterday?"

"I'm sorry, Hollie. Dawson Hollie. I got a little distracted."

"That's okay. It happens." With her light hazel eyes locked back on the computer screen, she stood up and scribbled down a note on a pink sticky note. "So, Mr. Hollie, experienced serious head trauma. They've taken him up to the second floor, room A15. You're his next of kin, right? We have to ask."

She peered back at me with an eyebrow of volition raised, as if to warn me that my next response would determine my level of access for entry.

"We're related, yes." My eyes bounced around the cork bulletin board behind her.

"Okay, I'll just need a copy of your I.D. and I'll get you a visitor's pass in just a second."

Pa'Rys picked up the phone and started multitasking again. "Good afternoon, this is Cedar's Pointe Emergency Triage desk, how may I assist you?"

I took a deep breath, bracing myself to see the state of Dawson's condition. Pa'Rys took my license, photocopied it, and slid it back over to me. I'd rather bend the rules now and ask for forgiveness later.

"You're all set."

To be one of the best hospitals in Andersonville, it sure seems disorganized, but at least I can use it to my advantage. When I made it upstairs, I reached yet another barrier that prevented me from seeing Dawson.

Doctors were currently in the room, so I couldn't see him. I waited two hours in the sterile visiting area with old carpet and cushioned chairs lined along the wall like airport seats before a doctor finally walked out to provide an update.

She trekked over to me in a white coat, black shirt, loose high-waisted slacks and tennis shoes. A stethoscope dangled around her neck as she untied a mask from around the back of her head. I stood up to greet her.

"Hi, I'm Lizah Burrows. Mr. Hollie's doctor. Are you his next of kin?"

"Yes, ma'am," I replied confidently. "Is he okay?"

"We've seen some progress since last night. His vitals are in a suitable spot. He experienced a stroke, most likely because of the cold temperature and his high blood pressure. Thankfully, a very mild one."

"Is he awake? Can I see him?"

"He's not awake right now. But we're showing signs that as the medicine wears off, he'll likely awaken by morning at the latest. He needs plenty of rest. Physical therapy may also be an option. Of course, we'll need to run more mobilization tests over the next week. But thus far, his reflexes are still strong."

"Oh, that's a relief." I blew out my breath after suffocating myself for hours.

"My only concern is the amount of blood he lost from the fall."

"Where's the blood coming from?"

She casually pointed to her temple with a frown. "He has a nasty gash. About three centimeters wide, a few inches deep. Looks like he may have hit his head on some gravel, a log, or a rough-edged stone judging by the interior damage. I'm assuming he slumped forward when the stroke began and demobilized, which made him lose control of the reins.

Good thing he didn't get thrown from the horse head-first. No broken bones, fractures, or tears, but given his age, recovery time may be longer without a blood transfusion."

She kissed the roof of her mouth to express her disappointment, but there wasn't much concern behind her bright blue eyes, just a blank stare. With her hands folded in front of her, she appeared unmoved. She probably delivers devastating news to families every day. Dr. Burrows leaned forward authoritatively. "Do you have any questions?"

"So, how soon will the transfusion take place?"

Dr. Burrows glanced over her shoulder at the clock on the wall to ensure she stayed on schedule.

"Depends. We have to find an exact match for his blood type."

Just as I opened my mouth to speak again, a woman who appeared to be around the same age as me walked in with her family in tow and a toddler on her hip.

Her pink scrunchie held her sandy-brown hair in a messy bun. She was fair-skinned, an olive complexion with red undertones. Aside from a few beauty marks on her chin, a birthmark on her neck, and dark circles from a lack of rest, her skin was flawless. Her dark brown eyes, thick brows and upturned nose made her facial symmetry even more striking.

She wore a navy blue jogging suit with a spit-up stain on her chest and no socks to cover her ankles inside her gym shoes. Her trench coat took over her petite frame as she spun away from the front desk and walked over in distress. She left her husband behind to tend to their two other children strapped into the double stroller.

"Sorry to interrupt, but you're Dr. Burrows, right?" The woman struggled with the squirming little girl on her hip.

"I am." Dr. Burrows' eyes shifted from me back to her.

"I'm Jilly. Dawson Hollie's my grandfather. I need to see him. My family's on their way from out of town."

"Ah, yes, I was just telling your brother here—"

Dawson's granddaughter's head whipped over at me as if it's the first time she realized anyone else was standing there.

She leaned sideways and blinked rapidly, confused. "He's not my brother."

"Jilly, I'm Dakota—"

"Dakota Callahan?!" Her eyes pinched.

I nodded. "Yeah, I was Dawson's client."

"Tell me something I don't know. He talks about you every day." She wiped her eyes and sniffed. "I didn't expect to see you here." She put her daughter down and outstretched her hands to embrace me. And there's that jolt of energy down my spine again.

"So, you two aren't related?" the doctor inquired.

"Not at all." Jilly perked up.

"That's strange. You all look like you share the same gene pool to me."

"Is he alright?" Jilly's eyes raced, longing for someone to anchor hope in her heart while the entire world crashed down around her. I knew that feeling all too well.

"The sooner we find a match for the blood transfusion, the better."

The doctor instructed one of her nurses to fill Jilly's family in on the details as I stood back to respect their privacy. Jilly's his first and only granddaughter out of three children, two daughters, and one son.

We've both agreed to get tested to expedite the process, Jilly's husband included. Results could take anywhere from two to three hours. Now it's just a waiting game filled with awkward bouts of silence, forced laughter, and small talk mixed with grief.

When the nurse approached us, we all stood up at once.

"Got some good news. We've got a match." The pudgy nurse grinned from ear to ear as Jilly naturally stepped forward.

The nurse pretended to check her clipboard to double-check. "It's Dakota, actually. You have a rare match for Type B negative."

Shocked, Jilly joined her husband's side, who looked just as confused as me.

"Are you ready? I can take you back."

I looked over at Jilly for confirmation, and she nodded vigorously. "It's okay, please, I insist."

I followed the nurse through the door, wondering how the hell I was a match. As soon as we turned the corner, she stopped me.

"Now that I have you alone, the blood tests were so close of a match we wanted to ask about your familial connection to the Hollie's?" Her eyebrow ticked upward as her pudgy hand rested on her hip.

"None that I know of." I shrugged.

"Anything said from here on out will remain in confidence between you and Cedars Pointe just as a reassurance, Mr. Callahan." Her ginger eyebrows raised suggestively.

I shook my head. "Dawson is an old friend of my grandmother's. We recently worked together on a civil lawsuit case. That's the only connection that exists."

"Hmm... I can't pressure you to look into this further, but when we see results with close percentages like this, we're required to bring it to your attention." Her country accent sounded deeper than anyone I've heard down here in a while. It had a southern, home-grown kick to it, like the people of Louisiana. She placed a few sheets of paper in front of me with several words like *ancestry*, *bloodline*, and *familial lineage* underlined.

"There's no way I'm of any kin to the Hollie's." I dismissed her findings with a slight chuckle.

"Alrigh', but from the looks of this, *you* may not be next of kin, but one of your parents might be."

My eyes shifted from the revelation, and then everything instantly clicked.

Meemaw was always good at keeping secrets.

EPILOGUE

"I THINK we've finally found our team, Aunt Jacquee!"

"I think you're right. Blythe is so talented. I'm excited she's joining us as the Head Baker. She's young, but her work is impressive."

"I knew you'd like her. She'll start next week since *Chassidy's Choc-O-Latte* is shutting down."

"It didn't sound like they were treating her fairly over there. I'm sure working at The Raspberry will feel like a breath of fresh air after dealing with Gallienne."

"For sure." I stacked the resumes in my hand and put the pens back in the cup on the folding table in front of us. We've started interviewing to fill new staff positions for The Raspberry's grand opening this spring.

Due to the overwhelming amount of interest, it took my aunt and I three days to conduct them. Lines wrapped around Greater Hope from nine o'clock this morning until sundown. I'm exhausted, famished, and couldn't take another walk-in candidate if I tried.

"Are we going to repost the pastry chef job description?"

Aunt Jacquee patted my hand. "Let's table that discussion for now. I'm going to call it a night." She stretched and grabbed her suede Bottega handbag. "Your uncle's been outside waiting for me forever."

"Are you sure it's not too late for the long drive back? Y'all are welcome to stay with me and Dakota."

"Unh-unh. I'm not invading you and Dakota's privacy. We were young once, too, ya' know?" She winked, and I shook my head.

"Dakota is busy scouting for his hockey minor league. He doesn't get home until late. And why would we fool around with ya'll there, anyway?" My lips twisted.

"I doubt our presence would stop the two of you. Y'all can't keep your hands off each other." Aunt Jacquee wrapped her arms around my shoulders and left me with a peck on the cheek. "What time are you heading out of here?"

"I need to do a little more prep for Sunday. Easter's around the corner, and there's a lot of foot traffic picking up around here."

"Okay, but make sure you get some rest. And remember to call me when you get in. Last time I waited up all night looking out for your call."

"Alright, Aunt Jacquee, I will." Even though Dakota and I lived in a gated community with security less than fifteen minutes away, Aunt Jacquee still required a 'I'm home' text.

"You need to get a head-start on making those wedding plans. Venues book up years in advance." Aunt Jacquee wrapped a checkered alpaca scarf around her neck.

"Yeah, I do, but I'm sure Dakota's name can pull a few strings."

A slow grin stretched across Aunt Jacquee's face. "I'm so happy for you two. Goodnight, baby girl."

"Goodnight, Auntie, love you!" I called over my shoulder, pulling out a few pans of fresh sourdough I'd refrigerated for the past two hours. A knock on the door caught me off guard as I tied my apron in the back.

"We're closed!" I yelled out without turning around.

"I'm actually here for the interviews."

My mother's voice compelled me to look back. "Ma? What are you doing here?"

"Oh, I was just around the way and saw this job posting on the church bulletin."

"Job posting?" I quizzed. "You're moving to Sunflower Falls?"

"Not sure yet." She walked over to the table, bundled up in a peacoat, snow boots on her size five feet, and a hand-knitted beanie with an orange flower design woven into it. "I need to find a stable job first. Are all the roles for The Raspberry filled?" She drummed her fingers on the counter as if she had already exhausted all of her options.

It's the first time my mother mentioned stable and job in the same sentence. She's never been forthcoming about her financial status. When she visited last year, she couldn't give me a straight answer about her occupation. But I knew she was barely getting by; the signs were all there.

I grabbed my notepad and pulled a chair out from the folding table. "Have a seat."

"Okay, I'm with it!" Dimples danced on her cheeks as she removed her coat.

I held out my hand to reintroduce myself. "Thyri Richards, soon to be Thyri Callahan." I twiddled my fingers in front of my mother's face.

"Ooh-wee! Girl, that rock is blinding." I gushed as my mother examined my ten-carat princess cut, engagement ring. "My future son-in-law is a triple threat: smart, handsome, and filthy rich. Baby, you hit the jackpot. He's perfect for you."

"He really is." I picked up my pen. There was so much I wanted to catch my mother up on, but I could tell she wanted a fair shot at working at the bakery without any family favors. "Okay, let's get back to business."

She folded her hands in front of me as if she had spent hours preparing.

"Why are you interested in working at The Raspberry?"

Our interview lasted for almost an hour. I learned more things about my mother in this short sitting than I've ever known in my life. She held several positions as a pastry chef in restaurant kitchens, school cafeterias, and grocery stores. One of her dreams was to return to culinary arts school and start a catering business of her own. I leaned back, resenting all the time we'd lost at odds with each other.

"Last question, Mama...I mean, Dauntrice. Name an accomplishment that you are most proud of."

"Well, I have two." She beamed.

"Okay, shoot."

"...I'm most proud of giving birth to one of the most beautiful, intelligent, and successful daughters a mother could ever ask for and..."

I smiled back at her, blinking back tears.

"Remaining sober for the past seven and a half years."

"Aww, Ma." I walked around the table to give her a hug. She held onto me tightly, as if she never wanted to let go.

"Okay, Thyri." She wiped the tears from her face. "Give me some good news, dammit. Did I get the job or what?"

"Congrats! You're The Raspberry's new pastry chef."

"Oh my God, I was so nervous!"

"Ma, please. You had it when you walked through the door."

* * *

"Surprise!"

Applause erupted as I walked through the door of Rooby's Bar and Grill to a room filled with the faces of everyone I loved. A long banner with "Callahan #17" painted on it hung above the old-fashioned bar.

Mirrors reflected fragments of our faces behind countless floating shelves of dark liquor bottles. Finger foods filled the top of the bar as rows of silver serving trays covered clothed tables with my old team's logos embossed on them.

I pressed my hands together, grateful for the weeks of planning Thyri put into my retirement celebration. Somehow, she pulled off getting my old teammates, coaches, and college buddies together in the middle of a busy NHL season.

I went around the room, greeting and chatting with friends, devouring Rooby's thumb-sucking hot wings that I just couldn't put down until I felt a tap on my shoulder.

"Jilly!" I spun around and hugged her tightly. "I wasn't expecting to see you here."

"Oh, I would not miss this for the world."

"Where's Brett and the little ones?"

"Back home, I needed a break, but I brought along some other special people in their place."

She happily stepped aside, and for the first time in my life everything had come full circle.

"Papa Dawson!" My grandfather walked in, leaning on a shiny metal cane with a slight limp in his step yet a cheerful smile on his face. "You made it!"

"Of course, anything for you, buddy!" We embraced, and I closed my eyes.

My bloodline didn't end with me. It extended far and wide through a lineage of aunts, uncles, and cousins hidden in plain sight. All it took was a one-way flight back to Sunflower Falls to get back to my roots and to find my soul mate next door.

Grandpa Dawson introduced me to his sons and his other daughter, who reminded me of my mom.

"It's such a pleasure finally meeting you in person! Welcome to the family, kiddo!"

They welcomed me with open arms, and life never felt better. I spotted Thyri eyeing me from across the room, and I made my way over.

"Excuse me, gorgeous. I was looking for my fiancée, and she looks a lot like you."

"Then she must be me, because I'm one of a kind, honey."

"Thee, Mrs. Thyri Callahan. It has a nice ring to it."

"Well, you might as well get used to calling me by my new last name, because you're stuck with me for liifffeee."

"I wouldn't have it any other way." One sensual kiss placed all eyes on us as our guests popped champagne and whistled in celebration.

"Save some for your honeymoon night!" Aunt Jacquee blurted, filling Rooby's with laughter and a lot more love.

I didn't have to search the depths of the Earth to find my happiness, my family, or my wife. All three found me in a valley when I was at my lowest. There was a time in my life when I didn't believe in fairytales or happy endings. But despite all my adversity, I can finally bask in the light at the end of the tunnel with Thyri at my side. Together, we're invincible.

I leaned forward, wrapping my arm around her neck as she stood in front of me.

"Hey, turn the television up! It's Logan!" one of my old teammates shouted over the crowd.

The music volume decreased, and all eyes were on the two flat screens hanging on the wall.

"Why does this feel like déjà vu?" Thyri rolled her eyes as Logan adjusted his mic while sitting in the dimly lit NWHL podcast studio.

Monica fanned herself as he squinted his honey-colored eyes in her direction.

"Whew! Did someone turn the heat on in here?" Monica blew her raspy voice into the mic. "Okay, Logan, now we all know you as the mysterious bad boy of the National Hockey League."

Logan shrugged. "There's a lot more to me than my past."

"It's rumored that you're quite the ladies' man too."

"And proud of it." Logan peered back at the camera, rubbing his hands and licking his lips.

He had enough extra hold gel and hairspray on his jet-black hair to last a week. The flashy gold jewelry glistened around his neck. He wore his signature outfit: a black leather jacket with no shirt underneath to show off the tribal tattoos across his sun-kissed chest. Logan might be a professional hockey player, but he's a rock star at his core.

My upper lip hiked. "This guy."

"So, let's clear the air once and for all regarding the controversy between Dakota Callahan and your sister, Laila McDermott, last year. You all graduated from the same high school, right?"

"We came out of Magnolia High in different years, but Kota's my dawg. That's my brother, fa' sho."

"Is it true that he was in a relationship with your sister?"

Logan shook his head visibly annoyed. "Nah. None of that was true, just rumors."

"Well, we spoke to your sister a few months ago, and she said otherwise." Monica lifted an eyebrow at the camera as it zoomed in.

"This show is a joke." Thyri uttered, and I smiled.

"My sister says a lot of things. She was going through a lot with me in rehab. Now that I'm out, she's good."

"Really now? The last time we saw her, she was pregnant. How's the baby?"

"You're messy, Monica." Logan peered at her sideways. "But I like it; drama keeps the ratings up."

"So, can we get an update, uncle Logan?"

"I'll do you one even better. My sister's in the back. Bring her out and ask her yourself."

"What do you think, chat? Should we bring Lala out?"

Logan shook his head at the spectacle, slightly amused.

"Alright, the chat voted. Tell Lala to get her ass in here."

Seconds later, Lala entered the studio, her stomach flat as a board in a form-fitting cocktail dress. She held a prosthetic belly over her head like it was the *WWE* championship belt.

My jaw dropped.

"I told you Lala was faking it all along." Thyri shook her head.

"Welp! Guess we won't be seeing a Baby Callahan running around anytime soon. Logan, any final words?"

"Yeah, I would like to send a message to my hometown." Logan stood up, instructing the camera to zoom in closer. "I just signed a fat contract with the Sunnyvale Kings. Sunflower Falls, I'm coming back to you, baby! Yah—hooo!"

SUNFLOWER FALLS SERIES

Saved By The Puck - Book 2

(Bear & Wisdom)

A LITTLE FAVOR

If you laughed, swooned, or maybe even yelled at a character or two (in a good way!), I'd *love* to hear about it.

Your reviews mean the world and they help other readers find my stories to keep the romance alive.

So, if you have a minute, please rate and leave a few words (or paragraphs, I won't complain!), wherever you purchased my art.

Xoxo from the pages,

Leigh Ryann

BONUS EPILOGUE

If you loved *A Pinch Of Puck And Spice* and aren't quite ready to say goodbye to these characters... don't.
As a thank-you for finishing the book, I've written a **bonus epilogue** ... a little extra peek into what happens after the "happily ever after."
Scan the QR code below to download!

Printed in Dunstable, United Kingdom

76294485R10198